ADX FLORENCE

THE KIDNAPPING ANNA TRILOGY: BOOK 2

A. B. ALVAREZ

BRUSHED STEEL BOOKS, INC

To All The Daughters
But Especially
To Lindley

CONTENTS

PART III
LOCKDOWN

PART IV
20 MINUTES

Does not man, perhaps, love something besides well-being?
Perhaps he is just as fond of suffering?

- *Notes from the Underground* by Fyodor Dostoevsky

PROLOGUE

Early October 2012

Late that night the man came upon the corpse halfway between the cemetery to the west and the complex to the east.

His slow, silent steps took him from the lightly used road by the cemetery and over the low fence, made of thin crooked rods spaced about fifteen feet apart with four thin wires that joined them together. The air hummed, not from the street lights on Arrowhead Drive (there were none), or the surrounding buildings (also none), but from all around him: the insects, the small animals, and the buildings in the distance that gave off just enough light that you knew something was there but couldn't be sure what. He thought that if he stood still long enough, he would hear the low brush growing, stretching, trying to come to life in the arid ground.

The waning moon left the dark almost impenetrable. It was easier to describe the fenced-off area as a dry patch of earth with swaths of green than as a flowering grove covered with patches of brittle ground. Small puffs of dirt rose from his silent steps, reminding him of Arizona. He shook himself alert. It was late and he felt cold even with the windbreaker zipped up to his neck. He wore dark clothes and a matching black flashlight he hoped not to use attached to his leg.

He stopped. He thought he heard a helicopter in the distance.

Stars filled the sky with glittery fuzz. He would have heard any inbound choppers long before they would have seen him.

A pair of night vision goggles weighed on his face and he allowed it to pull his attention toward the ground. If anyone had seen him, they would have thought his head misshapen; a human-sized insect that stood straight.

The bloated body was missing pieces of flesh, chewed up by passing animals as expected. Given that parts of his face were missing, it would be difficult to tell what happened to him in the moments before his death. The man crouched and gave the body a cursory examination. Rotting flesh never smelled good and the body gave off a horrific scent.

It's been two days. Two days! Had no one noticed he was missing? Not even the people who'd sent him?

The scene was set. The dead man had all the accoutrements required: heavy boots, a backpack filled with supplies, light pans, and plates. For all intents, a hiker out in the middle of nowhere who had a heart attack and died. It would all check out until they figured out who the corpse was. How long would that take? Would they ever figure out who he really was? Had his cover been that deep? It hadn't taken the man long to find out, but then he had been looking for impostors.

And he had help.

He checked his cell phone, which had its screen backlight reduced to almost nothing. Two bars. He could call for help and they would come, though it might take them ten-to-fifteen minutes to make the five-minute drive. A vehicle did a round every night, but he gave them too much credit. In this part of Colorado, it was easy to become lax. Besides, who took security seriously anyway?

To call or not to call. That was the question.

No point in making an example of someone if no one noticed.

He reached into his coat pocket and pulled out a pair of unpowdered latex gloves. He hated having to move the body, but he needed it found. Making its discovery accidental was just as much an art as killing him with as little damage as possible. Moving the body, and then making the site look like the original, was just tedious. He would have to make the first site disappear.

He got to work.

Within the hour, with the repositioned body in place, he returned to the original spot to begin the process of cleaning up. His eyes watered; the heavy goggles tired out his vision.

Too much green for too long.

If someone examined the first location, they would find nothing. There might be shreds of skin somewhere, but the animals would make short work of them, and his considerable landscaping skills took care of the rest.

Something crackled, disturbing the still air. The brief sound could have been anything. He chose not to worry. He was still alive because through the years his subconscious did a better job of protecting him than his conscious. He wished he understood that more, but he was accustomed to letting the back of his mind run things on occasion. It gave him comfort, especially in the cold.

The man stood and flipped the unwieldy goggles up. He listened. Without the goggles, he had just enough light to look around. He couldn't see much past the growth that surrounded him and the former crime scene.

The dry air scraped the inside of his throat. *Not a cold. Not again.* Being sick meant drugs and drugs meant being sluggish on the job. No time for that. He looked at the time on his LED wristwatch.

Time to head back. He didn't want to be late for work.

PART I

BLACK SITE: RANGE 13

1

HOUSE CALL

Special Housing Unit (SHU)

The siren was still blaring when the Special Operations Response Team (SORT) arrived at the cream-colored hallway of the SHU, the Special Housing Unit. The isolated area, like the rest of the prison, had no windows, poorly circulated air, and flat fluorescent lighting. The residents were inmates who posed a peculiar risk to themselves, or the workers at the prison. Range 13, within the SHU, was even more isolated than that with only four cells. The siren, activated by the Corrections Officer in the Master Control area, was the one that announced a forced cell situation in Range 13, letting the four male and two female SORT volunteers know that their services were needed.

Until now, no one had been allowed anywhere near that particular cell.

The SORT team jogged the short distance. Their shoes occasionally squeaked on the plastic laminate floor; otherwise, just the dull thud of their soles echoed down the narrow corridors.

The officers had sounded off the various body parts they would be responsible for prior to arriving at the cell door. There would be no mistakes. The inmate would be subdued with a minimum of fuss, and if anyone got hurt, it would be the inmate.

If they resisted.

The SORT member closest to the door held a large canister of pepper spray. He stuck the canister hose into the slot at the bottom of the green metal door and began to fill the cell with the pungent fog that would cause the inmate's eyes to become inflamed and teary, followed by pain, which would incapacitate them. One SORT member had a camera videotaping the event.

The padding and pepper spray were for the safety of the officers.

The video was for the lawyers.

The door slammed open in the 7x12 foot cell, the officers ran in, and jumped on the unmoving body in the orange jumpsuit. Through the fog, and their plastic protective helmets, they didn't notice the copious amounts of blood all over the floor. No one touched the leather mask that encased the inmate's head and part of the throat.

They carried the prisoner out of the cell and performed a by-the-book extraction: each officer held onto a body part, placed the inmate on the cold dusty floor, pulled the prisoner's arms back, and clicked on handcuffs.

Their job was done. The blood on their suits went unnoticed.

The SORT lead pulled off his helmet and spoke into a radio.

"Prisoner X is extracted. Get medical ready."

———

Federal Medical Center (FMC), Carswell
Fort Worth, Texas
Female-Only Federal Prison, All Security Levels

Special Agent Terrell Garrison sat in the office of Warden Belinda Rollins, after she kept him waiting over thirty minutes for their appointment. The room was standard prison fare even for a women-only facility. She had done her best to make the room habitable, but the institutional feel was overwhelming. The faux wood bookcases behind her held various books on criminal justice and prison management but were lined up to show off that they were here, not that she had read them. Was the smell from the books or the ancient heater?

The single window into the office let in dusty yellow sunlight. Particles floated sharply and marked the rays of light cutting into the room which revealed which table was used and which ignored. The walls were a dirty yellow.

I'm going to have my suit dry cleaned after this. The cleaning staff must avoid this room. Who paints their office the color of mustard?

When Terrell had disembarked from his flight, he'd been sure the worst was over. The weather didn't bother him, the long flight in the middle seat didn't bother him, and having to drive himself to Carswell didn't bother him. How could it? Terrell thought the uphill battle was over when he managed to get the Bureau to approve the National Security Letter for his visit. After Anna Wodehouse's trial, he had kept as close an eye as he could on her, but his patience wore thin. He knew what it was like in Federal penitentiaries even in the best of facilities. She had killed the man who might have told him more about the death of his friend, Del Kirby, but somehow nothing about her case felt right.

Warden Rollins had other plans.

She sat at her rather large desk with her meaty hands folded on her blotter and gave him a calm stare. The color of her red wool jacket seemed too bright for a woman of her advanced years.

"What do you mean I can't see Anna Wodehouse? I have a federal letter that says otherwise." Terrell wore his regulation gray FBI suit. He almost removed his jacket when he entered the room, but keeping it on turned out to be a better move. No point getting comfortable.

"Special Agent, I understand what you're saying, but you obviously haven't been listening to me." She leaned forward.

"You cannot see Anna Wodehouse."

"This letter says otherwise."

"I told you on the phone. She is here under a National Security Directive. That letter doesn't mean anything."

"Warden, please. I called ahead. I sent my questions to you ahead of time. I will Mirandize her to make sure that she understands that anything she tells me could be used against her." The chair felt awkward. He had heard of wardens purposely making their office uncomfortable to keep the annoying visits to a minimum, but this was business. He had done his research; he had crossed his T's and dotted his I's.

"I'm sorry you came such a long way. You were told many times that this was an unacceptable visit."

If she was a grandmother, her grandchildren were going to have a rough time ahead of them.

"Not to mention outside of your jurisdiction."

————

"What the hell are you guys thinking?" Hawking said. The wheels of the aluminum gurney made a loud clacking sound as the officers pushed it into the prison medical center. The unpainted concrete floor was smooth in some spots, not so smooth in others, and was a dark blotchy gray.

Doctor David Hawking, wearing a white lab coat, ran over to the gurney with its unconscious passenger and blood-soaked sheets. The SORT officers strolled in as if from a long walk.

"Doc, we got him here as fast as we could. Not our fault that your offices are in the basement." The man was still dressed in his bloody, padded outfit, like a linebacker for the football team from a horror movie. "We didn't tell 'em to do this."

Jesus Christ. How am I supposed to do my job? "Get him up here." He pointed to the examination table. His patient was leaking life. He reached for the mask. The officer grabbed him by the wrist.

"Sorry, Doc. That you can't do." Four of the SORT team grabbed a corner of the sheet under Prisoner X, counted off, and moved the body onto the table.

"I need all of you out of here. And what the hell are you talking about? This is my patient." He pointed to one of the female officers. "You stay."

"Doc," the bloody man said, "you haven't been here long enough. The mask stays on."

"Everyone except her needs to get out." Hawking called out to a woman dressed in blue scrubs. "Nurse! Get me the charts," Hawking said.

"I'm sorry, Doc. You can't do that either," the officer said.

"What the hell are you talking about?"

"This isn't the first time this guy's been examined. Warden's rules."

"This is the first time I'm seeing this inmate. This is my patient."

"You can save this guy, but you can't know anything about him."

"A little late for that," the doctor said.

"It's never too late."

The doctor turned, slipped, and looked down at the bloodstained floor. "But we're getting close."

———

"I'm outside my jurisdiction when the U.S. government stops being my boss," Terrell said.

A woman stuck her head into the room around the door.

"Something's going on in medical. You're being called."

"What's going on in medical?" Terrell asked. He could care less. His neck tensed as his frustration began to gain speed.

"Nothing you need to concern yourself with." The Warden stood and walked toward the door. "I have a facility filled with concerns."

Terrell stood as well. "Please. Warden." His anger rose with his helplessness. "I just need to know that Anna's okay." He wasn't sure if he should tell Rollins what he knew. "She saved my life."

Warden Rollins shook her head. "She took a life. Let's not forget that." The man Anna shot, Garth Donnell, had been involved in programs the government wouldn't normally acknowledge and died thinking he was finally going to see his family again. As one of the last people to have seen Del Kirby alive Terrell wanted to question him more than anything and now would never get the answers he was looking for. Anna's involvement, though striking, seemed peripheral. "And based on some of the things she did, she is an obvious threat to the security of this country," Rollins said.

"I'm not here to argue that. I chased her across the ocean, so I know. There are questions related to a case that I think she can address that will have minimal," *wrong word!*, "no impact on her sentence or her status."

This was insane. They were both officers of the court. What was the problem?

"Special Agent, you are not allowed to speak with her. I understand that this may seem arbitrary, but it is not. There are other branches of the government at work here and you will have to deal with them."

"Is she in her cell?" Why did the Warden look away? "Is she in medical?"

Rollins tugged down her lapels. "This is a normal day for her. She will be in her cell." She folded her hands. "Where she will normally be twenty-three hours every day."

"I understand. In isolation." Terrell had to find a way to let Anna know she wasn't alone. "I need to see her." He gave the Warden his best Bureau look. "There are lives at stake."

"Take it up with your boss."

Something clicked. Terrell decided to take a chance. "Where is she?"

The Warden paused for one second too long.

What's going on? "Where is she?" He took a step not knowing where it would lead. He didn't want to start the process all over again, but something was happening. Something wasn't right.

"I have to go," Warden Rollins said.

"Warden, where is she?"

———

The United States Penitentiary, Administrative Maximum (aka: ADX Florence)
Located near Florence, Colorado
Male-only Facility

The heart rate monitor wailed a steady beep.

Hawking cursed. Prisoner X's heart had stopped. The only way this was going to work was CPR. The defibrillator was for later, if at all. He had the arms already bandaged so now blood loss was the problem. He put his head against the prisoner's chest. Nothing. He continued beating on the center of the chest. He listened. Nothing. No, something.

"Paddles!" Hawking grabbed a pair of scissors from a tray. The officer who was closest to him motioned to stop him. "Get out!" The doctor pointed to the door. None of the officers left.

He cut the orange suit and tore it open. He needed bare skin.

The doctor grabbed the defibrillator from the nurse after putting the conductive gel on the metal surface of each unit. He rubbed them together to get an even amount. "Clear!"

The high-pitched whine of the unit charging increased in pitch until it hit just the right tone. He placed the paddles on the inmate's chest and pressed the switch. Prisoner X moved just enough that he knew the charge was having an effect.

Again.

He listened.

Again.

The heart rate monitor registered a charge.

The inmate was alive.

Hawking picked up a hammer that was on the ground in a corner of the dark room. He walked over to a locked filing cabinet and broke off the lock. Everyone else stood in surprise at the prone figure on the examination table.

"Doc!" one of the officers called out.

"Go get the Warden," Hawking said. He opened the cabinet. There were a handful of files in it. *What a waste of space.* He looked at one and then the other. Prisoner X's file had to be there.

There it was.

He walked back over to the still unconscious form. He unzipped the mask from behind the prisoner's head. He did it carefully and then pulled the leather accessory off Prisoner X's face. One of the SORT officers put a hand on his shoulder and he shook it off. "Get the damn Warden, and I already told all of you to get out." He pointed at the female officer again. "Except you." All the officers except one filed out.

Hawking opened the file and looked for a name. *Bingo.* The information he needed.

He looked at the bald-headed inmate and read the name on the form.

Name: Carpenter Poole (aka: Anna Wodehouse)

2

NEGOTIATIONS

Seven Years Earlier

"This surveillance is for the birds," Anna said.

"Finish up, or I'm not helping you with your app." Anna heard her father calling from the backdoor.

The back of their Brooklyn house looked like an entire forest had deposited their leaves in the narrow slice of land behind the brick structure they called home. Overhead, the clouds made the late afternoon unseasonably cold and everything look flat. Anna loved the cold. Maybe they could move to Vermont for college. UVM was a good school.

Anna heard a car go by in the distance. Even being in the middle of nowhere Brooklyn there were still plenty of sights and sounds that reminded her of the city. Her high school was mediocre, and Manhattan was next door. She would never understand why they hadn't moved to Manhattan begin with. Her father had no imagination. One day she was going to have to sit him down and explain to him how things were.

She smacked her forehead with the palm of her hand. *This man needs a hobby!* He worked from home one to two days a week and was home early enough the other days that he was just an annoyance. When would she ever have the time to get in trouble if he was always around?

Dinner was probably ready, but on a normal night, he would let her come in when she'd had enough of being outside. She knew he was calling out for another reason.

"You're using your frustrated voice," Anna said.

The smell of the leaves was awesome. This was the perfect afternoon to try out the new wireless camera. Sometimes she felt lonely, but today was one of the days when she just felt fantastic. One with the world. Her skin felt that tingling she always remembered when it was about to snow or she dug herself out of a snowbank into which her father had tossed her when she was younger.

She cradled her silver notebook PC on her left arm, and typed with her right hand. It was an early chill for October. Even though she enjoyed the cold, she wore her purple coat, unbuttoned, with a thick black scarf. The fuzzy wool leaned against her neck as if it had always been there, an extension of her. When she first came out to accomplish her mission, she couldn't help but look out at the world with wide open eyes, imagining how incredible everything around her seemed. Even if her domain was a tiny sliver of land in the borough time forgot.

But that was an hour before. Her frustration was growing. Just another trait she'd inherited from her dad.

Today's obsession: the single tree growing toward the end of the yard. The wireless camera in the birdhouse she had set up wasn't transmitting. "Maybe you should try dating," she said.

"No sex jokes, please. Only I'm allowed to make those," Marshall Wodehouse said.

She turned to her right and saw him approaching. No coat. No hat. He got cold at the mere mention of fall, and here he was walking around like he was Ernest Shackleton, impervious to the frigid air of the South Pole. He looked past her at the screen. When was he going to buy a new pair of glasses? His current pair were old and the lenses looked like they were used as a cat-scratching pole. "No signal?" he asked.

"No." She turned back to the notebook. "Could you climb in there and see if I screwed up the camera placement or something?"

"Ha, ha. Funny."

He reached over to the keyboard and she lightly tapped his large hand away.

"Dinner is ready, you need help with your app, and I need help with my bug."

It's the bug in his code that has him anxious! "I want to go to the dance." *Now is as good a time as any.*

"You don't dance." His voice took on that edge. The edge that always said *No*.

"I volunteered to be a monitor." Maybe some boy would be friendly to her. Maybe a meteorite would take out her nemesis Jennifer's house.

"They let the students monitor themselves?" He took a deep breath, ran his fingers through his hair, and sighed. "What is the administration thinking?"

"Let me go or I won't help you with that bug." *Keep it light. Don't make him feel like he's being ambushed.*

"I don't negotiate with terrorists." He stuck his hands in his pockets. "Oh, wait, there was that time..."

"Now who's being funny? I don't have to work on my app the night of the dance. I can finish it before then."

"When's the dance?" he asked. His earlier attempt at a smile curled downward.

Anna tapped on the keyboard a few more times. Why wasn't the video coming up? "Tomorrow night."

"You're going to finish a health care app between now and sunrise before you go to school? And help me with my bug?" He looked over her shoulder. "And figure out why your video isn't working? And have dinner? And do your school work?"

"Yes." She flipped a few windows open. Where the heck was the feed? "I don't have any homework, dinner will take fifteen minutes, and I'm great at hand-waving code into existence."

"You can't go."

"I'm seventeen. Yes, I can." Anna gave him her best defiant look. *Always look a lion in the eyes.*

"If you go, we might have to move again."

"Are you never letting that paranoia go?"

"I'll have the house on the market and sold by Monday."

"If you put the house up for sale, I'll put a bigger bug in your code."

"What do you mean 'a bigger bug'?" He stood before her. She continued to look at the screen and search for the video. Where the heck was the picture?

"Remember, last week's three-day adventure?" she asked.

"Yeah? The one that made me miss my deadline?"

"That's the one. I saw the bug when I was talking to you about my calc problem. I was going to point it out, but I figured you would solve it soon enough." She looked him in the eyes again. "Dad? Seriously? Three days?"

"I'm not as fast as I used to be." Marshall's shoulders curled inward from the cold.

"Your loop is going to index its way out of your array and leave you with an out-of-memory exception that's going to look like your garbage collection is causing the problem, and that's just from the glance I gave it." She wasn't as sure as she sounded, but she knew it sounded reasonable enough.

"I see you decided to check on your patient." He motioned to her notebook.

"I am going to make sure that little bird gets better and flies."

"That bird is defective. You're fighting evolution."

"Aw, her mother pushed her out too soon. She just needed a little more time." She opened another window and looked over the driver configuration to the webcam. Again, everything was fine. "Mom would never have done that."

Marshall looked into the neighbor's yard. The five-foot fence had green metal interleaved to stop the prying eyes of the vertically challenged. "You're right. She would never have done that," he said.

"Do you still miss her?"

He looked over at the fence. "Yes, I do."

Anna thought she could almost see the memories of her mom playing out before his eyes. Ingrid Wodehouse. The mother taken from her by a car accident Anna didn't remember. Anna had been two years old and in the car along with her parents. Her father didn't like talking about it. "She would be so proud of you."

Anna smiled and was sad.

"Why don't you put on some gloves?" he asked.

"Hell-o?" She turned her hand back and forth. It was red from the cold. "Typing?"

"You'd really let me fight over a bug you already found?"

"Am I going to the dance?" Anna peeked a glance at him.

"Is that Jorge whatever-his-name going to be there?"

"Yes, but he knows better than to come near me. I'll break his arm next time."

"Spoken like a true caregiver."

"Can I go?"

"A monitor, huh?" He started the short walk back. Each step was a little faster than the last. "Yes, you can go. Just show me where that bug is." He stopped. "Oh, and Squirrel, just so you know there are no hard feelings." He pointed at the notebook. "If you want to have a prayer of saving that bird, try picking the right video source." He spoke over his shoulder as he opened the door. "You're smart, but you have a habit of looking at the problem wrong."

3

THE DOCTOR IS IN

ADX Florence
Intake

"Nice mask." A tall man stood in front of the cell that held Anna.

She was lying on a metal frame recliner that had clamps holding down the dirty white straitjacket that enclosed her torso. The Intake area, a collection of claustrophobic chambers just large enough for their recliner, had walls made of Lexan, which was a bulletproof transparent polycarbonate. The clear walls permitted the nearby corrections officer posted within viewing distance to look in. Suicides, while not common, were possible even for a completely restrained inmate. Four had already proven that since the maximum-security prison, also known as Supermax, had opened in 1994.

Anna's exhausted eyelids opened at the sound of his voice. The musky cloth mask scraped the inside of her dry nasal cavity as she moved her head to get a better view of who was speaking. It was as if she were inhaling ether but never falling asleep. *I'm still alive.* Breathe. *Damn it.* Breathe. *I'm still alive.*

Her arms tingled like someone had cut off the blood flow. Her fingertips hurt. Were there needles under her nails?

"Ms. Poole?" There was that voice again.

She tried to blink in rapid succession, but her head felt surrounded by a thick gel. The fluorescent light bathed everything in a movie-studio white that muted the colors around her.

"Can you hear me?" There was a figure at the transparent wall. His left arm was up over his head pressed against the glass wall, and his other hand was in his pocket. *White shirt. Pressed. Tie.* She held her head up for a moment and let it fall back onto the headrest. *Who is this idiot?*

"Wodehouse," she said through the electrolarynx attached to the mask against her throat that made her sound like a cyborg. The name escaped her parched lips. A glob of phlegm collected in her throat. Maybe she could choke on it.

"I'm sorry. I can't hear you."

She hissed a low *harrumph.* "Wode-house." She couldn't understand why they made her wear a mask, or disguise her voice, when it would have been easier to simply bury her alive. Maybe they already have.

"I'm sorry?"

"My name," she fought to find energy, but there seemed so little left, "is not Poole. It's Wodehouse."

"I saw your file. It said Carpenter Poole."

"That's...my other life." *The one I should have settled into.* The one that didn't involve looking for her father, the man who kidnapped her when she was two years old. The one that involved her having a boring life knowing that her past wasn't real, but a joy compared to her present. Anna's head rocked back and forth. Was that her brain she felt flopping like a too-small meatball? She forgot that she never got anything right the first time. She supposed she would never get anything right at this rate.

"I was just in your cell."

Who was this guy? And why was he allowed in her cell? *Oh yeah, I don't have any rights. Anyone can violate me.*

"Are you going to rape me?" She felt nauseous. When did she eat last?

"Excuse me?"

"It's not a very big room, but I suppose there's nothing I could do about it." *What did it matter?*

The man pushed away from the glass and stood straight. "Has anyone touched you?"

"No." *Not yet, so far, anyway, whatever. Go away.*

"Ms. Poole..."

"If you're not going to do the one thing I ask for then please just go away." She looked up at the concrete ceiling.

More yellow. "Without the please."

"What happened?"

"Can I get a DNR?"

"What do you think that means?"

"*Do Not Resuscitate.* What the hell do you think it means?"

"Why would you want one? Not that you can get one anyway."

"It's very obvious why I want one. Why can't I get it?" If she had had it in place she wouldn't have had to go through the humiliation of waking up. Would she ever get another chance?

"You have to finish out your sentence first. What you do when you get out is up to you." Nonchalant. Was he pretending not to care? Or was he pretending not to care to make her care about his not caring?

"I'm never getting out."

"Then I guess you have a long wait." His stance relaxed. He wore a button-down shirt and a tie that was loose around his collar. She couldn't make out the color. Cream?

"Where are your cigarettes?" she asked.

"I don't smoke."

"But you used to," Anna said.

"What if I get you more time out of your cell?" He leaned against the glass with his right shoulder. "And I never smoked. Bad habit."

"If I can get me a DNR, your doctor never has to waste his time again."

"What makes you think I don't want to treat you? Or that treating you is a burden?"

"Oh," she exhaled, "you're the doctor." Her arms turned sore. The pain in her hands felt worse. She laid her head back and closed her eyes. *If only I had a happy place.* "With a DNR you never have to treat me again," she said with her eyes closed.

"You already have one hour out of your cell for every seven you're in. That's more than anyone else." He gave the surrounding area a glance and then turned back to her. "In fact, that's almost unheard of. You have regular shipments of books. You were allowed to write." She knew she wouldn't be seeing a pen any time soon. The last few weeks had been passable until they weren't. He licked his lips. "You shouldn't kill yourself. Even for an atheist..."

"Okay."

"Okay?"

"I won't kill myself. You can trust me on that. Can I get a DNR now?"

"They're going to take your books away."

My books. Whatever. She leaned back and closed her eyes again. She saw the concrete walls of her cell. The old mattress she slept on. How long had she been here? She felt cold even wrapped up in the rough canvas restraint-ware.

"If you keep this up, the state will force me to put you on medication the likes of which you've never seen or felt before," he said.

"I thought you were a physician."

"I am."

"Then why are you playing psychiatrist?" Anna asked.

"We're a little understaffed. This is the federal government after all."

"So you're the lowest bidder psych," she said.

"I suppose I am." He pushed off from the window. "But it doesn't take a genius to see you're depressed and by all accounts you were fine up until a few days ago."

"I need a DNR."

"I'll take it up with the Supreme Court. In the meantime, do you think you can wait for their decision?"

"I told you I won't do it again. If a DNR is in place, the guards will be more apt to let me die if I have a sudden onset of natural causes."

"I'm afraid they won't. They don't want to lose their jobs."

"Something that I'm sure keeps them up at night." *This is a waste.* "What kind of meds?"

"Nothing you can overdose on, if that's what you mean."

"When does this thing come off my face?" What was the point of the mask? To dehumanize her more than she already was? Why disguise her voice? Was no one supposed to know who she was, or what she did?

"The warden won't say. Does it bother you? I mean, is the mask causing you any discomfort?"

Anna sighed. *He really is an idiot.* "Have you ever tried wearing a mask 24/7?"

"Not even for Halloween."

"Yes, it's bothering me."

"I'll see what I can do."

Anna sighed. She had hoped not to live since failing at suicide meant the humiliation of coming back. Nothing changed; Groundhog Day continued.

It doesn't matter, does it?

"Next time I'll get it right," she muttered. He didn't respond. "What kind of meds?"

The doctor looked down at the ground and motioned as if he was stepping on something. "What happened to your hair? The file photo showed you with long hair."

"You're creeping me out." Were those goosebumps? Anna shifted on the metal frame. Every muscle of her back, butt, and legs ached.

"Something light at first. Maybe some Xanax."

"My hair wouldn't fit under this thing."

"Maybe push you to Seroquel. You already look like a chemo patient."

"Does that stuff actually work?" Anna asked.

"No, but it'll make the Warden feel better. He'll look like he's being proactive about the prisoner no one is allowed to see except for a select few. And you'll turn into a drugged-up lump of jelly."

"Like you."

"I'm special." He leaned against the glass with his shoulder again. "Like a snowflake."

Like a snowflake. Like a random number. Like a random event.

He cleared his throat. "You know, your father sent me. I'm here to take care of you."

She blinked. "What did you say?"

"I said, you know, you bother me, but I'm here to take care of you," he said. He lightly tapped the window. "Hello? Is this thing on? What do you think I said?"

She held her head up for as long as she could and then flopped back from the exertion. "Don't bother with the meds. When I get back to my cell, I'll put in the request to my lawyer." Her father would never have sent this clown. "I want that DNR."

4

LAUNDRY

"Special Agent, all I'm asking is for you to stop looking into Consolidated."

Terrell was outside the FBI offices at One Justice Way, in Dallas, about forty miles from the Federal Medical Center in Fort Worth where he had just struck out with Warden Rollins. Rather than fight her with what little influence he had he did what he usually did in situations like this: he found someone else to use their influence. As he drove east on I-820, feeling as frustrated as he could possibly feel, he knew the one person who could help was someone he hadn't even met yet.

He made the call anyway and set up a face-to-face at the local FBI office. Forty miles away.

The quick drive was uneventful. Traffic was light heading into Dallas, and he kept the windows rolled up in his full-size rental car so he could blast the air-conditioning. The air was dry. How did people live in an area where fall temperatures meant ninety degrees? How could kids wear Halloween costumes? Maybe it got cooler as the month progressed. Who the hell knew. At some point outside of Fort Worth the clouds disappeared and shoved sunlight through his windshield until he found that even his sunglasses weren't protecting his eyes enough.

Terrell turned right onto One Justice Way off Storey Lane. If he felt this wound up, he wondered how annoyed the U.S. Attorney was going to be.

After he parked the Impala (*why the hell did they give me a black car?*) he walked across the steaming pavement, the back of his shirt already sticking to him, into the cool air of the front lobby where he found his new best friend: U.S. Attorney Joseph Russell.

Russell was a large man with clothes that had a sense of humor. His white shirt needed to be tucked, his gray suit jacket hung too tight across his shoulders, and his pants bunched up on his shoes.

Please let him not be a good ol' boy.

Russell turned his attention to Terrell, smiled, and took four large steps toward him with his hand outstretched. "Why, Agent Garrison, it is a pleasure and an honor to finally meet you. When you called and said you wanted to meet, I knew that the good Lord was smiling down on me this fine Texas day."

Oh, God, help me.

Russell led him outside and began to tell Terrell all the great things he had heard about him. Terrell did his best to smile and decided to stand on Russell's left where his bad ear could muffle some of the noise radiating from the sweating giant. Maybe having someone fire a gun close to his head wasn't all bad.

Yes it was.

As they crossed the parking lot, heading back to Justice Way, Terrell heard Russell say, "Special Agent, all I'm asking is for you to stop looking into Consolidated." Terrell, tasked with drawing a connection between Biological Lab Consolidated and unexplained money, knew his knowledge of money laundering would be stretched in all sorts of new ways.

Terrell stopped so fast he almost fell forward. "Excuse me? You want me to what?"

"We're in this together, right? You just joined the task force," Russell said.

"A month ago. Transferred."

"So you just joined the task force. I'm happy to have you here, and I'm ready to help you in any way I can." The sun headed toward the western horizon, ensuring Terrell's shirt remained pasted to his back.

"Joseph, right? Can I call you Joe?" Terrell wasn't sure if he should be trying to make new friends or tearing this man a new one. "I'm here to discuss Anna Wodehouse. I just came from Carswell and it didn't seem to matter that a federal judge gave me permission to talk with her. The Warden wouldn't let me anywhere near her."

What does Biological Labs Consolidated have to do with any of this?

"That doesn't really matter." Russell waved his right hand up and down at Terrell. "I can get you in to see her. That's an easy one."

"You know the case?" Was Russell even paying attention? His eyes looked everywhere but at Terrell. A warm wind scattered dust all around them from a nearby road construction. The smell was thin and acrid.

"Can we get a coffee or something?" Russell asked.

"Too cold for you? It's like eighty degrees right now."

"Better than New York," Russell said.

"Sixty degrees is fine. I grew up in the Bronx." Terrell's boyhood bedroom was on the fifth floor of a five-story tenement. No elevator so a lot of stair climbing. "Can you get me Anna Wodehouse?"

"Why won't they let you see her? We check up on her on a regular basis."

They did?

"She's one of those inmates who doesn't cause trouble. She's in there because she gave away classified info, isn't she?"

Damn it! He doesn't know the case. "She killed someone in WitSec. But that's not a propensity."

"Listen, Special Agent," Russell began to walk again and Terrell followed as they continued along the Justice Way loop that led away from the FBI campus, "I didn't realize that you had another case you were working on along with the stuff you have with the Finance Task Force."

"Like I said, I got transferred about a month ago. Anti-money laundering related to terrorism. During my free time, I work on a cold case or two," Terrell said.

"Free time?" Terrell said nothing. "You must be very bored and single."

Terrell did his best to make his smile include his eyes. "Oh, and it's so much easier for you with a wife," he pretended to think for a moment, "and child. You've got a two-year-old, right?"

"They warned me about you when I told them we were meeting." Now they were on the shoulder where the road would meet with Storey Lane after a bit of a walk. "I want to help you. Tell me what I can help you with?"

They warned him? Terrell shook his head. "Anna Wodehouse."

"Done."

Terrell straightened up. *That's it?*

"What can you tell me about the case that brought you down here to begin with?"

"I can't believe it's taken us this long to actually get together on it," Terrell said.

"Tell me about Biological Labs."

"What's to tell? You already seem to know about them."

"My mistake. You're following a money trail," Russell said.

"Maybe talking about this outside is not such a good idea," Terrell said.

"Outside is perfect. Lots of wind, noise from the cars on Stemmons. Construction. We'll be fine."

Terrell looked around. His paranoia was off the charts. He loosened his tie. Texas in October. "Money is coming in. Since we received the first reports a few years ago, it's been interesting to see the patterns. The trail is hot then it goes cold. Then it's hot and then it's cold. At first the agents in charge were sure there was a leak somewhere because they changed conduits so often, but looking over the case's paperwork it's obvious that whoever's moving this money is a pro."

"How's it involve Consolidated?" Russell asked.

"I'm not telling you anything you don't already know."

"Indulge me."

"BLC is one of a number of start-ups being backed by a consortium of venture capitalists. The consortium is clean for the most part, but five of the members are hooked into dirty money coming from overseas."

"You're right. I've heard this all before," Russell said.

"I'm a little concerned about something." They stopped. "The money is coming through friendly countries before arriving here. France, the UK, Germany. The furthest back we can trace the funds is to Taiwan. But the Chinese wouldn't siphon funds through there. That would be too obvious. They would go through India or Russia or some other country with a low barrier to entry."

"And your concern?"

And now the fun begins. "What if it's us?" Terrell asked.

Russell stopped and stuck his hands in his pockets. "Us?"

"Us, us." Terrell had mentioned this to his colleagues on the task force and that led him here. "We're getting indications that some of that dirty money might be coming from us."

"Who is 'us'?" Russell asked.

"I don't know, but it smells like Intelligence."

"We fund overseas companies clandestinely all the time. Why would we do that here?" Russell walked a few paces, stopped, and rubbed his belly that spilled over to cover part of his belt buckle.

"That's what has me concerned. I know why we do it overseas. I don't know why we'd do that here."

"Okay, then this is what we're going to do. I will look into what the deal is with BLC and you lay off them for now," Russell said. "I'll make a few calls with some contacts I have at Central Intelligence and NSA and see what they can tell me. Or not tell me. But if they tell us to lay off, we have bigger problems."

"You're telling me. The deeper I go into this the worse it looks. Why is so much money flowing into the US into a bunch of companies that don't seem to be connected in any way?"

"And I'll take care of Anna Wodehouse," Russell said.

"I'm out here now. I want to see her in the next few days," Terrell said. He would be sure to head back to his hotel for a full change of clothes. Between the sun and the walking he felt well done.

"I can't promise you anything."

"At some point keeping me from seeing her is obstructing an ongoing investigation."

"Her case is closed. What are you talking about?" Russell asked.

"Her case is related to the murder of a Bureau agent who was a very close friend of mine. I don't appreciate anyone standing in the way of my asking questions of potentials."

"Remember, she's a security threat."

"I thought you didn't know her case that well?"

"If there is information you want from her, we can always have her rendered."

"Now talk like that is what pisses me off. I don't need her sent to Egypt to be tortured just so I can ask her a few simple questions."

"If your questions are so simple, why didn't you just email them?"

Yeah, why don't I just email them? Maybe because I still don't feel like I have the answers I need. Maybe because I think Anna is as much a victim as Del or Garth Donnell.

"I work better in person."

5

LOSING BOOKS

From where Anna stood, she had a full view of the long and narrow walk-in closet in which she lived. She had her back to the door with her hands in the slot behind her at waist level.

The cell was neat except for the short piles of books up against the gray wall to Anna's left. When she had attended UPenn, she would have given her left arm to have a room to herself. While she was there on a scholarship, her aunt and uncle really couldn't afford to help her other than with occasional expenses. Her part time jobs didn't do much more than let her go to the occasional movie. Mixing with the college population was just a reminder how much she didn't fit in, and the movies a reminder of the few times she could escape whatever haunted her. Back then she didn't know enough about her father to know if he really had kidnapped her. She still didn't know. Maybe the DNA test was a fake. The peek she had of his classified file was enough to convince her that he hadn't done anything wrong professionally, but his personal life was still a closed box. Was he a kidnapper, or just her father? Why abandon her?

Where was he?

Anna felt the handcuffs click on her wrists; they were cold, and looser than usual, but she knew the drill. Due to her mask and its own collection of interesting smells, she stopped noticing the smell of sweat within a few days of arriving. Today she wore a beige jumpsuit. If she had to be moved, she would put on the orange suit. Both were baggy enough to conceal most of her body shape, but the number of people she interacted with was also minimal. It was easier to keep a secret within a small circle.

Of course, part of her secret was out.

The doctor had cut open her jumpsuit. Whoever was in the room with him knew she was not just another inmate. How many others? She didn't care. Let them work out what a woman in an all-male prison meant. Of course, they might try rationalizing it by saying that she, as a he, was going through hormone treatments to become a woman, but that wouldn't make any sense, now would it? Who would be paying for the treatments? She'd read about serial killer Richard Speck who grew breasts by smuggling hormones into prison and how, a few weeks ago, a Federal judge told the state of Massachusetts that they had to use taxpayer funds to pay for the sex change of a transgender inmate.

Would she be thought of as a male inmate being given unfair privileges? Not quite a serial killer, but not quite normal?

She bowed her head and gave thanks for loose restraints.

Any day she didn't have to spend fifteen minutes massaging her wrists was a good one.

"Step away from the door," the muffled voice said.

Probably wearing the plastic mask the Response Team always wore. She heard another voice as well, one she recognized. He was the kind, but firm one. Older. Must have kids.

She took a few steps forward, and turned to let them see that she didn't have anything in her mouth. She wasn't sure how she would attack them wearing her mask, but she also didn't make the rules.

The door creaked open. It needed an oil bath. It looked new but was so noisy she would wake up the prison if she tried to get out on her own.

The first man to come in, wearing the regulation marshmallow suit, stepped toward her and motioned for her to stand against the wall in the corner.

Her cell was seven by twelve feet, which meant that there wasn't a lot of maneuverability to be had. *Whatever. Now I just lose what little knowledge I called my own.*

Two additional Corrections Officers walked into the room and looked around. One, the older man, looked like he had his uniform tailored to fit. Tall with a square build. The other officer, a much younger guard, skinny and awkward, couldn't control his eyes from darting back and forth around the room, looking for something comfortable to rest on.

The COs looked at the pile of books, and she had about twenty, and then grabbed a few at a time, putting them on a pushcart just outside her cell. Seeing the COs touch the books twisted something in her chest.

"Could you...?" Anna's electrolarynx cyborg voice said.

"No talking!" CO Marshmallow stood with a baton at the ready in case he needed to take immediate action. She had never given him cause to worry, but then this was a Supermax.

The older CO stopped. "It's okay, Kenny." He put the stack of books on the cart and re-entered the room. "You know we have to take them all away. You did this to yourself."

Anna caught herself at half a sob. "Please. Not all of them." The man continued grabbing the mix of hardcover and paperbound books that the prison had allowed her to have these last few weeks.

CO Marshmallow nodded at her. "Is it true you're on hormone treatments?"

"Kenny, stop talking." The older guard walked toward CO Marshmallow as he held a stack of about ten books.

"You're just a freak." He turned toward the older guard. "Just a freak. What is wrong with you, Justin?" CO Marshmallow turned back to Anna. "Never had one like her before."

Anna looked down. The words simply went through her. CO Justin left the room, placed his cargo on the cart, and returned to get the next batch with the other CO.

"You're obviously very smart," CO Marshmallow said.

"Kenny!"

"How fast does a cheetah run?" He chuckled to himself.

Anna mumbled something.

"I can't," he nudged her left shoulder, "hear you."

"So this is institutional rape," Anna said.

"Are you a virgin?"

Time for the other CO to chime in, she thought. The young one who looked like a praying mantis. "Not after this," she said. She leaned back against the wall. Cold. Now she knew what it was like to live in a black-and-white world. Even the TV was black-and-white. The only colors were the dark hues of the CO uniforms.

Her throat hurt. Had no one checked out the impact of leather fumes on the throat of round-the-clock wearers? She flashed on how she had cut her arms with the pen. Her heart had been beating faster and faster, and her breathing shallower and shallower. *I'm not just in prison. I'm not just in solitary. They're hiding me from the world.* Why put her in a Supermax unless they were putting a shovel to her life?

She was never getting out. Was she forgotten? Was she so well-hidden that no one knew where to look?

Justin entered. "Are you okay?"

"Don't talk to her."

"Kenny, I swear to God, I am going to write you up and stick the report up your ass." He looked at Anna again. "Are you okay?"

"Cheetahs run at about seventy miles an hour, but only in short bursts. Enough to catch prey, but not enough to avoid a determined hunter." She shook her head. "Maybe it's faster. I'm not sure anymore." Anna glanced at Justin and then looked back down. "Please. Just leave the one by Julian Jaynes. I'm," she shook a tear that escaped from the bottom of the mask, "I'm almost done and he makes a great argument for the evolution of the brain."

The younger CO walked in, grabbed the last batch of books, and walked out.

"Please." Anna's voice cracked.

Justin tapped CO Marshmallow on the shoulder. "We're done

here." He scanned the bare cell. "Don't forget to put in a kite. The doc wants a follow-up."

The kites, requests for medical treatment, were the lifeline to the system. If you had anything that needed looking at, but didn't put in a kite, you were as good as invisible. Usually it was to have the doctor examine you if you were sick, or bored, but Anna never submitted kites. All she ever wanted were books and computer time. She was determined to find a legal way out.

CO Marshmallow shoved her shoulder again with his baton and followed Justin out. He walked out backward, following protocol. The thought of breaking his neck by kicking his head occurred to her.

The door slammed shut. She shuffled over to the door as the hand-level slot opened and she put her hands through again. The sound of keys, the movement of metal rings removed from around her wrist. She pulled her hands back in and took a step forward.

Out of routine, she massaged her wrists, but there was no soreness this time. She gave the room a quick look and took a step toward the bed.

There were sounds outside her door. No one was yelling, but most of the time the hallway was as silent as the dorms during exams. She wasn't sure where she was in the facility, but she was sure she was nowhere near the front door.

It was definitely a disagreement.

The voices stopped. Some muffled steps came close.

The slot opened for a split second and a book spilled in. *The Origin of Consciousness* by Julian Jaynes.

6

JEKYLL AND HYDE

The last woman in the world sat alone in a locked room.
There was a knock on the door.

Anna sat up. The banging on the door was insistent. Was it that time already?

———

With her hands bound behind her, the handcuffs were tight this time, and her ankles chained a short distance apart. Anna took a few shuffling steps forward on the smooth gray floor to stand away from the door to let her two guard escorts in. Between the black leather mask, the electrolarynx, and the orange jumpsuit she was sure she would never mind wearing a too-tight dress or super-comfortable loose gym pants ever again. If she ever managed to find a legal way to get out. That was her only choice. Federal inmates, by law, were not eligible for parole so proving her innocence was all she had.

But even she had to admit that she was anything but innocent.

The dark tan door creaked and clanged open. *Jekyll and Hyde, again.*

———

Once they left the area of the Secured Housing Unit the hallways all looked the same. The never-ending patterns of white on white gave Anna the impression of being in a hospital, or a sanitarium. Everything was bright, but flat. Disinfectant floated in the air. The occasional scream or bang greeted them as they passed.

Anna shuffled forward and the COs remained behind her.

They met no one.

Anna preferred not to speak. That worked out well as the guards were not supposed to speak with the offenders either.

"So how was the game last night?"

"Do you still think your wife is cheating on you?" Blah, blah, blah.

"The cameras don't always work all the way down this hallway."

Why would he say that out loud? It spooked her. Her heart skipped a beat.

Both COs had thick black batons with Jekyll's nestled in its holster. She thought she remembered seeing Hyde's baton in his hand, but she was mistaken so often that she didn't give it another thought. Their procedures meant nothing. She didn't intend to cause any problems so whatever protocol they had for her was for their own edification.

Then she felt the baton touch her behind.

"Are the rumors true, you think?" Hyde asked.

She felt the baton again. An explosion of pins and needles enveloped her skin. Her face felt hot. "All this time I thought we were protecting some guy who gave away state secrets and it's some woman convicted of murder." Behind her mask, Anna felt her cheeks and ears go red, and her stomach clench. She nicknamed him Hyde for a reason. His clothes looked neat, but his appearance felt sloppy. He couldn't keep two thoughts straight in his head. His hair looked like he had just woken up and his eyes might as well be bloodshot.

"How they hell did she end up here?"

"She's not a woman. Not officially," Jekyll said.

He scared Anna because she knew that he and Hyde were friends.

If not on the outside, at least behind the walls of the prison. Her abnormal psych class had a name for men who fed off each other's psychoses. The professor was one of the best in the department and even though he might have flirted with her, she loved the way he made everything make sense. What was the term he used? She couldn't remember.

She settled on *assholes*.

———

The pool, the name given to the recreation area of the prison where offenders spent their mandated hour, was larger than the cells. With a vaulted ceiling, and a four-inch by four-foot window, it allowed outside light to stream in, but not enough of a view where an inmate could tell where they were.

On a previous visit to the pool, Anna returned to her cell and found a present waiting for her. It wasn't meant to be a present, but it was a welcomed surprise.

When she lay down on the thin mattress with the green bedsheet, she felt something in the crushed bone colored pillowcase of the otherwise lifeless cushion that passed for a pillow. There was a camera in her cell. She could never tell when they were looking at her so she decided to be discreet and examine the pillow on her own terms.

The books were still in her room at the time. She grabbed the nearest one, Steven Pinker's latest, opened it up and began reading. She sat on the concrete bed and read where she'd last left off. Her shoulders loosened; reading was her best and most powerful relaxant.

She heard yelling outside. The other inmates in Range 13 were trying to talk to each other again. She wasn't sure who else was in her neighborhood, but Wikipedia said perhaps Ramzi Yousef. Timothy McVeigh might have lived out a few of his last years in her cell, but it was hard to say. She didn't like being included with them.

Given what little she had managed to learn since arriving, the one thing she was certain of was that civil rights weren't high on the list of the federal prison system, even if the worst of the worst really were housed here.

She lay down and felt like she was lying down on the sidewalk. The thin mattress did little to change that. Whatever was in her pillow was hard enough that she could feel it through the pillow fabric.

She turned her body and the book so that the book was now on the pillow and her body was in between her and the camera. Using her free hand, she reached in and pulled the card out. Anxiety tensed her shoulders. This was not the first note that had arrived unbidden to her cell.

But they never made any sense.

She slipped the latest card into a fold in the book. She had all the time in the world to read it but also couldn't wait to see what it said this time.

The card was always in an unmarked white envelope. She sat back on the bed and pushed herself to the wall. With the book as a shield, she opened the envelope and extracted the card.

The card read: *If this prison is like a haunted house then during construction someone must have gotten caught in the pouring of one of the concrete beds.*

She slammed the book shut and jumped off the bed. Who would send something like this to her?

With her back to the camera, she put the card away with the others she had received since her arrival.

————

Anna entered the pool area as Jekyll and Hyde stopped behind her. The door slammed shut behind Anna. She took a few steps backward and stood against the door with her hands in the slot and her feet against the bare metal. A few seconds later, she was uncuffed and unmanacled. She had read that offenders had one hour out of every twenty-four to leave their cells, yet she was out almost three hours every day. The last time she was here, she ran in circles for almost the full length of her time and then practiced Tae Kwon Do the following hour.

That was before. She looked at the gray walls and the slit of sunlight streaming into the large empty room. Energy slid from her shoulders.

She walked to the middle of the room and sat down on the floor.

7

LOOKING FOR THE DEAD

Walking through the corridor of the Hart Senate Office Building on his way to Hart 216, General Malik Palma noticed almost nothing about its his surroundings.

The 9-story atrium with its vaulted ceiling and white marble floors. The giant black Alexander Calder sculpture with its unmoving clouds. The pedestrians who walked through on their way to other Senate offices. The landscaping. The marble walls.

The cold air. The bright lighting.

Too many other things to think about.

Palma wore his uniform. Sometimes he thought of it as a costume, but most of the time he embraced it for the symbol it embodied. The promise of security and protection. Serious subjects with serious consequences.

Testifying before the Senate Select Committee on Intelligence held none of that. A mere formality that included posturing, and cameras, and giving the government the chance to look good because they could ask questions of people whose answers didn't matter. When was the last time anyone went to jail after Senate testimony?

The weather outside was just chilly enough for October, but he drove himself to the Hart building instead of walking. The cold air in the atrium incented the pedestrians to walk faster. Palma unconsciously walked slower. His drive to the Senate Office Building already forgotten. Muscle memory controlled the speed and direction of the vehicle to the building that opened in November of 1982, named after Senator Philip Hart of Michigan.

The Division Chief for Collection and Analysis at the NSA thought about missing people, slipping schedules, perceived treason, and unthought of obstacles.

He thought about the hearing and its pointlessness. Reality happened in the shadows, not on television or in newspapers. All history was secret history.

The Intelligence Committee hearings were tiring. Not getting tiring. Tiring. Palma had been doing them for years and his new countdown was changing his perception of time.

He felt an unwelcome vibration in his jacket pocket and became instantly aware of his surroundings. The people in front of him. The ones behind him. Where the exits were.

"Good afternoon, General."

Palma had heard the voice before. "Good afternoon," Palma said.

Why call him in the middle of the afternoon?

Palma did his best not to look around. His burner didn't ring that often. It wasn't supposed to.

"Please forgive the call. Accept out apologies, and expect that we would not be calling if it were not important."

"I understand, but I'm in a bit of an inconvenient location. Please. How can I help?"

"This is about Anna Wodehouse."

The General turned his body toward the nearest wall.

"Some of the people I speak to on a regular basis were wondering why she is still alive."

————

The headquarters of the NSA had been Fort Meade since 1957. The decision to move within the environs of Washington, DC, instead of

Fort Knox, quelled the rebellion that almost occurred when it was discovered that none of the civilian employees and contractors wanted to live there.

Palma sat in one of the Fort Meade offices reserved for military brass at his level. He just did not like working in the large glass building off the Patuxent Freeway. The agency had plenty of smaller nondescript office space in the area. Most of the time he preferred to work with the analysts who performed the intense signal and communication analysis needed to cull through the billions of communications that came in every day.

Their tools were many, but there were only so many hours in a day and only so many brains they could trust to the task. The psychological shift that had occurred in the wake of 9/11 was one that would never roll back.

"Excuse me, General." Andrew Yen walked into the office through the open door. Andrew strode with a military bearing that belied his origin. His paperwork said he was born and raised in Chicago.

Palma knew better.

"Yes?" From behind his large oak desk Palma looked up at Andrew and thought, *I have to get rid of you one day. But not today.*

"You wanted me to remind you when you had an hour available before heading up the Hill. Your briefing with the Oversight committee."

"Yes. Thanks." Palma folded his hands. "Did the reports come in from the projects I asked for?"

Andrew reached over and placed the rather full file folder on Palma's desk.

"What would I do without you?"

Andrew pursed his lips and nodded.

I suppose I should be nicer. But also not today. Andrew stopped at the doorway with his back to Palma.

"The weather is changing," Andrew said.

"More alerts from the National Weather Service?"

"Yes."

Do you mean to sound like a smart-ass? "Sounds like someone has a problem," Palma said.

"Yes. It sounds like you do."

––––––––

"The plan is to leave her in place. She's my problem." Palma stood even straighter in an attempt not to turn his head and look around. He didn't need to run into anyone in the Hart building atrium. "An asset is in place." Palma was used to giving his people a wide latitude. This was a bit ridiculous. Should they have rendered her?

"We're getting reports that she is receiving communications. Are they yours?"

Communications? "I don't...I haven't received any indications of communications getting through to the subject. What are you telling me?"

The call was taking too long. This might be a burner, but he was in a Senate building and he knew they monitored cell phone traffic. His use of an encrypted burner only made it worse. There were only so many encrypted calls expected and his phone, while registered and official, was for As-Needed use only. Palma was paranoid enough, and informed enough, to know that this kind of call, especially in this location, was something to avoid.

"We are telling you that our mutual friend..."

"Who is dead," Palma said. *He had to be dead. He was always playing risky games and maybe one of them did him in.* There had been no sight or sound from Marshall since his daughter's arrest. Palma had hoped to surface Marshall while eliminating Garth Donnell, but that didn't happen. Not coming to save his daughter told Palma something much more important: Marshall was probably dead.

Yet, even in death, Marshall was still being a pain in the ass. What was it about him that made otherwise reasonable people do stupid things?

"Perhaps, but the dead might be sending his daughter messages in a location that no one is supposed to know about, and that information appears to be spreading."

"Spreading?"

"She," the voice took in a breath, "needed medical attention recently. Certain aspects of her examination were quite revealing."

"How do you know this?" Why wasn't Palma getting these reports? What the hell was Andrew doing, anyway? This would be an easier call to be taking at home. This was not important. This was just annoying.

"If her whereabouts become known then we would need to speed up the timetable."

"You can't deliver a premature baby," Palma said.

"It's done all the time. The doctors in your country have made it into a science. Premature and alive is better than on time and stillborn."

Palma took his hat off and clawed at the top of his head through the thick black hair that was one of his signatures. He placed the hat under his arm.

"Well, then we shouldn't deliver a premature baby." Delivery of Halon was not trivial and Palma was nothing if not thorough. "Why the rush? This baby can be delivered on time."

"Perhaps. We would like to take possession as soon as can be arranged. Perhaps next week?" *Are you kidding? There are still people there. They have to be moved, debriefed...*

"There's a skeleton crew in place. They will not be able to..."

"We will take up where you have started and have taken so long to complete. We have previous experience in the proper closure of American projects."

"Yes, you do." Palma wondered where this was going and where it came from. "Is there something you want to tell me?"

"Of course, General, but first I wanted to have a nice chat with you as we have not had one in so long."

Palma's jaw tightened.

"I understand your wife is traveling to California today. The time with your children is something to which I know you look forward."

Palma took in a breath. "Tell me what you want to tell me."

"You have not found Marshall Wodehouse."

"Yes, we've already made that clear." Palma looked down the hallway. No familiar faces. "I can't do my job if I find myself under investigation."

"Deliver what you promised. Find our friend. Eliminate his daughter. You don't know what she knows and she could use it to set herself free." Palma glanced at his watch. He only had another few minutes. Maybe he could delay his testimony. "If you are using her as bait you should reconsider your decision. He was never that deluded."

"I will take that under advisement."

"You don't need to look at your watch. You are on time as usual."

Palma hung up.

The weather is changing.

8

VISITOR

Anna felt like she had blinked and she was back in her cell. More gray, more walls, sweaty smells. Was it a trick of her mind? Did she just come back from the pool or was that yesterday? Had any time gone by? She wasn't sure.

The Warden sat on the concrete bed. He looked like he was visiting his daughter's room.

If his daughter were in prison and dressed in orange.

He was a middle-aged man. Could have been her father. Tall. A little overweight. Thinning hair. Lucky for him the manacles held. Or maybe it didn't matter. Caring about anything leached out of Anna with every movement. With every breath. With the firing of every neuron.

Her bound ankles hurt.

Did time matter anymore?

"You don't exist," he said.

"How Kafka-esque." Anna, wearing her mask, was still not used to her new voice. "I don't care. I just want a DNR."

"I've spoken to Hawking, the doctor. You're not getting it through him." He sat on the bed while she stood at attention.

His heavy cologne was starting to bother her. "Could I sit on my bed?" she asked. She was so done with the violation of her space. "It just seems weird that you come along and suddenly what little space I have isn't mine."

"Nothing here is yours. But I'll concede..." He stood and they traded places. The feel of the solid bed comforted her, but she wasn't sure why. Maybe the thought of a body encased in the concrete.

The Warden wore a gray suit and blue-pattern tie. Was that what it meant to be professional? Wear a suit and no one could question if you were an idiot? Her father would have said to cut him some slack. He was just doing his job. *Well, forget that. His job is keeping me in prison.*

"I can get you a DNR."

Anna shook her head. "That would save me a bit of time."

"Has anyone come to visit you?"

"You know they haven't."

"I wonder why?"

Anna thought a moment. Why hadn't Aunt Marcie and Uncle Ray come to visit? Because the prison was all the way out in Guam (i.e. Colorado)? Or because...?

"I don't wonder. They don't know I'm here."

"Of course they do." He slouched against the wall with the closed cell door to his right. He knew she wouldn't attack him. She would have to care.

"You're lying," Anna said.

"Believe what you want."

At twenty-four, Anna was full of her own beliefs. She knew that her aunt and uncle would have come to visit if they knew where she was. They were those kinds of people. They believed in you no matter what you had done.

At this late juncture, she realized that she loved her aunt and uncle. They would always be there for her even if she hadn't managed to show them the same level of affection they had shown her. She would make it up to them. Anna would move mountains to make sure they were safe.

"Do you know what I'm going to do when I get out of here?"
Anna asked.

"Run like hell?"

"I am going to take over the Bureau of Prisons. I'll head the
Bureau, and I will fire your ass." She had been doing her research.
Even a lifelong bureaucrat like the Warden could go to prison for
allowing stupid things to happen, not just causing them.

"Not a lot of murderers running the Bureau of Prisons."

"I didn't kill anyone."

"Ah." The Warden crossed his arms.

"Ah?" Anna clasped her hands together. "Ah?"

"Prisons are filled with innocent people."

Was this man going to parrot all the usual prison aphorisms? "I
didn't kill anyone."

"So the gun went off by itself?"

"Yes." Anna had no problem remembering that she had put her
finger on the barrel of the gun away from the trigger. There was no
way she could have fired.

"I can see why the jury took so little time in returning its verdict."

"Screw you."

"That would be illegal and I'm married."

Anna could feel her anger well up. He was baiting her. "I didn't
kill anyone."

"The gun and the paraffin test say otherwise."

He was right. She held the gun that killed Fletcher Burkholder,
the man she thought was her father. The man she had wanted to kill.
And the paraffin test was positive. She was holding onto the gun
when it went off. *Damn it. How did I let Benson do this to me?* Benson,
the man who knew so much about her that he led her to believe he
could help her find her father, tricked her into being at the wrong
place at the wrong time and set her up.

"I don't...it doesn't matter," Anna said.

"Apparently not. But even if you didn't kill him, passport fraud,
assault and battery, obstruction of justice...You were busy. Should I
go on?"

"Why are you here? If baiting me is part of your job description you can just call it a day and give yourself a high review." The clawing smell of the leather mask twisted in her lungs and chest.

"That's not why I'm here." He uncrossed his arms and pressed his hands against the wall.

"And?"

"I am prepared to grant your DNR."

Anna looked up at him. He didn't seem to be kidding. "I don't get it. Why would you do that?"

"DNR is not a privilege. Usually."

"I know. I have to file paperwork..."

"DNR is a privilege here."

Anna sat up straight. Great. More negotiations.

"I didn't kill anyone."

"Then why give up? Why decide it's okay to die?"

Anna paused. *WTF? He's playing armchair psychiatrist?* How could she explain to this lifelong bureaucrat what life really meant? That to live was more to her than just sitting around a cell the size of an SUV. Or, as the Warden, to come to work and supervise the implicit torture of people who had committed crimes, but who didn't deserve to be treated worse than they treated their victims. "I didn't kill anyone."

"I have to admit that my curiosity has gotten the better of me. Do you want to die out of remorse? Out of guilt? If you believe that you didn't kill him...?"

Anna wanted to answer. It took all her strength not to throw the words at him. *I failed. I failed to find and resolve the one thing that was most important to me.*

Why did my father leave me?

"I'll get you the DNR you want. You can go ahead and file whatever paperwork you think you need, but I'll take care of making it real." His face was impassive.

"Thank you." She wasn't sure what he was looking for. She felt a measure of gratitude. Would she get to thank him one day? Or would wardens come and go and she would still be here trapped in solitary confinement waiting for someone to realize that she had been set up?

"Of course, paperwork like that has a habit of getting lost."

She looked at him, framed against the gray wall like a pinned insect, and realized he was no better than Jekyll and Hyde. "It doesn't necessarily make it to the eyes of the on-the-ground CO. The guys you need to respect your final wishes. These officers are professionals," he said.

"Like the guy who raped the female inmate just before her release from FCI Danbury? You know, the CO who ended up here? Or the two guards you have escorting me who poked my ass with a baton the last time they took me to the pool?"

The Warden squinted. He crossed his arms.

"DNR is a privilege."

"DNR is a right once I get the paperwork done," she said.

"My people are professional."

"Famous final words."

"You know your paperwork says NHC. 'No Human Contact'. I thought that decision was too extreme even for you."

"Then I guess I have you to thank for the baton."

9

A BODY IN THE WOODS

Warden Stephen Coleman's office at ADX Florence was comfortable. He'd thought that on his first day on the job and almost every day since. Comfortable. Not spacious, though it was. Not ostentatious, though he could have made it that. No. Comfortable. A place where he could make a difference because he knew he had made a difference at every other penitentiary he'd had the privilege of working at. He had various degrees, certificates, and letters from politicians and activists hung up on the cream-colored walls in different places where he could stare at them when he needed to think. So much nonsense. The education was priceless, but the letters were pointless. The politicians had nothing to say, and the activists didn't have a clue. Was the justice system perfect? Hell, no. But the fact that it was right most of the time was all that counted. Kept those bastards off the streets. Apologies to the innocent fucks who got caught in the gears of the system, but that was how it rolled.

Anna Wodehouse was not one of the innocent. *She doth protest too much.* He figured he would never find out what really happened with her, but he was also past worrying about the crimes and punishments of his charges. They simply had to be taken care of, and kept indoors.

Sitting at his mahogany desk, Coleman had the usual collection of tasks and paperwork to accomplish, and as much as he liked to delegate, there were certain things that were his to do. He made sure they stayed that way. In this case, he had a new first priority even before he left Prisoner X's cell. Not because it was important—it was —but because it would hurt him later.

He spoke to the duty officer on his way back and re-assigned the two officers who had been escorting his latest special resident. Coleman was used to working with guards who didn't seem to know their ass from their elbow, but put a woman in front of them...Coleman had no intention of finding himself embroiled in a scandal caused by a pair of Colorado yahoos who thought that any woman they ran into was fair game.

Wodehouse might have put herself in this situation, but he would be damned before he let a pair of idiots ruin his retirement over a sexual indiscretion because they couldn't get dates. The buck stopped with him and he would make sure that it sure as hell didn't get past them.

Bunch of fucking yahoos. I wish I could just fire them.

"Where the hell is the new CO who was supposed to start earlier in the week?" He dialed the Bureau of Prisons directly. This sort of thing was exhausting. That bastard had better be dead. Or worse.

"Warden, I've told you before." The voice on the other end of the line sounded like another sassy New York black woman. This wasn't going to be an easy call, but he would show her. "The man was assigned. He checked in last week. Has your shop steward tried calling him? Until he hits the three day mark he might just be sick," she said.

"Sick?" *You have got to be kidding. Listen, honey, I've dealt with enough lazy white boys to know better than you.*

He picked up his favorite paperweight: an acrylic obelisk engraved with the number of years he had served as Warden at the last prison he administered in Texas. The acrylic felt solid. Dense. *Doesn't get any harder than running a prison in Texas.* He ran his thumb over the engraving. "All I'm hearing from you is that you don't want to take care of this. You assigned him. He's not here. Send me somebody else."

"I can't do that, sir." She accented the last word. *Oh, this one was a doozy. Must be from New York.* "You understand that under federal law..."

"I don't give two flying sticks of crap about federal law. Your office promised me two new officers and all I got so far was a doctor I didn't even ask for."

"That's not my department, Warden. I can look into it if you want..."

"I want my men." He carefully placed the obelisk at a corner of the tabletop. "I'm short-staffed and I've been asking for months." What a load. This didn't happen when he ran that facility in Arizona. "And about," he opened the folder on this desk of the AWOL corrections officer, "Jonathan Hardin. He's fired. I don't want him showing up here. He knows how to use a phone..."

"This is out of my hands now. It's up to the union to decide what to do."

Always passing the buck. "This is not out of your hands..."

"Yes, it is, Warden. That man is in the union that is under your jurisdiction so there is nothing I can do for at least another seventy-two hours."

"This is insane. I don't want him and I'll probably arrest him when he arrives."

"That's your call, sir." *She did it again!* "All I can say is I can't send you anyone until we have final disposition of his whereabouts." He hung up before she did, but he didn't slam the phone. *I'll be professional even if you are incapable of it.*

Coleman's forty-something assistant opened the door to his office. While always judicious about interrupting he kept her afraid in any case.

"Sir," she pushed her black plastic frame glasses up the bridge of her nose, "the state police are here."

———

"Warden, with all due respect, this is not a courtesy call." The two Colorado State Troopers stood before him with as close a military bearing as Coleman had seen in all his time in Colorado. They all shook hands and took their positions: one by the door; the other before the Warden.

"I understand, son." Coleman motioned to the chair next to the trooper closest to his desk. This was unexpected.

The man stood with his hat under his arm in a relaxed position. Coleman could use a few men like this.

"Thank you, sir, but we won't be long. We know how busy you must be and we have to return to the crime scene."

Words he had not thought he would hear inside his prison. "Tell me what happened," Coleman said.

"Sir, we received a call from a passing motorist about an hour ago. He and his daughter saw someone they thought was unconscious in the brush just outside the prison perimeter. When they stopped to assess the situation, they determined that the man was dead." The trooper spoke with a tone as crisp as his uniform shirt.

"Well, I appreciate your concern, Officer. I suppose you'll call in the FBI to begin an investigation..."

"Not at all, sir. The wooded area is outside of the prison grounds and does not fall under the jurisdiction of the BOP. The troopers will be running this along with local law enforcement."

"That's nonsense, son." Coleman sat back. This was his land. His prison. "Has a cause of death been established?"

"No, sir, but from the looks of it he was out there for a few days before he was found. We'll have to wait until the coroner returns with an opinion."

A Colorado coroner. Another yahoo.

"Son," Coleman pulled himself up straight in his chair, "I am certainly appreciative of everything you and the other fine members of the Colorado State Troopers have done for us in the past and in keeping this area safe." *Safe, my ass.* "But this is all under federal jurisdiction. I have to call the FBI and let them know that someone has been found dead on federal land and they need to..."

"Sir, as I have stated, the body was found well onto Colorado state property. We already have a call into the Bureau letting them know that we have everything in hand and that while we appreciate their assistance, we will be in touch if anything of interest occurs."

"I think it already has, son." Coleman looked down at the file folder labeled *Jonathan Hardin*. He flipped the file around and pushed it toward the trooper.

———

Colorado State Trooper Maynard Ferguson walked out of the Warden's office with his partner Trooper Gaynor in close tow, with a copy of the file the Warden had supplied. Ferguson had asked to be the one to deliver the news because he'd heard the stories. They would appear to be true. The one thing he could see with his own eyes was that the feds in Colorado thought they owned the place. Time to teach them otherwise. He would let his superior officer know and the news would make its way to the only political office any one cared about in Colorado.

10

THE GOVERNOR

The office of the Governor of the State of Colorado, located at 200 East Colfax Avenue, in Denver, had been open for business since 1894. There had been thirty-six governors in its history along with seven appointed by the President of the United States when Colorado was still part of the Kansas Territory and the U.S. still part of a growing nation. The people of Colorado thought of themselves as quite self-sufficient given that while New York City had a population density of approximately *twenty-seven thousand* people per square mile, the entire state of Colorado had a population density of about *fifty-two* people per square mile. Lots of elbowroom and lots of independence.

"Has my wife called yet?" Governor Fermin Hollingsworth asked no one in particular. He turned and looked past his Chief of Staff, Eli Hidalgo, hoping that his administrative assistant would poke her head into his office.

The governor's actual office, the one where he conducted most of his business was spacious in the same way the White House was. The entire building was his and he used it fully. The main office was filled with books he'd inherited from the previous governor. The smell of old paper permeated the room along with the scented candles his assistant used to hide the smell of age. Today's scent was Cut Roses.

"You just have to play nice with the Federal government," Hidalgo said.

Hollingsworth met Hidalgo at a fundraiser but had already been following his career in and out of the public eye. His work at one of the largest law firms in the state, and his ties to some large multinational corporations, made him a natural for the position of Chief of Staff in so many ways. Managing the day-to-day operations of the governor's office was child's play for him, but his virtuoso performances at election time made him the most valuable.

"I always play nice with the feds." Hollingsworth turned the padded leather chair toward his longtime friend and colleague and considered how much more to respond. "You know, we've done a lot for them in the past."

"And they've done a lot for us," Hidalgo said. He always looked good wearing a tie. He wore the same one he wore the last time they'd discussed campaigning.

Either he had a strong subconscious or he was hoping to sway Hollingsworth with the gold.

Hollingsworth wore a full suit and tie only when he had to. The citizens of Colorado were an informal bunch.

"Not as much as they seem to think. I delivered for the President this November," Hollingsworth said.

Money was not a concern. It was never a concern. At one point in the campaign last year the DNC, the Democratic National Committee, had threatened to pull funding on him. After Hollingsworth laughed at them for a few minutes he reminded them that he was self-funded, thank you very much, and they could find a dark place to shove their pittance.

"Why are we having this conversation?" Hidalgo put the file he'd been holding onto the governor's desk.

Hollingsworth was proud of the fact that Hidalgo knew when he was about to be engaged in a rather long diatribe.

"You know what I like about the feds?" Hollingsworth asked.

Hidalgo looked like he was about to roll his eyes. "Their endorse-ments? Like the one you're going to need in two years?"

Here we go!

"Their money. I like their money. It pays for a lot of things around here." Hollingsworth leaned his head back. "And they stay out of our business. I think that is their best, and my favorite, trait."

"What's on your mind, Governor?"

Hollingsworth took in a deep breath. "ADX."

"You mean the dead body? That's not even over the wire yet. Why do we want to get mixed up...?"

"Our land. The body was found on our land. I'm tired of giving things up. I wasn't happy when the prison was built back in '94 and I wasn't happy when they started transporting the most dangerous people they could find into our backyard, but I understand why it exists, etc., etc., etc." He waved his hand in the air. "I know we're short-staffed in law enforcement. I know it; God knows the polls show the voters know it. But every time we take care of business it's something we can point to as ours."

"Your numbers are low."

"This could bring our numbers up."

"They are not 'our' numbers. They're your numbers."

"My numbers are not that low." Hollingsworth swung the chair toward the window. He cupped his chin. Something was bothering him, and he wasn't sure what it was.

"If you stand up to the federal government, that does give you a short-term boost," Hidalgo said.

"Check with counsel's office. I don't want to get involved in some-thing we can't finish, but check with Carma as well," Hollingsworth said.

"You know she's going to have something to say about this." Carma Mobry was the Governor's Chief Strategist. If an opinion was to be had on the governor's moves, it would be hers.

"This is nothing. It's not like we're taking over the prison and letting the inmates run free." He hated this. What a waste of time. Chasing the kittens out of his backyard. Federal damn kittens. Carma, his spare brain pack, would bring a sense of sanity and balance to the conversation. "I hope it's all good. I need her to help me figure out what we need to do over the next few months. We've got an ornery constituency. I like to keep them on my side."

"Fighting the feds does appeal to them."

"It appeals to me too. You know we have the marijuana vote coming up again and the President is going to make a lot of calls on that one."

Hidalgo smiled. "Yeah, that's going to be fun."

"No, it's not going to be fun. It's going to be another showdown and I'm quite tired of those calls. Colorado doesn't need the federal government as much as it thinks we do."

ADX. That prison had been a boon in some ways, but a thorn in his side in others. While most of the US fought to keep prisons out of their backyard the town of Florence was so enthusiastic in their support of the prison that they purchased the land it was built on and gave it to the federal government for free.

That's how much Florence wanted the prison.

Hollingsworth's issue was the behavior of his guests of late. He appreciated the political expedience of the War on Terror, a joke if there ever was one, but at some point, the saber rattling took on a somber tone of reality that couldn't be shaken or taken away with the ease it arrived. Fear gave control to the government in ways they had not even considered until they found themselves with a terrified electorate.

But not in Colorado. If he could do one thing while governor, it would be to maintain a sense of sanity on the ground. There were too many citizens walking around with guns to allow any sense of disarray to take effect.

The reports he was getting in and around Florence had him concerned. Overall the town kept to itself, like so many of the other towns and cities here, but as of late...

"The Blackhawks. Eli, I swear it's the damn Blackhawks. Why are they performing so many flybys around Florence?" He pointed at Hidalgo. "Mark my words, they've got something going on over there and they're going to cause some mischief that they won't be able to get out of.

"Especially if I have anything to say about it."

11

ALARMS

CO Kelly and CO Anderson, aka Jekyll and Hyde, were on their way to accompany Anna back to the pool for her third hour of the day. While she received one hour of exercise out of every eight, her schedule was set at a more standard pace: once around breakfast, again after lunch, and then sometime after dinner. That made it possible for a single shift to take her out twice and another only once. Jekyll and Hyde, on the later shift, took her out twice.

When they met two other officers heading in the same direction down the tan-colored hallway toward Range 13, Hyde decided to poke at the green-eyed monster. He recognized the two men right away. Howard and Price. Hyde worked with everyone at the facility in some capacity or other and while he had a terrible memory, he always remembered the things that irritated him.

If it wasn't because one was white and the other black, Hyde would have thought they were brothers. Even their sense of humor was similar. They walked like soldiers. Their uniforms fit. Their shoes were polished. Their steps echoed on the white and gray tile like a metronome.

They were even the same height.

"Hey, Howard," Hyde called from behind, "you look lonely. I can introduce you to someone if you want. I'm heading over to her right now."

"Well, look who's here to help us personally walk our mystery guest to the pool," CO Steven Howard said. He gave the two men a quick glance and continued walking with CO Price.

"What are you losers talking about? This is what we do every day at this time. It's her turn. Again." Kelly chuckled. "I don't know who she's sleeping with, but she gets more books, more time, more food, more interaction than any of the other losers here." His voice sounded flat in the empty corridor.

"Well, she just got rid of you two," Howard said over his shoulder. "Didn't like your looks."

Anderson, aka Hyde, put his hands on each of the shoulders of the men before him, stopping them in their tracks. They bladed toward him.

"Well, hold on there, guys. Since when does an inmate get to decide who escorts them? Or who beats the crap out of them?"

"That's the kind of talk that gets you into trouble,"

Howard said. "Your names got pulled from the roster. You guys aren't her favorites anymore."

———

And this is how the game is played, Anderson/Hyde thought. *I scratch your back; you scratch mine.* Howard and Price had owed them a favor and now Kelly and Anderson would get to bring a measure of joy to their new BFF.

It was time to show that bitch who was boss.

Hyde banged on the brownish metal door. "Hands in the slot." He opened the slit and Anna's hands appeared for their usual cuffing. *I can't believe I never noticed her hands before. Girly hands if ever I saw some.*

"Are you sure this is something we should be doing?" Jekyll asked. He looked up and down the deserted corridor. "We were off rotation for a reason. Maybe we're being set up."

"Shut up." He clicked the handcuffs into place. "Not likely, my friend. Not likely."

Hyde knew where the cameras were positioned so he didn't look at them. It would only draw attention, and he just needed enough time to go into the security hut and delete the few minutes from the official record. The record that was useless to the woman on the other side of the door, and dangerous for them.

Jekyll crouched down and manacled Anna's ankles.

Anna took a step forward and Hyde opened the door.

"Hello, darlin'," he said.

––––––––

Anna's head felt numb, or more accurately, her feelings had checked out. There was a hole in her chest where her heart used to be. She had spent the last few hours sitting on the edge of her concrete bed wondering what she should do next. The flat mattress had no perceivable bounce, creating a thin layer between her backside and the solid gray surface beneath. Without books, or paper, or even a pen or pencil all she could do was either sleep or try to visualize analytics.

Visualizing was getting difficult. Like a blind girl trying to remember braille after a period of inactivity. She wasn't sure what was going on, but her mind needed the stimulation information supplied. Without it, after the last few weeks, she just felt lost.

The door opened. There were Jekyll and Hyde. Jekyll behind Hyde. Hyde a little taller. The tan wall behind them had a black scuff mark (from a gurney?). Their batons were holstered. With her hands firmly braced behind her, and her manacled feet, running was out of the question and she wouldn't be able to show these two jokers even the most basic of lessons in manners if they touched her again.

It doesn't matter. Her shoulders sagged. She had already lost the last two hours of her time in the pool and she couldn't work up the caring to do anything this hour.

"I don't want to go. I changed my mind." She turned around, giving the two men her back.

"Oh, don't be like that. You like your time in the pool."

She didn't turn around. *Was that Hyde? Whoever.* She wasn't going out. *I have to go to class tomorrow. I need my rest.* She remembered saying that to a lot of people at UPenn. The guys especially so they would leave her alone. "Let's go," Hyde said.

She didn't move. She felt a tug on her handcuffs. He repeated his words. She bowed her head. *Just leave me alone.* She took a few steps toward her bed and sat down. A pair of legs stood before her.

"I said, let's go."

Whatever strength she had was gone. Her legs felt tired. Her eyes wouldn't stay open.

As she started to fall back Hyde pulled her up by her arm. "Time for a walk."

Whatever.

Hyde swung her out the door and into the corridor. She almost fell, but not because they pushed her. Neither man had touched her. The metal around her wrists and ankles were dead weights. Her feet had a harder and harder time lifting themselves off the ground. She dragged her feet across the white and gray checkerboard floor that she had looked at for the last few weeks and contemplated the color scheme. Again. Plain. Boring.

She felt a tug and she turned down another corridor. After what felt like forever, she turned another corner and another. Were they still heading toward the pool? What was Jekyll saying?

"I don't think...," he whispered.

"Shut-up," Hyde said.

"You're not married. You don't have attachments," Jekyll said.

"Oh, and you do, Mr. Childless Wonder?"

Where was the pool door? Every corridor looked the same. It was mind-numbing.

"I have a wife. A pension. I like it here."

"You'll like it more after this," Hyde said.

More steps. More turns. Even with the mask against her face, she had tunnel vision. The outline of the leather was visible in her peripheral vision. It was impossible to push it back far enough. Would she always see those edges?

Hyde opened a door. Was this a new entrance to the pool?

Anna shuffled in and looked around the room.

Sacks of concrete powder, sawdust, tools, and metal shelving all around. The lighting was bad and the musty smell of mold and concrete filled her head. Where the hell were they? Hyde spun her around. His face was calm, relaxed. He pushed her down.

"And this is where we find out if the rumors are true."

Jekyll pressed back against the door and looked out the square window in the upper half of the door.

Anna couldn't keep her eyes open. *So this is it. My brain is shutting down and I want to care but can't find the energy.*

Hyde loosened his belt buckle. He undid the front of his pants.

His pants fell. Anna chuckled. *What foolish looking legs. Why is the light so dim?*

"She's never getting out and she's never going to tell anybody." He reached down to the zipper on the front of her jumpsuit.

He pulled it down slowly and when the zipper was about halfway down her chest, he yanked it to her waist.

What the hell? Anna screamed and struggled to get up.

No! No! NO! NO! NO!

A siren began to blare through the room. The two men looked at each other and while Anna struggled to stand, Jekyll grabbed her zipper and pulled it back up. Anna tried to head butt him, but her disorientation kept her from finding the right position.

The two men grabbed one arm each, pulling her up to the standing position, and dragged her back into the corridor. Her pace wasn't any better than before and she stumbled more than a few times. She felt a hand slam her hard on the side of the head. She walked with them best she could as her heart beat faster than she was used to, but slower than the day of her panic attack. Officers ran past ignoring them.

12

ORVILLE

Anna closed her eyes and let the sunshine heat up her eyelids. The rest of her face just felt hot. It was October in Colorado and the leather mask stuck to her skin even in the dry air. She held onto the wire fencing of the cage and tilted her head back. She thought she smelled manure or dead animals nearby. A heavenly fragrance. If anyone had been looking, they still wouldn't have seen the barest of smiles behind the mask.

In the center of the USP Florence ADMAX facility there was a recreational area that included an outdoor basketball court. Just to the south were cages where, on occasion, and with the warden's blessing, an inmate could go to exercise outside. Ted Kazinski, Tim McVeigh, and Ramzi Yousef would go there to exercise and talk for their one hour out of twenty-four.

Anna stood in the same exercise area and held onto the hot wire. The sunlight on her face was like a walk through Coney Island during the summer. Warmth. Air. The smell of diesel and sand. She breathed in deeply.

She put her hands up against her face and pressed down against the hot leather under her palms. The muscles of her face hurt from the effort to relax. Her small smile had made her cheeks feel sore.

She stepped away from the wire mesh that surrounded her and thought about sitting down on the dirt floor.

Waves of heat from the ground seeped through her shoes. If she sat down, her butt would be scorched. Was orange a good heat reflector? She touched her arm. *No, it's not.*

Through her leather tunnel vision, she saw a barbed-wire fence to the east of her cage, the basketball court to the north of her, an unknown building to the east, and high walls surrounding the entire area around her. She could be anywhere. *Prison technology had certainly gotten better since the days of the sheriff's lockup.* At least she was in a federal facility. She had never heard good things about city and state prisons.

There were so few clouds in the sky. Nothing to stop the sun from burning her body and bleaching her bones.

She closed her eyes again and took in a deep breath.

She began to cough. *I could really use an inhaler.*

"Are you alright?"

Anna opened her eyes, saw one of the two guards who had escorted her over, and turned away. She hugged herself and shuffled over to a corner. Every step sapped energy from her. She could feel it sliding off her shoulders and down her arms, but the feeling of running away was a knee-jerk reaction.

"I'm sorry. I thought you might like to talk."

Anna stopped. "We're not allowed to talk," she said. "You want to get us both in trouble?"

"I'm already in trouble." He had a soft, smooth, southern drawl.

"You mean given that you work at a maximum-security prison?"

"No. I don't mind it here," he said.

Anna looked at the CO. He was young. Dusty blond hair. Probably had blue eyes.

"Are you okay?"

"What do you care?" Anna asked. It had been weeks and she still wasn't used to the sound of the electrolarynx. Her secret was out. Would they care if she at least stopped using the cyborg voice?

"I," he looked away, "I guess I don't. I just wanted to..."

"To what? Take a look at the latest freak at the show?" She looked down at her shaking hands. What happened? Was she flashing back on what almost unfolded in the supply room? Would she have fought back? The entire scene was like an out-of-body experience.

"I don't think you're a freak."

"You're wrong." Anna gazed up. The wire mesh ran all the way around the sides and the top of the cage. Even with her hands and legs free, she couldn't do anything more than just jog a few feet before having to turn around. Running in circles. If she ran fast enough, maybe she could turn back time. "I am a freak."

"Okay." He turned and headed in the direction of the basketball court.

Anna watched his slow deliberate movements. He was tall.

"What's your name?" she asked.

He stopped and turned his entire body toward her.

"Orville."

You have got to be kidding. "Seriously?"

"I like my name." *A Colorado farm boy. Playing guard at a prison.*

"You married," Anna stressed the next word, "Orville?"

"No." He hesitated. "I'm seeing someone."

"No, you're not." Stop. She had to stop talking.

"Okay," his mouth did contortions Anna had only seen on YouTube videos, "the last time I dated was about a year ago."

"Was she a high school sweetheart?"

"No." He put his hands in his pockets. "College."

"You need to legally change your name." Anna leaned on the wire. "And disown your parents."

He smiled.

Oh, a nice smile. Devoid of agenda. Maybe even of complex thought.

"Are your parents still alive?" he asked.

"Do you know who I am?" Her heart hurt long enough for her to remember she had one. A heart, not parents.

"No one knows who you are. Just that you're the only female here. Even then, only a few since what happened in medical." He jerked his head to one side. "Well, now we know that."

"The warden knows."

"Now you'll get me in trouble." He took another step away from her. His pants were crisp, but silent in the afternoon air as he took step after careful step. He stopped again and looked over his shoulder at her. "I just wanted to make sure you knew something." He shrugged. "I wanted to tell you something." He paused then said, "I set off the alarm. That's why I'm in trouble."

Anna had to close her mouth when it opened unbidden. "Why did you do that?"

"You might be a dangerous criminal. I might even die because of you one day," Orville turned away, "but you're still a human being. Part of your sentence didn't include taking your dignity away."

Anna stepped forward to the wire mesh closest to him. "Take me back to my cell, Orville."

He walked back. "Your time isn't up yet." His radio was attached to his shoulder, but he didn't reach for the talk switch.

When he got close enough, Anna looked in his eyes. "Sorry, I lied." *He does have blue eyes.* "Can you stay a little longer?"

"I can't stay here. I shouldn't be talking to you, but I just wanted you to know God was looking out for you." He turned and walked away again.

When he rounded the corner, Anna let go of the wire.

"Thank you, Orville." She was sure that her cheeks were the color of her jumpsuit.

Did he have to mention God?

The public-address system screeched its non-emergency code. How anyone understood was beyond her.

"Officer Moss, call in to Master Control." The message repeated twice more.

Orville came trotting back, talking into his shoulder radio. He released the shoulder strap and stood before her. "I have to wait for the other CO to come over, but we're taking you back. You have a visitor." He leaned in. "I got docked for four hours pay."

Now I know the price of my dignity. Half-a-day's wages.

13

FRIENDLY CHAT WITH THE FRENCH

Terrell Garrison deplaned in the America Airlines terminal of John F. Kennedy International Airport with an ocean of people around him that he could not seem to get around. He wasn't just coming home. He was also going to work. Not in the morning (tomorrow was Saturday after all. He would go into the office in the afternoon), but in a few minutes. His first thought: someone was trying to set him up, but having gone through this multiple times in the past he knew it was just the fact that it was Friday afternoon and people wanted to get home.

As he descended to baggage claim surrounded by expectant travelers, Terrell saw a middle-aged man in a dark suit holding an iPad before him like it was a sign. The iPad read: Garrison. *There goes my coffee.* Terrell hoped the man was a driver but knew better with a second look at the man's face.

The French equivalent of the FBI was known as the DST or Département de la Sûreté/SécuritéTerritoriale. The man standing before him was neither smiling nor welcoming, and Terrell wondered why working with his counterparts overseas was sometimes such a chore. Not always, but in his recent duties with the Financial Action

Task Force on Money Laundering, he found more and more humorless co-workers and colleagues.

Terrell's carousel was behind the man. There was no avoiding him.

The man extended his hand. His eyes did not share his smile. "Special Agent. Good to see you again." They shook hands. "Alexandre Corneille. DST." Corneille was Terrell's contact with the French in Terrell's new role on the Financial Task Force.

"I thought I recognized you. You could never be a limo driver. New York drivers aren't so courteous." Terrell chuckled and, seeing the humor not reciprocated, became serious. *Fine. I just want to go back to Texas anyway.* "You're certainly a long way from the office on a Friday evening. I thought that perhaps we could sit and chat over there or maybe over some dinner," Terrell said.

"Special Agent, I would love to, but I am in a quandary. I must return home and continue our investigation from France. I brought some information with me that you need to look at, but I need to leave."

"You can't leave. You just arrived. We haven't even set up basic protocols," Terrell said.

"All true, but your time is not as valuable as mine. The information that has just come in has lowered the import of several organizations we have been following." Terrell's caring also lowered. He turned and walked over to the baggage carousel. "We need to discuss this back in the office."

"There is no need. Also, I already have my ticket and my flight leaves tonight."

Terrell turned back to him. "What? You can't just leave. You only just arrived a couple of days ago. I need to go back to Texas to complete an investigation I'm in the middle of." He looked around. Where the hell was his bag?

"That may be true, but I am leaving." Corneille crossed his arms. "I have a very sick child I need to attend to."

Terrell thought about a conversation they had over dinner in the past. "You're not married."

"Please do not mention that to the boy's mother. She will insist we wed."

Was this his attempt at humor? Where was his bag? Why were there so many insane people on this planet? He knew he shouldn't have arrived so early for his flight. First in, last out. The florescent lighting sucked the shadows out of baggage claim. He heard someone call out and thought he recognized the voice. He looked around for the face that couldn't be there. A woman hugged a man.

He focused again on Corneille and smiled. "In America we would consider you a philanderer."

"That would be true if I were married." He looked awkward holding the iPad.

Terrell still didn't see his bag. "I have to go back to Texas on another case."

"And yet you came here. Quite important, of course."

"Monsieur Corneille, you are my day job. You and the task force. I did as much as I could from Dallas, but I was told that I was needed here and so," he spotted his bag, a large black monstrosity that had seen better days, "here I am. Was I brought back so that you could leave?"

"You and I are the leads on this case. I have been on the Financial Task Force for a few years now with this case being my prime respon-sibility. Information about the laundering of US funds into alleged illegal projects here in your own country was given to you as a cour-tesy. The FBI's involvement is quite recent. As is yours," Corneille said.

Terrell grabbed his bag from the carousel and lifted it clean off the ground. Why was it so hard to find loyal people? His bag was loyal. He has used it for years and it never failed him.

"I have to return to France. I am briefing you as a courtesy. You have been very professional and I appreciate that."

"Oh, you appreciate that." Terrell put the bag down and turned it so the handle was facing upward. The handle had a dirty white tag attached to it that simply read *TG*. "And briefing me as I arrive on my flight is how you show me your professionalism?"

"You are the Agent-in-Charge," Corneille said.

"You are the Agent-in-Charge, as well." He grabbed the handle of his bag and started walking toward the door. "I'm here long enough to get briefed and find out why I had to be here."

A group of young girls were giggling as they took a selfie.

"This is the age of the Internet, but we're still allowed to use primitive communication devices like the telephone to convey information."

"I wanted to make sure that you agreed with my assessment of Piercing Ventures."

"What about Piercing Ventures?" The task force had decided months before that Piercing Ventures had to be one of the biggest conduits of laundered money next to the Colombians.

Corneille handed his iPad to Terrell who was compelled to put the bag down. This was going nowhere. He needed Corneille to stay, not fly off, leaving Terrell holding the bag.

Terrell glanced at the paperwork. "There's nothing new here."

"That is precisely my point." Corneille retrieved the tablet. "I suspect the money going into Piercing is from hardworking loyal Americans who are trying to avoid paying taxes." He stuck the tablet under his arm. "No drugs, no human trafficking. Illegal, but not my problem. I have a dozen other firms that are funneling money into truly illegal things and I need to focus on them."

"I'll make a deal with you: stay for another week." Terrell grabbed his bag again. "I'll take over then."

"How about if I make a deal with you: do your job."

Terrell stopped in mid-step as the handle on his suitcase tore off. The bag fell to the ground and tipped over onto its back. He gritted his teeth and then he had a flash of a memory.

"Can I see that file again?" Terrell asked.

Corneille handed the iPad back after unlocking the screen. Terrell flipped a couple of pages and then reread one input field.

His old partner, Del Kirby, had been tracking down a firm involved in money laundering. He had entered the information into his case files and two weeks later he was gone. The firm, Eleras Brannan, was a venture capital firm that had been started by some people with shady backgrounds to begin with and the talk was that it was really a conduit for intelligence money. US intelligence money.

Piercing Ventures, while in business for over twenty years, wasn't always called Piercing Ventures. After much digging it was discovered that after a major corporate restructure it had changed its name. Its previous corporate identity: Eleras Brannan.

"You're right. I need to stay."

14

SHOT IN THE DARK

The parking garage was cold and smelled of exhaust and motor oil. Somehow, Terrell had found the strength to make the four-hour-drive down to Virginia after he called one of his contacts. She'd agreed to meet him after a bit of horse-trading. *Why the hell did she pick such a cliché place?*

The sun was almost gone and the large overhead lights gave off enough light for walking, but deadened the color and detail of all the cars that filled the grimy concrete structure. Given the difficulty he had finding a spot, business at the garage must be good. He was up five stories before he found her car and then he drove up another two stories to a quiet spot once she got in the vehicle with him. He could have driven another three stories up.

Terrell was exhausted. The flight from Dallas was one of the few flights he hated taking. The trade-off was one he was willing to make: he would check in on Anna, make sure she was okay, and...and what? Tell her she was never going to get out of prison? That the story she told the courts was so farfetched as to be an out-and-out lie? She might as well have told them a secret government agency put a tracking device in her right butt cheek.

But Terrell was certain there was something to her story. It couldn't all be true, but it didn't have to be. She said she didn't pull the trigger on the gun she was holding, and he didn't make it through the door until after the shot was fired.

The district attorney refused to allow Terrell's testimony into the record. Terrell believed her. He was not sure what part he believed, but someone like Anna Wodehouse didn't go from introverted honor student to cold-blooded killer without prior questionable behavior. She just didn't have any. The before and after in her file made no sense.

Which led him to the lonely, but crowded garage where he hoped his contact could tell him something that would help him with his current case so he could return to Dallas. He could continue his slow, but steady push against the Bureau of Prisons. He had met his contact here once before, but only once. Terrell's paranoia didn't let him use a place more than once or twice. If something was going to go wrong, he wanted his adversary to have as much difficulty with the location as he would.

"Why do you need to know about Piercing Ventures?" she asked.

"I need to know," he said. Terrell had only been using her as a contact for a few months and even then on an irregular basis. She was mixed up in an investigation of government fraud in the Intelligence community and had come forward as a reluctant witness. Her immunity was contingent on cooperation.

"Something is wrong and you don't want to tell me," she said. She sat with her hands on her lap when her right hand wasn't pushing a lock of hair away from her blue eyes.

"I don't have to tell you. You're supposed to tell me." The woman sitting next to him was in her late thirties, early forties. She wore a stylish gray coat over her dress, but he couldn't make out any detail. Blue? Black? The first time he met her, her eyes were brown; a lighter brown than her hair.

"How did you find out about Piercing?" she asked.

"Now I'm gonna be very serious here. You're dancing and I'm not. You're in a position to tell me something about these people and I just need to know."

"This is part of another investigation, isn't it?" She sighed and shook her head.

"This is the part where I threaten to take you in if you don't tell me something."

She shot him a quick look and then relaxed. "You're an idiot. You don't want me. You want," she waved her hands toward the windshield, "them. 'They' are doing something that you care about. 'They' are moving vast sums of money 'they' are not supposed to."

"And ending up in Piercing," Terrell said.

"Why did you call me?" Now she clenched and unclenched her hands.

"Cold?" he asked.

"Stop pretending to care."

"What's going on? You tend to just answer my questions and leave." He saw worry lines around her eyes. "You're still here."

"You have to go."

"I don't have to do anything."

And then Terrell saw it. Her focus shifted for a split second as if she remembered something. She turned to him in surprise. "It was you."

"What?"

"It– It was you." She grabbed her bag that she had placed at her feet earlier. "Something is wrong. You have to go."

"What something is wrong?"

"I read something. I didn't think anything about it until just now."

"And?" Terrell wanted to reach out and hold her hand.

"And, nothing." She reached for the handle but didn't open the door.

"If you're in danger then I have to stay."

"If you don't go, I won't meet with you anymore."

"You'll go to jail." *That sounded weak. She's panicking.*

"I have immunity. I'll ask for another handler." She looked past him. "You're under surveillance."

"Tell me about Piercing."

"You have to go. You're being surveilled."

"I won't surveil you."

"Not me. You. I'm oversight. I see some of the most insane memos cross my screen. Sometime I understand them and sometimes I don't. The ones I don't want to know about I ignore, but..." She shook her head. "I can't believe they meant you." She opened the door. "I hope I'm wrong." She looked at him one last time. "Go."

"But what about..."

"I'll tell you all about them next time." She closed the car door. "If there is a next time." She walked into the shadows and started to run.

————

Damn it! What a wasted meeting! Something was going down and the one person who might have been able to tell him spooked herself. Piercing Ventures. He had something. Maybe too much. Del died and Terrell had been tortured just a few months back. He was not looking forward to that again. There would be no Anna to save him next time. How she had managed to find him, escape, make it back to the US, evade capture, and still manage to be framed for murder was beyond him, but something he would be forever grateful. Anna got him out before anyone even knew he was missing.

Now, she was tucked away at the Federal Medical Center with no hope of ever seeing the outside world again. Unless. Unless Terrell could figure out if she really was just a victim caught in the crossfire.

A dark blur smeared the edge of his vision. Terrell slammed on the brakes of his rental. He looked left and right. No one was hiding in the space between the cars to either side of him. His gaze stayed on the windshield as he reached over to his glove compartment, opened it, and extracted his gun.

Nothing moved. Without changing his focus, he put his gun, butt up, in the cup holder and took his foot off the brake. The car rolled. He kept his eye on the cars where he last saw the shadow. As he approached, he counted off the vehicles.

One.

Two.

He pressed the brakes again. Left. Right. Nothing. Crawled forward in two tons of metal. In the confines of the garage he was a sitting duck. If there were two men looking to ambush him, it would be all over.

The car stopped at the top of a down ramp. He grabbed the gun with a deliberate motion and opened the door, not moving his head from the direction he thought he saw the movement.

At his 3 o'clock someone stood. Terrell dropped to the ground as explosions of multiple gunshots echoed in the concrete structure. He got behind his door and leaned his back against the fender.

Was there another shooter? He didn't see one.

"FBI! Come out with your hands up!" Terrell knew that never worked, but he had to do something to buy time.

The shooter blew out light after light after light until the only illumination came from the street. Buildings, traffic lights, cars.

Terrell ran in a crouch in between the cars to his left. Running down the ramp would have left him exposed. He was going to have to stand his ground and hope that someone heard the shots.

How long would he have to keep this guy busy? However many bullets were in his clip. And that would be nine.

He looked under the car, but it was too dark to see anything. Was the man where he started or had he already run?

Was shooting out the lights his way of escape?

The driver and passenger windows blew apart from the shot. Terrell felt glass particles falling around him. He cursed at himself. Why the hell didn't he think she was serious?

He chanced a peek around the fender of the car and pulled back. A shot rang out where he had been a split second earlier.

Great. He's got night vision and I'm blind.

Crunch.

Terrell stood and fired in the direction of the sound. His assailant fired and Terrell felt the bullet hit his shoulder. He dropped and leaned against the fender of the car acting as his shield. The flash of the barrel gave him a snapshot of someone walking toward him wearing something on their face. Night vision goggles? Did he have on a vest? No. They flinched when Terrell fired.

Had he hit him? Terrell felt moisture running down his arm.

Goddamn it.

He heard steps running into the distance.

15

BIOLOGICAL LABS CONSOLIDATED

The ambulance, escorted by the Alexandria police, took Terrell to Inova Alexandria Hospital. His car impounded to a safe location, the local police would begin their forensic work while they waited for the FBI to join the investigation.

They also knew that once the FBI showed up they would take the car away from the locals. Everyone knew the protocol.

The local police felt compelled to prove that they could find something the feds couldn't.

The Bureau didn't care and probably wouldn't look at any but the most basic paperwork.

The inside of the ambulance was bright. Terrell was already nauseous and lightheaded and the strong smell of disinfectant did nothing to calm his stomach. The endorphins that kicked in at the garage wore off after a few minutes of reality seeping back into his brain. Once he was in the ambulance, the paramedics had done three things: dressed his shoulder with an occlusive dressing (a bandage that applied slight pressure on the wound), put him on IV fluids, and radioed in for permission to give him morphine. There was nothing like a bullet crashing through your shoulder to remind you bone breakage was painful.

———

"Sir, this is not how I like to work," Terrell said. His first thoughts were: *A private room? I should get shot more often.* Of course, the room, done in late 20th century antiseptic, could have been one of a million hospital rooms across the country. He motioned to the police officer sitting by his bed. "Can't you sit outside?"

Tolsen's voice was tinny through Terrell's cell phone. "You mean with a shoulder wound, round the clock medical care and twenty-four hour security? My heart bleeds for you," he said. "I suppose the food's not that good, but you can't have everything."

An IV tube led down into Terrell's left arm. Blood. He wondered how much he'd left behind on the garage floor. The starchy sheets felt rough on his cold legs. He didn't want to know how they got his clothes off. The shreds of material were probably in a plastic bag in the narrow closet on the wall to his left. Why couldn't he expense clothes to the Bureau?

"Sir, with all due respect..." Terrell said.

"Why is it that every time someone starts a sentence with that they just want to tell me I'm wrong?"

Tolsen had graduated from the FBI Academy a year before Terrell. While they were close in age Tolsen was much more ambitious. At least that's what Terrell thought given that Terrell was still a Field Agent and Tolsen was management.

"You're wrong," Terrell said.

"You see? I told you." Tolsen's voice was still light, but Terrell knew what was coming next. "But I don't really care, now do I?"

"No, sir," Terrell said, "you don't." A nurse walked in holding a tray of food. Terrell pulled the rollaway table toward the nurse who set out his meal. Terrell motioned him away with his right hand, and missed part of what Tolsen was saying. Having only one working arm was going to be a problem. "I'm sorry, sir. What was that?"

"I said, you're going to stand down. Not forever, but you need to get well enough to get out of the hospital. At that point you're going out with a partner because you can't defend yourself."

"Sir, I need to find out what the hell just happened. I need to find out why." He stopped and looked at the police officer sitting next to his bed. He put the cell phone against his chest. "Excuse me." The officer did not look up. "Officer? Could you?" Terrell gestured to the door.

The burly man stood up, put down the magazine he was reading, and stepped out, closing the door behind him.

"I need to find out why Piercing Ventures is so important. Del..."

Tolsen cut him off. "Are you still working Del Kirby's angle on this?"

"Yes, sir."

"I would call you insane, but that would be calling the kettle black since I'm going to hear you out and then eviscerate you."

"Thank you, sir." Terrell looked toward the door and lowered his voice. "One of the last things Del discovered was a funding company named Eleras Brannan. Major money movement into that one funding company. They disappeared since they were a private firm. They showed up a few years later as a new firm."

"Piercing Ventures."

"Piercing Ventures. Not the same company, but with a lot of the same players so the same company. Tankers full of money and all sorts of interesting companies getting funded."

"All kinds?"

"One in particular, but I want to get more on that before I say too much."

"You know, Terrell, every time I reassign you I keep hoping to get you out of your obsession with Del, but it seems he was onto something and you keep slamming into it."

"I need to go back to Texas."

"No."

"Sir..."

"Don't make me pull rank on you. You stop. You stay home and continue the investigation from your bed. You will allow us to protect you and you will continue when you have a working left arm."

"She knows something."

"Who? Your contact? The one who probably led you into this trap?"

"Wodehouse. She knows something. Why did BOP seal her off? I keep getting complaints from her lawyer about denied access and I can't do anything."

"She's not your problem anymore. That case is done."

"She doesn't know she knows."

"She's in prison. She's not going anywhere."

"I'm not going into hiding."

"I don't pay you to go into hiding, but I do pay you to do your job and right now that means staying alive."

"What if I took administrative leave?"

"Then I'll place you under house arrest," Tolsen said.

Terrell closed his eyes. He was tired. He was in pain. The surgery was almost a symbolic gesture since the bullet had passed clean through, leaving a few very broken bones. How was he going to do this?

"You win. I'll work with a phone glued to my ear."

"The one that still works, I hope."

———

Terrell was asleep when his cell began to buzz. The room was dark and it had taken him more than a few minutes to relax enough to get any rest.

He opened his eyes just enough to see who was calling.

Joe Russell? His eyes opened a bit more and he shook his head to clear the cobwebs. His shoulder throbbed with pain as he moved the wrong way in the softly lit darkness. His protection detail was outside and he knew he could call out to them if needed. He decided to stay silent.

He cleared his throat and answered the cell. "Joe?"

"Yes. Special Agent Garrison?"

"The one and only."

"How are you doing? I haven't heard from you in a few days."

"Doing fine. Doing just fine. What can I do for you at," he looked at the clock on the nightstand, "4:16 am?"

"Don't be upset with me. It's only 3:16 am here in Dallas."

This can't be real.

"What can I do for you, Counselor?" Terrell asked. He tried to reposition himself with his right elbow while holding the cell. Instead his elbow slipped and he almost dropped the phone.

"I think I have confirmation about Biological Labs Consolidated."

"Confirmation?"

"Yeah, you know. We spoke about them last time."

"Yes, you were saying that you wanted me to stop looking into them so your folks could do it." Terrell pushed down on the bed with his right leg to reposition himself. He moved a few inches and slid his back just fast enough to know that he should stop. The firm mattress gave enough for him that he knew he would be safe for the moment.

"Well, they've passed our litmus test with flying colors," Russell said.

"Litmus test?"

"Yes, they're not involved in any illegal activities that we were able to ascertain. They manufacture medical equipment, most of which is assembled here in the US, and get most of their funding through private equity."

"Private equity?"

"Yeah. You know, venture capital. They're well into their fourth or fifth round of funding, but we haven't found anything that would indicate suspicious activity."

Terrell pushed against his pillow. There had to be a way for him to find a more comfortable spot. "Private equity?"

"Yes, there is consortium, you know, of private equity firms with guys like Bright Future Health care, and some others that it's just too early for me to think of."

"Really? Do you have any of the other investors?"

Russell started to read off a long list of names. Terrell recognized some, but others were new. He would ask for the list and do his own checking.

"I'm sorry. What was the last one?"

Russell stopped reading. "Some hedge fund or something. Lots of health care investments." Russell took a breath. "Piercing Ventures."

16

THE INTERVIEW

"Who is this guy?" Anna's electronic voice asked.

"He's a journalist," the warden said.

He and Anna were in a windowless interview room. The room was smaller than her cell, but wider.

The metal table in the middle of the room had a 2-inch hole cut through it, and two aluminum chairs positioned opposite each other. There was a standard pockmarked drop ceiling with flush fluorescent lighting that buzzed enough for Anna to notice.

Anna sat with her hands on the metal table, her handcuffs attached to another chain attached to the floor.

There would be no friendly hand shaking for her.

"I thought you said no one knew I was here." Anna's butt felt the cold of the cushion-less aluminum chair through her jumpsuit. "How does a journalist..."

"He has connections and agreed not to print anything until you have a more public place to live." Was the warden lying to her? It was hard to tell. He had the face of a used-car salesman: his eyes never matched his smile. What was he trying to sell her? There was no way that a reporter could have found her, but not her aunt and uncle.

"I want my DNR," she said.

"You're not entitled to take your own life," he said.

———

"How would you prefer I address you?" The young Asian man placed his cell phone on the table and tapped the Start button of the voice recorder app of his cell phone. He draped his jacket on the back of the chair before he sat.

Anna ticked off: Plain white shirt. Dark suit. Average height. Kind of built. Nicely built.

"Ms. Wodehouse or Mr. Poole?"

His accent was very light, but there was something in the way he held himself that told Anna he was not American.

"Does that matter?" Anna asked.

"I very much appreciate the opportunity to speak with you. I would not want to disrespect you in any way."

"Anna is good," she said. She folded her cuffed hands together and looked down at the table.

"I just want to know what happened the day you were arrested." He mimiced her folded hands. How would she be able to tell where he was from, or at least his ancestry? Was he Japanese? Chinese? Korean?

His eyes were very focused. Anna met a number of guys with that look at UPenn. There weren't that many of them, but they were the ones who didn't date. They usually closed the libraries every night.

"As long as you know it's me," she turned to the warden, "could we turn off the Darth Vader voice?"

Warden Coleman had been standing at attention by the door. The CO was outside the door. No witnesses for this private episode of Oprah.

The warden nodded. Anna pulled the electrolarynx off her throat, then looked at him for a reaction. When none was forthcoming she said, "Let the record show that the warden has agreed to let me use my own voice." She rolled her eyes.

"Ms. Wodehouse?"

"Nothing happened." She tried to sit back, but the chain attached to her wrists would only let her go so far back. "Other than the gun I was holding went off, a man died, and I was shot." She looked at her hands. "I'm sure you must have read that in the court transcripts."

"I did. Thank you for that." He opened his iPad and gestured to find something. He read for a moment. "You mentioned that you don't remember what happened on the roof."

She shook her head in a deliberate motion. "I went up there to talk to," *my father?* "someone who turned out not to be my father. He refused to talk to me. The gun I was holding went off and when I tried to help him, a police sniper shot me."

The man studied her. "Police sniper?" He placed the tablet on the table. "The gun you shot Mr. Donnell with disappeared so there was no way to confirm that it went off on its own. Since you failed the paraffin test there was no doubt you pulled the trigger, or at least held the gun that shot him. But, Ms. Wodehouse, there was no police sniper. Haven't you spoken with your attorney?"

"No, I have not. Perhaps you can explain that to the Bureau of Prisons," Anna said.

"She is being kept here for her own protection," the warden said.

"What do you mean there was no police sniper?" Anna asked. Her chest felt hot and raw as if someone ripped off hair-removal cloth too fast. *Is he kidding? Someone shot me.*

"The US Attorney's office suppressed part of the New York Police report on the shooting. It was considered irrelevant to the proceedings and a panel of federal judges agreed. The man who shot you was not with the police."

"Who was he? How can that be considered irrelevant?" Anna pulled at the table restraint.

"How do you feel about that? Was there anything that Mr. Donnell might have told you that would explain why you would be shot as well?" the journalist asked.

How would she know? He said so little to her. "'I'm tired of hiding.'"

"I'm sure you are."

"No," Anna remembered part of that day in a visual flash, "he said that my father screwed up and that he was tired of hiding." *How did Dad screw up?* Anna looked off to the side. "I just remembered that."

"Did he say anything else unusual?"

"I was on the roof about to be arrested for tracking down my father who I thought was in Witness Protection. I found the wrong man, he died, and I was shot." Anna folded her hands again. "Seems unusual enough for me."

"But did he say anything?"

"Whatever your name is, I don't know any more now than I did at the trial. Those two sentences are the best I've come up with in all this time." Anna stopped.

His hands were around my throat. She looked at the man again.

"He strangled me."

The warden, who had been leaning against the wall, stood up straight. The journalist angled forward. "Is that why you shot him?" he asked.

"No," Anna, lost in the memory, looked to her left again, "I was crying." She blinked. "I didn't shoot him. The gun would have proved it."

———

Ewan Brown was grateful to enter his car. He was used to the cooler climate of the east in October and he expected to see snow; this was Colorado after all. Disappointing weather and disappointing interview. Whatever Anna knew she was going to remember little by little and that was not acceptable.

17

PRISONER X

The ADX medical center, designed and stocked with all the latest state-of-the-art equipment money could buy back in 1994, showed its age. Dr. David Hawking, who arrived at ADX a few short weeks earlier, thought he had fallen into a medical hellhole.

Boxes everywhere. Well, maybe not everywhere (he hadn't found any in the bathrooms), but the examination rooms had at least two boxes each. The equipment was either dusty or had a thin layer of grime that didn't look like it was coming off anytime soon.

He wondered how the larger inmates would make it if they were ever brought in unconscious.

The heavy, dark green, metal front door to medical, locked at all times, led to a well-laid-out area with a lobby/reception area (staffed by a nurse), multiple examination rooms, a triage area, and private rooms with individual hospital beds.

Echoes did not exist.

Hawking was tired. It was almost the end of his shift and the list of inmates never seemed to end. If this was what it was like to have a private practice then he was glad never to have opened an office.

The last inmate shuffled off with the same constipation complaint he had the first thirty times he showed up in the last two weeks. If past behavior was any indicator, the next patient would also have constipation problems coupled with diabetes. Or high blood pressure.

He was sure he wasn't being paid enough for this.

The nurse stood in the doorway.

"Last patient of the day." She held the folder out to him. "Prisoner X."

————

"Doctor?" Anna walked the best she could without trying to appear threatening. She knew how much that freaked out the guards (*why do they call them COs? They're not correcting anything*) so she walking as fast as she could without walking as fast as she could. "I'm sorry, I don't remember your name," she said through her electrolarynx.

"Hawking. David Hawking." He held out his hand and pulled it back as she extended her restrained right hand. "Sorry, I forgot I'm not allowed."

"Oh, that's okay." *That was rude! What kind of a doctor is he?*

She shuffled over to the examination table and hopped on to the crinkling of paper.

"What can I do for you today?" He peered at the file. "Your kite says that you're not feeling well. Considering the reason why you were here last time, I'm not surprised."

Anna looked at the COs behind the doctor and then at the doctor himself. "Hawking? Your parents must have been pretty lame not to have named you Stephen."

Hawking did a double take.

Yes, I just made a joke. Anna took in a deep breath and gave it all she had. "I need a private consultation."

"Excuse me?"

She spoke out of the side of her mouth. "I need a private consult."

"That's not happening," said CO Shaped-Like-A-Refrigerator standing behind Hawking.

"I'm not sending him away," Hawking said.

"Then tie me down." Anna started to lie back. "As long as you send them away."

"I'm not sending them away," Hawking said.

"We're not going away," CO Refrigerator said.

"I'll tell you every last medical secret you could ever want to know," Anna said.

"You mean like the cure for cancer?" He waved her file in the air. "I already have your file."

"Half the stuff in there is wrong. I'll tell you which half if you," she looked off to the side, "see me in private."

"Can I have a nurse in here?" Hawking asked.

"Doc, we're not leaving you alone with her."

"Ah." Anna thought for a moment. "I suppose, but I really just want to speak with you."

Hawking turned to the CO who had spoken. "How dangerous is she? Any write-ups?"

"Until the event the other day we barely knew she was here," the Refrigerator said.

Hawking rolled his eyes. "Oh, my God, this is stupid." To the CO, he said, "I'm going to take a chance here. I hate questioning your experience in this, but I'm going to ask that the two of you step out for a few minutes."

"Doc, this is crazy."

"I know. I've never gone against my better judgment like this before either." Hawking turned to Anna. "Are you going to kill me?"

Anna folded her hands. "Not today."

———

Hawking closed the door of the office with a low chick of the lock. Anna was worried. She had never really had this kind of talk with anyone except her dad.

"Okay," he said, "how do we do this so I feel like you're not going to kill me, and you feel like you can tell me what's on your mind?"

"I promise to stay sitting on this table for the entire visit. If I hop off for any reason, you should run like hell." Anna did her best to look unassuming. While wearing a black leather mask.

Hawking looked at Anna and then at the door. "If you hopped off that table, you could easily knock me over and kill me before I reached the doorknob."

"I promise not to?" She reached up and turned the electrolarynx off.

"I'm going to place this chair between me and you, and I'm going to hope it slows you down." The chair made a dragging sound on the dry tile.

Anna slammed her hands onto her lap. "What kind of a doctor are you? I'm here for a confidential visit and you're acting like I'm a convicted killer."

Hawking slid the chair closer to her with his foot.

"Okay," Anna said, "maybe you're right. But you have to help me with something."

"Can I ask how you've been doing since your last visit?"

"Just great. I was almost raped by two guards, all of my books have been taken away, and I think I have a crush on somebody."

"Let me write that down." He picked up her folder and took a pen out of his shirt pocket. "Almost raped. No books. Feeling frisky. Anything else you'd like to tell me?"

"I want you to find out everything you can about CO Orville Moss. I think that's his last name. If I'm wrong, there can't be that many Orvilles working here." Even though the examination table was uncomfortable she did her best to sit up straight.

Always appear confident during negotiations.

"Should I write that down or should I just call your escorts back in?" Hawking pointed his thumb at the door.

"No, you don't understand." Anna was confused. How could she explain this? "If I were on the outside and I met some guy and I thought he was cute, or whatever, I'd do a background check on him. Facebook, Google. Pipl. I'd pay a few bucks and find out the basics. Is he married? Kids? Convictions?"

"Setting the bar a little high, aren't we?"

Anna shook her hands in frustration. Hawking twitched. "I need you to check him out and I'm willing to cut a deal."

"Oh, this is going to be good."

"I promise," she forced the words out, "I promise not to attempt suicide again. Well, at least not until the end of the week."

"What a tempting offer."

"If you could see my face, you'd know how much this means to me. This will keep me out of trouble."

"Any chance you might be able to stay out of trouble without my help?" Hawking uncrossed his arms.

"I'll make more trouble if you don't help me," Anna said.

"If I help you? Whoever this guy is doesn't know what's about to hit him and you want me to be the bat?"

"Is that a reference to the pen being mightier than the sword? If it is then you just went up a notch in my estimation."

"Really? I was kind of hoping that making sure you had at least one book would have done that."

Anna's mouth dropped open. "That was you?"

"Or someone suspiciously like me. Anyone who still thinks reading about the evolutionary beginnings of consciousness after trying to do herself in is someone worth cultivating as a friend." He put the folder back on the table.

I think I like this guy.

"Nurse! We're done here." He shook his head. "By the way, I'm a career civil servant, so the answer is no."

18

DEJA VU

Palma was sure that the sub-committee meeting had gone well, but it seemed that the chairman had a few things on his mind. Palma could see it from a mile away. There was something in the way he'd both framed his questions and avoided asking others. Palma wasn't surprised when he received a call from the Senator's office asking him to stop by before heading back to Fort Meade.

The Senator's office was on the third floor of the Hart Senate Office Building. When Palma walked in, the Senator's receptionist, an impressive woman whom Palma had known for years, greeted him. She offered him the usual coffee or seltzer before she showed him into the Senator's office. The woman had been with the Senator for over twenty years and was someone Palma would have liked to have had on his staff. She was sharp, well-educated, well-traveled, and respected by everyone who knew her.

The reception area was dominated by her rather large desk and a thick dark coffee table where it would be possible to sit and chat for a few moments while waiting. The window treatments matched every other reception area in the building (white curtains with off-white shades), with rare exception. The Senator's office, in contrast, was more of a cacophony of rich colors and textures. His desk was an antique he had acquired during his tenure in the state legislature and dragged along everywhere he went. The deep burgundy wood was the perfect match to the two antique chairs in two of the room's corners by the bookshelves that lined the walls and extended to the ceiling.

Palma thought the office ostentatious. *A public servant has a duty to his nation and symbols of power are self-serving. Do your job or don't do your job, but don't posture and stop others from their appointed rounds.*

If there was one thing that he prided himself on it was looking the way he felt: sharp and on point. When they shook hands, Palma noticed the Senator had put on a few more pounds. They sat down, and spent the next minutes on pleasantries he didn't feel.

"I'm sure you've been hearing some of the rumors flying around," the Senator said.

Finally.

"Sir, there are so many I gave up trying to keep track of them a long time ago." Palma crossed his legs. "If it doesn't come from my analysts, I don't pay attention." Palma smiled. "Except for the Patriots." Both men laughed. They had run into each other at too many football games.

"General, I hate having to bring this kind of news to you, but the group is about to begin proceedings on an operation that has come to our attention and, quite frankly, I need your help."

Palma had heard that kind of entreaty before. The wording was always the preamble to his subordinates just before demoting them or throwing them under the bus for disobeying combat orders. And in the military all orders were combat orders.

"Senator," Palma said, "you know that my office is always open to the sub-committee. In fact, to no one else except for the President. I respectfully request that this investigation be postponed or stopped.

"If there is a true problem I would prefer we work this internally rather than putting assets at risk." He gave the Senator as calm a look as he could muster. Requests like these came in every few months. People on the outside, especially oversight groups, had no clue what was going on and how sensitive the work they did was. Intelligence gathering wasn't for the faint of heart.

"Heard it all before. I can tell you something that you've heard before: it won't be stopped. I've got a whistleblower giving me details that only an insider would know and the things I am hearing about," the Senator reached for a pen and tapped it on his desk, "remind me of another program we had to go on the carpet over. You might remember: it was when the Secretary of State was in your shoes."

Palma remained impassive. A leak? Was he going to have to start another internal search? It always became a witch hunt and would raise the cost of doing business, not to mention put his people on edge. There was a literal army working in the Intelligence community. To find the small faction of malcontents was always a nightmare that led to early retirements, good people leaving, and the firing of scapegoats to uphold the symbolism, and pointlessness, of the hunt.

Some of the smartest people in the country worked for him. It couldn't be helped if some of them misheard their conscience or misread their job description. "An internal investigation is exactly what this needs. All I need is some congressional staffer taking classified documents into an unclassified area to make things worse. Much worse."

"That's for me to worry about." The Senator rubbed the surface of his desk. "I know that we run programs all over the world that would cause untold repercussions if they became public, but," the Senator pursed his lips, "any program running in this country, with or without authorization means people are going to jail."

"Ah. Melodrama. Our institutional memory isn't that bad even if it was almost ten years ago."

"Eight. We're coming up on eight years since we shutdown PRUDENT RAINBOW. Easy to forget how time flies."

"Programs like that have budgets. If they have budgets, we can find them. Last time it was a rogue group, but we stopped them in time," Palma said. *Yes, a rogue group.*

"The committee caught them in time. Remember, George didn't

see it coming. It was us." George Monahan, then General Monahan, head of various special projects, and now Secretary of State.

What was the Senator looking for? What did he know? Palma had an uncontrollable urge to cross his arms, but instead folded his hands on his lap and crossed his legs again. "Senator, you know I came forward and took the brunt of the exposure on that. If anyone remembers, it's me."

It was a painful time for Palma, but it was the price to pay for what was needed. He had almost gone to jail, and Monahan had quietly stepped down. While not planned, it gave him the ability to do something he had wanted to do for a long time: run for office. While in the middle of planning his resignation, he shook enough hands and got appointed instead. A much better outcome and not as expensive as a political campaign.

"Then find the program," the Senator said.

"Does it have a name?"

The Senator spun the pen in his hand. Palma thought twirling objects in your hands while having a serious meeting was a waste of time and a distraction he couldn't afford. He was always happy to see it in others.

"Not yet. As soon as I know it I'll let you know. Whoever this guy is I expect he'll be dropping more Easter eggs before this is over," the Senator said.

"Get me more information. I can't look for something with a description like 'an Intelligence program that might be illegal'."

"I'll have the cleansed information sent to you."

"Cleansed?" Palma asked.

"I don't want you looking for this guy."

"Sir, with all due respect, if we have a leaker we need to know who he is and what he's managed to leak," Palma said.

"I understand, General," he said. "But the committee needs this guy to wander the halls and tell us what he sees. There may be something going on that even you don't know about."

"That would be highly unlikely. However, I understand that the committee needs whatever information it can get even if from unvetted sources." Palma gripped the arm of the chair. "My office will cooperate fully. As always."

The Senator walked to the door. Palma stood and pulled at the bottom of his jacket to straighten the lines along his shoulder.

"General," the Senator had opened the door, but appeared to reconsider it and closed it again as he spoke, "I don't want this to be like that other program. It was sensitive, and put too many people at risk. Would have been a major disaster for us."

"Understood. This is under control. Send me what you have and I'll have my people figure it out." Palma shook his hand.

The Senator didn't let go.

"General, I don't want another PRUDENT RAINBOW. We barely got that under control and it was all you could do to bring it down. Whatever this is has got to be contained, understood, and shut down." The Senator let go. "There is no negotiation here. Whatever it is has got to be shut down."

19

HEART-TO-HEART

Dr. David Hawking walked into the ADX Florence cafeteria, after deciding his civil service career was going to be short-lived anyway, and decided to hunt. The cafeteria was larger than it needed to be given the inmates were fed in their cells, but it made for a comfortable place where the COs and support staff could go when they were hungry or bored. The tables were heavy gray metal bolted to the floor with thin aluminum chairs that didn't match. There were windows to the outside in the far corners that lit up the end of the palatial room, yet there weren't a lot of takers. Most of the diners sat around the tables further in avoiding the heat and the light. Hawking was a fan of sunlight. He just didn't get out often enough.

He hoped his prey was near a window.

Today, he discovered that work had left him rather hungry. Hawking stood on line for the requisite five minutes it took to get through the queue to select the wide variety of food available and scanned the room as he held onto his beige plastic tray stocked with just the right selection of proteins and carbs. He walked up to an officer who was on his way out.

"Is there a CO Moss in here?" Hawking asked.

The officer pointed over to a table in the half-full dining area where a single man sat eating the remains of his lunch. Hawking strode in silence on the streaked tile of the room. The sparse shadows and muted sounds gave the room an oppressive feel. The smells were a mix of institutional cooking and recirculated air. Hawking felt nostalgic.

"CO Moss?"

"Yes, sir?"

This guy really is young. Hawking extended his hand and Moss shook it with a weak grip. *So he might be young,* and *stupid.* Moss's shirt looked pressed one too many times; he had double crease lines along part of his sleeves and a bit of a shine in spots.

"I don't think we've met. David Hawking." He motioned to the table with his tray. "May I join you?"

"I'm almost done, but sure," Moss said. Moss motioned to stand while Hawking sat.

Soft voice, slight twang. He could see why she liked him.

Hawking scrutinized his lunch. *They call this a sandwich?* "No problem, Officer. I just wanted to have a quick chat." He grabbed half of the turkey club and took a bite. The mayonnaise had more taste than the meat. "About one of my patients."

"Aren't they all your patients?"

"You catch on fast. The warden is going to want to see you."

Moss's eyes grew wide.

"It seems you've been seen talking to one of the offenders."

"I," Moss swallowed, "I talk to all of the prisoners that don't have an NHC. They don't usually talk back, but some do and I can tell they appreciate the conversation."

Did anybody buy this aw-shucks routine? "Son, you're talking to one of the NHC inmates. Most of the guys here will cut your throat open if you give them half a chance. They'll compromise you, get you to do things for them that you're not supposed to, and then you'll end up in a local or state prison doing time for just being plain stupid."

Moss put down the can of soda he had been drinking from, eyes opened wide. "Am I in trouble?"

"Of course not." Hawking took another bite. *Yeah, the mayonnaise is definitely tastier.* "But you have to stop talking to Prisoner X."

Moss looked unconcerned for a moment and then disappointed. "Doc, what's a girl doing in here?"

"That is not your concern and I'm sure the warden will remind you of that when you see him."

Moss shrank a little bit in his chair. "You talk to her!"

A couple of COs walked by and gave them a look that lasted more than a few seconds. Moss's admonition had drawn attention.

"That's my job. If I don't talk to them, I can't find out what's wrong with them." Hawking took another bite of his turkey. "And most of the time they don't tell me anything useful. Maybe you can come down one day to Medical and listen to some of the BS stories these guys give to convince me to prescribe pain killers so they can trade them for favors. Or sometimes they're just bored." Hawking leaned forward. "But they're always looking to game the system and get nice guys like you in trouble."

Moss's eyes were glazed and unfocused. "She reminds me so much of my little sister," Moss said. "Smart, pretty." Moss looked up. "How do you do it?"

"Do what?"

"You know. Keep from helping them," Moss said.

Jesus. He wants a heart-to-heart. "Listen, you can't befriend these guys. At the last prison I was at there was this one inmate who was never in trouble. Never. And this was a State facility so these guys weren't in for jaywalking." Hawking opened his bottled water and took a sip. "But this one guy was different. The few times he came to see me were for real issues. I did what I could for him because he wasn't trying to game me. At least that's what I thought." He took another sip. "Turns out he had gamed the last doctor who was there and not only got him in trouble, but got him sent to jail. That doctor should have known better." He paused. "Son, you should know better."

"And yet that didn't stop you from treating him like a human being, did it?" Moss emphasized "did it?" like he was poking Hawking with a stick.

The dining area was starting to fill up. Hawking didn't want this conversation to go on for much longer.

"Listen, son," Hawking said.

"Listen, doc," Moss said. "I appreciate you taking the time to chat," he made air quotes with his hands, "with me, but since the warden wants to see me I guess I might lose my job at the rate that I keep getting in trouble for trying to treat people like people."

"Officer Moss," Hawking softened his voice. "Orville, right? Orville, I'm not saying not to treat them like people, just to watch out for yourself. Trust me when I tell you this has happened to me more than once and I have the scars to prove it."

"So you still see them as human beings deserving of mercy?"

"Of course I do." Another sip of water. His throat felt sore. "But they're here for a reason: they've done wrong things. Make your peace with God about that. You're helping the rest of the world by keeping them here."

"But you still care for them," Moss said.

"Okay, so maybe I'm a bad example. You'll lose your job. You might go to jail. Don't do that. You've got a bright future ahead of you."

"I guess you're right, Doc. I won't talk to her anymore. Such a pity 'cause she sure seems like a nice girl."

"Don't forget she's in here for murder."

Moss's eyes grew wide again. "I swear, Doc, I didn't know that. I thought, I thought..."

"What?" This was going to be good.

"That she was here for her own protection. Why would anybody put her here otherwise?"

"No one goes to jail to be protected," Hawking reached for the second half of his sandwich, "and certainly not at a Supermax." He took a bite. "Go to your appointment. I'll bus your tray."

———

Hawking watched CO Orville Moss walk out of the dining room. He waited an extra minute before standing, hoping that Moss wouldn't be too upset when he found out that the warden didn't really want to see him. Hawking needed him to leave with a sense of urgency that wouldn't bring him back. He put the various items from Moss's tray on top his own, and then stacked the trays.

He walked over to the trash, took a last sip of his water, and, item by item, threw everything away that was on the tray except for Moss's can of soda. Hawking picked up a napkin, wrapped the can, and shook it empty. He reached into his jacket, extracted a pen, shoved it into the can and lifted it without touching it. Then he placed the now empty tray onto the holder above the trash bin, and walked back toward medical.

20

GENERAL SUSPICIONS

It was the morning of the second day. Terrell was in another rental car, a white 2012 Ford Focus, and on his way to get what no one seemed to be able to give him. Answers. At Inova Alexandria, he had managed to convince the attending physician to give him a mild painkiller along with a prescription for a stronger drug he could take once he was home.

And paperwork he could sign on his way out.

The one break he had for the last few days was that he had spare clothes at the home of another agent who kept clothes at Terrell's apartment. You never knew when you would need a fresh change of clothing.

He didn't mind the protection detail; he didn't mind the constant poking and prodding of the nurses and doctors. He didn't mind the pain in shoulder. What he minded were the unanswered questions. Terrell was certain he was never going to like the answers, but he sure as hell was going to find them. So after two nights, against the advice of his physician, he checked himself out and headed to the environs of Virginia just outside of Washington, DC.

He called one of the Bureau-approved car rental companies, took a cab to the nearest rental facility, and drove away with a new car. For a few hours, his main goal was to simply get in the car, and get to his destination.

His final goal of the day: return the car and take the train back to New York. He would rather take the Amtrak than risk the long trip with his left shoulder feeling like someone was poking a hot iron into it.

He left the hospital around 6 am to pick up the rental car with the sun cutting through the cool air, leaving sharp shadows where the clouds had parted, and gray blotchy marks where the clouds did not.

I-395 at 7 am. At that time of the morning, traffic was moving. That would change in another hour when the commuters would hit in full force and bring the road to a stop like they did every morning.

He opened the window. His shoulder ached and the cold would numb it (he hoped). The frigid air did wonders for the skin on his face.

He was awake.

Going where he didn't want to go. As much as he didn't miss his NYC apartment he disliked being outside of New York in general. Either fly him out to some remote location to do work or leave him in the center of the universe. Being born and raised in the Bronx had left him with very strong feelings about the city and the boroughs. He wasn't about to waste a trip from Dallas to question someone who didn't want to talk to him and whom he did not want to talk to either. Even if he was the one who'd rented a car and drove down to meet with his own version of Deep Throat.

He had also done something that he hated doing: he went against protocol and left his protection detail behind. The man he was going to meet would not take well to seeing Terrell if he showed up with the police.

Terrell saw the black SUV parked out front and knew he had arrived at his destination long before the GPS announced it. He pulled up behind the vehicle, pulled out his ID, and stepped out with his hands out to either side of him. The motion was made all the more difficult with his left arm in a sling.

A soldier in full garb came out to greet him. His right hand was on his service revolver.

"Special Agent Terrell Garrison. I'm here to see the General."

———

General Palma greeted him at the door dressed in civilian clothes. He had exactly the sort of home expected of someone high enough up the chain: immaculately manicured, perfect lawn, white door, and great paint job. The bright yellow siding was exactly as Terrell had pictured his home would look the day he decided to settle down. He also suspected he was never settling down.

"Special Agent, good to see you." Palma motioned to Terrell's left arm. "Problems on the job?"

"As we're fond of saying, good day at the office." Both men smiled and shook hands. Terrell relaxed his face to keep the look on his face passive. No point giving the man ammunition he could use.

The General led Terrell into his home, through the sparsely furnished wide-open front entrance. An antique table to the side held photos of children. Cutting through a living room or den Terrell saw some child-like paintings here and there. The General motioned to the soldier at the door and closed the door. "I assume we should be alone when we talk."

"I think that would be a good idea," Terrell said.

The two men walked through the house, passed a carpeted stair-case that led to an upper floor, and cut through the living room to the kitchen.

"It's too late for breakfast, but can I offer you something to eat? You look like you've had an interesting few days."

"You have a nice house. Not very big, but I'm sure it cost you a pretty penny."

"Yes, the perks of having deceased parents with insurance policies."

"I'm sorry, sir," Terrell said.

"No problem, no problem. It's convenient to live and work in this area. I would have found some way to make this work." The General poured himself some orange juice and took a sip then leaned on the marble-topped island. "What brings you to my humble abode?"

"Any children?" Terrell sat in a high-topped chair opposite the General.

"At school."

"Wife?"

"At work. She's a partner at a law firm."

Terrell smiled. "Good for her. I'm sure she's earned it."

"Special Agent?"

Terrell ran his tongue over his teeth. "Tell me about Piercing Ventures."

The General took another sip.

"I'm here in an unofficial capacity, but something tells me that Piercing Ventures is something I need to get clearance on." Terrell looked at the General's face. Impassive.

"Are you looking for me to tell you if Piercing Ventures is an Intelligence front? Are you serious?"

Terrell scrutinized Palma's hands, his eyes, his bearing. *Oh, this guy is good. I can't read him at all right now.*

"The answer is no. We do not funnel funds into the United States as that would be considered money laundering. While it is well-known that we use overseas companies outside the US to do that for us we sure as hell don't do that here."

"Well, General, I am so glad to hear that."

"Are they a company of interest?" Palma held the glass of juice close, but didn't sip. He was waiting.

"That would make my visit one in an official capacity. But I think you know how we do business. I have a team that is going to look at every last hair on their ass until we find something." Terrell swiveled his chair. "And why would you care?"

"I was going to ask that about your interest in Anna Wodehouse."

Terrell's face revealed his surprise.

"Don't worry. I'm not having you followed or anything. I just happen to get regular updates on the inmates who have committed crimes against the US from an Intelligence perspective." He took another sip and drained the glass. "And she has certainly committed some rather interesting Intelligence-related crimes. Entering the UK after hacking into their persons-of-interest system, their citywide camera infrastructure, who knows what else."

"Are you offering to get me in to see her?" Terrell wasn't sure if he felt lucky or terrified.

"Not offering. You just have to ask." He placed the glass in the stainless steel sink. "But I have to ask why."

"She's a person of interest in an ongoing investigation."

"I thought that case was closed. She killed that man after chasing him halfway around the world."

"That man? He was one of your men, wasn't he?"

"Not one of my men." Palma stood up straight. "Don't insult your host."

"Garth Donnell was one of your men."

"Are you admitting to stealing classified information?"

"Are you admitting to lying about someone in WitSec?"

The General didn't take his eyes off Terrell.

So this is what it's like when you're uncomfortable.

The General turned, grabbed another glass, and stuck it in the refrigerator door. The only sound in the room was spurting water. "Like I said, I can get you some time with Ms. Wodehouse, though I fail to see what you would gain from it."

"I can keep you up to date on Piercing Ventures, though I fail to see what you would gain from it." Terrell stood up. The audience was over.

"Then I suppose we won't have much to discuss the next time we get together," the General said.

They shook hands.

Oh, yes we will.

21

SHOT IN THE ARM

Anna was out for her second hour of the day and decided to make the best of it. But it had nothing to do with Orville. No, nothing at all. She was in the wire cage to the south of the basketball court, and she had extra energy that she knew she wanted to burn.

However, she caught herself hoping he would walk by.

If only she knew where she was. There was no sense of direction at the prison. She was never out long enough to get a good fix on the sun, where she walked, or where her cell was in relation to everything else. If Anna had to find her own way out, she was toast.

She gave a silent thanks to whoever had the pull to get her three hours of outside time every day. Even if she didn't do anything during that time at least she had the opportunity to stretch her legs. She had been lucky that there hadn't been a lot of rain in the last few weeks. Would they have taken her outside in that case? She wasn't sure, but she didn't want to find out. The sun was out in all its blazing glory. She would feel the heat of the sun on her mask and her jumpsuit even as she felt the cold of the surrounding air.

She used to love fall.

Orville and the other CO had walked her over to the cage and undid her wrists and ankles like they always did. No one spoke. It was like any other day in her new place of residence. They left her alone as she stood by the cage wall and looked toward the basketball court and the high walls that formed a large, solid, unmoving triangle around her. The outside world felt unreal. She could never leave, yet no one from the outside could do her harm. It was a strange scenario she hadn't thought about when she was in school learning advanced psych. An interesting dissonance: in danger and not in danger at the same time.

Yet, even with the high walls, she felt less alone now than ever before and wasn't sure why.

Her heart jumped. She heard the jangling of keys.

Orville turned the corner and gave her a small wave. She smiled because she knew he couldn't see it. She wondered what he looked like in civilian clothes. And, for a brief moment, not in civilian clothes.

"Hey, sailor. Come here often?" *Argh! That damn cyborg voice! And that was lame!* She tried again. "Come with me if you want to live."

Orville smiled a sad smile. He took small steps toward her as if the size of the step meant something to the cameras that were on twenty-four hours a day watching everything they did. The dirt barely noticed his passing.

"How are you today?" he asked. Orville stood close, but not enough to alarm anyone.

"Dandy. Top of the day." *If I turn off the voice, they'll send storm troopers over and maybe even perform surgery to implant it where I couldn't disable it. Whatever.* She flipped the electrolarynx off her throat. "And you?" *That is so much better!*

"Why are you here?" He walked along the perimeter of the outside of the cage. There was a wire fence behind him (Twelve feet?) topped off with barbed wire, and behind that a structure built into the eastern vertex of the surrounding triangle.

Anna felt her heart drop. "What do you mean?" She walked parallel to him at a non-alarming distance.

"You killed someone." Orville pushed some dirt aside with the side of his shoe. "Would you kill me?"

"I did kill someone, but I didn't do it."

How the hell was she supposed to explain that? Her attorney couldn't even do it. She thought and thought and thought, sometimes late into the night, about that last day. The day she thought she was about to see her father and it turned out to be a set-up. "We don't have to talk anymore. You can go back to your shift, or whatever it is you call it."

Orville stood in place for an extra second and then said, "You remind me of my sister."

His sister? Her heart sank. "She tried to kill your dad?"

"You tried to kill your father?"

Orville's reaction caught Anna by surprise. *He doesn't know why I'm here?*

"Oh, this is a long story." Anna walked to the middle of the cage, and then started to walk back. As she approached the fence, she turned around and walked back again. She smelled the dirt coming up from her steps. Her feet ached and her throat felt dry. Pretty soon she wouldn't need the electrolarynx to sounds like a cyborg.

Her spirit felt sore.

Neither of them spoke as Anna hunted for the words to explain what was going on. What she felt. What she wanted to say. To someone. Anyone. Even in the dustbin she now called home.

"Are you going to...?" Orville started to ask.

"What's your sister like? I never had any siblings."

"Not like you." Orville put his hands in his pockets and crossed his ankles.

No one is like me. "I didn't kill my father. I was looking for my father and found someone else," Anna said. "Can you answer a question of faith?"

Orville looked up. "I can try."

"I just need to know something. If you believe in God then can't you forgive me for something I didn't do?" She walked up to the fence and held onto the crisscrossing wire.

"What?" He swung his right leg like a pendulum. "I can't say. I leave forgiving to God. What I think doesn't matter. You have to atone."

"I'm atone deaf." *Oh no! Did I just say that?*

"I know you think this isn't serious, but it is. You can stay here for the rest of your life or you can begin the road to salvation."

My head is starting to hurt. He is looking less cute with every passing word.

"You can leave this place if you really want to."

How naïve. I'll probably leave this place in a body bag. Anna glanced up at the too-blue sky. At the wispy clouds overhead that looked painted in 3D. "It doesn't matter if I do or not."

"Don't say that. There are people here who want to help you. To protect you."

Yeah, like Jekyll and Hyde. Orville took a step to her left. All she could see was his face though she had a clear view over his shoulder. His facial hair was almost nonexistent. She could see his light blue eyes in the bright daylight. His chest was close to her hands.

"I'm going to tell you something nobody else knows about you."

Anna felt a ball of heat form in her belly. *Oh, this is close. This is way too close.*

"Everybody thinks you're so tough, even you. You think nothing can touch you, but you feel everything. And it hurts. Just as much as the day you thought you found your father and it turned out to be somebody else." He reached up with his hand and touched the fingers of her black glove.

As Anna felt electricity run up her arm the sirens began. Orville's eyes went wide and Anna saw a puff of dirt pop up from the ground behind him. And then another closer to her. As Orville turned, his right sleeve puffed and something tore through his arm just missing her shoulder. Later she would swear that she saw the bullet come out of Orville's arm with shreds of his skin trailing behind it.

Orville fell to the ground close to the door, and Anna threw herself as far away from him as she could get. Did anybody hear that? What the hell was wrong with the guards watching the cameras? Why was the siren going off? Were they under attack?

Anna stopped moving and waited for the next shot. She tasted dust in her mouth and felt sand in her nose. When no other shot came, she crawled as fast as she could and, when she got to the cage door, pulled off her right glove, reached through the bottom slot in the door and reached for Orville's radio, the one on his shoulder. Would they hear her over the siren?

"Officer down! Officer down!"

PART II

STAGING REALITY

22

TARGET PRACTICE

The officer in the South tower was the second person to see the object enter prison airspace.

The seven towers surrounding ADX were usually manned, but budget cuts being what they were, there wasn't always an officer on duty. CO Wesley had been at his post for the mandated amount of time, but his replacement at the South Tower hadn't yet arrived.

Wesley scanned the grounds and looked at the various people coming and going, mostly ADX personnel, when he saw Dr. Hawking, outside the fence, going for his irregularly timed walk. He wasn't sure if the doc was trying to keep a schedule or if he just escaped from medical when he could to get some air and sunlight. Not a lot of that once you were in the prison proper.

The early afternoon sun made everything bright, but the tinted windows that surrounded the circular tower made visibility the easiest part of the shift. The rows and rows of monitors and panels gave the room the feel of Air Traffic

Control without the constant worry of lives at risk in the air. Now if Wesley could just get them to install a better coffee machine life would be good. The smell of burnt grounds seemed to have made a permanent home in the walls.

The doc had just gone well past the South tower heading east when he looked up. When the doc turned around and ran back to the parking area, the officer looked back in the direction Hawking had been observing. *What the hell is that? A plane?*

He grabbed his binoculars. *What's hanging off it?*

Whatever it was, it was moving toward the prison. There was no doubt about that.

Wesley saw Hawking run like he was being chased by a lion back from his car in the direction of the unidentified object. *Holy shit, can the doc move!* He had a gun in his hand.

"Central, this is South Tower. We have an inbound from the air. I repeat, an inbound from the air." Wesley was about to put his radio down when he remembered Hawking. "Be aware: we have ADX personnel outside the perimeter and they are armed. Repeat, they are armed." He saw Hawking aim up at the intruder.

Is that a fucking drone?

Hawking fired into the air as the drone flew into prison airspace. Wesley could see Hawking's shoulders shake as they absorbed the recoil.

Wesley slammed the palm of his hand onto the main alarm switch.

23

CANCELLED LEAVE

Hawking was worried. *Who the hell took a shot at Anna?* He would worry about that later. There was already too much going on. He had run back into the prison, and to the secure outside cage area, as soon as the alarm went off.

And his clip ran out.

He had missed. Every shot. The drone did its job and took off. If he had gotten to his Glock sooner, would the extra few seconds have made a difference?

Let everyone else worry about the fatality. He had a job to do.

Amazing that in a place like this, that was so understaffed, five officers could find the time to help their own. Hawking caught himself. He would have done the same.

In fact, he had done the same.

It helped that the prison went into immediate lockdown with the alarm activation. Didn't matter. The COs were people surrounded by numerous sociopaths and psychopaths. The only ones they had to rely on were themselves. That was their problem, in any case.

Hawking's immediate problem was lying down in the bed in the infirmary. The sheets had seen better days, but new sheets didn't matter as much as an IV of blood. Two officers had been shot. One lived, the other didn't. The one on the IV would live to see at least a few more days (especially if Hawking had anything to say about it). The other was on a slab in the morgue.

How the hell had he missed every shot?

Hawking hated the smell of the ammonia used to keep the area clean. There were five other beds in the room (high-value inmates would never be treated in a room with others); otherwise, it was empty. *He doesn't have any visitors.*

The room had no windows. Hawking grabbed the chart at the end of the bed, gave it a quick glance to see if any of the nurses had updated the numbers, and then returned it to its holder. He rubbed his neck with his right hand.

"Officer Moss, I see you're still conscious," Hawking said.

Moss opened his eyes. He had morphine eyes. "Hi, Doc. What happened to Vasquez?"

Hawking squeezed Moss's left arm. "He won't be going home today." Moss's eyes widened, taking in the news. One of the first shots from the drone had killed CO Vasquez who was simply waiting to take Anna back to her cell. "You okay?"

"No, I'm fine." Hawking walked around the bed to get a better position to begin his examination. Even for something like a flesh wound Hawking knew that Moss would be sent home for a few days to get his thoughts together. They might even offer him an early retirement.

"I see you didn't listen to me," Hawking said.

"What?" Moss shook his head in slow motion. "You lied to me. The warden didn't want to see me." Moss clenched his right hand but opened it again before finishing. That kind of movement was going to hurt for a while.

"I wanted you to realize how serious this was without having to deal with him. I like you, Moss. I never married, never had kids. If I had one, and I almost did, he would be about your age." Hawking looked at Moss for a reaction. "Now this is serious."

"I want to go home."

"To Mommy, a warm glass of milk, and cookies?"

Moss's stony gaze looked past him. Moss was upset.

"Sorry, you just don't seem like the type to live alone."

"Send me home. I guess I'm done here now." Orville's jaw swung back and forth. "I won't talk to her anymore."

"A little late for grand gestures. Getting shot means lots of things. The police. HR." He checked Moss's vitals. All normal. "Maybe they'll even give you an award." He pulled off the blood pressure sleeve. "What they're not going to give you is a ride home."

Moss stared at him. Impassive.

"At least not yet. Doctor's orders."

"I don't understand. If they don't want to pay for an ambulance..."

"Nothing to do with that. You're fine. I have two nurses and myself all saying the same thing." Hawking placed the blood pressure cuff on a nearby cart. "The warden is afraid for your life. It seems that if they killed Vasquez and didn't kill you, they might be back. Sending you home is just a bad idea."

"But I want to go. Can't you tell the warden that I'm well enough to defend myself?"

"I would, except you're not." Hawking grabbed Moss's chart from the bed. Pointless updating numbers that weren't changing. *This guy's got ice water in his veins.* He updated the number anyway.

"I'll tell the warden that you've been doing special favors for some of the inmates." Moss's voice was shaking. "I'll tell him that you've been seeing Prisoner X and that I've been helping you."

"I'm so scared. That would take us both down," Hawking said.

"I'll get an early retirement for this. You'll lose your pension and go to jail."

"So will you."

"I'll get immunity."

Hawking walked over to him and poked at the wound. Moss squealed. "Wrong answer. I've already written you up for fraternizing and if you keep talking, I'll make sure it takes a few weeks to heal." He leaned over the bed. "Retirement will be a be-otch."

Moss frowned and tried to cross his arms. It seemed painful.

I enjoyed that too much. I must be getting soft, Hawking thought.

"I have friends," Moss said.

"I hope they like you enough to help you out."

"I have friends who'll take care of you."

"I don't need any more friends." Hawking pretended to trip and hit the wound again.

Moss cried out.

"Sorry, sorry!" Hawking stood up straight. "Ready to listen to reason?"

Moss put on the face of a recalcitrant teen. "You're right. I don't live alone. I do live with my mother. And a cat."

"I just want to keep you here for observation. I know you and your medical history better than anyone else right now. I looked at your records. You've only just moved here a few months ago. I'm sure you don't have your own GP yet, so an EMT is a poor substitute."

Moss pursed his lips and took a few shallow breaths. "I'll stay."

"The warden will be happy to hear that," Hawking smiled. "I know I am."

———

"Send him to St. Thomas. I don't want him here. We can secure him from over there," Warden Coleman said.

St. Thomas More, twenty minutes away, was the nearest hospital to ADX. Hawking had called him instead of taking the long walk to the warden's office. He almost hung his head at the warden's response but was afraid of the duty nurse walking in on him.

"Warden, listen, I don't know that much about Officer Moss, but I can tell you the he was begging me to let him stay. Since there's no reason for someone to want to shoot an inmate, it only makes sense that the two officers were the target. He's afraid for his life."

"I'll come over to talk with him."

"Do it in a few hours. He's still quite overwrought. And," Hawking took a breath, "I had to sedate him. He's very excitable and the only way I could get him to rest was to put him to sleep."

The warden cursed under his breath, but loud enough for Hawking to hear him. "That boy has been nothing but trouble from the day he arrived..."

"I understand, Warden, but I don't need details unless they have a direct bearing on his health. I can take care of him for now and then we can send him home." Hawking stood up from behind his desk. He was using his desk phone and the cord was long enough for him to take a few steps. He thought better of it when he was on his feet and the phone cord was taut with within two steps. Primitive piece of crap.

"Dr. Hawking, I know you mean well, but no. I want him out of here. I don't want anything to happen to him, he is one of my men, at least for now, but the state police can guard him night and day. I don't have the personnel."

Or the caring, Hawking thought.

"Were you in the military?" Hawking asked.

"No, and I don't need a story about military camaraderie and Band of Brothers."

Hawking chuckled. "None of that." He lowered his voice. "The boy looks up to you. He told me that himself. Besides, you really want the state police involved in this? It's bad enough they've been here twice in the last few days."

Hawking waited. No more words.

"How long do you want to keep him here?" the Warden asked.

"No more than forty-eight hours, probably just twenty-four. I'll do a better job than the local hospital and I know he'll be grateful," Hawking said.

"This is an HR problem now, Doc."

"Understood, but let's not send him out to be a sitting duck just in case someone really is gunning for him. Let the locals do their job and when the Bureau shows up, we'll let them do theirs."

"If he doesn't retire, I'm having him transferred."

"I'm with you, Warden."

"And surrender your firearm. I hope Vasquez wasn't done in by friendly fire."

"Done."

"Keep me abreast of any developments."

"As always, Warden. As always."

24

PROFESSIONAL COURTESY

In the distance, the man saw his target.

The sun had already gone down and it took him a long time to follow the tracks into the forest about twenty miles from the prison. But he'd done it. The satellite intel had come in handy, but the only way to take care of this was on the ground. The tracks were fresh even as his target did his best to cover his trail.

The target had worked from an RV. He flew the drone right off the highway a few miles away, and the rest was history. The man found the abandoned trailer burned and gutted; its contents destroyed and unusable.

The moon gave off just enough light to allow him to see the terrain. The woods were dense, but he could move without making any sounds. He loved the smell of the forest. Working outdoors was always preferable to being inside. The chill on his skin, the feeling of wild life all around him, the promise of the dark. He felt at home.

The going was slow, but that was fine. He had all night.

———

A few hours later, he sat and aimed. If only he could kill him now.

That would make his job so much simpler. He looked through the scope at the man hidden up in the branches of one of the larger trees. He was so close that if he moved the wrong way, the sound would give away his position and he would have to either run or hope that the man wouldn't shoot faster than he could react. These guys were pros. No point taking any chances.

He pulled out his cell phone and dialed. Ahead of him, about a hundred feet to the target's right, a light came on. The cell phone he had set up thirty minutes earlier. The man moved. Some behavior was just too hard to suppress. Now he knew where the target's head was.

He pulled the trigger and the target fell out of the tree onto the pile of rocks. If the target stood, he would have to kill him without waiting.

Wait.

Wait.

No movement. Approach and reassess.

———

The man built a small fire to do two things: take the chill out of the air and make it easier to see how his target would react. He didn't have a lot of time, but he didn't want to appear impatient. He cleared the area around the fire to make sure he didn't start a fire he couldn't control. The smell of burning wood permeated the area. He could feel the air around them getting warmer with pockets of cold sliding onto his consciousness.

His target came to.

"Good evening."

The target squeezed his eyes shut and blinked numerous times. Good. He was going to be coherent even after falling onto the pile of rocks he had set up on both sides of the branch. In addition to shooting him, he wanted to make sure that the target was somewhat battered.

The target looked around at the fire. At the dark. At the duct tape holding his arms to his side, his legs in a crouch. His wrists and hands securely taped onto a large rock. His multi-day stubble gave him the look of a survivalist. It was difficult to see what the man was wearing, but it was probably standard issue camo. The target's face was covered in mud. The target swallowed.

The man stood up and splashed some water on the target's face from a water bottle he held in his hand. The plaid flannel shirt absorbed the liquid, leaving a spreading stain on his shoulders and chest. He brought his face down level with the bound man. "This isn't going to go well if you don't talk to me." Their eyes met. The man knew not to show concern or anger to his prisoner. "And to answer your question: yes, I am going to kill you."

———

He held the target's fingernail up for examination. They never looked the same as they did when attached. "You have seven more. And ten toes. But I'm hoping you don't make me take off your shoes because I probably won't be able to take the smell."

"Let me go and I promise not to kill you."

"Ah. Signs of life. I thought the only word you could say was 'Argghh!'" He dropped the fingernail onto the target's lap where the other two nails lay. Sitting on the ground was uncomfortable for sure, but the man stood when it bothered him. He reached down and picked up a small, thin branch. He twirled it around then tapped it against his ear.

"Who are you?" the target asked.

"The question is, why are you shooting at inmates in a prison? Have those men not suffered enough?" The man took the branch and outlined the target's ear. The target tilted his head away from the stick. "Are you a mercenary or an unfortunate victim caught in the crossfire? Collateral damage, perhaps?" He tapped the man's face with the thin stick of wood. "Who sent you to shoot someone at the prison?"

He had torn off each of the target's two fingernails with little fanfare or flourish. The rock on which his hands were attached was splattered with blood.

"Who are you?" He reached down, jammed his own thumbnail under the man's index finger, and ripped the target's index fingernail. He splashed more water on the man's face as a scream left the target's throat.

"If I have to ask again..." He tapped the target's hand with the branch.

"I was given orders. I don't know by who, but they were approved by the brass." Gasps escaped from deep in his throat.

"Hmm. The brass have given up your ass." He sat on a nearby rock. "Were you here to shoot guards or inmates?"

The man gritted his teeth.

"Or a particular guard? Or a particular inmate?" He splashed water on the target's hands. "Just to show you I'm not a cruel man."

"An inmate."

"Which one?"

"The one at the location. I don't know. I was told he would be there and he was."

"And yet you missed."

"The damned second guard stepped in the way. The first one was in the way so I took him out to get a clear shot."

"You certainly did." He stood and walked. This was a useless conversation. Time to bring it to a close. He kicked at the fire. The burning embers shook and smoked. The man loved camping. Building a fire was like breathing. Just like getting answers. Just like knowing when there were no more answers to be had.

They were so far into the park that no one would see them.

"Why kill him? The inmate?" the man asked.

"Not my call. They tell me who to do and I do it."

"But you're a soldier. Do you really just do whatever they tell you?"

Of course he did. The man had done it many times, but he did it because he was good at it. The bound professional on the ground was a tribute to his skill. "You could not have done what you did without knowledge of scheduling." He bent down to face the target again. "Who helped?"

"Hell if I know! They told me where to go and I went. I did my job."

"I'm afraid you didn't. The inmate is still alive."

The target bent his head. He'd failed at his task and got to die anyway. Dying knowing he had completed a job well-done might have been comforting. Or not.

"You're not going to let me go, are you?"

"If I did, you could ID me. You could tell your high-powered friends to come get me. You might come get me out of revenge. Your children might chase me down even though what you were asked to do was not only illegal," he outlined the target's other ear with the branch, "but just not fair. I mean, shooting an unarmed prisoner in a cage. Do you train for that?"

The target's breathing was shallow. "If you're going to do it then do it."

"Don't tell me how to do my job."

He kicked dirt onto the fire until it was completely out. His pace was deliberate. Building to a crescendo.

In the dark, a muted bang sounded simultaneously with a bright flash that lit up the small area.

25

BLOODY NAILS

What was the last thing she told him? She couldn't remember. Anna sat on the cold hard floor of her cell with the image of Moss falling to the ground playing over and over before her.

I should probably put in a kite. No, that would be a waste of the doctor's time. He shouldn't be bothering with me.

The words streamed through her mind in a slower and slower pace, like floating shreds of skin in a transparent gel. She scratched at her arm through the bright orange sleeve. Imagined what her scars looked like. Scabs. *You should always tear scabs off as quickly as you can.*

A pattern on the linoleum floor caught her attention. Was that a blood stain? Or an outline of Manhattan? She closed one eye and then another. Her breathing slowed. A sense of calm came over her. The cell was the same as always. Solid, hushed.

Anna stood and walked over to the wall. Felt the solid surface with her hand. Closed her eyes as she pushed the side of her face on the concrete. The coolness relaxed her shoulders. *If I slammed my head against this, would it hurt for more than a few seconds? Yeah, I'm sure it would. Is it normal to think about death all the time? Do I think about death all the time?*

She scraped her nails on the wall. She didn't feel anything. Her eyes unfocused as she thought about rainbows and fall leaves. She scraped her nail against the wall up and down and up and down and felt a nail break. Blood streaked the wall. She stepped away and started to scratch at her mask. *Make it stop!* She scratched over and over. What was going on? Why wouldn't it stop? She reached under the mask, reached behind her head, and tried to find some hair, but all she felt was stubble. Where was her hair?

The mask fell to the floor with the sound of an uninflated water balloon. Her neck felt like ants were crawling all over it. Her hands, her nails didn't make it feel any better, but she scratched anyway, over and over.

She heard a scream and wasn't sure where it was coming from and all she heard was that it went on and on.

She pulled up the sleeves of her jumpsuit and tore at the bandages and scabs until CO Marshmallow came through the door and knocked her to the ground.

———

Anna woke up, but nothing seemed normal. Her vision was blurred and she couldn't move her arms.

"Nice job, Anna."

The punctuated words stabbed her.

"How's it feel to fail again?" A female voice. Her own.

Thoughts were hard to come by. Where was she? She opened her mouth, but nothing came out at first. A storm formed in her chest and drove its way through her throat until she started to sob in frustration. The sobs started low and gained in intensity until each one wracked her body and the restraints felt like they were going to break her bones. Pain crackled through every part of her body, but she couldn't stop herself from trying to sit up and failing over and over again.

She felt a hand on her shoulder. "Stop. You have to stop." The voice of authority. A pinch on her arm. She wanted to keep going, but stopped and blinked asleep.

———

"Hello, sunshine." Hawking's voice was unmistakable.

When did it become an insurmountable task to open her eyes?

What did he give her?

"I want to go home."

"Why does everyone start their conversations with the same request?" He put his hand on her forehead and held open her right eyelid open. Bright light. "You dilate like a pro."

She thought back. Her memory was starting to go because all she remembered was...scratching at the walls. CO Marshmallow.

Right.

"You've been out for a few hours. Do you remember what happened?" Hawking asked.

"I need to die."

She had never been in this part of Medical before. It looked like a storage closet. Crappy colored walls. Crappy colored job. Is this the best he could do with his life?

An awful smelled wafted around her.

"It's not that I want to die. I don't have a reason to live. Even a small, empty, pointless friendship..."

"You mean Orville?" Hawking walked around the room tidying up. "He's fine. A little shook up, some blood loss. I think we might have to cut his arm off."

"What!"

"Just kidding, just kidding." Hawking held his palm out. "For someone who professes not to care you certainly got yourself twisted into a knot."

"Is he okay?"

"He's my patient. Of course he's okay."

"And me?"

"You're my patient." He pulled her chart and paged through it. "Of course you're okay."

"I think," how could she say this? "I think you need to put me under."

"Planning on some surgery?"

"Please." She took a breath and swallowed. "You don't know how much it hurts." She leaned back on the hard bed and paper-thin pillow. Anna could feel the wire-mesh under the mattress. "Please."

Hawking slammed his hand down on the tray by his side. "You are exhausting my patience." He thrust the chart back on the foot of the bed. "You have no reason to give up. None!" He looked behind him at the closed door and shook his head.

"I almost killed someone today."

"Technically that was yesterday. And, no, you didn't almost kill someone. You definitely saved someone." He walked around to the left side of her bed. "My daddy hates me. My daddy abandoned me. Where oh where has my little dad gone? Where oh where can he be?" He swung back and forth as he sang the last two sentences.

Tears crawled out of Anna's eyes. "Do you know why your father left you?"

"He didn't want to be arrested."

"No..."

"He left because he had died on the way home." *He couldn't think of a single reason to come for me.*

"No."

"He left because he loved me." The words felt acidic leaving her mouth.

"No..."

Anna felt a sob escape her lips, causing her heart to tear open, leaving her hemorrhaging inside.

"He left because he got tired of your incessant whining," Hawking said.

"Why are you so mean?" She screamed out the words. "Why do you hate me?"

"Do you think that seeing you like this would make him proud? Do you think that all the years that he took care of you that he ever expected to see you give up? I thought you were a head-strong, no-nonsense, intelligent woman? *The Origins of Consciousness*? Why don't you just curl up with a nice Harlequin romance and drown your sorrows in your broken dreams?"

Her chest heaved up and down. "I'm so tired. I'm so tired." She wanted to get angry. In her previous life, she would have cut him open and fed him to the neighborhood strays. She just didn't have the energy.

Hawking leaned over and examined her face. "Anna, he can't wait to see you."

"Where's my father?"

"I don't know." He pulled back and turned away. "Orville can't wait to see you."

"Where is he?"

"In another part of the facility. He's resting comfortably and is just fine." He loaded up a syringe and pushed it into the top of her left arm.

"When can I see...?"

26

JUDICIOUS DECISION

Time to amp up the level of security theater.

Terrell had commandeered a black Chevrolet Suburban to give his next task the proper level of seriousness. In Bureau circles, to get a judge into the right frame of mind everyone knew that you had to do three things: make them understand the gravity of the situation, the negative impact of moving too slowly, and the time pressure involved. In other words, make him feel like part of a TV episode. Sad, but psychology worked on both sides of the table. Such intelligent people, but still just people.

The sun was going down. At various times, Terrell opened his windows and let in the cool late afternoon air as he headed north into the environs of upstate New York. As soon as the skin on his face felt chilled he rolled the windows back up again, but within a few minutes he lowered them again. The air conditioner was tempting but emitted stale smelling air that reminded him too much of his captivity, as short-lived as it was.

Was this trip going to help? His last attempt had gone nowhere so it was time for a fresh start.

————

An older woman opened the door of the regal two-story home that sported an immaculate lawn with lights that outlined the driveway. She wore a flowery print dress and black flats. Her blond hair was short, pulled back around her ears, revealing emerald earrings that highlighted eyes that were startled to see him. Was she startled because she was expecting someone else, or because he was black? Terrell stopped caring a long time ago, but every so often reactions like hers reminded him.

"Good evening," she said.

"Good evening, ma'am. Is Judge Burke available? I called ahead and I believe he's expecting me." Terrell stood at the door with his hands behind his back and a respectful distance from the door.

The judge had every right to be skittish about late afternoon visitors. His wife not so much.

The judge appeared a few seconds later. He extended his hand. "Good evening, Special Agent Garrison. A pleasure to see you again." He smiled, and they shook hands.

———

US Federal Judge Silas Burke sat with Terrell in a stereotypical setting: Queen Anne chairs before a fireplace with a single log burning more for show than for heat. Burke's wife had disappeared as soon as she saw her husband greet the man at the door as more than a stranger and left them alone.

"How are you doing, Judge?"

"Just fine, Terrell. It's always good to see you, though I know it's always about some business I would rather not have to know about." Burke was one of a select number of judges who knew about the classified programs run by the United States. While not related to his position as a member of the Foreign Intelligence Surveillance Court, or FISC, sometimes referred to as FISA, Terrell knew that this problem was firmly in his bailiwick.

"You and me both, Your Honor. This has to do with Carpenter Poole, aka Anna Wodehouse," Terrell said.

"Yes, that young woman. Can I get you a drink?"

"Only if it's a single malt." Terrell was still on painkillers for his shoulder but was good at partaking even when he wasn't partaking.

"I think I can arrange that. I'm partial to single malts myself." The judge walked over to a table and held up one of the many bottles long enough to look at the label. He poured them both a drink. "I've heard you were driving Judge Harrelson crazy about that a month or so ago."

"All in the name of a case, Your Honor. Always in the name of a case." They both smiled again.

Judge Harrelson was in his 70s and sided with the government as a knee-jerk reaction. Always useful when you wanted to win a case.

"You know I rarely turn down requests like this from the Bureau," Burke put his drink down on the end table, "but the reverse engineering of evidence is starting to piss me off."

Terrell took the glass Burke offered him and watched Burke sit down. He was still wearing a white button-down shirt with dark pants; he must have just arrived from another busy date in court. With all the crime statistics showing that things were getting better, why did there seem to be so much work left to be done?

"As am I, Your Honor. But none of those agents would be me." Terrell took a sip. The hot taste of the whiskey left a burning trail down the back of his throat. The judge wouldn't remember that Terrell drank nothing after that first sip. "I would rather come to you too many times than not enough. And today would be one of those times."

"Personally, I don't care. Either follow the letter of the law to do your job or get another job. Or go to jail first. I'm not particular about which."

Burke was a stickler; Terrell was always happy to work with him. Burke did his best to keep everyone honest even if he made the higher-ups upset, which Burke did on a regular basis.

Terrell was going to miss him when he retired.

"What's with the girl?" Judge Burke asked. He crossed his legs.

Terrell knew that was a sign of a long conversation.

He hoped the small talk wouldn't take long but was prepared to indulge him. "What do you mean?"

"You're the second request the court's received in as many weeks."

Terrell blinked. "Second?" *What the hell is going on?*

"Yes. Maybe you should see her together," Burke said. He sipped from his snifter.

"Who would I see her with?" Terrell asked.

"Maybe you need to do some investigating. Talk to some of your friends in high places."

"I need to see her," Terrell said.

"Didn't you already get permission to do that?"

"Apparently not. The warden at Carswell refused to let me see her, citing a National Security Directive that I'm not even allowed to look at much less circumvent."

"Ah, yes." The judge took a sip. "I'm hearing more and more of those all the time. I suspect you're going to lose on this one."

"She's instrumental in another case."

"Aren't they always? The problem is that whatever she tells you can be disclosed in open court and lives may be at risk."

"I need to see her. Whatever restriction the directive dictates can simply be set on the court ruling for my visit. This is an old case, she's a new witness, and it has a bearing on a possible money laundering case being handled through FATF."

"What do they have to do with anything?" He put down his drink on a small table to this left toward the fireplace. "Having foreign law enforcement involved in a case on US soil makes my job harder. I haven't seen anything on it, have I?"

"No, Judge Cornier is familiar with the case, but he wasn't available."

"Oh, so you thought to saddle me with this?" Burke's eyes smiled.

"I could use the help," Terrell said.

"If you talk to her, even with the permission of the court, they could bring you in on administrative charges or even obstruction."

"What would I be obstructing? She's already in jail."

"That's classified, as well."

"And if I see her anyway?"

"If you got past Warden Rollins, you mean? Good luck with that. She's a bigger hard ass than I am. You could end up in the cell next to Wodehouse."

"Sometimes I think that might be the only way to question her," Terrell said.

"Let's not go that far." Burke grabbed his drink and took another sip.

"What do you need to get this moving forward?" Terrell asked.

"You mean what would convince me? Honestly, nothing. You might have wasted this trip. Usually these kinds of judicial decisions are easy even if I have to take time to make them. I can't give you authorization to see her because to see her would open up possible classified programs to exposure they might not survive. Not to mention piss off some people who don't want their operations known or examined."

"Give me authorization to speak with her for one hour, in a totally classified setting, where someone from DIA or whoever the hell has her locked away can decide what I'm allowed to use or not."

The Judge took another sip and nodded to himself. "That sounds reasonable. What's the problem?"

"There's a chance that the information she knows will point to an illegal intelligence op here in the US."

"Great. A toxic op." Burke gazed at Terrell over his wire-frame glasses. "That's pretty dangerous. Even for the Bureau."

"I understand, sir. That's why I'd like to interview her alone, but I'll take whatever I can get."

27

VANISHING LEADS

Ewan Brown. The address was in the Upper West Side of Manhattan. Nice neighborhood but pretty nondescript as Manhattan neighborhoods went. Terrell was grateful for the side trip, but he had other things that needed doing. He was going to have to return to Virginia tomorrow. Another visit with the General he wasn't looking forward to.

Judge Burke was an old friend. They never talked about their commonalities or met for drinks or dinner, but there was something about the judge that led him to think (to hope?) he had an ally in the older man. That was good. Terrell thought he was running out of friends both inside and outside the Bureau.

A friend who gave him a name. And not just any name.

Ewan Brown.

As Terrell shook hands with the judge he felt a slip of
paper in his hands. He read it in his car, and called it in.

The morning air was brisk. It was fall in New York, and Terrell enjoyed the biting feel of the air in his nostrils. It was cloudy enough that chunks of the neighborhoods had no shadows, but sunny enough that when the sun poked its way through the cloud cover, everything looked bright. Terrell needed bright.

The man he was coming to see had better have answers or he might break Terrell's autumn-induced mood.

Ewan Brown, journalist. The paperwork was as devoid of information as Terrell would expect from someone who didn't want to be known or tracked. The paperwork that Ewan Brown submitted to DOD for permission to visit with a federal inmate. To visit with Anna.

How the hell did this asshole get permission and Terrell didn't? *Breathe. Just breathe. Lessen the paranoid thoughts.* No one was out to get him, but if this kept up, Terrell was liable to become someone else's paranoid nightmare. He would subpoena this guy's notes. If he took pictures, recordings, he would subpoena it all. He probably wouldn't be allowed to, but right now Terrell was not in a caring mood and the more he thought about this stranger getting in to see Anna the angrier he felt.

Terrell looked up at the five-story Upper West side building. Short enough not to have an elevator, but tall enough to make walking the stairs annoying. Terrell entered the front door and looked up Brown's apartment. There it was. 3R.

He pressed the buzzer. What did this man know?

No answer. He pressed the buzzer again.

A Latino man came in behind him. Mexican? Guatemalan? It didn't matter. "Excuse me, but are you the super here?"

The man shook his head and responded with a heavy accent. "Yes, yes. You looking for an apartment?"

"No. 3R." He held aloft his ID. "FBI."

———

The man led him upstairs and, after looking at his ID a few more times, a call to the management office authorized Terrell to enter the apartment.

It was moments like these that always worried him; he didn't have a warrant. He didn't have probable cause (he just wanted to talk to the man!). And he sure as hell didn't have any reason to break into this guy's apartment.

If Ewan Brown had ever lived there.

Terrell stood in the middle of the empty apartment. Freshly painted off-white walls. Clean wood floors. Ready to be occupied. The disconnect that Terrell confirmed: a deposit was paid. A month's rent was also paid.

Yet empty. No furniture. No pictures. No dishes. Nothing. If it wasn't because the apartment was already renovated, there was no saying if Terrell might have found the apartment stripped to the rafters.

No one lived at the apartment Ewan Brown had given as his address. He had either moved out as soon as he'd interviewed Anna, or he had never really been there to begin with. The super had never seen anyone come or go from 3R in the last few weeks.

Terrell thanked the super and left the empty shell.

He bounded down the steps, flipping open his cell.

"Jonesy, what the hell is going on?" Terrell called his partner in crime back at the NY Bureau offices. "You got me this paperwork and it's all bogus."

"Listen, it's not like I did a background check on this guy."

Special Agent Howard Restinack, who Terrell always complained couldn't get rid of his Brooklyn accent, had worked with Terrell for many years. Terrell called him Jonesy as a throwback to old school New York. The moniker reminded him of the NYPD at the turn of the 20th century.

"Yeah, I know, but it isn't like he might be on vacation. The place was down to the walls," Terrell said.

"Maybe he took his furniture with him. Hold on while I do a quick check on his forms."

Terrell, for all his complaining about turf wars among the various federal law enforcement agencies, was grateful for one thing: what little information they shared they shared in full. He knew Jonesy would find something.

"Well, isn't that interesting?"

"I don't need interesting. I need his warm bottom sitting in a chair in front of me so I can ask him who the hell he is," Terrell said.

He stepped outside. The weather wasn't cold enough for coats, but he could see that New Yorkers were already pulling out their winter clothes. It was going to be a cold winter.

"His name comes up, but I gotta tell you I have never seen paperwork go through that fast."

"How fast?"

"Like forty-eight hours fast."

Terrell stopped. Forty-eight hours? That wasn't even remotely possible. "He was able to get that fast, authorization to see someone I've been spending months trying to see?"

"He has clout. You on the other hand..."

"Ha, ha, ha. Remind me to send you a funeral card on your next birthday."

How could he have done that? The invisible man got clearance to see someone at a maximum-security prison in the middle of Texas that no one else was allowed to get. A journalist?

My ass.

"Hold on a second."

Terrell was confused but willing to live with it. He had to talk to the General again. If there was anyone who might know about Ewan Brown, it was him. Maybe he'd sent Ewan Brown. Now that *would* be interesting.

The scenarios ran through his head faster than he could think. He closed his eyes for a moment and let the moment wash over him. Did Brown make it to Carswell already? Did Warden Rollins know and not tell Terrell?

"You still there?" Jonesy asked.

"Still here."

"I've got another good thing for you."

"How good?"

"Confusing good."

"I'm going to get on a train in about five minutes to get a car and start a long drive. Can we just keep it to good?"

"This woman you keep trying to see? She's in the Federal Medical Center, right?"

"Right. She's a woman. It's an ADX facility for women. She was sent there after her trial."

"Then it's probably just a mistake." Jonesy sounded apologetic. "Maybe this isn't the guy."

"What are you talking about?"

"Well, why does this guy's authorization list ADX Florence?"

28

TELLING TALES

"General Palma's office."

The voice on the other end of the line sounded soft, but male. Shouldn't there be a Rottweiler on the other end? The muffled noise of the passing traffic penetrated the closed windows of Terrell's car and reminded him how much he missed having two good working ears (Was his other ear ever going to show up to work?)

"Yes, good afternoon. This is Special Agent Terrell Garrison. Is the General available?"

"I'm afraid he's not," the soft voice on the other end said.

Damn it. He didn't want to appear unannounced again at Palma's house, but it looked like he might have to. At some point, the General was going to be within his rights to either file a complaint or call Terrell's immediate supervisor. Tolsen would not be happy to get that call.

"Is he expected back?" Terrell asked.

"In the morning, but if this is an urgent request..." the voice on the other end trailed off.

"Yes, this is an urgent request," Terrell stretched his neck, "but it can wait until morning."

"Excellent, I will pencil you in."

Terrell slowed down. He was on his way into Maryland, but he might as well pull into a hotel and go over the latest FATF paperwork on Piercing. "You are in for eight am. Of course," the soft-spoken voice on the end of line said, "perhaps you and I could meet?"

———

The Cigarette Outlet and Truck Stop is, on a good day, ninety minutes outside of Washington, DC, off Route 81. It took Terrell almost two hours to arrive at the truck stop on Martinsburg Pike in Clear Brook, VA. He considered himself lucky to have gotten there that early. The Olde Stone Diner, located in a cream-colored vinyl-sided converted home, wasn't exactly what he had hoped for, but they would get the anonymity they needed.

Terrell had been to upscale restaurants and little holes-in-the-wall in various locations in New York and always preferred the hole-in-the-wall. Sometime the smells weren't right (though they were today), or the menu sparse (which it was), but he felt in his element. Growing up in the Bronx meant that he felt at home in the local places more than in the large, well-managed, efficiently run restaurants of Manhattan.

A young man came in and looked around. Terrell had been there before and really enjoyed the basic breakfast menu. *If you must eat at a diner, it should be for breakfast. And this young man looks to be on today's menu.* Terrell glanced at him and the man walked over. He was average build, wore glasses, and had on a very pressed navy blue suit. He and Terrell shook hands and they sat.

Weak handshake.

"My name is Andrew Yen. There's no point hiding my name since you can find it out very easily enough." He folded his hands on the table.

"No need to be paranoid this early in our conversation," Terrell said. He put his hand around the bottomless, steaming hot cup of coffee. He stroked the cup to keep his fingers from scalding.

"I need to know that whatever I tell you is in the strictest confidence."

Terrell smiled and chuckled. He tapped the surface of the light blue table. "Going fast. I know it was a long drive, but you'll beat the traffic on the way back."

"I won't be staying long." His smile didn't reach his eyes. Andrew's hands remained folded.

"Oh, please, you have to have some of their coffee. It's the best," Terrell said.

"You've eaten here before?"

"No," Terrell lied, "but it's always great in places like this." Terrell had taken a quick scan of the diner before he sat down, under the auspices of going to the men's room. No exit to the back; you came and went by the front door.

"General Palma is a good man," Andrew said.

So this is what betrayal sounds like.

"I know he is," Terrell said. No perspiration, but Andrew now squeezed his hands. *He's comforting himself.*

"You're looking for Anna Wodehouse," Andrew said.

Terrell forced himself to relax his jaw. *How does he know my button?*

"I need to know about Piercing Ventures," Terrell said. There was very little this twerp could tell him about Anna. Even hearing him say her name tugged at Terrell's chest like a soft hook in his rib.

"The General knows all about her. He actually has a special briefing once a week and she is always the first agenda item."

"Can I get you boys anything?" The waitress came over and pulled Terrell out of a glare that strained his neck muscles.

Thin with a stained skirt apron, she grabbed their menus before they could respond.

Terrell blinked. *First item?* He looked up to break eye contact with the man sitting before him. "Yes, some more coffee please. And a toasted corn muffin. Butter on the side." He flashed his best smile at her and she smiled back.

"And you, son?"

Hurry up and order so she can go away.

Andrew did not return her gaze. "Nothing, thank you."

She walked off after giving Terrell a look that questioned his choice of companion.

He put both his hands around his coffee cup. "Piercing Ventures."

"My work in the General's office means that I get to look at information that others would take years to find."

"Yes, what with all those pesky subpoenas and warrants. Especially not knowing what you're looking for.

"What are you looking for?" Terrell asked. *Money?*

"I am just a concerned citizen," Andrew said.

"I can see concern just dripping off you." Terrell draped his arms around the booth. "Tell me about Piercing Ventures."

"If what you want is to question Ms. Wodehouse, I can help you with that." Andrew stared Terrell in the eyes. "Or perhaps you care more about the General's work when he was doing covert operations."

"One of us isn't listening. Piercing Ventures. What can you tell me about Piercing Ventures?"

"For example, about eight years ago, the General was a manager working under then Operations Chief George Monahan."

"Oh, so you know something about Secretary of State

Monahan. Democrat." Terrell took a slow sip of his black coffee. "Is this a long story or a short one?"

"I want to know that anything I know will not land me in prison."

"There are laws, you know."

"I'm a federal employee. I'm protected by federal whistle-blower laws, unlike Mr. Snowden." Andrew's eyes were calm. No hint of stress. His words were in conflict with his appearance.

"You seem concerned. Tell me about Piercing Ventures."

"You are looking for one of your colleagues."

Terrell put down his cup. "And?"

"I want to know that anything I know will not land me in prison." Andrew unfolded his hands and placed them on his lap under the table.

"Which colleague?" Terrell's eyes felt hot. The palms of his hands tingled.

"An agent named Del Kirby."

Terrell took a deep breath. *Do I grab this throat now or later?* Was he even serious? "How do you know that name?"

Andrew looked down at his empty place setting. He was playing an interesting game.

"How can you help me get to Anna Wodehouse? And who is Ewan Brown?" Terrell asked.

"I have not heard Mr. Brown's name before."

Terrell didn't take his eyes off Andrew. That was lie number one.

"Perhaps I can get you information about him."

"Don't worry about him." Terrell thought for a moment that he might be getting set up. "What can you tell me about Anna Wodehouse?"

"She's a criminal. Del Kirby, on the other hand..." He shrugged. "He was in one of the files I accidentally looked at about some work the General was involved in approximately eight years ago."

"And?" Terrell relaxed his jaw. *Don't scare him off.*

"The General was involved in many things back then. As he is today." Andrew raised his right eyebrow. "The General is a very busy man."

"Aren't we all?"

"He was almost arrested, but instead took a plea in exchange for his resignation. But part of the deal was that he could remain in the military. It was decided that the operation he was involved in didn't reflect on his military honor," Andrew said.

"Did it?"

"Did what?"

"What he did. Did it impugn on his military honor?" Terrell asked.

"You'll have to ask him. Apparently he was one of the last people to see Special Agent Kirby alive."

29

TEAM-BUILDING

"General, I know you're not going to be happy about this, but I just gave the go-ahead on the internal investigation," Senator Bigelow said.

It was morning and Palma was sure that he must have misunderstood the senator. He stood dressed for work in his pressed uniform with the phone against his ear in the foyer of his home. To his left was a winding staircase that led to the second floor where he and his children slept in their three-bedroom house. To the right was the door that led out to his driver. Another few minutes and he would have been out the door with his private cell phone, out of touch from people like Bigelow. Andrew would have told him about it when he got into the office.

Maybe his phone was broken. Maybe someone was playing a practical joke.

There was nothing practical about this call.

"So all of our conversations were for nothing," Palma said.

"I don't know where to begin explaining how disappointed I am. What more do you want from me?" Palma had assured Bigelow that he would get him all the information he needed...up to a point, but he didn't need to get into that right away. Palma had no way of knowing where that point was if the senator wouldn't at least work with him before letting something like this happen.

"Senator, this is unacceptable. You and I spoke just the other day. I've always been cooperative and you know how sensitive our work is here."

"Oh, stop it. You know how this works. You create one or more programs that are legally questionable and at some point, the things you're doing are going to become known," Bigelow said.

Just another bump in the road, Palma thought. *We'll work this one out.* Legal paperwork meant nothing these days. He would make sure it stayed that way. There was no way for an Intelligence organization to achieve anything if it had to worry about the law. The law was for everyone else.

"How long have we been doing this?" Bigelow asked. "Almost as long as you've been running the Agency, that's how long. When you were sworn in, one of the things I asked from you was to clean things up. Clean them up! Now couldn't you have done that? You would have made both our jobs easier."

"You didn't appoint me to leave the country unprotected though, did you?"

How many years had it been? This morning it didn't matter. Every morning Palma woke up, looked around at his bedroom and his life, and appreciated it all for a few moments. The day was coming where the comfort, warmth, surroundings he knew would be gone. A day coming like the falling of the hand of God. He seldom remembered the day he never thought would never come. Monahan assured him, but somehow it seemed like a fantasy.

A moment created by their hard work and determination, but a fantasy nonetheless. The day of his appointment. That was a day he didn't think that Monahan and he could pull off. As good as a coup. Only better.

"I managed to keep it internal for now. You should at least be grateful for that," Bigelow said.

Internal was just code for hoarding political points for some time in the future when he could stand up and show how noble and gallant he was. How instrumental in taking down the big bad administrator running the only machine that consistently found the information needed to keep U.S. foreign policy on track. *Chew the hell on that.* "I am, Senator, I am."

He was. As soon as news of the committee's findings hit the media, it was going to take more time than he had patience for. The incessant questions would pile up, and the shell game of moving programs around would begin. Just knowing that his people were wasting their time with this level of pettiness always bothered him. What they needed was more autonomy, not less.

"This is how it's going to work. We don't go back into session until next week and by then I expect that most of our members will be less worked up about some of the allegations."

"Which one broke the camel's back?" Palma asked.

"What broke the camel's back? We've received dozens of documents about projects that you are allegedly running on US soil. If you know about them then you already know what broke the camel's back."

Dozens? Not hundreds? Not thousands? Maybe things weren't as bad as he thought. "Senator, none of that is true. I, again, respectfully ask for access to the raw content so we can work out what is going on."

"You'll see it when the paperwork arrives at your desk next week. Start putting your team together, General. The one thing I can tell you is that you're going to be on a very short leash for the duration of this investigation."

"I'm already short-staffed."

"You have the largest budget next to the military. You can complain to somebody else. Find a team and get them ready. We're going to expect answers from you and expect them fast."

"Understood," Palma said.

Short leash? The job didn't pay enough to cover all the nonsense he put up with.

But making history did.

Next week looked like the target date after all. If he was removed from his position, whether by choice or circumstance, there was nothing that could be done by anyone at that point.

Halon would be in place.

"I'll take care of assembling the team, General," Andrew Yen said. "This is a distraction from your real work."

Palma took a quick look over his shoulder at his assistant while he walked over to the glass table that held bottles of water, soda, and juice. "Yes, it is, but it's also part of my real work."

Palma's jacket hung on the back of his desk chair. He would hang it up behind the door when Andrew was gone. The hanger would keep it wrinkle-free.

"I meant no disrespect."

Andrew looked almost perfect. He didn't act anything like an American his age would act. They would be professional, but there was something different about him.

"Stop talking to me like you know anything." He twisted the cap off a bottle of water and drank a few gulps. How did Andrew pull off being condescending while still being so efficient?

"I don't." Andrew folded his hands with a smooth silent move. "Know anything."

"Why did I agree to put you on my staff?" Palma knew. He wasn't happy about it, but he knew.

"As a sign of good faith, sir." Andrew stood at attention. "Will you be needing anything else?"

"If it wasn't because I know you have a single goal, I would have you arrested as the leaker," Palma said. Maybe he was the leaker. Monahan was an expert at finding traitors. Palma couldn't understand why he'd let Donnell live for so long. Why let him hide under the auspices of the FBI and Witness Protection?

He had ordered other men disposed of for less.

"Thank you, sir. I appreciate the vote of confidence. I have no reason to do something that stupid." Andrew had a file in his hand.

"Did you have something for me?" Palma asked.

"Yes."

He placed the file on Palma's desk. Palma had his back to him. There were days when he was tired of seeing Andrew around. He was efficient, courteous, terse.

"Vendor invoices. They need to be paid so the vendors can leave."

"Do you see the long view? Does history mean anything to you?" Palma asked.

"It does, sir. That's why I'm here." Andrew stood by the desk.

"I know." Palma waved him off. "Go build me a team. Just like the ones we keep busy every few months when another ridiculous request comes from the Hill."

"I will, sir."

30

MALL WALKING

Palma had his driver take him to the National Mall. The sky was a steel gray, almost like rain was on its way, but the air was arid and thin. He tasted the dryness on his tongue and felt it in his eyes. When he got out of his black SUV, he told the driver to meet him by the Washington Monument, and started to walk. Normal behavior. Drop him off. Pick him up. Nothing was wrong. Everything like any other day.

He was sure the driver saw him on the phone and knew he needed alone time.

That was how he felt at times. Alone. At least for the moment. There was much to do and no one else could understand the gravity of why time was the enemy of all projects. This project in particular.

The National Mall, in Washington, D.C., had the Capital to the east and the Lincoln Memorial to the far west though it extended as far as the Constitution Gardens. The Washington Monument was somewhere near the middle and Palma's target for the afternoon. He had walked the Mall before when he needed to clear his head.

Today he needed to clear his head.

He felt the burner phone buzz. *Right on schedule, but why the hell are you calling me?*

"Good afternoon, General. I hope you're feeling well today."

The all-too-familiar voice. The one he'd hoped not to hear until this was over, but not the voice that had called him earlier. He walked on.

"Is there a reason why I'm feeling an unusual level of anxiety these last few days?" Palma asked. He held his head up high with his right hand holding the cell to his ear. "Because I'm pretty certain that there's no reason to have your people applying additional pressure. We are on schedule."

"We understand. We are on your side just as much as you are on ours. I must admit that I called just to let you know that you don't need to worry about our friend at the Supermax."

Palma stopped for a moment and lowered his hand. He took in a quick breath and continued. "My confusion knows no bounds. You have no reason to worry about her. As I have mentioned to our colleagues on previous occasions, I am taking care of this."

"It would appear that your plate is full, General. Your people are not doing their jobs, or forgive me, not doing the level of work that you expect of them. Your man has not done his job if you sent him there to take care of business."

He knows which men I sent? Andrew was going to be the death of him. Literally. "Please accept my gracious appreciation for your concern, but the one thing I have to do is handle her." A chill wind came up behind Palma and gave him a slight push.

"My men are in position. They can handle the job quite well and no one will know what happened. Your man does not appear to be doing anything so far as they can tell."

"Then you must be looking at the wrong person. I get almost daily updates on her and what she is doing, seeing, and saying." *Why did he say my man? Is providence smiling on me? Does he not know about the second man?*

"The choice of location, while inspired, is not what we would have preferred. We mentioned our displeasure weeks ago. Even if no one's allowed to see her, she appears to be having plenty of contact and mobility. She would not be receiving such things if your office were not authorizing them."

Palma froze in his tracks. *What the hell is he talking about?* "There must be some incredible misunderstanding. She is flagged so that no one, and I mean no one, is allowed to see her except in the case of a medical emergency and then I would be notified immediately. I have received no alert since her attempt to take her own life a few days ago."

A runner flew past well south of him, but Palma took note of her. Neon green shirt with a neon yellow jacket and reflector tape on her shoulders. Late twenties, early thirties. Brunette with her hair tied back in a ponytail. He took a quick look around. There were the usual walkers in addition to the runners and they all seemed self-absorbed. White-and-black wire ear buds disconnected them from the surrounding world. None appeared to be paying attention to him.

The grass was patchy. It would be turning into permafrost soon enough. Palma thought about how hard it was to bury someone once the ground got that hard.

"I need you to leave her alone. She's my problem," Palma said. "You are not in control of this. You'll be busy enough in a few days. I hope that your preparations are in place."

"We prefer not to discuss such a sensitive matter while you're walking the Mall. It is enough that you gave us some of your time today to consider this sensitive topic."

Palma wasn't sure what was going on. "What have you heard that perhaps you think that I have not heard?" An industrial-strength lawn mower came to life and made an ear-piercing drone that caused Palma to miss the caller's statement. He asked them to hold on until the man and his over-sized John Deere went by.

"General, what I can tell you is that in two days if Anna Wodehouse is not taken care of, she will be taken care of."

"And if that happens then next week is off. Not because I want it to be off, but because there will be such a stir over the death of a prisoner at ADX that I will have to explain how someone I purposely sent there, and that no one else is supposed to know exists, is now dead."

He was tempted to loosen his tie but straightened it instead. "The prison is run by human beings. They know someone is there even if they don't know who she is. Her anonymity is part of what is keeping us both from having to worry about her."

Every so often, a runner would chance on by and give him a second look. While he wasn't well-known to the public, it was not every day that a decorated high-level military man walked the Mall. He knew that his appearance was a novelty, which meant that others would remember that he was there. But he counting on the noise level making it hard to overhear his conversation.

"Don't worry, General. The death will not cause a stir."

"Perhaps you don't understand me. If you do anything to her, I will call off the hand-off. There is already a level of attention falling on me that I'm not happy with." He could feel the blood running up to his head. How could he get them to understand something they didn't seem to comprehend?

"Understood. We do not seek to make your job harder. We are looking to lighten your load. We understand how much pressure you're in and are just offering to help," the voice on the cell phone said.

"I have already done a few things for you in the last few days that are going to stick out like sore thumbs if anything happens to her," Palma said. *Like give that journalist access. Like speed up the time line.* There was a mistake if ever he saw one.

"You concern yourself where none is needed."

What was it going to take to convince them to let him do his job? They were already going to own one of the most expensive pieces of real estate in history. "This has been going on for years. Let's not stumble this close to the finish line," Palma said.

"We appreciate everything you have done for us, General." The voice on the other end wrapped up. "Please, do not be afraid to ask for help. Keep us apprised of anything you might need."

31

ICE CREAM AND LEAD

When Palma arrived home, he was greeted with silence. The usual chitter-chatter of his children reading to each other or fighting over some snack was absent.

"Violet?" He put his bag down. "Milda?" He walked around the first floor, found it abandoned, and ran upstairs. Also empty. His jaw clenched. *What the hell?*

Palma opened the door and stood looking out on the lawn. One of his security detail saw him and strode over.

"General? Is there anything I can help you with?"

"Where are the children?"

"Sir, they are with Mr. Yen. He called ahead and said that you had asked to have them out of the house for a few hours." The officer reached his radio.

Palma held out his hand. "No, no. You're right. I. Forgot." There were two other men out by the SUV who turned and put their hands on their hips. "I do have a lot of work. I was looking forward to putting them to bed early, but this works out better." Palma turned back toward the house. "When Andrew returns, please ask him to come by my room before he leaves."

"Yes, sir."

———

Palma heard the door open and strolled over to the foyer as his oldest, Violet, walked over to him and gave him a hug. He kissed the top of her eleven-year-old head, and she smiled at him. He pushed her bangs off her forehead. She needed a haircut soon. His six-year-old ran over, slammed into him, and hugged him as best she could. He grinned through his tension. "At ease, soldiers. I understand you both went AWOL."

"Daddy," Milda, the youngest, said, "you told Mr. Yen to take us to the library, and then to the mall, and then to Mr. Wilson's ice cream parlor." She nodded her head with each destination. She looked puzzled. "Daddy, what's a parlor?"

"Your older sister should have told you. At eleven she knows almost everything." He ruffled Milda's hair, sending it into disarray.

"Daddy!" Milda said.

"Go upstairs. The both of you. Wash up and then let's see how much dinner you can eat now that you had dessert first."

They both voiced assent and Milda ran up while Violet walked the walk of a precocious pre-teen learning to be twenty. She was looking more and more like her mother, but walked with an assurance she'd learned from her father. Palma looked at them both and smiled. They were home.

They were safe.

He turned to Andrew, who was still wearing the same dark navy blue suit he had on at work. "Would you join me in my office?"

———

Palma closed the light wood door behind Andrew. It was bulletproof. When he played hide-and-seek with his girls, the goal was to get them to learn that his office was the place to go if they needed some place safe. He knew that everything he did with them was a learning opportunity.

Much like this.

"Please sit down," Palma said.

"I can't stay long." Andrew stood his ground.

"You will stay as long as I say if I have to break your legs to do it."

Palma walked over to his desk, unlocked a drawer, and slid the solid compartment open. "I will say this only once. And I am not speaking figuratively. If you ever do that again, I will kill you."

"Yes, sir." Andrew folded his hands over his crotch.

"Do you understand?" Palma looked down at the drawer. His military service revolver peeked out from under some papers. "I'm not sure that you do, but if you do then this conversation is over."

"You have lovely children," Andrew said.

"Perhaps you should get your own," Palma said. He slid the drawer shut. If Palma called out, he was certain that the officer by the door would hear him and enter.

"I was just trying to take some pressure off you." Andrew stood still. It was almost as if he could immobilize his body while his head continued functioning. The suit he had worn all day, and on his unauthorized excursion, looked fresh as it hung on his slight frame.

"What pressure? What do you know about the pressure I'm under?" Palma ran his fingers along the edge of the desktop. The desk had been a gift from his wife. She would be along eventually, but being a partner at a law firm meant she would work even longer hours than before.

"As your assistant there is nothing I know better than your workload. Things have been difficult lately."

"Yes, but I'm starting to wonder if you're the reason for all of the problems that have been coming up." He walked up to Andrew and stood close enough to look down on him. "You're not the reason why," Palma stared into Andrew's right eye, "are you?"

"Your daughters are very intelligent and social. You must be very proud of them."

"You did hear me?" Palma asked.

"There is no reason for threats. My job here, my role, is to ensure that you get the support you need to do your job. After next week I will no longer be around and you can hire another assistant who will do a much more acceptable job." He returned Palma's stare.

This is one lion into whose eyes you should never look.

"We're done here. Get out," Palma said.

"There is no reason for your threats." Andrew looked away. "I'm here to help you. I would never have allowed anything to happen to your children."

"Where did you take them?"

"Exactly as Violet said. The library. The mall. Ice cream. We know their three favorite things. That should have given you two hours to work on this most important of projects because I know that is your highest priority." Andrew turned away and sat down in the nearest chair.

Palma towered over him. "Next week is important, but I have other things that are more important. You don't get to set my agenda."

"But I do, General. Once the team is assembled to help the oversight committee, you will be working with the White House on the hostage situation in Iraq, and making sure that security is doing its job to find who leaked the dozen or so documents. In addition, you will approve the termination of Anna Wodehouse in the next forty-eight hours or she will die anyway. Next week's schedule will go forward in any case." Andrew looked away from Palma. "And it will all happen because I will be here to help you in any way that I can. Next week is the culmination of years of work on your part. And the Secretary of State's, of course."

Palma strolled over to his desk and opened the drawer. He looked down at the gun. He hated empty gestures. He picked it up and felt the weight in his hand. It felt like an overly large scotch glass.

"This timeline is going to go forward," he walked over to Andrew, grabbed him by the collar of his jacket, and crumbled the material in his grip as he pulled Andrew up toward him. "It shouldn't and I am certain, no, I predict, that next week is going to go badly for all of us." He took the gun and pushed it at Andrew's forehead. "In fact, I can predict with 100% certainty that it will go very badly for you. I will give your employer..."

"And yours," Andrew said.

Palma pushed the gun harder onto Andrew's head. "I will give your employer what he is asking for so that sometime next week I will be done with this." Palma brought his face close to Andrew's. "I am very unhappy."

"I can see that."

Palma, still holding onto Andrew's jacket and the gun pushed against his forehead, called out, "Corporal!"

A few seconds later, an older soldier opened the door and took one step into the room. "Yes, sir?"

"Would you please check on my girls and let them know that dinner will be read in a few minutes?" Palma stared down at Andrew. *If I shot you now, this man would help me bury you.*

"Yes, sir," the Corporal said.

32

TOR

"I need to get on a computer," Anna said.

She saw Hawking stop and think for a moment, and then glance around the empty examination room. She had put in a kite in the hope he would be receptive to the idea of losing his job.

"Computer? You already have one. There's a computer set up specifically for you and your other close friends here at the club," Hawking said. He pulled the blood pressure cuff off her left arm with a loud crackling of Velcro. "Looking for the latest graphics to play Halo?"

"If you keep talking like that, I'll stop coming here. Halo is so 2001. I stopped wanting to play that right after Halo 2." Besides, she couldn't find anyone who could fight the Covenant as well as she could, and no one at her schools had a clue beyond point-and-kill.

"I'll talk to the warden about it, but he and I are becoming not-so-fast-friends," Hawking said.

Frenemies. Great. "I only need a few minutes. I have a legal right to communicate with my attorney and they won't let me send her email," Anna said.

Hawking contemplated her face for a second and continued his examination. "You see that there are no guards in this room, right?"

Anna nodded.

"You also notice that there is no chair between me and you, right?" She nodded again.

"So, I'm trusting you with my life, yet you're asking me for things that are beyond my control." He stood up straight. "This is a maximum-security prison. You can't go to the bathroom without twelve people knowing about it."

"Well, three, but I get your meaning."

"Just need to what? Set fire to Chicago? Launch nuclear weapons?" Hawking asked.

"You're certainly giving me more credit than I deserve."

He pulled off some of the bandages on her left arm, revealing the stitches he had given her a few days before. "Maybe I am," he said.

Anna looked away. *Why am I doing this? It's not going to work. He just has a job to do.*

"The guards told me stories about you," Hawking said. "That you may have caused the blackout a few years back. That you made airplanes disappear off the air-traffic control radar screen." He shone a light in her eyes. "There is so much damage that you could cause in a few minutes that I'm not sure I would let you use my home computer, much less the authorized unit here at the prison."

Anna's shoulders sagged. "So my rights can be violated even though I'm in a sealed box with no windows and no way to get out. I can't participate in my appeals process. I can't email my friends..."

Hawking held up his hand. "Wait."

Anna thought the way he furrowed his brow was attractive.

"You have friends?"

"Ha, ha, ha." She leaned forward. "You're lucky my hands are cuffed."

———

Two days later, Anna was back in the examination room feeling her cheeks get hot as she sat on the table in her orange suit and matching manacles. In his beige pants, and a white shirt with a blue and silver striped tie, Hawking let the guard out. His close-cropped hair looked provocative. A stethoscope hung from his neck. *Hoping to die one day, and wondering when I'm going to have sex the next. What is wrong with me?*

He had removed her mask at Anna's request.

"How many more kites are you going to send me about menstrual problems?" Hawking asked. He held aloft a stack of a dozen kites. "Should I just call the blood bank and lie about where my donations are coming from?"

"How many is it going to take before you let me use a computer?" Anna asked. She adjusted her butt on the examination table, causing the paper to crackle. "And I am having menstrual issues. I need pads."

Hawking smirked at her.

"And tampons. Just because I'm not dating doesn't mean my body's not getting me ready to be pregnant."

"You want to be a mother?"

"If I have kids, I will be." Anna felt her neck flush. Mental flashes of Aunt Marcie, and her mother, Ingrid, tickled her forehead. Ingrid, the mother who wasn't. The mother she had never known. Anna would never have children. She was never getting out of the federal penitentiary. Her quest for closure sealed her future before she'd even had the chance to consider that she had a future.

Closure? Was that what she was after?

"Whoa." Hawking looked concerned. "What just happened?"

"Nothing." Anna reached up and felt her cheeks. No tears. She really was out of them. "Nothing." She took a breath and closed her eyes for a second. "Pads. Tampons. A PC."

"You really think that pushing me is going to push the warden to get you a networked PC that they won't monitor? I thought you were a smart woman." He put random items away into a cabinet: cotton balls, tongue depressors, bandages.

"Look, you're no better off than I am. You get to go every night, or at the end of your shift, but you come back. You've got a sentence here, too, only they trust you enough to come back."

He looked over his shoulder. "I wouldn't trust you enough to come back."

"I don't want to leave. I just want to communicate with my lawyer so she can find out why evidence was suppressed."

"What?" He rolled his eyes. "Of course, there's always evidence being suppressed. Why wouldn't there be?"

"Alright. Wrap up here and send me back." This was going nowhere. Time to go back and wait a few weeks for her reading privileges to be reinstated so she could at least read while she waited.

Waited for what?

Hawking didn't move. He looked at his own PC. "How long do you think you need?"

Anna's ears perked up. "Ten to fifteen minutes."

"Will you let me look at everything you're doing?"

"I can, but..." Was he really going to let her use his computer? "Wouldn't you rather have plausible deniability?"

————

"Do you know why I'm letting you do this? Because I don't believe half of what I've read about you. Besides, what you want to do isn't anywhere as dangerous as the stuff I do."

"You do dangerous stuff?" Anna asked.

His eyes widened and he pointed toward the door. "Have you seen some of the people I have to treat here?"

————

Hawking was sitting in a chair in front of Anna reading the paper. "Remember, I don't usually take this long with my patients," he said, "so don't take long."

"Don't worry. I'll be done soon." Anna was downloading Tor, a web browser that kept users anonymous on the Internet. Her were sweaty. The download speeds weren't exactly snappy and she had a lot to do with the little time she had.

But she had been practicing. She was ready to send messages to a few people she knew asking for help, including her attorney.

But this was far better. On the prison computer, they would be monitoring what she was doing as she typed. On Hawking's computer, they would have to do forensic analysis and they would find nothing. At least that was her intention unless she was wrong about the prison not monitoring the PCs of their personnel. If investment banks did it, why wouldn't the Federal Bureau of Prisons? In a word: laziness. She knew she was making a bad tactical move, but she had to bank on some weakness to get through.

She wanted to get out of here and there was only one way she could think of: put pressure on the people who put her here to get her out. Job number one: Find out who Benson was and threaten to expose him. If the sniper who had shot her was not a police sniper, and the gun she allegedly used to kill Garth Donnell, some guy who knew the-man-who-was-not-her-father, went missing almost immediately then there were other things going on that she had to get help with. She knew she was over her head, but by how much? She needed some metrics, and she wasn't going to get them here.

Download: done. She started up the Tor bundle so she wouldn't have to install or configure Hawking's PC. It would do its job without interference.

The moment of truth: If the PC was being monitored, they would come into his office within the next few minutes as soon as they saw an encrypted stream leaving the prison.

She started up Tor. "What time is it?" she asked.

"Just after two. Are you done yet?"

"Almost." She logged into a cloud account she had set up a few years before. While everyone else was posting their pictures in public she had been storing them in a private cloud service. Anna stopped. What if they knew about this account? Too late to worry about that now. She navigated to a folder named *Stuff* and found the photo. It was still there. If this was a trick, they would be storming the door soon.

She copied the link to the photo and navigated to another site. It was an instant message site where only the insane would go. It was an IRC channel for black hats. She had found them as part of her research into cybersecurity and had kept in touch with a few of the developers she had met there. They had regular jobs, but after hours they were breaking ground in all sorts of areas that the average person didn't even dream about.

She typed a private message to *CrapIsKing*.

HarlequinNinja: Hey! This is your old buddy.

CrapIsKing: Heard you're incapacitated.

HarlequinNinja: The news of my death is greatly exaggerated.

CrapIsKing: Are you around?

HarlequinNinja: No. But I need some background on someone. Can you get it?

CrapIsKing: Sure

She pasted the link into the chat window.

CrapIsKing: Your dad?

HarlequinNinja: No. My so-called dad is uglier. Gotta go.

It was her one and only photo of Benson.

————

"Excuse me, General?" An analyst poked her head around Palma's door. He had decided to go into the office. Things were going to go as planned if he had to arm-wrestle them there.

Palma had moved himself to an office on one of the upper floors where he could be closer both to the people he directly managed, and to a certain analyst group. The group created and directed to follow the movements of various people due to their potential to involve themselves in projects tied up in national security. "I think you should see this."

Palma strode out of his office over to the room where the twenty or so analysts were busy monitoring various events, countries, and people around the world.

The analyst led Palma over to her desk and found him a chair. "So, nothing has been coming out of the subject in Colorado for a number of days, but I noticed something strange happening a few minutes ago."

The analyst was one of the few who didn't wear glasses. She tugged her hair behind her ear. "The Bureau of Prisons has a given number of desktop computers in use at the maximum-security facilities, and ADX Florence is no different. They do standard auditing and so on, but they're no better than home users. While they have web logs of everything the user is doing they don't do keylogging or regular audits of passwords and so on."

Any other day Palma would have been quite impatient, but the thought processes of his people always took him in. These were the brightest people he had ever had the pleasure to work with and ranked high in comparison to the work he had done in the military during active duty. He appreciated the group that had raw courage as much as he did the group that had raw intellect.

"Of course," she said, "if they did do it then our jobs would be harder. Anyway, I made sure to put a tap on network activity coming out of the prison and something came up." She typed a few keystrokes and the screen changed to a graph. "There was nothing special about their network traffic, but all of a sudden there was a burst of encrypted packets that looked like Tor traffic. On the assumption that BOP isn't smart enough to ask their people to use something like Tor, I can also conjecture that the subject has found an unmonitored PC."

"Can we tell what?" Palma asked.

"I'm afraid not. There's a project working exclusively on solving the Tor problem, but for now all we can tell is that it's Tor traffic. Is the subject generating the traffic? No way to confirm without someone on the ground. We could be wrong. Maybe some guard or administrator couldn't wait to go to a porn site and heard that their traffic could be anonymized using it." She swiveled her chair back toward Palma. "My recommendation is to have someone check it out.

If the subject is sending out encrypted communications, we probably want to find out what it is."

Palma thought for a second. It might be worth a call to the prison. The security breach might not be Anna. It might be his asset trying to reach out.

33

NIGHTMARE SCENARIO

What if the shot at the guard was meant for me?

Anna paced her cell and lost count of her steps as she pondered the possibilities.

Orville thought it was meant to be him, but why would the other guard have been killed? Did they want all three of them? Then it would have been a random shooting. Did Orville mention that?

She didn't remember.

How many steps was that? She started counting again.

What if Jekyll and Hyde were behind this? What if Benson and his minions were behind it? What was more likely? Damn it, she didn't know. Anna slammed her fist into the gray wall, fleshy part first. She side-punched it again and again.

That concrete is pretty solid. She opened her hand and placed the palm of her hand against it. *No super-powers to be had here. If I'm going to get out of here it's going to be through the legal powers that be and not by waiting for heroic measures. I never had those.*

But maybe I do.

Someone banged on the white metal door. Her eyes opened wide. Guards? She wasn't scheduled to go out yet.

The door swung open silently and she found that she couldn't move. The fear was a dense ball in her chest. The mask suffocated her. In the doorway, someone held a rifle. She asked something but couldn't hear herself. She reached behind her mask for the zipper but felt the back of her head instead. She panicked. Where was the zipper? It was getting harder and harder for her to breathe. She opened her mouth as wide as she could in a silent scream.

The guard, wearing her mask, stood next to her. Why would they want to kill her? Because they didn't finish last time?

Because being with others was unauthorized.

———

Anna rolled and tumbled off the concrete bed onto the hard, tiled floor. Her arm and shoulder ached where she hit the ground, her head still groggy from the nightmare. She used to like dreams. They used to be about things that frustrated her, but always things she knew she could overcome or that didn't matter. She had read up on dreams when she was ten and after she discussed it with her father she decided that symbolisms, while cool, took too much time to decipher. At that young age falsifiability of dream symbols seemed too difficult, like trying to falsify evolution or string theory, so she let it go knowing she would revisit it when she and her father were older, and maybe she could explain it to him instead.

The specific visuals of the dream faded as she replayed bits and pieces of it over in her mind. Punching the wall. The guard with the gun in the doorway. All traces would be gone in a few minutes, but the feeling of immovability, of fear, of despair hung on like a scratchy blanket meant to warm her, but caused discomfort instead.

The banging on her door continued. *Great. So that part was real.*

"C'mon, darlin'. I've got your magazine for you."

Was that Hyde? Anna knew that when the Warden said he had reassigned her escorts what he meant was that he had done nothing. She pushed herself off the floor, brought her knees under her, and straightened.

"Drop it in the slot. I'll send you a nice Christmas card later," she said with her electrolarynx voice. She didn't want to see him. What if he wore a mask like hers? She froze for a moment, and realized a move like that would take too much foresight on his part. Between Jekyll and Hyde there wasn't even a complete thought.

Her perspective shifted. If he made even one false move, she would do something she would regret, but no one would credit as self-defense. They would make things worse for her.

"Hands in the slot."

"I'm not going out," Anna said. Even if it was time for her to go out, she wondered if maybe Hyde found out about her time with Hawking.

More and more scenarios piled up in her mental queue. Hyde was an idiot, but he seemed to know people. She didn't want to find herself having to defend what she did with a demented lunatic. Or one of the COs.

"Hands in the slot."

She was going to regret this. Her hands were shaking. Should she cover them? She reached over to her desk and put the black gloves on that matched her mask. Fear built in her chest. *Please let this not be a sneak attack. Please.* Helplessness flooded her brain. Her shoulders sagged, her face relaxed, her eyes teared.

Do I kill him if he touches me?

Yes, I will do everything in my power to kill him. Even if it means he might kill me.

She turned around at the door and placed her gloved hands into the slot. Anna trembled. The handcuffs ratcheted closed. Pain shot up her arms as he closed it one more notch. The ankle bracelets came next. She was sure that he wasn't going to try anything stupid. Another guard was always supposed to be with him and maybe Jekyll had a day off.

Please, let Jekyll have today off.

She stepped away from the door as it slid into the wall. Hyde was there with another CO, who stepped over to the left and stood behind the wall. It looked like he didn't want to see what was about to transpire.

Hyde held up a magazine. "I brought you the latest issue of Nature."

Every step he took into the cell Anna took a step back. *Don't let him get close.*

"I thought we could kiss and make up."

"You need to go." The robotic voice fueled her disconnection.

"Don't worry," he said. He tossed the magazine onto her bed. "My shift is almost over and I just wanted to say hi."

"You need to go."

"You're nobody here."

"You're nobody out there."

"The cameras will show that you attacked me first," he said in a lower voice. "You're gonna be mine."

"As long as the cameras are going to show it anyway." Anna took the small steps she needed to bring herself within a foot or so of Hyde, jumped up, and kicked out to his chest. Hyde flew out of the room onto his back and slid across the floor in the otherwise empty corridor. Anna landed on her butt. A sharp pain ran through her back and ribcage.

Anna floundered to stand. As she stayed within the confines of her cell she had dozens of thoughts fly around in her head.

Would the other CO shoot her? When would the siren go off? Should she try to make a run for it?

Hyde stood before she was completely up, and came at her like a freight train. He grabbed the chain holding her hands to her waist, brought her up a few inches, and punched her in the face. Pain shot through her as she tried to get her bearings so she could stand. He swung her against the concrete wall.

He hit her again. And again. Her mouth went slack. She tasted blood. He let her go and she dropped to the floor. He turned his back on her as he exited the cell. "Sound the alarm," Hyde said.

Anna was able to get into a crouch and slammed into him. He fell on the floor with the umph of air flying out of his lungs. As he turned over Anna kicked her legs forward and landed on him with her feet toward his head.

Her leg chains pushed down on his neck. He started to pull her legs up so she sat up and put as much weight as she could to change her center of gravity. Hyde slipped his hands over his neck and under the chains. She struggled to get a better position when she felt some-one's hands under her arms. The other CO dragged her off Hyde and flipped her onto the ground. He pulled out his gun and held her at gunpoint.

The siren went off.

34

EMERGENCY MEASURES

In the medical center, Hawking heard the siren and tried to understand the super echoey words scratching their way through the PA. The local fast food joint had a more intelligible speaker. He turned to the Head Nurse who was at her desk ignoring the cacophony of fuzzy sound. "Where the hell is that happening? What's happening?"

"That's code for a prisoner attack. SORT is probably on its way." She turned back to her paperwork.

"Which block?"

"Range 13."

———

Hawking knew he wouldn't get there fast enough so he went out of the nearest exit and ran across the hot, dusty ground to the entrance closest to Range 13. Running was forbidden on the grounds of the penitentiary. Lucky him. He would deal with that later, if at all. The guard towers weren't always manned or, if manned, short-staffed so they would probably leave him alone with an alarm distracting them from their full-time tedium.

He knew something was going to happen if he let her use the

computer (he knew it!), but he didn't think it would be this fast. How could he be so stupid?

After going through the master station, he ran down the narrow corridor toward the three figures. On the other side of the figures was the approaching SORT team. He ran even faster.

The siren blared in the confined space. This was going to be dangerous.

"Everybody, step back!" Hawking yelled.

The SORT team saw him and one of them yelled back, "Doc, step back. Dangerous situation."

Hawking stopped running. They saw him. *Good.* He walked the rest of the way to the unfolding scene with his hands in the air. He looked at the CO who was pointing his gun at Anna, who was still wearing her mask and gloves. Also good.

He saw blood coming out of the mouth area of the mask.

Someone was going to pay for that.

Hawking crouched down and turned to the CO on the ground. "You okay?"

"Doc, I told you to step back!" The SORT leader, CO Petroski, he thought (Hawking was still learning names), came forward. "Everyone step away from the prisoner."

Hawking needed him calm first. "You have everything under control here. Let me take a look at the CO." *And the inmate.*

"You can look at them once we have the inmate restrained," Petroski said.

Hawking examined Anna's hands and legs. "Still in the same restraints that allowed this, only now also unconscious.

I'll file a much more accurate report if I do this now. Besides, the inmate looks subdued."

The CO seated on the floor with red welts on his neck looked angry. Very angry. This was going to be interesting. He scratched at one of the CO's cuts, and the man yelped. *Good.*

Hawking stood. "Alright. I need them both in medical." He nodded at Anna, who wasn't moving. "I'm also going to need a gurney or a stretcher. Make sure the inmate is properly restrained." He didn't want them thinking the CO wasn't his first concern.

———

The scene in medical was out of control. What the hell was going on? Hawking banged his palm on a nearby table. "If all I'm going to get here is noise then I will ask everybody but my patients, medical staff, and one officer, to leave the room."

Quiet descended. He gave the SORT team a glance and turned to the CO on the examination table. There was only one table in the room so Anna was still on the stretcher.

Someone had attached additional restraints across her arms and legs. That was for the best. He would make sure she wouldn't get blamed for something she was incapable of doing.

"I'm fine, doc. Really." The CO on the bed nodded over to the stretcher. "She attacked me out of nowhere. I went to drop off a magazine that I thought was part of the stuff she's allowed to read."

Hawking blinked. "Magazine?"

"The mailroom. They noticed that they forgot to deliver this magazine," the officer waved into the air, "that came in the mail for her and it hadn't been dropped off. I knew part of my detail was down there so I brought it over for her." He looked at the officer who had been holding Anna at gunpoint even after she lost consciousness. "You know, to be a nice guy." His eyes bulged open. "And then she attacked me."

The CO nodded his head in agreement, but his eyes darted away.

Hawking returned his gaze to the CO on the bed. *So this is Hyde.*

"That's quite interesting, Officer," Hawking said. "Since the warden gave me authorization to give, or withhold, her reading material and there was nothing in the mailroom when I called earlier today. I'm not sure what to say."

Hyde's face remained impassive. "You can say, 'You're welcome.' I did you a solid. You're welcome. It must have come in after you called."

"It must have," Hawking said.

The Head Nurse was in the room with them. She examined the marks on Hyde's neck, dabbing at them with a peroxide-drenched gauze pad. Hyde's face twitched at her touch.

Hawking felt the walls closing in. "SORT team, thank you very much for a job well done. I'll take it from here. You can all go back to your normal details."

It took them an extra second to start moving. Were they hoping that they would get a look at Anna the way the other officers earlier in the week had done? *Rubbernecking rednecks.* The new COs in charge of escorting Anna stood by the door. He pointed at them and then at Anna. "You guys stay with the inmate," Hawking said.

"Margaret," Hawking said, "could you please take a look at our other patient behind the partition?" The Head Nurse nodded, wheeled the stretcher a few feet away, Anna's two COs in tow, and pulled a curtain between her and Anna, and the rest of the room. That would hide the nurse from him.

"Can I go home?" Hyde asked. "That lunatic almost killed me and I would rather not be here for a while."

"I agree." Hawking took a syringe filled with morphine and jabbed it into Hyde's thigh after pulling up his pant leg. "I think you should go home right away," Hawking said.

"Ow!"

"That was just something to dull the pain. Make an appointment with your regular GP and come back when he says you should." Hawking held out his hand and when Hyde took it, Hawking pulled him off the bed. "Don't let me stop you from taking care of that." He let go of his hand. "You really must see your GP. Today. To start a paper trail."

Hawking was sure that the man's brain cells were blowing up in confusion. Was Hawking kidding or serious? Hawking hoped that the man would question him in some way. He pointed Hyde toward the door. "Really. Today."

"Okay, Doc." Hyde took a step and hobbled toward the door.

"I'll check in with you once I know one way or another."

There was a scream behind the curtain. Hawking looked at Hyde. "Go. Get out of here." Hawking pulled the curtain back and saw the two COs poised to do something. Anything.

Anna's mask was off, blood dripped from her cheek onto her jumpsuit, and onto the floor. Hawking knew she was screaming from the pain.

One officer grabbed her already restrained legs and the other held down both of her arms by throwing himself across her diagonally. Hawking spun a bottle of sedative and a syringe, poked the needle through the top of the upside-down bottle, and plunged the needle through her left arm.

"Get off her." Hawking stood there looking at the two guards acting like Anna could rip through the restraints. *What is wrong with these people?* "I said, get off her!"

When neither man moved, Hawking pulled the one leaning across her and threw him off her slowly relaxing body. The other guard released her legs, took a step back, and put his hand on his gun.

Hawking put his hands up. "Stop." He took a step back. "Stop. Go help your partner up. One or both of you can stay, but you guys have got to calm down." He turned Anna's face to him. There would be minimal scarring, but she would hurt.

"You know the warden is going to hear about this," the officer said as he stood up from where Hawking had thrown him.

Hawking began Anna's examination.

35

STEALING MAGNOLIA

Terrell walked over to the agreed upon park bench. Again, they had only met there once before so Terrell felt comfortable going there one last time. He would change the spot next time. They would never return here.

The air was chill for October and the talk of an oncoming storm seemed like the predictions of a blizzard. Terrell would believe them when he saw snow on the ground or gale force winds.

He saw her sitting on the metal park bench. She wore the same charcoal gray coat from their last meeting. The meeting before he'd been shot in the shoulder. Her hair was not as blond, but this time he noticed blond streaks. Terrell's jacket, one of his older Bureau uniforms when he'd been heavier, hung loose on his left side. He hated wearing a sling, but at least it was on his left arm and it relieved the pressure on his shoulder. Having to use his gun was always a possibility even in a low risk situation like this, but that was not a worry. While he had a sharpshooter rating with either hand, he still favored his right.

He sat down on the bench behind her. The metal was cold and the light breeze did nothing to make him feel better. A bird above them gave a chirp and flew away.

"Why do I feel like you're about to tell me you're taking your marbles and going home?" he asked.

"I think they know," she said.

Terrell snuck a glance in his peripheral vision. Her head was bowed down. A passerby might think she was sleep, or praying.

"I don't want to go to prison."

"You're not going to prison. You were granted immunity," Terrell said.

"I'm a contractor. The laws don't cover me."

"You're covered," Terrell said. "By me."

"I don't want my family to hate me."

"They're not going to hate you." *No, but nobody likes a hero.* She chose a path that never led to tranquility. "How can they hate you? You're one of the few people around here asking the hard questions. Questions I didn't know I was supposed to be asking."

Like why blatantly illegal operations were still going on in defiance of the law. Terrell wanted to make her feel comfortable, but something told him he was running out of time.

"Look, we'll have plenty of time to talk this over, okay? Everyone goes through this. You think you're doing something wrong, but you're not."

"Oh, God." She panted. "What am I going to do?"

Terrell scanned the area then tilted his head toward her. "Nothing is going to happen to you or your family. I promise. The committee is behind you. Even if nothing is found, you walk away scot-free with the thanks of a grateful nation."

"It wasn't supposed to turn into this. The bad actors were supposed to go to jail and I was supposed to...I don't know, find a measure of peace for helping put them away," she said.

She needed reassurance. She was an innocent who believed in the system. He needed to calm her down and strengthen that misguided belief.

"Piercing Ventures." Terrell wasn't sure how much time he had left with her. He could feel the walls closing in. Was it just her? Were his internal feelers telling him something?

It was just after noontime. There was a man walking his dog. The usual traffic going by. A couple holding hands. A tall hedge. Bare trees. A helicopter overhead.

The woman put her hand up to her mouth and then stuck both her hands in her coat pockets. "Piercing Ventures is a front, but you already know that or you wouldn't be asking. The problem is where the money is coming from. Money flows from overseas into three cleansing points in Europe and ends up at Piercing Ventures. Piercing takes the money and funds domestic programs that are used to equip other programs using money meant for clandestine operations in other countries."

"Overseas? What is the money doing here?"

"The operations that are being funded are all over the place, but there is at least one taking place here. This isn't the funding of fake cell towers to monitor domestic cell phones. Those are legal even if their funding isn't white bag. This is funding to create an operation in the U.S. that you only find overseas. Piercing Ventures is one of several termination points for Intelligence funds. Funds meant for overseas ops are being funneled back into the U.S. for operations that are illegal even under the current Intelligence laws."

"How many operations?" Terrell asked.

"I've only found one, but I found it because some documents were misrouted and ended up on my desk." She turned to him. "I wasn't looking for them. They found me."

"Take a breath." He waited. "Now sit back." He placed his arm on the back of the bench. "What happened? You were on high-alert before and you're even worse now. What's going on?"

"There's talk of an internal search for the leaker. I don't know if they mean me or someone else, but if they find me, I'm going to need protection right away." She wasn't crying, but her voice cracked. "And my family."

Terrell could read her mind: *I'm just a contractor. What have I done?*

"You have to pull me out."

"Okay, but I can't do that right away."

That was when car after car pulled directly in front of them on the street and onto the park lawn. Terrell stopped counting after eight.

"Hands up!" Police cars screeched to a halt as officers poured out of the vehicles with guns drawn. Others screamed, "On the ground! On the ground!"

Terrell turned to the woman. "Do as they say! Don't run and don't do anything." With his hand up he called out, "FBI!"

Two police officers ran up to him and pushed him onto the ground, ignoring the sling and pushing him shoulder first.

"Are you guys crazy? What the hell is going on here?" Terrell saw legs and shoes. He lifted his head up. "She's a witness in an ongoing..." Someone pushed his head back onto the cold grass. The last thing he saw before tasting the ground was her hands in cuffs and people walking away as quickly as possible. "Where are you taking her? This is Bureau business!"

"Magnolia Sams, you are under arrest for the passing of classified information under the MacCarran Internal Security Act and provisions of the Patriot Act. You have the right to remain silent..." Terrell had heard enough. The words were all boilerplate.

Car doors slammed and a flurry of vehicles took off. The two officers who had pushed him down grabbed him by the arms and pulled him up. Terrell pushed the officer holding his left hand away, closed his hand into a fist, and pulled his right arm back almost taking a swing at the officer. Both police put one hand on their guns and their other out in front of him. Pain scraped along his shoulder.

"Drive me to a hospital," Terrell said.

The men walked back to their cars and drove away, leaving him the center of attention as dog walkers, lovers, and gawkers looked on.

36

PILLOWCASE MEMES

Anna lay prone on her bed. The mask was off, as per the doctor's orders, and she floated in a Vicodin enhanced haze. The air smelled sweaty and all she could hear was the hum of the light fixture. She rubbed the top and the back of her head. She crossed her arms and patted the sides of her torso. The few times she tried touching her face she set off shards of needles through her cheek bones that hurt so much she was on a self-imposed mission not to move.

Things to remember: When your hands and feet are restrained, make sure to land as hard as possible on the intended recipient. That and change my center or gravity sooner. Things she should have learned when she was taking Tae Kwon Do. She would practice that when her face felt better in a day or so.

The next thing she needed to remember was to look at the magazine that had somehow made its way into her sphere of influence. Was it really *Nature*? She would be surprised if that were true. Pleasantly surprised, but surprised nonetheless.

And the next thing was to retrieve the latest message sent to her by the Unknown Correspondent. She had lost all the others messages when her books were confiscated, but she wondered if she had lost the opportunity to find a code in them. Could they really just be random thoughts, aspiring aphorisms, which dropped from the sky like manna from heaven?

If a meme was an idea that spread like a virus then her pillowcase was the viral vector. The genes were the delivered message, and the pillowcase was the virus that delivered it.

As she lay with her mostly numb head on the sack of flatness known as her pillow she thought: *the viral vector has succeeded once again.*

She felt the paper in the pillowcase and knew not to rush.

Waiting to read the message would be the same as waiting for her Christmas presents. Her dad used to look worried that she didn't pester him about her presents, but what he didn't know (did he?) was that she knew where he hid everything and that she was content to get everything she wanted except for the really expensive toys. Yet somehow, she found the occasional gift that she didn't see hidden away and was always surprised when she unwrapped it. It was always the toy, or book, or kit that she had wanted the most but didn't find in the hidden stash. In fact, it was always something she didn't realize she really wanted until she got it.

The messages were like that. The present she didn't know she wanted until she received it.

So this is what painkillers feel like. I think I want more of these. She tried to stretch, but her muscles were both sore and loose. Closing her eyes, she thought of amusement parks with fun houses and make-believe monsters.

Anna sat up and stretched her neck. She felt a dull throb from her shoulders all the way up to the top of her head. The beauty of self-defense was you weren't supposed to let anyone land a punch because punches hurt and they became a distraction. Not at all like in the movies where people land on their side or their backs or get pummeled over and over again until the hero regains a bout of newfound energy, able to beat the villain just in time.

If she hadn't restrained Hyde, she would have been lunch.

Anna swung her legs over the side of her bed. Blinking was interesting. Every third or fourth blink she saw flashes of light in a circle around her vision. It reminded her of having a migraine without the actual sensation of one. Fast or slow she felt puffiness around her eyes. Were painkillers meant to be so numbing?

She crouched down and picked up the magazine that somehow made its way to the floor. *Well, what do you know?* The magazine *was* the latest issue of *Nature*. She had never had a subscription but loved reading it in the UPenn library. Since it came out every week, she couldn't keep up, but Anna loved going through the latest research. Even the titles were exciting to her.

Maybe she could try doing theoretical research in genetics.

If she could convince them to let her have pen and paper again she could work on a cure for some niche genetic disease the pharmaceutical companies would never work on.

A siren cut through the air with all the subtlety of a sand blaster. Did they have to use such a piercing frequency? Did they think being in a cell meant they were deaf? The sound was different though. That much she knew.

The ear-piercing sound stopped. The intercom kicked in with its usual echo and hard-to-understand voice.

Anna strained to understand and heard a word she had not thought she would hear in a maximum-security facility like Florence.

Lockdown.

37

JEKYLL'S LAST TOUR

The body was found shortly after lunch.

Correction Officer Patrick Crutch, aka Jekyll, was a career civil servant. Having dropped out of college, he had enough credits to take the corrections officer exam a few years earlier and passed with a high enough rank that he made the eligibility list after a year, working for the Bureau of Prisons shortly after. His assignment to the U.S. Penitentiary, Administrative Maximum Facility was not his first, but after getting married and moving to the small town of Florence, Colorado, it was meant to be his last.

It was.

Hawking looked over Crutch's file, closed the folder, and placed it on his tired wooden desk. *You will no longer get to play the part of unwilling accomplice.* The Head Nurse was giving Crutch's body a basic examination in preparation for the arrival of the coroner.

"Forget it, Margaret," Hawking said. "Give me a few minutes and we'll do it together. If anyone's signature has to be on the preliminary report, it has to be mine."

Head Nurse Margaret Gregory, dressed in her medical blues, nodded at Hawking and left him in the examination room reserved for the few inmates who had completed their life sentences. The

room was larger than the main examination room and had lockers
where the bodies lay in cold storage for the few days it took for the
coroner or the mortician to arrive. It was larger than the examination
room where he performed the physicals on the inmates, but then
again complaints about overcrowding would never happen in
this room.

The phone rang. The Warden.

"So what did him in?" Coleman asked.

Hawking was sure the Warden had already been apprised of the
situation by the CO who found the body, but who was he to tell the
warden how to run an investigation?

"I'm not a forensic pathologist. You should wait until the coroner
files a report," Hawking said.

"I don't pay you to let someone else tell me things. What do you
think happened?"

"Blunt force trauma. Given that his head was badly crushed and
that there was no sign of a struggle, I think he was surprised by
someone with a large solid object." *Like a tire iron.*

"What do you think?" Coleman asked.

"What do I think? When are the police arriving?"

"The FBI is sending someone over right away."

"The FBI? We're still waiting on the first agent to come in and talk
to our guys about the shooting. And the other body found before
that. Why not the locals?"

"Not your call. This is a federal facility," Coleman said. "I have to
ask. Is there any chance Prisoner X did it?"

"This is a murder. You're acting like he was hit by a falling piano
or a dropped air-conditioner." Coleman was an interesting man to
deal with. Hated the locals. Preferred to delay findings rather than let
someone he didn't trust do the work. *He should let the police come.*
Hawking would never understand the anxiety of ego protection but
was grateful for Coleman's inability to handle distractions.

"Do they understand that the body count is starting to rise? And
that she is in a locked cell under the influence of painkillers?"

"They do and have someone coming soon."

"Fine. I'll be here ready to help out in any way I can. And Warden?"

"Yes?"

"Don't forget that he was found in one of the dumpsters. He wasn't meant to be found." Hawking wondered what the others made of that. What kind of killer hides a body in a nearby dumpster? He would never have done that.

"Something I had already considered. Thank you for your observations." Coleman hung up.

PART III

LOCKDOWN

38

FOLLOWING PROTOCOL

Warden Coleman stepped into the darkened central control area and surveyed the dozens of screens that were shifting even as he looked at them. Nothing could happen at ADX without someone seeing and reacting. Of all the locations in the prison, it was these that gave Coleman the confidence that everything was under control. The well-lit room had an officer who staffed the station at all times. There was a multi-hour overlap and the only thing that could make it better would be for the security system to surveil itself.

The other two locations that constituted the remainder of the facility known as the Florence Federal Correctional Complex each had their own security station with dedicated personnel.

"Is everything secure?" Coleman asked.

"We had the usual rotation of inmates in transit to their cells or to the exercise area." The officer typed in commands and a number of the screens changed again. "They were immediately called back and are all where they belong, sir."

"Good." *Time to talk to the troops.*

The warden stood on a bridge overhang looking down into a common area where most of the COs of the facility had reported on his orders. He would keep it short. There were not enough men if something were to go wrong. Nothing would go wrong, but he was not a veteran of the prison system by underestimating the odds of unplanned events.

"I don't need to tell you the obvious. The BOP will be here in the next day or so if we haven't lifted the lockdown status by then. We will have no problem maintaining control of this facility. Given that three men have been found dead in the last week I want to eliminate the possibility that one or more of our residents, or their associates, is somehow responsible." A few of the men looked at each other.

How could Coleman explain this without sounding alarmist? "Since the inmates can't get around without at least three officers then we will have eliminated them as potential suspects," Coleman said. He would have to increase the detail on Prisoner X. He could only spare two officers before; now she would get the regulation three.

"Keep your eyes open. There may be someone in or around the facility that we need to stop."

———

"How can you lock down a facility that's in lockdown all the time?"

Coleman knew the call from the Federal Bureau of Prisons would come soon enough. He had to notify them of the change in status.

Within the hour by Coleman's estimate.

"Sir, I understand your concern. I have many of my own, but this is the third death this week. At some point, I expect the media to get involved and at that point anything I do will seem extreme. The lockdown is tame by comparison," Coleman said. He sat alone in his office knowing that he might be interrupted at any time, but he didn't expect to be.

"But you've also locked everyone else in. Officers, medical personnel, custodial staff. While I agree with your assessment, you have to lift the lockdown. This isn't a situation where you have prisoners running around like hormonally-challenged teenagers. You may have some of the worst of the prison system, but you also have some of the least dangerous as well."

Coleman had had the pleasure of speaking with Bureau of Prisons Director Allan Berry only a handful of times before this. He had been appointed a year or two ago to head the Federal BOP and was known as a reformer, but not a liberal reformer. He wanted sentences to be served and the convicted to either be genuine before the parole board or stay in their cell.

The government was paying too much to waste anybody's time with someone who was tried and convicted. Coleman had heard that he felt there wasn't enough time, moreover, not enough money to go around wasting effort on convicted criminals.

"I understand, Director, but my biggest fear is that there is some terrorist group out there trying to release one or more of our charges and that we will be unable to sustain an attack." Coleman had already made a few calls but wanted to make sure that his request for help wasn't seen as posturing.

"Stephen, I've already escalated this. I have officers coming out of the academy. I have the FBI looking into this. You should have people arriving this afternoon or evening. Is that going to work for you?"

"Yes, sir, that will," Coleman said. The thought of letting some of the COs leave crossed his mind for a few seconds, but he thought better of it.

"When can you lift the lockdown?" the Director asked.

"I don't know, sir. I will keep you apprised."

"You don't have a reason for the kind of lockdown you're executing."

"Maybe, but here we are."

39

PASSING NOTES

Anna heard the steps echo outside her cell but thought nothing of them. Her face hurt, her back was in pain, and the Vicodin haze was lifting. All that was left was for her to take off the mask and breathe the stale unmoving air. There was always someone coming through to check on the few people in Range 13, the location where the worst of the worst lived, but that really just meant making sure the cells were locked and that no one was trying to kill themselves.

Even the worst of the worst had bad days.

Anna felt her cheeks go hot. Was she still drinking the Kool-Aid about surviving this?

"Anna?" A loud whisper came from the slot where she would normally place her hands to be cuffed.

Sliding off the gray solid slab that held her mattress, Anna walked over to the green door. She leaned against it and considered whether she should answer.

"Anna? It's me, Orville."

Was that possible? She tried to stop from smiling but decided to endure the muscle pain instead.

"Orville?" She crouched down a little and looked through the slot. Sure enough, there he was. "Hi."

He smiled. She felt a butterfly in her stomach. "How are you doing?" he asked.

"How are you doing? You're the one who was shot." Anna could see the sling through the slot. It wasn't very big, but she examined every detail she could. His tan shirt, very pressed, his blue eyes, his dusty blond hair. The blue sling with white trim. His twang.

"I'm fine. I hope I didn't disturb you."

Anna rolled her eyes. Why did he always seem so...simple? "Yes, I was in the middle of a very important meeting that I really need to get back to."

"Does it involve getting out?" He looked around. "I can help you get out."

Anna stood and leaned against the door again. *What the hell is he talking about?* "Orville!" She was almost hissing at him. She opened the slot again. "Stop talking like that. You want a cell next door to me?"

"Don't worry. There's no audio."

OMG! What is wrong with this man? "There are cameras, you idiot! They can see us talking like we're passing state secrets because we are. There is no escaping here. I'll be lucky if my lawyer can find a loophole to get me out."

"You won't need a loophole," Orville said.

"Yes, I do. I don't want to be chased around like a fugitive for the rest of my life. I didn't do anything!" Except accidentally shoot someone in Witness Protection. Other than that. This was not going to look good if Orville was just trying to find out if she was planning anything. What if he was setting her up?

"If you didn't do anything then leaving is the best thing you could do." He glanced to his right. "You're the first woman to be in this facility." And then he said it: "You could be the first escape."

Oh, please make him take it back. "This is bad. This conversation is being recorded by the cameras in this cell and outside in the corridor. Audio or not."

"No," Orville said, "it's not. I have a friend who," he made air quotes, "'accidentally' shut down the cameras that would show us together." He put his hand in the slot and Anna reflexively put her hand on his. "You can do this," he said.

"No, I can't." She remembered something. Was this a newfound opportunity? "Are you sure he turned off the camera in my cell?"

"Yes, he told me he would."

Oh, simple, simple Orville.

"Be right back." Anna ran back to her bed and stuck her hand in the pillowcase to pull out the latest message. Plain envelope with the flap folded inside. She pulled out the note.

Opportunities are like sunrises. If you wait too long, you miss them. - William Arthur Word

Anna sighed. *Great.* She stuck the note back in the envelope. She scanned her cell. Stainless steel sink. Concrete desk, but no drawers. No bureau since she didn't have any clothes to store. Gak! There were no hiding places. Where could she hide the note so she could look at it later?

On the floor!

Nature.

"Anna?"

"Be there in a second!" she whispered. She spun, grabbed the magazine, and stuck the note about three quarters of the way in. The note would have a harder time falling out of there than in the middle.

She looked behind her and saw Orville watching what she was doing. Damn it, she didn't want him to know.

"What are you doing?"

"Nothing. Close the slot. I don't want you getting into any more trouble." She threw the magazine on the floor by the sink so that when the camera came back on, it would look like she hadn't touched it.

She stuck her hand in the slot. He didn't reach in with his hand. Another lost opportunity. "Are you sure the camera is disabled?"

"He mighta lied to me, but he hasn't so far."

OMG, trusting too.

"Why are you here? You should be home getting better."

"Didn't you hear? We're on lockdown. I came back just as the warden announced it. I'm lucky to be here."

Only Orville would consider it lucky to be in a prison surrounded by murderers, traitors, and high-value Intelligence assets. "They let you come back in? Are they that short of personnel?" What kind of prison was this?

"I guess I'm kind of lucky too."

How long had they been talking? What if Orville's connection had to change shifts or go to the bathroom? "You should go. Your friend might only be able to disable the cameras for so long."

He knew Dad. Marshall. She was still confused about her feelings for him. She didn't think about him at all anymore, yet it felt like she still thought about him all the time.

And Donnell.

You're Marshall's girl? But you can't be. She's dead.

Anna stretched her back. She felt so sore. What a mess she had made of things. Hyde had goaded her and she fell for it. All she had to do was nothing and she blew that chance.

She crouched down, peered through the slot, and looked into Orville's eyes. "You have to go. I'm glad you came back. Don't get into any more trouble. I'm not worth it."

"God thinks you are." He leaned forward just a bit more.

She memorized more details about his eyes.

"And so do I," he said.

40

PROTECTION UNDER THE LAW

"Senator, I think we have a problem," Terrell said.

The first person Terrell called was Senator Lyndon Bigelow, the Chairperson of the Senate Select Committee on Intelligence Oversight.

"I appreciate your taking my call, but this is only going to get worse before it gets better," Terrell said. The wind was picking up. Terrell had tried brushing the grass off his suit and only succeeded in moving it down to his pants. What the hell was wrong with him? Why didn't he see this coming?

The passersby at the park ignored him or didn't see him as he walked along the edge. Every step jostled his shoulder and tightened his jaw.

"Where has she been taken?" Bigelow asked.

"No idea. I have charges I'm bringing against two Metro PD cops, but that won't help us at all," Terrell said. He tried flagging down a cab to no avail. His arm throbbed.

"Do you think this was the General?" Bigelow asked.

"They read her her rights. They knew she was talking to me and didn't care who I was."

Terrell saw another cab and tried to hail it down with his right hand. No good. There just weren't enough cabs in metro D.C. In New York, at least ten of them would have ignored him as they drove past, but he would have gotten one to stop even if he had to step in front of it. He put the cell phone back to his right ear and cursed to himself. "This has to be the General."

"She's probably being held for arraignment and will spend the night in DC Jail. We can't let that happen."

"You have any friends in the judiciary?"

"Not in DC. They don't like me very much here."

———

Terrell entered the police station of the Metropolitan Police Department of the District of Columbia with a wobble in his step. He needed to sit before he fell down. He knew there was a hospital in his future, but he was going to do his best to avoid that.

"Excuse me." He walked up to the desk sergeant. "I need to know the disposition of a woman who was just picked up by two of your guys." He held up his ID.

The desk sergeant glanced at it and then at him. "Are you posting her bail?"

"Has she been arraigned?" Terrell asked.

"What's her name?"

"Magnolia Sams," Terrell said.

"She's probably in lock-up waiting to be taken to DC." She looked down at some paperwork. "They'll arraign her in the morning."

"Yeah, that's not going to work."

———

"Captain, I need that woman," Terrell said. *And I need to sit down.* The station house had narrow corridors with dirty walls and glassed-in bulletin boards. The smell of gun oil and locker room mixed with the scent of expensive perfume and makeup.

"I've already told you," Captain Naoma Keck continued to walk as if Terrell were just another sycophant, "you can't have her."

Terrell walked alongside her doing his best not to trip, but found it harder and harder. Even getting her to speak with him had taken over thirty minutes. Thirty long minutes when he felt every minute, every second, of his wait going by, and felt Magnolia Sams' panic growing as well. His pulse felt like it was moving from his chest to his shoulder.

Was his vision getting blurry?

Please have at least one damn chair in your office.

"Captain," he swerved around a bench chair, "you don't seem to understand. She is my prisoner, my witness, not yours." His shoulder ached. He reached over and massaged it. His shirt felt wet. *Please let it be from the running.*

"I would love to accommodate you, but the problem is that you don't have jurisdiction, and I have too much work to do." She didn't bother looking over at him. Her hair was pinned up in a bun behind her head and it looked like one solid piece of her head.

"How can I not have jurisdiction? You think your homeys have enough to keep her?"

Keck turned her head enough to give him a quick glance. "She was brought in by DOD. She's not even here. They took her straight to DC lock-up and I expect she'll be there in the morning when she'll appear before a judge and then be remanded somewhere more accommodating."

Where the hell was her office? *A chair! My kingdom for a chair!* "Then what are you doing with her paperwork?"

"A courtesy, Special Agent. Your colleague at the Bureau sent a few of your men, with a few of my men, and a few DOD men." She stopped in front of door, opened it, and turned before looking at Terrell.

Was she not letting him in?

"We filed the initial paperwork, but the Bureau is in charge of her. You should be taking to your homeys." She crinkled her nose, entered her office, and closed the door.

———

The afternoon was on a fast burn. Terrell found that his peer at the Bureau, the Special Agent in Charge, or SAC, wasn't in the office. What the hell? He contacted his boss. No answer.

He headed to Tolsen's office but on the way decided to sit. He was light-headed. He should have gone to the hospital. He decided that if he found Anna, he'd go. Where the hell did they take her?

Screw this. He got up. Tolsen's office was on the far side of the floor.

———

Terrell put his cell phone on Section Chief Bernard Tolsen's desk with a restraint that belied his anger. He hit the speaker button on the flat surface.

"Good afternoon, Section Chief," the voice from the phone said.

"Good afternoon, Senator. What can I do for you on this fine Washington, D.C. day?" Tolsen asked. He folded his hands on the desk. His receding hairline looked like he had combed it back one too many times.

"The question is, what can I do for you?" the senator asked.

"I don't follow, Senator." Tolsen eyed the cell phone.

"You have someone who is under the protection of the Intelligence Committee. I want her back." Terrell kept his eyes on Tolsen and wondered who would blink first.

"I'm sorry, Senator, you can't have her."

"You have no right..."

"Forgive me, Senator, but this woman has been leaking highly classified information in violation of more laws than I can count."

Terrell was confused. "Sir, she was working with the Committee and with me."

Tolsen held up his hand to stop Terrell from continuing. He mouthed, *We'll talk later.* The look on Tolsen's face told

Terrell it wouldn't be a happy conversation.

"Senator, we don't know to whom she may have been passing information. She may have told you that it was only you, but we have no proof of that." Tolsen stood up for a moment and removed his shiny gray jacket. He draped it on his chair. "We'd been notified by NSA that they had reason to believe there was a leak and we found her in record time."

"Yes, I noticed that. You are to be commended for your speed. I want to see all the paperwork involved in bringing her to justice seeing that she had been given immunity by this committee," the senator said.

"Again, please forgive me, Senator, but her paperwork, the paperwork submitted by the committee, has been stayed by a federal judge. As a federal contractor, she has no protection under the law. The information she was passing, and she appears to have passed quite a bit, was all highly sensitive and she should have taken it internally first." Terrell felt his stomach drop to his knees. Where did they take Magnolia?

"Please see to it that I have a copy of all of her paperwork. If I find that you're reverse-engineering the charges against her, I will bring charges against the Bureau," Bigelow said.

Reverse engineering was a new process at the Bureau and little discussed. It involved two things: illegally obtained evidence from any Intelligence agency, and legally created paperwork to make the collection of that information look like it came organically from an investigation, which of course, it did not.

"Understood, Senator. I will send everything over with Terrell," Tolsen said.

This was going to be good, Terrell thought.

"Thank you, Mr. Tolsen."

"My pleasure, Senator."

41

AUTHORITIES AT THE GATE

Warden Coleman met the State Troopers at the gate just outside the perimeter of ADX. It was late afternoon and the air was dry and the ground dusty. He had asked the guard at the entry point to stop the troopers from coming onto the facility grounds, and had one of the officers drive him to the gate leading into the prison. His shirt felt itchy and he was tempted to take off his jacket and tie. But he wanted them to see he could stay professional even if they were not.

"Warden," the taller of the troopers accepted Coleman's outstretched hand, "we have some news for you." He adjusted his hat while his partner stood at attention.

"Trooper." Coleman tried to read the nameplate and gave up.

Either his eyesight was going or the lettering was too damn small. "Who was the man found outside the gate?"

"That man's name is," the trooper avoided eye contact, "still unknown. We have been waiting patiently for the local FBI field office to send someone, but they appear busy with other matters. We have put in an official request for their help."

The local FBI field office was located two hours north of Florence. This is exactly the kind of thing the FBI office should have been involved with from the beginning. Were the Colorado State Police playing a game?

"Perhaps you should wrap up the body and drive it up to Denver yourself. Are you saying that the FBI has refused to help you out?"

"No, sir, but given that the man was found on state land I suspect they're doing the prudent thing and allowing us to conduct our own investigation first." The trooper adjusted his stance. "We have been told that they'll have someone here in another day or so."

"On a body that was found spitting distance from a federal maximum-security prison three days ago?" Coleman couldn't believe it. These guys were bigger jokers than he gave them credit for. "Has a request even been submitted to the FBI?" He knew the trooper would want to interrupt him so he soldiered on. "What are you allowed to tell me about this man's death? Or are you not allowed to tell me due to the sensitive nature of the investigation?"

The trooper looked uncomfortable.

Good.

"While the results are preliminary the coroner has determined that death was due to asphyxiation. There were some fibers found in his lungs, but their source has yet to be determined."

Coleman was sure the trooper stood as straight as his back would let him. *He looks like he has a stick up his ass and he knows I put it there.*

"Alright." Coleman extended his hand again. If these men worked for him, they wouldn't have a job anymore. He thought so highly of them just a few days prior. "Thank you for your time."

"May I ask why we were not allowed on the grounds?"

"We are on lockdown, Officer. There have been a few incidents and we need to stabilize the situation," Coleman said.

That was more than he wanted to tell them, but they weren't stupid either. The warden of a federal penitentiary came all the way out to the entry guard station to hear their report. He didn't want to take their call because it would have been too easy to dismiss them. This gave him the Intel he needed and the details he wouldn't have gotten over the phone.

They knew nothing. CSP was useless to him. Life was so much easier in Texas.

"An escape? Or did it have to do with the drone attack from the other day?" the trooper asked.

Coleman did his best to hide his surprise. They must have monitored the frequencies to the military base. "As soon as I feel a need for the assistance of the *state* police I'll let you know." He looked at both men and then turned away. "Have a good day, gentlemen."

———

Hollingsworth asked his police-assigned driver to take him to the Colorado State Patrol headquarters in Lakewood, a short twenty minute drive west of Denver. While he was never happy with the black SUV purchased by the previous administration it made it possible for him to get work done in relative comfort on most days. Today, instead, he took in the sights that constituted part of his constituency.

The warden has every right to keep the troopers off his property, thought Governor Hollingsworth, *but I don't rightly care.*

When he arrived at the Colorado State Patrol headquarters, a four-story brick-facade building, Chief Brian Diaz met him at the door. Diaz, a tall barrel-chested man who had been chief for less time than Hollingsworth was governor, was going to be chief for a long time. Hollingsworth would make sure of that. The locals loved Diaz but, more to the point, he owed Hollingsworth. Hollingsworth wanted to keep it that way.

They shook hands and after the standard pleasantries, went for a stroll around the building's black asphalt parking area. Taking a local tour, as Diaz was fond of saying.

"I need you to take care of this," Hollingsworth said. He zipped up his black windbreaker as the chilly air surrounded and lifted it.

"Not a problem, Governor."

It wouldn't take them long to circumnavigate the building, but

Hollingsworth could use the walk even if it only took them a few times around.

"I have to ask. Why are we purposely pissing off the feds?" Diaz asked.

"We are not pissing off the feds." Hollingsworth rubbed his chilled hands together. It was brisk even for October. "We offered to help and they brushed us off. I think we need to help them with their problem."

"I assume you mean the three deaths," Diaz said.

"Precisely those. The first was done by a man on the state side of the property."

"True. Hard to argue that," Diaz said. He took off his hat and repositioned it. Diaz didn't wear a jacket, which showed off his tan uniform, but it also showed off the gun that was nestled against the right side of his belt.

"The attack happened in your jurisdiction. There was no need to call in assistance from Cheyenne Mountain." Hollingsworth wondered at what point Warden Coleman would realize that he was treating his host like an undeserving relative. A call to the Cheyenne Mountain Air Force Base was the same as calling in tanks to find a lost pet.

"And the second we know almost nothing about as we only have an anonymous caller to thank for even letting us know," Hollingsworth said. He put his hands behind him and stretched. "As for the third, well, we would have never known about it had the lockdown not happened." He scanned the parking area and gave Diaz his election gaze. *I see what you mean. I can see what you want.* "The good people of Florence need to know that we have their back. There is something going on and we're not being told."

Diaz pressed his hands against his face and sighed.

"Governor, you know I owe you the world, but..."

He turned to Diaz and extended his hand. "Then we have nothing else to discuss, and I will let you get back to your work. It will be great to see you at dinner next week," Hollingsworth said.

"Yes, Governor. Please give my best to your wife."

42

WILLING CONFESSION

"You're still not leaving," Coleman said.

Two officers flanked Corrections Officer Todd Peterson, aka Hyde, in Coleman's office. Coleman had had Human Resources start a file on Peterson months ago, but this might be the moment Coleman was waiting for. He was the kind of worker who got others into trouble, but did a great job at keeping himself clean. Coleman despised people who could do that. Dysfunctional and Teflon. Peterson was the kind of guy who could have been on the other side of the cell door. Coleman decided he would read Peterson's background check to see what the hell the investigator thought when he let Peterson through.

"I get that, Warden, but I just wanted to bring this to your attention."

Was he drunk?

"That little witch, who has been getting far more privileges than she should be," he poked at Coleman's desk with each word, "has been thumbing her nose at you."

Peterson was in his civilian clothes. His hair was disheveled and he looked confused. How the hell did this guy manage to keep from getting fired? Or arrested?

"You know, Officer Peterson," Coleman pushed his chair back and put his hands behind his head after looking at Peterson's personnel file, "Todd. When I ask your co-workers about you, all I ever hear is that you're a bottom feeder. You're a low-life scumbag who can't keep himself out of trouble if he tried. Even the union doesn't like you."

Peterson's face turned red. The smile that he had on his face became a thin line as he pursed his lips. "I brought you these things because I thought it would help," Peterson said.

"And yet somehow everyone owes you. How do you do that?" Coleman asked.

"I'm a guy who knows how to take care of his friends," Peterson said.

"Officer Crutch was your friend, right? At least as much of a friend as you seem capable of having," Coleman said. Coleman had been to the morgue earlier without Hawking's knowledge or permission. This was Coleman's facility after all. He didn't know what Crutch had done to deserve being ambushed and thrown in the dumpster, but he was still one of his men. Crutch could have been any of the hundreds of people who worked for him and Coleman was loyal to his people. He would make sure that whoever killed Crutch would be brought to justice. Coleman would even ask the courts to have the murderer sent to ADX. Just because.

"Yeah." Peterson looked away. "I miss him."

Yes, the evil villain always missed his minion.

"But I'm sure that girl," Peterson emphasized that last word, "had something to do with it. She has a hold on a lot of the people here."

"Oh." Coleman tapped the tips of his fingers on his desk. "Like?"

"Like, like," he let his gaze float around the room, "the doc."

Coleman became serious. Let him put the noose around his own neck even as he indicted others. Maybe there were others worthy of being fired.

"The doc sees her alone," Peterson said.

Now *that* was interesting. "And?"

"They talk a lot."

"Imagine, a doctor talking to his patient," Coleman said.

"I bet you she's doing him."

"I hadn't considered that." What an idiot. If he could throw him out the front door, Coleman would have done it immediately.

"That's why he gives her so much attention. I bet you she's doing everybody," Peterson said.

"Everybody?" Coleman asked. What must Peterson have been like in grade school?

"Yeah, yeah." He stopped and thought for a second. "Orville! He's another one! He's always being nice to her." Peterson slammed the palms of his hands on Coleman's desk. "He talks to her." His gaze wandered all over the room.

Coleman was sure this man was on something.

"Is she doing you?" Coleman asked.

"Of course not. That's against regulations," Peterson said. The sweat was starting to show on Peterson's shirt.

"Good to see you remember that," Coleman said.

"You've done so much for her, sir. She's never showed you any kind of appreciation. Instead she decides to attack your officers."

Here it comes.

"She almost killed me!"

"Did you kill Officer Crutch?"

Coleman thought you could hear the screech of tires on that one. Peterson hadn't thought he would be asked that.

"What?"

"Did you kill Officer Crutch?"

"That's insulting, Warden. Why would I kill my friend?"

"Because he was getting favors from her and you weren't?"

"He was?" Peterson rolled his eyes. "He wasn't getting anything from her. You're just sussing me." He looked like he was on the verge of saying something and then caught himself. "We didn't even know she was a girl until a few days ago."

"You and the rest of the planet," Coleman said. This was a point-less conversation. Peterson was bringing contraband that he should have brought to his attention a long time ago.

"Warden," Peterson shook himself like he realized he needed to go to the bathroom, "can I go home?"

"Not until you get interviewed. You were on shift when Officer Crutch's body was found. No one goes home until then."

Peterson sighed then sighed again. His hair was sticking up and his eyes were red. Coleman looked down at the contraband that Peterson had brought him. He returned his gaze to Peterson and motioned to the officers to take him away.

A collection of open envelopes and notes. Strange quotes. Why would someone go through that much trouble just to give her self-help advice?

43

TAKING NOTE

Anna, not wearing her mask (what was the point?) stood in the furthest corner of the cell and watched as Warden Coleman took her last bit of reading material. The issue of *Nature* that Hyde had used as bait. *Oh, don't look. Please, don't look. Please, please, please.* As he leafed through the magazine he stopped and held up the tiny piece of paper.

"You went through a lot of trouble to get this," he said. He put the paper back into the magazine.

Anna bowed her head and sighed. Just another failure. When would the denigration stop? Would it ever? It didn't matter, did it? She didn't bother responding.

The warden was wearing gloves. "Who gave this to you?"

Anna blinked.

Blink. Blink. Blink.

"Alright." He turned and started to walk out. "Let's go."

"Please." The word that came out of her mouth hurt as it scraped its way up her chest.

"Excuse me?" Coleman asked.

"Please, don't take that from me."

She couldn't find the energy to lift her head. It was a pointless gesture, asking for the note, but her sense of helplessness was over-whelming.

I didn't do anything! I didn't do anything! I didn't DO ANYTHING! Why are these things happening to me? I know I don't matter, I know that no one can do anything for me...

She started to sob, first slowly, then faster and faster until her body shook from the anguish-filled sound. Her voice was barely audible. "Oh, please! Oh, please! Leave it for me! I don't have any other connection to him!"

Anna thought that the Warden looked at her. She wasn't sure as she could barely see him as she fell onto her knees and bent her head as far as it could go. The cold floor on her knees. The manacles on her ankles. The cuffs on her wrists. Could this be how it works out? All that work, all that time and effort and the only thing in the world that mattered to her right now, at this very instant, was a piece of paper that came from the outside world. From someone who remembered her.

Coleman and the Marshmallow Men left her cell and slammed the door shut.

44

IMPLIED DIRECTIVES

Palma walked the antiseptic corridors of the NSA building looking for yet another conference room for yet another briefing in yet another operation. *If the public thinks we take these things lightly, they have another think coming.*

Andrew was falling behind. Maybe he wasn't super-human after all. Maybe Palma would let him live. As he walked past a connecting corridor, a senior analyst caught up with him. Janine Ammons. "Good afternoon, General," she said.

"Good afternoon, Janine. How are you doing?" Palma continued walking. Whatever she had to tell him could be told on the way to the next briefing.

Janine wore her usual business attire: navy skirt, white blouse, and black shoes. He wished he could clone her; she was that good.

"Just fine, General."

Her stride was off. Was she wearing high heels?

"You look worried." Palma smiled. "Big date tonight?"

"No, sir." She took her glasses off, folded them, and hooked them into the fold of her blouse. "I had something I wanted to bring to your attention. I asked Mr. Yen to put me on your calendar yesterday, but he didn't and since I've found you wandering the hallways..."

"I'm not wandering. I'm trying to stay on schedule." He stopped. "Are you going to throw off my schedule?"

She looked up at him. The high heels weren't helping. "No, General," she said, her eyes wide, "but maybe, yes."

Palma sighed and continued walking. "Give me the short version."

"I've been tracking some communications from the Chinese," Janine said.

"Well, that is your job."

The NSA had been tracking the communications of most of the world for over a decade now. There had been a few embarrassing leaks over the years, but the depth of surveillance that was in place was nothing compared to what would be in place in a few years.

And a few years after that. All things he had pushed, and pushed, and convinced the powers-that-be were necessary in the new century. He would have pushed for more if he was staying until retirement, but he would leave the country safer than when he started. The thought gave him a second of satisfaction until he thought about next week.

"Yes, sir, it is, but you also made it my job to track communications that might pertain to PRUDENT RAINBOW." He stopped. PRUDENT RAINBOW was HALON's original project name.

———

If there was one thing that Jeanine Ammons enjoyed doing it was talking to the brass. When she first started as a junior analyst out of school, she couldn't believe her luck. Doing foreign signal analysis was something she had always wanted to do when she first read about it in high school after she got the bug to follow the Intelligence community in the U.S. and the kind of things they did overseas. Now that was changing the world!

Promotion after promotion gave her the reputation she was looking for and always made the next move easier and easier even as the job got harder and harder. And here she was, working for the director and making sure he was kept up to date on specific communications on projects that he kept his eye on due to their sensitive nature.

This time he wasn't going to like it.

"I think the Chinese are sending over a team to assassinate someone," she said.

He didn't react. Was she not speaking clearly enough? "Assassination. As in killing an American. Of course, they might already have a team in place waiting to be activated, but that's splitting hairs. No matter what someone has a target painted on their back."

"What have you got?"

"Something from a satellite embassy office. They don't usually say much from there, but the satellite offices are the best way to distribute Intel since no one is really watching them. Except us. I think this is serious," she said.

"Are you sure?"

"If this were my asset, I'd move them."

"What else have you got?" the General asked.

"The communications were from a handful of encrypted emails, but since we have their keys reading them it's a non-event. The email didn't name names, but from previous coded messages they were talking about a person in isolation who would be terminated."

She was excited about this. This was a breakthrough for her and the project. She hadn't encountered information like this in years. As an analyst, she knew that the career-making assignments were far and few between. She was bucking to lead a group like the one she was in now. If she was right...

"I don't know, Janine. This isn't up to the quality of work you lead with."

She felt her cheeks go red. What the hell was he talking about? She kept her face impassive.

"Sir, this is a clear indicator. They did everything except say, 'We're sending a team to kill an American located in an American prison.' That would have made my job easier, but a lot less interesting." Was she still on the side of the argument where she wouldn't be transferred for insubordination?

"Any information about the team being sent?"

"We're working on that, sir. The fact that there were no direct or indirect indicators of one or more people entering the country, I'm predicting that the team is already here."

"Seems a bit forward for the Chinese, wouldn't you think?" Palma asked.

"That's what I was thinking as well. The Chinese are a lot more patient than we are so they avoid confrontational situations where they won't win by default. This breaks a lot of rules for them. They must have a strong reason for wanting this person removed, but I don't have any Intel on that yet."

45

STATUS

"Good evening, General. It's great to see you," George Monahan said.

Palma entered the office of Secretary of State George Monahan as the sun was setting to the west.

Monahan greeted Palma as he always did: with open arms and a warm handshake; not the standard politician's handshake, but with a man hug and strong respectful grip. A greeting of equals, or brothers. Through the years, Palma had remained loyal to Monahan, though Palma had been having doubts of late. During the Senate hearings eight years ago, when HALON was almost made public, it was Monahan who had offered to give himself up to allow Palma to continue the project. From Palma's perspective that was unacceptable and Monahan knew it. Monahan's position and experience in the Intelligence community meant that his absence would be felt. Palma couldn't allow that given the sensitivity of many of the programs they were working on. Palma sacrificed himself to prove it. Temporarily losing his position in the Intelligence Community was the cost of entry to the long game. What were the choices? Shut down a program they both believed in or play the long game and do what they could to continue under the radar.

Soon after, Monahan left the NSA, was appointed by the Presi-

dent to be Secretary of State, and he pulled every string he could find
to get Palma back into Intelligence.

He knew beyond everything that Monahan was there for him. He
was a man who knew the value of loyalty and protecting his people.
And yet.

There were days.

Monahan closed the door to his office behind Palma. The room
was ornate but furnished in typical early American. White walls,
antique ceiling moldings. Palma enjoyed the difference compared to
his office. While he overspent on making his people comfortable there
was something off-putting about late American office architecture.

"It's after five. Care for a drink?" Monahan asked.

"Thank you, sir. Yes, please."

"I'm glad you were able to come on by. I know how crazy things
can be this time of year and given some of your operations I know
you're burning the candle on both ends." Monahan walked over with
two glasses and handed one of them to Palma. "Cheers."

Their glasses clinked and a drop splashed on Palma's hand. He
took a small swallow while Monahan took a full gulp.

Monahan, the taller of the two, patted him on the back. "Please sit
down. These chairs are very comfy."

The men smiled at each other. They were a long way from the
days of waiting for war, going to war, and coming back. War changed
things, but the change they had in mind would have a greater impact.

Change it forever.

"So what can I help you with, General?"

"Our friends," Palma said, "seem a bit impatient." He crossed
his legs.

"Oh yes, they are." Monahan took another sip. "They're chomping
at the bit." He smiled.

Palma knew the look. Sitting in the third chair from the presi-
dency didn't change the man he knew.

"I know we can't get it to them next week. They're insane."

Palma relaxed. "Thank you, sir. I have been getting some rather interesting calls and reports. None of which make me feel like the project is under control."

"The one thing we can never allow is the slippage of control. No, this will go on your schedule, not theirs," Monahan said.

"Do you happen to know what's going on?"

"Not really. I've had a few calls myself." Monahan twirled the glass in his hand. "I understand you've had a few encounters."

Palma thought about his girls for a flash of a second. He almost smiled and then remembered Andrew's indiscretion. "I have. If we don't know what they want...?"

"What they want is to unwrap the present early. That has never worked out in my estimation and will not work out here.

"So what's left to be done?" A smaller sip. "Anything extraordinary?"

Was he repositioning? Did he really want the project delivered early?

The sun streaming through the white lace curtains went behind a cloud or building and all the shadows disappeared.

"No, not really," Palma said. "We have staff and contractors who are still going about their business and they need to complete their work. Everything they're doing is important, and can only be done by people who know what the hell they're doing."

Palma had been to the work site a few times in the last few years. While a bit of a bother to enter, it was quite impressive and claustrophobic at the same time. He thought about the delivery date. "I realize that traveling to the site might be a problem for you, but do you expect to be there?" Palma asked.

"When we hand the new tenants the keys?" Monahan took another sip and emptied the glass. "I wouldn't miss it for the world." He lowered his voice. "Do we still have to ride the subway?"

"Yes, sir. You'll be happy with what you see."

Monahan and Palma both looked away and smiled.

Hard to believe this is almost over. "Once this is done," Monahan said, "it will be time for another promotion."

"No, sir, I think I'd rather retire. It won't be that many years before I'm replaced. It would give me time with my girls," Palma said.

"Yes, yes, maybe. But I'd rather you get appointed to something a little more visible where you can use your background to make even greater strides than you already have."

Palma nodded. "Maybe. I'll worry about that after."

"You always were the one to get things done first," Monahan said.

Palma remembered Andrew. "Their insistence is rather worrisome."

"You think? The only way to get them to leave us both alone would be to do what they want." Monahan stood and sauntered over to the bar. After throwing some more ice into his glass, he reopened the bottle of John Walker Blue and splashed in more of the bronze liquid.

Palma had been considering some options since the first call a few days before. *What if we gave them what they wanted?* "A hand-off next week would never work. We couldn't leave our contractors. All our personnel would have to be extracted long before anyone else arrived. There are storms being predicted for the latter part of next week as well," Palma said.

"Like that's going to happen," Monahan said. "I don't trust the National Weather Service to tell what the weather is outside their window." Monahan sat and loosened his tie. "What would happen if we got the contractors out in the next few days?"

"Everyone?"

"Everyone."

Palma put his glass down on the table next to his chair. "There will be uninstalled equipment, equipment in various stages of being installed. If they bring their own people, they can probably complete some of the set-up, but if they are sloppy about anything..."

"What about the failsafe?"

"What about it?"

"We're good with it?"

"Of course. It was the first thing that went through extensive scenario testing. Our friend took care of that." *Yes, Marshall was some friend.*

Monahan frowned. His eyebrows curved down. "I guess that should make me feel better, but somehow it doesn't."

Palma saw Monahan's eyes focus into the distance and then returned his gaze to him.

"If you're good with this, I think we should do the hand-off next week."

Palma tapped the armrest with his left hand. Yes, they could do it, but he was just not comfortable. Something didn't sit well with him, but he couldn't tell what it was. "I suppose we can, sir."

"If you really don't want to, we don't have to. We've come this far by telling everyone to go screw themselves. I don't see a reason to change attitude," Monahan said.

"If we let our people do what they can over the next few days, evacuate them, and then hand over the keys, perhaps we can make next week."

"Unless we get an early snow or a hurricane." Palma smiled.

"In that case I'm opening up another bottle of scotch and waiting for the following week." Monahan tilted his glass toward Palma in a mock cheer and took a full gulp.

46

FREE HUG

After a few weeks at the prison Hawking had pretty much seen it all. The worse of the worst really were bad and their visits to medical were just to waste time. But there was another type of inmate. The ones in for white collar crimes, including treason. Hawking had had a chance to meet with them all, and being a somewhat vindictive person, considered what it would be like to hurt one or more of these men.

He read the kite that was mixed in with the few that had made their way to him: *Help me. -Prisoner X.*

————

Anna entered medical at the speed of a snail. She looked terrible. Had he failed?

The sound of the leg irons scraping against the floor reminded him of his time as a mechanic in the Iraq War. Her speed was slower than he had ever seen from her. Her mask still crusted with the blood from her teeth after Hyde's attack. The first thing he would have to do was examine her face. Something had to be broken. Possibly a cheekbone. The amount of pain she must be in must be considerable, surpassed only by the depression she must be feeling. The chemicals released or suppressed from a deep depression, serotonin, norepinephrine, and dopamine, would allow her to endure that much pain, but for a limited span.

She was a walking symbol of defeat.

Anna stood in front of the examination table. Three COs had escorted her this time and two of them lifted her by the armpits while the other stood by holding a Taser. Hawking understood their precautions but knew it was unnecessary. They lifted her onto the examination table that buckled under her weight. Hawking was going to have to put in for a new table. Someone was going to get hurt on it. He didn't want it to be him.

Hawking stepped up and looked into her eyes as they jumped back and forth. "I'm going to take this off. I want to take a look."

She barely moved her head. As he reached behind the mask, he stopped and stared at the small army of men standing there to pounce on her at the least provocation. He wondered how they felt about her getting the best of one of their co-workers even when restrained.

Anna was one scary woman.

He turned to the three COs. "Gentlemen, I know you're tired of hearing me say this, but I will examine her alone. I take full responsibility if anything happens to me, and you can come in and shoot her after if that will make you feel better."

There was no point pretending there wasn't a young lady in their presence. With any luck, the warden had had his talk with them and they knew enough to value their jobs to stay quiet about her existence.

It was the umpteenth time Hawking had been alone with her, and the officers walked out. Hawking knew they would be waiting outside. Would she snap and hurt him?

He had defended himself against worse.

He reached behind Anna's mask. "I'm sure your cheeks must be in pain right now."

She was silent, but he could see her eyes moving as he unzipped the leather shroud on her face. He peeled the mask off to reveal the bald, and bruised, Anna Wodehouse.

The mask went on the examination table to her left. She placed her hand on it as if it might fall, or leave her.

"Okay, I'm going to touch your face and I want you tell me how much it hurts."

Her eyes changed. Something was up.

"On a scale of one to ten."

She peeked around him and saw the closed door. "Okay, so the depressed me is probably going to need a really long examination and talk with my federally appointed therapist," she whispered. Her eyes were almost gleaming. "We have to talk in whispers or else they might suspect."

Hawking crouched down an inch or two to look at her eyes. "If we spend the entire time whispering, I'm pretty certain they're going to suspect anyway."

"Well, whatever." She grabbed the mask and put her hands on her lap. "I don't care what happens next."

"Oh, Anna," Hawking said.

"Will you hear me out? Jeez, you're no better than my father." She looked down for a moment, as if she realized what that meant, and appeared to push the thought away. "My life is over. As long as I have you and Orville, I might be able to survive in this clean room version of hell, but it's like being grounded for life. Trust me, Dad threatened me a lot with that because there was no point grounding me for a week since we never did anything anyway. I guess I'll never know if it was because he was that boring or if he was really afraid of someone finding us."

Hawking felt mixed emotions. Should he feel upbeat that she felt better, or upset that she was playing a con? He stood up and crossed his arms. "Go on," he whispered.

She sighed. "I am so grateful to you. I would hug you if I could, but the chains would make too much noise. You don't know me and I don't know you, but you and Orville are exactly who I needed to know to survive this. I think I can make it here for the next few years knowing that you're here even if I can't talk to you all the time."

"Shut up."

"What?"

"I said, shut up."

"I don't..."

"Let's get something straight." He massaged his chin. "I am not your friend. I work for the prison and the last thing I want to do is jeopardize my job. I get to retire in twelve years and I don't want that derailed."

He found the whispering to be annoying but figured it was better to carry on. The guards would be able to listen otherwise. "You are an incredible young woman. I'm sure that your father, if he were here, would tell you how proud he is of you." Anna started to object. "Stop. Stop! What you did, and remember, I have seen the court transcripts, was incredible.

"So maybe you were a little misguided. Deciding to kill your father was probably not one of your best moments." She became serious. The bruises on her face made her look like the fighter she was.

"But you tried to warn him that someone was after him. You knew you were going to be arrested, yet you went up on that roof."

"I didn't do it for him."

"Like hell you didn't. You wanted to save him. You didn't kill that guy. Any fool could see that."

A tear escaped her eye. "I...I..." She leaned into him and chuckled. "This is where you have to hug me because I'm cuffed."

He put his arms around her. She shook a little and then pulled away.

"I need to get back on your computer."

"I knew I was being scammed."

47

OVERSTAYING A WELCOME

Sitting in Hawking's chair was awful. A creaky black monstrosity, the chair shed pieces of its cushion at random intervals like a creature pooping chunks of crumbling black foam that didn't smell much better. Hawking sat with his back to her.

Why does he trust me so much? Or he is dumber than he looks? Anna knew that when she got the chance, she would have to talk to Orville as well. Maybe with more than a hug. She thought of his eyes and baby face. How could he be such a lunkhead to like her?

She would never be able to thank him.

She started up Tor on the beige-and-dirt colored PC and navigated to the link that would get her back to the IRC site where her friend *CrapIsKing* would be. At least she hoped. It was late in some parts of the world and she didn't know where he was. Her cold fingers hurt every few keystrokes, making her shake her hands to get the blood circulating.

CrapIsKing: Hey! Glad ur back.

HarlequinNinja: Glad to be back. Have anything?

CrapIsKing: God, ur such a pita sometimes. Ur lucky I like you.

HarlequinNinja: Cue the violins.

Anna waited. He didn't type back.

HarlequinNinja: Hey! Some of us have to get back to our cells.

CrapIsKing: I found your guy.

Anna's heart skipped a beat. He found Benson?

CrapIsKing: DMV match, but I didn't need to do that. That guy's name is not Benson. His name is Malik Palma.

HarlequinNinja: Not ringing any bells.

CrapIsKing: General Malik Palma. A higher up in NSA. You know, the guys spying on the world...including you.

Anna stopped a moment. She didn't want to waste time, but she wasn't sure what this meant. Why would the NSA care about her? Did they use her to kill that man? She felt like slapping her forehead. *What an idiot. To deflect attention away from them.*

Why the hell would a higher-up get involved like that? Anna was a nobody. Then she remembered what Donnell said. *OMG, Dad was involved with the government somehow. He did something that made him have to hide.*

HarlequinNinja: WTF?

CrapIsKing: Exactly. You are up to your ears in poop.

HarlequinNinja: Not the word I would use.

CrapIsKing: I found something though. About the guy who kidnapped you.

Anna almost got into a typing match with him and thought better of it.

HarlequinNinja: Whatcha got?

CrapIsKing: TL;DR I made a compilation for you. Can you download and read l8r?

HarlequinNinja: Well, no, but I guess you might as well post it.

CrapIsKing: I already put it in the same folder as the photo. Happy reading. WTF? THE COPS JUST BROKE IN RUN

Anna's eyes opened wide and she shut the browser down. She looked at Hawking's back and then at the door. Nothing happened. They'd traced him. They couldn't trace back to her, but if he didn't kill the IRC, they could read the text. Anna tried to swallow, but her mouth was dry. She didn't know what to do except feel awful for getting someone in trouble.

She re-opened Tor and went to the site where she kept the photo of Benson. *A General? What is that about? How does he know Dad?*

Anna shoulders tightened around her neck. Donnell's voice rang in her ears: *Marshall dropped off the radar screen when we needed him the most. People were dying.*

The words were strong and clear. It was what he told her as he purported to strangle her. Her father was involved in a government project gone wrong.

She changed the page view from Preview to Listing. There was the file: *HarlequinNinja.README.pdf.*

Was she running out of time? She clicked the link. Tor warned her about downloading files, but she had to read it. There was nothing gained by being shy. What could they do to her at this point? Kill her?

She thought about that for a moment and then shook her head. This was still the United States.

They got you to kill Donnell.

She tried to read the document and found herself going back and reading sentences over and over again. He wasn't kidding about this being *War and Peace.*

She decided to read faster. When that didn't work, she started flipping pages. Where was Marshall's name? She pressed Ctrl-F and typed *Marshall.* His name came up on page forty-two. *Head of IT. You have got to be kidding.*

Had her father been Dad a sysadmin for a runaway government Intelligence op? It wasn't possible.

She heard his voice: *If you go, we might have to move again.*

Anna put her hand to her mouth. The sound of the chains caused Hawking to turn around. She tried to change the look on her face but couldn't do it fast enough.

"What are you doing?" he whispered.

"Nothing, nothing." She had to get back to reading. What was the name of this report? She jumped back to the cover. Great. *Flagged as Sensitive.*

Hawking stood up and took a step toward her.

She held her hand up to stop him and he froze. "You don't want to come here." She motioned for him to sit.

He looked concerned and stood in place.

The title meant nothing to her. She couldn't understand half of the jargon in the report. They didn't need to mark this as secret. No one could understand it. What she did understand, though, was that her father had been part of something gone wrong. He'd gone into hiding, and she'd thought he was kidding.

The section with her father's name on it was an intro to a section he wrote. The page listed the various IT projects completed and in progress (over five hundred! He could barely cook dinner) and the stages they were at ten years before.

This is insane. Flip, flip, flip.

This was a massive project. Billions of dollars. Didn't anyone tell them that you couldn't plan software projects more than a year in advance?

Administrative tools. Electronic lab books. Failsafe mechanisms. *Dad?*

What happened? Why did he run? How did Anna fit into all of it? Her cheeks started to hurt. Pain distracted her long enough for her eyes to water which made it difficult to keep reading. She cursed to herself. Hawking tapped at his wrist where a watch should have been. She shook her head in acknowledgment, and he turned around again.

She blinked and the document disappeared. Whoever had gotten to her friend had found the link. Anna felt a shiver run through her. She exited Tor. She opened Windows Explorer and deleted the Tor binary. Maybe she could keep Hawking from getting into trouble.

She thought of calling out for pain-killers, but she'd already worn out her welcome. Dr. Hawking had already done so much for her. How could she ask for more? She would deal with the pain in her own way.

Classified documents. The police arresting her friend. If they came in looking for her, it was all over. She would never be able to explain how she accidentally found herself at the doctor's computer, or accidentally found an old classified document from ten years before.

She had a knot in her stomach. They would throw the key away, and she would never get to defend herself again. Dying in a prison filled with men did not seem that appealing at the moment.

Orville was right.

She had to get away.

She had to escape.

48

UNWANTED ADVANCE

It took Anna a long time to get back to the cell. She had to be Depressed Anna again to help deflect suspicion if they bought her act to begin with. The COs were surrounded by professional liars so they should know a con when they saw one.

But she made it to her cell, changed into her Sunday beige, and came to the conclusion that while she had nothing to read, she had plenty to ponder. The biggest thing was getting out. She had forgotten to check her email, but the best thing would be for her attorney to contact the FBI directly. What did Anna think she could accomplish, anyway, with that stunt? She might have gotten her attorney in trouble for receiving unauthorized communications. Would the FBI even care about her case anymore? They were in the business of finding the guilty, not freeing the innocent.

Maybe that one agent, Terrell Garrison, would hear about it and take an interest. She had started thinking of him more and more. Anna wasn't sure if he liked her, but she certainly liked him.

Oh, who was she trying to kid?

Her mouth was dry, but she couldn't get up enough energy to pour a glass of water. Her skin, one second warm, and the next clammy, was cold. She rolled the sleeves down and then rolled them back up. Why pretend comfort was possible? She rolled them down again.

She smelled something, took a whiff of her clothes, and contorted her face. Had these guys not heard of scented fabric softener?

She heard a key turning. Her movements felt a little delayed; Hawking had given her something to help with the pain, but it also put her in a bit of a haze.

The door opened and for a moment she imagined it was Orville doing something stupid (but welcome!) like coming to visit her.

Hyde peeked out from behind the door.

Oh, this is a new kind of stupid.

Anna felt a blast of adrenaline light her up. She looked at the camera and waved a couple of times into it.

"What are you doing, darlin'? Trying to put on a show for the boys back home?" Hyde asked. He looked under the influence.

How had he managed to stay in the prison? Was that what a lockdown meant? Keep the stupid indoors?

"You need to go."

He walked in carrying two books. He closed the door behind him.

"What are you doing?"

"Nothin'," he said. He held up the books. "I brought you a present. So we could kiss and make up." He waved the books in the air and seemed surprised to see them both. "Two presents."

Curses flew back and forth in Anna's head. The already small room got even smaller. Could she seal him in the anteroom?

Nope. He stepped into the main part of the cell.

"Ain't nobody seeing anything out of that camera."

Did all psychopaths have so many friends?

There was nowhere she could run. If she defended herself, she would get punished. If she didn't defend herself, she might get hurt or worse. And this absolute asshole would feel like he won.

"Take your books." Hyde held out his hands where the books rested like an offering to her.

Anna stepped back into the furthest corner of the room that was just a handful of steps away from him. How could she put this off?

"What do you want?" Anna asked.

"You killed my friend, didn't you?"

"What?"

"I don't know how you did it, but you did." He threw the books onto the bed and came at her. There was so much concrete in the room she wasn't sure how she was going to avoid doing anything but kill him.

She pushed him back hard enough that he fell onto the floor. He jumped up and reached for his Taser. Anna hit him in the face and he fell back, dropping the unit on the floor. They both reached for it and knocked against each other. Anna kicked it into the anteroom. When Hyde turned in the Taser's direction, she lunged for his leg taking him down to the floor again.

She felt sluggish and her vision blurred into focus. Hyde kicked at her face and while trying to avoid his boot, she hit her head on the base of the bed. She saw the concrete racing at her face and she did her best to stop it, but it struck her forehead. Her vision exploded into a million stars. *At least I didn't hit my jaw against it.*

Hyde got up as Anna pulled herself off the floor in a crouch. She lunged at his leg again and grabbed enough of his pant leg that he fell again. He kicked hard behind him, allowing Anna to get a better grip on his left leg. She hugged as tightly as she could and tried to dig her nails into his skin.

Where's the gun? He's not even in uniform! She tore at his pant leg. He stopped and tried to turn. He punched the top of her head as she reached up and squeezed his groin as hard as she could. Hyde screamed and swung his fist down against her face with such force that she let go and crashed against the wall.

The impact on the back of her head caused everything to go black for a few seconds. Hyde was heading for the anteroom.

No, you're not!

She pushed herself up, clutched the back of his shirt collar, and threw him to her left. Pain radiated up her arm as she turned in an unnatural direction to get the leverage she needed.

He stood up and she put out her hand. He stopped.

Anna took a step backward toward the cell door of the anteroom where the Taser lay on the floor waiting for a user.

She slid the door shut.

"You're not gonna win this one, darlin'," Hyde said.

He was gulping in air as Anna took in her chances.

Her face was partially numb, but being thrown around caused her blood to circulate faster which meant that the pill's effects sped up. Her face tingled, which would turn to screaming nerve-endings in a few minutes. The back of her head throbbed and she was having a hard time thinking.

She was willing to go with muscle memory.

Hyde screamed, "It's too late for you now! You assaulted an officer. Twice. You're already in here as No Contact. I'll be able to explain why I'm here, but you're a different story."

Anna relaxed her shoulders. Time to scare the hell out of him. "You're not leaving here alive."

"You're not leaving here."

He tried to run up and over her bed, but she

pushed him against the wall of room where he fell with the impact of a sandbag. Hyde seized one of the books that had fallen to the floor and swung it at Anna's head. She blocked it, punching him in the jaw with a right hook. A smaller person would have come off the ground, but Hyde's body had a low center of gravity.

She remembered her dad telling her once, *If you're in a fight, end it after the first punch. I'll straighten it out with the police later.*

One punch.

She snagged him by the front of his shirt and twirled him away from the wall. She pulled her arm back and gave her punch all she could muster. His eyes went wide...and he moved his head out of the way. The force of her punch made her fall toward him, and she lost her balance.

He gave her a quick bear hug. Anna felt the bulk of the air in her lungs forced out through her mouth. Her back hurt. He pushed her away, grasped the top of her mask with his left hand, walked over to the cell doors to the anteroom, opened them up, and reached for the Taser.

49
———

ESCORT SERVICE

The cell door slid with a crash as a SORT team officer entered the cell, extracting Hyde from the room. Hyde let go of Anna's mask at the first sign of the officer. When he vacated the cell, three other SORT members entered, each clutching a different limb.

Anna knew there was no fighting them so she went limp, letting them push her down to the ground. They cuffed her wrists and ankles. She wanted to scream in frustration, but instead let the exhaustion of her battle with Hyde wash over her.

This was not going to end well. For anyone.

———

Warden Coleman walked over to see what the commotion was all about. While surprised to see Officer Peterson standing amidst the SORT team, he wasn't that surprised. Was his job ever going to get easier?

"Warden! All I was doing was trying to be nice and bring her something to read," Peterson said. "I swear! I was just trying to be nice!" He panted his words.

Coleman continued over and restrained himself from latching

onto Peterson's throat. He stopped a few inches from Peterson's face. He looked into his eyes, and examined the pock-marked skin. *Usually Federal officers are so much better than this. College educated, nice family, good home life.*

"So this is what stupid looks like," Coleman said.

Peterson tried to step back. Coleman got closer.

"She has an active NHC on her. No. Human. Contact. You are off-duty, and here pending questioning on the murder of a Federal Corrections Officer. What part of 'stay the hell out of everyone's way' are you having a problem with?" Coleman's midsection twisted from the acid pouring out of his stomach lining. He knew that some of his men were doing stupid things, but he stood in front of the poster child.

"I can explain. I know the cameras haven't been working in that cell, but I didn't do anything," Hyde said.

Coleman blinked. There were still words coming out of Hyde's mouth. "You need to stop talking."

"But, I can explain."

"Stop. You need. To. Stop. Talking."

There were two corrections officers flanking Hyde just like last time.

"Gentlemen, you need to escort Mr. Peterson to the holding cells in A Block pending charges."

"What? What charges?" Peterson's eyes opened wide and he looked at his fellow officers standing behind him.

"Officer Peterson, I don't know what possessed you to enter that cell, but the camera was working just fine. In fact, Officer Moss had found it accidentally turned off and made sure that it was in perfect working order. The security detail saw you enter the cell and took care of calling SORT."

Coleman spoke to one of the guards to Hyde's right. "Make sure Intake is clear. If it's not, please clear it, and move Prisoner X there. She's going to need round-the-clock attention." To Peterson, he said, "I think you're going to lose your job, Officer Peterson."

Coleman started the long walk back to his office through the otherwise quiet corridor. "I also think you're going to jail."

————

Coleman had one last thing to do.

"Doctor, while we are in an official lockdown, I am making an exception." Warden Coleman was walking down the corridor with Hawking in tow. There was no mistaking his intention. "Just for you."

"Exception? Am I being fired?" Hawking looked and sounded surprised.

The corridor was hushed, just like Coleman liked it. He hated when inmates screamed or shouted. They were here for the duration and no amount of struggling was going to change that. Hawking, on the other hand, was more of a standard story. Coleman had seen this so often it ceased to amaze him anymore. Prison employees compromised by inmates was almost the norm these days. Was TV making people just plain stupid?

"No, doctor, you are not being fired, but you are being put on administrative leave," Coleman said.

"What?" Hawking stopped Coleman in mid-stride.

"Prisoner X happened. The attack on one of my men happened. And you assaulted two officers who were carrying out their duties to secure the prisoner." Coleman took a step toward Hawking. "What the hell were you thinking?"

Hawking looked like he had to ponder what Coleman was describing. That was fine. Nothing was going to change, and Hawking lived just up the road. They could find him if they needed him. Just another career civil servant.

"She was in pain. She needed help. Your men were physically assaulting her and stopping me from doing my job."

Coleman heard Hawking's words, but they didn't matter anymore. "Your job is to keep our inmates alive so they can serve out their sentences. As long as they're alive, damaged is allowed. Dead is not." Coleman continued to walk. "And we don't need you dead either."

"She was in full restraint. There was never any danger to anyone but herself." Hawking put out his hand and stopped them both. "Warden, if you put me on administrative leave, you've got an entire facility of about four hundred inmates who need medical care and won't get it until I return, or you replace me." Hawking put his hand on his chest. "I admit I screwed up. I shouldn't have pushed the officers off my patient. But Warden, things were rather crazy there. I was just doing my job as well."

Hawking was breathing hard. Was the doctor that out of shape?

"Your job made my job harder. You're out of here," Coleman said.

"Warden, your man hit her full in the face over and over again and then slammed her into a wall. A prisoner who was restrained and could have easily been taken down by the two of them. Speaking of which, regulation requires three officers escorting prisoners at all times, but no one has been saying anything about the fact that there have only been two for the last few weeks."

Coleman felt the blood rush up his neck. "We're running a lean operation."

"And I agree. I'm not saying you're doing anything wrong. My point is that there was no reason for his reaction to her attack. The two of them should have been able to subdue her with no problem."

"You should have sedated her quicker."

"Point taken, Warden, but I did it as quickly as I could." Hawking looked around. "I can't believe I'm saying this, but I would like permission to stay and continue to help out. And I continue to suggest bringing in the state police."

"They've already been notified. But nothing leaves the facility." Coleman pointed at Hawking. "Not even that boy's body."

They continued to the main gated area leading to the hallway that led to the foyer where officers and visitors alike entered and exited. An officer was standing by the gate.

"Understood. I'm in total agreement with you, Warden," Hawking said.

"Good." Coleman cocked his chin at the officer. "Please escort Dr.

Hawking off the premises. Have him wait by his car for his things to be brought out to him."

Hawking's mouth dropped open.

"Let Officer Hanson know what you would like him to retrieve for you and he will bring it to you at your vehicle." Coleman walked away. "You are now officially on administrative leave pending charges of assault and battery against officers of the law." He waved. "I would call a lawyer."

50

OFF THE CASE

"So, Terrell, it appears you're in the thick of it again." Section Chief Tolsen had called Terrell back in after an hour or so of busy work.

Tolsen's office looked more like a conference room than an office: an L-shaped wooden desk with the customary family photos and a round table for six for impromptu meetings.

Terrell wasn't sure what to make of his boss's reaction to what appeared to be a straightforward money laundering case. Unless you counted its involvement with one of the largest Intelligence communities in the world.

Terrell dragged one of the metal chairs from the table over to the desk. The thin pile carpeting muffled the sound of the chair legs. The air felt hot, or was it Terrell? The dim lighting, the lack of air-conditioning gave him a sense of dread. He had never felt that way before in Tolsen's domain.

"I'm sorry, sir. Could you explain to me what just happened?" Terrell asked.

"Your case is being suspended," Tolsen said. He pushed the palms of his hands on his desk as if he were keeping the desk from floating away. His focus was squarely on his blotter.

Terrell's shoulder throbbed and his face felt hot. "Are you freaking kidding me?"

"Don't start with me," Tolsen said.

Why did Tolsen look guilty?

"Are you telling me that I've run into a legally sanctioned Intelligence op? Being run by us in violation of I-don't-know-how-many laws?"

Was this to be the FBI of the twenty-first century? Always watching its back because its Intelligence siblings were nonchalant about breaking the law in the name of intelligence gathering?

"We run Intelligence ops all the time," Tolsen said.

"But they're legal. Well, usually."

Terrell knew that there were always operations that someone thought made the grade until someone higher up decided the operation was too sensitive or was about to make an ugly personal appearance. Maybe someone trying to box him in?

Had he inadvertently revealed too much to General Palma?

"The more we asked them about what we were investigating the more we were told they had nothing to do with it. I discover Piercing Ventures because of a concerned citizen," Terrell poked the top of the desk hard enough it thumped, "who just happens to be an Intel contractor who also wondered what the hell we were doing. And this woman, who's been a valuable asset in our investigation, did nothing more than do what we asked her to. And we told her we would protect her."

"The Committee told her they would protect her. She was never given any assurances from us." Tolsen opened a drawer, pulled out a stick of gum, and started chewing.

Terrell could smell the fruity aroma.

"No." Terrell shook his head, "Sir, you know that's unacceptable. We have a responsibility to the Committee. And to her." Terrell thought his head was going to explode. *How do you bring charges against someone who can do what they want and then gets retroactive protection?*

"We have a responsibility to this government, not to any particular committee or group or person." Tolsen chewed fast, watching Terrell. He seemed to be very concerned with what Terrell would say next.

Terrell focused on his boss. "I need to see Ms. Sams. We need to get her out of DC lock-up and get her home."

Terrell remembered her terror on the park bench. He stood. He was wasting time in this office. "She needs legal and she needs to let her family know that she's doing okay."

"I know you want to see her, but you're not going to."

Terrell reached for the doorknob and stopped. "What are you talking about? She's a valuable asset," he said. He didn't need another Anna on his conscious.

Tolsen raised his voice. "You are not going to see her because if you do, you'll end up on unpaid administrative leave. You're twisted in a knot with a woman who will be classified as a traitor no matter what the committee thinks it's going to be able to do for her."

Terrell was dumbfounded. "Sir, with all due respect, this is not the way we do business. And how can she be a traitor when all she did was what we asked her to?"

"It is since September 11," Tolsen said.

"That's a smoke screen. What are we doing here?" Terrell's shoulder throbbed.

"What you feel is none of my concern. Look, you'll survive this. It took a lot on our part to keep you away from this, but you'll survive. You were doing what the committee asked and we cooperated in full."

In full? Terrell stared at Tolsen. He could feel the acid rising in his throat, scorching the tender skin. "In full? We gave her up?"

Tolsen put his hands on his keyboard but didn't type anything.

It was Terrell's turn to raise his voice. "We gave her up?" Was this the moment he handed in his resignation? No. It wouldn't change anything, and there were others who still needed his help.

"We got word from someone at NSA. They knew all about you, and the investigation, and told us they needed to know who was talking to us. They reminded us of her status as a contractor and that they were bound by law..."

"Oh, give it a rest," Terrell said.

"Bound by law to arrest her immediately, which is what they did. They didn't have to notify us."

"They didn't notify us. They bugged our phones once they knew we were running an investigation and then gave us a call to look like the all-knowing assholes that they are."

How was he ever going to run an investigation like this again? Everyone recognized that the vast majority of the work done by the Intelligence community was useful and legal. But there were always projects going on that skirted the law and caused new laws to be put on the books to keep people from going to jail.

Even as the laws and the people the laws were protecting eroded civil liberties. Like Magnolia Sams. Because someone always needed to go to jail even if it wasn't the guilty. In the last few years, it was a point of cynicism for Terrell: economy-destroying events were occurring and no one was going to jail.

But that was a different problem for a different law enforcement agency.

"That may be, but we're still a member of this club and we have a job to do. Your asset is going to have serious charges brought against her. You're going to testify about what she's told you," Tolsen said.

Terrell's forehead hurt. "Are you kidding? If I have to stand before a grand jury, it will be to tell them about the good she did for us." Terrell had testified as a character witness before to keep someone from going to jail, or from getting a sentence they didn't deserve.

Interesting how, after so many years in the Bureau, Terrell could see the many distinctions between innocent victims and guilty perpetrators. It was much easier in the beginning when there weren't so many shades of gray.

"We can't shut this down. We can tell them that we have, but we can't do it," Terrell said.

"Agent Garrison, I'm afraid we already have," Tolsen said. "Go home. Watch TV. Get ready for a Bureau interview. This should be textbook, but just watch yourself."

"Watch myself?" Terrell felt his brain shutting down. *Watch myself?* "I have to see Magnolia Sams. She needs to know that we haven't deserted her. I need to know what pushed her so over the edge that she demanded to see me today."

"If you see her, there will be people watching, wondering why you're talking to someone who might have been leaking secrets to the wrong people," Tolsen said. He stood up.

The meeting was over.

"And since we found a potentially illegal project operating in the U.S., we would be the wrong people," Terrell said.

51

D.C. LOCK-UP

In for a penny, in for a pound, Terrell thought.

The Correctional Treatment Facility (CTF), located next to the D.C. Central Correctional Facility, was a medium-security facility meant exclusively for women. It shared the same institutional, brownstone appearance of many of the buildings in and around the seat of government. The Anacostia River to the southeast contributed to the humid summers, and again to the frigid winters.

Terrell was starting to wonder if he shouldn't move to the DC area. He seemed to be spending more and more time there. Given the reception he'd received of late he was sure New York was still the better choice.

———

"Hello, Agent Garrison," Magnolia Sams said.

"Hello, Magnolia."

They shook hands in public for the second time. The first had been when he'd first met her. His hand engulfed hers and he squeezed enough to feel her weak grip.

Medium security, and that she was being held for arraignment, meant that they could sit across from each other and not have to use telephones to speak. There were numerous tables in the rather large, dirty, gray room, but most of them were empty. The windows were frosted and let in only muted light. The room had the stale smell of rusting metal and sweat. Nothing like General Palma's modest house in the suburbs of DC. Magnolia and he wouldn't be sharing drinks this afternoon.

Terrell kept his jacket on. Magnolia was still in her street clothes.

"Are you here to get me out?"

Terrell's stomach twisted into a pretzel. "No."

"So this turned into exactly what I had told you and the committee so long ago. I was going to be left to twist in the wind."

"No, Magnolia."

"Just Maggie. Please. I feel alone enough."

"Maggie, we're not hanging you out to dry. I have a call to the senator and he assures me that they are doing all they can..."

Maggie laughed. She motioned around the room. "I can see that. I just have to look around to see that."

This case was spiraling out of control. She wasn't the one who should be in here. Should it have been the General?

"Maggie, I'm sorry, but I have to ask you some questions." Terrell couldn't remember when he felt this uncomfortable talking to an asset. Other assets knew what they were getting into. Knew that the information they were handing over would lead someone to go to jail but were safe in the knowledge it wouldn't be them.

"Do I have immunity?"

Terrell pursed his lips. "I don't know."

"What do you mean you don't know? I've been working with you in good faith for weeks and the best you can say is you don't know?" She was shaking.

Terrell wanted to put his arms around her. Why did you put your faith in me? What was he going to do as the Maggies and the Annas of his life accumulated in his head like bodies in a secret gravesite?

"I'm sorry."

"Ask your damn questions," Maggie said.

"Piercing Ventures."

"I'm sorry, Special Agent. I don't recall." She crossed her arms and legs. It was cold in the room, but Terrell was certain it wasn't the temperature that made her close up.

"Maggie, we've been at this for a while. You know things that can put people in jail and I want to help." He leaned forward as close as he could. "I can't do this without you."

"Do I have immunity or am I going to jail?" She clenched her jaw.

"The committee is doing everything they can, but..."

"But!"

"NSA got a federal judge to put a stop on your paperwork." She put her hand on her mouth as though to stop herself from crying.

How was he going to make this work?

"I need an attorney." She faced him. "I'm here because of them." She pointed at Terrell. "Because of you."

"Regardless of your immunity status you need an attorney. Don't kid yourself."

"It seems the only ones who've been kidding me have been the committee and you." Maggie turned away.

What must she be thinking about? Her kids? Her career? Her marriage?

"And to think I thought this was a country that cared about its citizenry. That illegal activities were anathema to our ideals and goals." She made a throaty chuckle. "Pretty stupid of me." She crossed her arms tighter. "Pretty damn stupid."

"Please, Maggie. This is important. What you know, and won't say, is affecting people. I'm still going on with this case. I can't without you."

"Then I guess you can't if you can't get me immunity."

"You know I'm going to do everything I can. I've never lied to you."

"You're with them." She motioned toward the door with her chin. "Lying is what you do best. For all I know all you meant to do was surface me so I could be arrested." A tear wended its way down her right cheek. She clenched her eyes shut and re-opened them. Her face relaxed. "I need to get out of here."

"And I'm going to do everything I can to make that happen even if you don't help me." Terrell put his hand on the table between them. "Even if you don't help me, I'm going to do everything I can."

"I want immunity."

"What is Piercing Ventures funding? Are they just seeding tech start-ups?" Terrell asked.

"I know," her voice cracked and Terrell glanced around the room to see if anyone heard her, "I know where that woman is."

The air changed.

"What woman?" Terrell's ears were piqued.

"The one from New York." Maggie's voice was almost a whisper. "I know she's one of your cases.

"I think she was set up."

"Anna...?"

"Yes, Anna Wodehouse." She covered her mouth.

"Talk to me, Maggie. You need friends, and I'm your friend. I took a bullet for you."

She nodded at his wounded shoulder. "I had a look at the list of aliases. She was on it. I thought, that poor girl."

"Where is she?" Terrell the FBI Agent took control. He stopped second-guessing himself. This is just information. *Let her tell you what she wants.*

"She's, she's at a black site."

Could that be true? Black sites were locations where the CIA would send terrorists for questioning or to simply make them disappear. The locations didn't exist as far as the government was concerned. Then-President Clinton had signed into law legal rendition to foreign countries so U.S. citizens could do what they couldn't do at home: torture suspects for information.

"She's overseas?"

"No." She leaned in as best she could. "We have a black site here in the U.S."

That is fucking impossible. The blood rushed up his neck to his cheeks and ears. The heat made him want to loosen his tie, but he sat unmoving, waiting for the next words.

She seemed to push every word out of her mouth with all the energy she had. "She's at one of them."

Black sites? In the U.S.?

"There's a black site at the Supermax in Colorado," Maggie said.

"I'm going to get you out of here."

"I just want to go home."

———

Terrell stepped out into the late afternoon air. The cold streamed up his face and into his hair while the sun's glare made him look away toward the other end of the street. He had to get back to the office. He unbuttoned his jacket and rubbed the back of his head.

Two men jogged up to him holding out Bureau IDs.

"Agent Garrison? Terrell Garrison?"

"Yes," Terrell said.

"We've been directed by Section Chief Tolsen to bring you in."

"Has there been news about my case?" Terrell asked.

"I don't know, sir. All I know is you have to come with us." The man paused. "And that if you refused we were told to arrest you."

52

AGENT SMITH

There was a rather large man sitting in the conference room at the J. Edgar Hoover Building, at 935 Pennsylvania Avenue NW, along with Section Chief Bernard Tolsen.

"Okay, I'm here. What's going on?" Terrell asked. He looked at the other man and then at Tolsen. *Please don't tell me I'm being fired.* "Is he with HR?"

"No," Tolsen said. "He's an observer."

Terrell felt the blood rushing to his face again. "Oh, like a bird watcher?" Terrell walked over to him. Just enough cologne. Large frame. Ill-fitting white shirt. Easily taunted. "Or my big brother?"

He extended his hand and the two men shook. Firm grip. Moist palm. Skeptical look.

"Terrell Garrison."

"John Smith."

"Oh, clever," Terrell said. He cocked his chin at Tolsen. "If he's not HR, is he cleared for the case?"

"Assume that he is."

"Are you sure?" Terrell asked. He walked over to Tolsen's side of the table, pulled a chair out, and placed it in front of the observer.

"Yes, assume that he is cleared for this case," Tolsen said.

"Perfect." Terrell sat down, looked at Smith, and thought for a second to make sure he worded his statement with minimal ambiguity.

"I have reason to believe that General Malik Palma is running illegal operations in the United States that include money laundering, attempted assassinations of U.S. law enforcement officials," Terrell pointed at his shoulder while maintaining his gaze on Smith, "that would be me, and influencing public officials making them accomplices in illegal domestic Intelligence operations." He eyed Tolsen. "Are you sure he's cleared?"

"Yes, I'm sure." Tolsen looked like he swallowed something unpleasant.

Terrell felt bad for him. He and Tolsen went back a ways.

"Anyway, you called me here under penalty of arrest," Terrell said, and continued to look at Smith. Close cropped hair. His mother cared too much.

"Special Agent Garrison," Smith said, "you were told to stay away from Magnolia Sams, yet you went to visit her not an hour ago."

"Mr. Smith, you were told to stay out of this," Tolsen said.

Terrell smiled and examined Smith's face. "Yes, she's a good friend of mine, and I always visit my friends before they get railroaded." He smiled at Tolsen. "Sorry, I meant arraigned."

Smith stood up. Terrell obliged and also stood. Smith was about half a foot taller and wide.

"She is not to be visited. She is not to be questioned. She is not to be looked at, sneezed on, hugged, and more importantly, heard," Smith said.

Tolsen said, "For your information, Mr. Smith, Agent Garrison is still allowed to make personal calls on whomever he pleases as long as there isn't a court order mandating that person's limited access."

"The paperwork is in progress," Smith said.

"You guys are getting slow," Terrell said.

Smith scowled at Terrell.

Tolsen said, "If you keep this up, I'm going to insist you two get a room."

"Gladly, Chief. As long as I'm taking it from behind anyway." Terrell didn't move from his vantage point six inches below Smith. "Let the record show that I went as a private citizen who knows Ms. Sams and to offer her any assistance she might require in her time of need. Her husband and two children still hadn't been notified of their loved one's arrest. I assume she still hasn't gotten her one phone call."

Terrell sat down with his good arm draped over the chair back.

"She's not our concern right now," Tolsen said. He looked at both men and motioned to Smith to sit.

Terrell swiveled his chair to face Tolsen. "And why is that, Chief Tolsen?" He heard himself and decided that he should cut back on the sarcasm. He needed Tolsen on his side, and Tolsen had never back-doored him before. He owed Tolsen the courtesy and respect he'd earned over many years.

"I called you back to let you know that you are now the subject of an internal investigation and on unpaid administrative leave," Tolsen said.

Terrell turned to Smith. "Well, isn't that a surprise?" So much for sarcasm control. He rotated back to Tolsen. "Any other good news?"

"No." Tolsen looked embarrassed.

"I think this is perfect timing. I need a vacation while I wait for the slow wheels of justice to crush me underfoot." He swiveled the chair again. "What do you think Agent Smith? Should I head out to Poland, Romania, or maybe Saudi Arabia?"

Smith walked over to Terrell and bent down. "I don't know, Agent Garrison, but wherever you go, watch your back."

Terrell laughed. "Oh, that's so funny. 'Watch your back.' If I didn't know better, I'd say you just threatened me." Terrell stood up, forcing Smith to step back into the wall. "But you would never do that, would you? We're all on the same team."

Smith gave him a last look, and exited the room.

Terrell sat back down. "I didn't mention the General just to get a rise out of Sneaky Pete over there."

"Really? I would never have known."

"What Magnolia Sams knows is dangerous. She needs protection and they're the ones she needs protection from. She could send high-level officials to jail. And not just the General. RICO would make sure all the people who've been aiding and abetting him all these years would join him. She needs to move out of CTF and into protective custody." How could he arrange that? Would he have to start leaking information that would both endanger her and make her more valuable? This was not where he wanted to use his adrenaline. "I don't want to read about her death tomorrow morning."

"She's under the control of counter-intelligence, but that doesn't amount to much. It just means that it doesn't matter that she was your asset. She's now theirs. She's considered a flight risk, and if she takes off after you to help her out then you become their target," Tolsen said.

"I'm sorry, Chief, but did you say that I would become a target? For helping one of our assets out of prison? An asset who's there on trumped up charges when she holds all the cards on an investigation that may put the head of one of our Intelligence organizations in jail?" Terrell slid his hands on the tabletop. Something he did had struck a nerve with someone. He knew it wasn't Tolsen, but he also knew there was only so much Tolsen could do for him. "Or did I mishear you?"

"I don't think you know how deep a ditch you're digging."

"But you'll always be there for me, won't you, Chief?"

Tolsen stood and buttoned his jacket. He left his tie loose. "Your unpaid administrative leave," Tolsen turned to go, "hasn't actually started. But you are involved in an internal investigation. You're a pain in my ass, and yes, I will watch your back. What that means is: don't go far and certainly don't go putting your foot into it. There's only so much I can do for you once you've got a target on your back and a dozen red dots on the target."

"The only thing my foot will end up in is a pile of shit."

Tolsen smirked. Terrell had seen that look before. They both knew the game could get serious, but in this case they were still in control. But for how much longer? "I know you're not taking this seriously, but we're talking about something that could destroy your future at the Bureau. Do what you always do. Make sure her family is told so they can get her a lawyer, recommend one if you like, and then step back into the shadows."

Terrell didn't do well in the shadows. "I think you're right. I need some time to re-think my life. What are my goals? My ambitions? Where do I see myself in five years?" He smiled. "How much vacation time do I have?"

53

PRIVATE TRANSCRIPT

Almost every conference room in the NSA building that did not have an outward facing window was designed as an SCIF, or Sensitive Compartmentalized Information Facility. In short the room was a Faraday cage: there was enough metal mesh in the walls to make sure that no radio frequency emanations came in or out of the room. Entry into the SCIF, forbidden to unescorted non-cleared personnel, meant quarantining any form of electronics someone might be carrying. No cell phone, no recorders, no WiFi-enabled electronics of any kind.

Any room, at any time, designated as an SCIF was a room purposely designed to keep information in and not let information out.

Of course, people were the weak link in that security chain.

Palma sat in the SCIF-enabled debriefing room along with the internal investigator selected by Andrew Yen. The search should have been conducted by FBI counter-intelligence, but Palma didn't have the patience or latitude to allow that to happen. He would notify the Bureau about his findings the same way he notified them when he discovered Magnolia Sams: he sent his men along with Metro DC cops and the FBI to pick her up.

There was no long waiting time or preparation. Magnolia Sams was a lightweight. She hid in plain sight, which made finding her that much easier.

Tracing Terrell Garrison's cell phone was a help as well. As opposed to the FBI, Palma didn't have to wait for a warrant for permission to track his phone. He just had to ask his people to do their jobs.

"I think you'll find everything you need in the report, sir."

The analyst chosen by Palma, both for his ability to think in a holistic fashion and his discretion, had turned the task around in a few days. He had worked on the problem, given the depth and breadth of information available to him, and made his initial findings in record time.

The breadcrumbs were too obvious.

"Is there anything I should be concerned about?" Palma asked.

"No, sir. There was no indication that you knew or were involved in any way."

Palma shook his head. That was good considering that he knew nothing about it. An internal investigation that found him guilty of anything would be a bad outcome.

"My recommendation is to set up overhead surveillance to catch the real leaker in the act. He doesn't have a reason to transfer any more information to Ms. Sams, now that she's in custody, but he may have other assets in place."

Other assets? Palma was willing to risk it. "Understood.

You know your recommendations carry a lot of weight with me," Palma said. "I will take them strongly under advisement."

The investigator was sure it was only one other person and Palma agreed. The questions were always who and why. Was it a lone leaker? Someone with a conscience gone astray? Or someone who was fed information so the actual leaker was not discovered?

It appeared that Magnolia Sams was the latter; the lone leaker, the former. At least Palma had a name.

"Remind me again. What is the status of SAC Garrison?" Palma asked.

"He's supposed to be on unpaid administrative leave, but his paperwork is still pending. There is very little chance that any charges brought against him will be considered as the FBI was brought in at the request of the Intelligence Oversight Committee. Of course, no charges would be brought against the committee even though they had unauthorized access to classified materials."

"Alright then."

Both men stood and shook hands. Palma had his point of failure and the Bureau would take longer to look into anything related to clandestine funding for HALON.

"I'll take it from here," Palma said.

———

Palma drove home. He had to prepare for a showdown that he had often thought would happen but hoped to avoid. It would also give him a chance to change clothes. Anything he did now had to be done with the utmost discretion and care. The good news was that he'd also hid in plain sight.

His home office, designed to his specifications, was set up to the highest standards of security of any office in the country. If he was ever under investigation, he would never know, but no one else would ever be able to intercept his communications in any way. In effect, his home was a giant cone of silence.

He was ready. He sat down to check his email before leaving when he saw an automated email alert had come in. He had a number of emails waiting for him, but the alert was something he had been anticipating since the arrest of Magnolia Sams.

He looked at the time stamp of the email and the attached transcript. As the NSA had speech-to-text technology that put the most advanced commercial technology to shame most analysts didn't have to read many of the conversations they were in charge of. In fact, they didn't have the time or the wherewithal to do so. A computer created the transcript, did the initial screening, and, if any of several keywords came up, created a transcript sent to the proper parties.

The transcript arrived at Palma's computer shortly after the automated analysis. He knew it would, as he put in the request for anything related to Terrell Garrison and Magnolia Sams for his eyes only.

His computer screen was sharp. Palma wondered at what point the old practice of reading a transcript would go away along with the paper on which it was printed.

Sams: I just want to go home.

Garrison: Do you know how long she's been there?

Sams: No. I never followed the case.

Garrison: Why would they do that?

Sams: She's there now. Put her in a Supermax? They think she knows something.

Garrison: About an op?

Sams: Yes. I think they think she knows something about Prudent Rainbow.

Garrison: Why would they think that? I have information that the man she shot was a sleeper.

Sams: I don't know anything about that.

Garrison: Tell me about the op. Prudent...

Sams: Rainbow. Prudent Rainbow.

Garrison: Yes.

Sams: I'm not sure, but General Palma is one of the few people who has access to anything about it.

She said it. Palma tilted his head back and took in a breath. Confirmation that Sams knew too much. She might not even know what she knew, but the one thing she did know: his name. His name and the hidden line between him and PRUDENT RAINBOW.

And this was why they needed to move both faster and slower. Get the new tenants in place as soon as possible, but make sure that everything was ready so the transfer would go off without a hitch. That was all he was asking.

While Palma would be happy to delay it, Monahan had a point.

The sooner they did it the better. Palma would make sure there was one less point of failure.

———

The General pulled up to the front of NSA HQ in his GM Yukon XL where Andrew was waiting for him to arrive. Andrew wore his signature dark suit and carried a black satchel. Palma knew the satchel was where Andrew kept his notebook PC, a yellow pad, and pen. *A simple man with simple needs*, Palma thought. Palma wore a lined suede jacket and clean, but worn jeans.

Andrew opened the door and climbed in. "No escort today?" he asked.

"No," Palma said. "Put on your seatbelt. This one's for us."

54

A WALK IN THE WOODS

The two men drove for about an hour. Andrew briefed him about upcoming meetings with Intelligence Oversight, and the State Department. Andrew always had interesting insights into the process, not shy about injecting suggestions that

Palma thought were quite useful.

If only Andrew had been someone else. Someone who belonged.

Palma pulled over onto the shoulder of a heavily wooded area. There were no highway cameras, and only the occasional car. The evergreens were close enough together that the two of them would disappear into the foliage within a few minutes. This would do. "Let's go," Palma said.

He climbed out without waiting for a response. He was quite a bit more comfortable and more mobile not being in his uniform. His green button-down did a better job of keeping him warm. He heard Andrew get out on the wooded side of the vehicle, and walked over to him.

"We're not leaving here until we have solved one of our little problems," Palma said.

"Yes, General." Andrew looked as excited as he ever did, meaning not at all. Palma wondered how Andrew reacted to surprises.

They both stepped into the woods. There was no guardrail so they simply walked in, leaving the SUV behind. Palma didn't bother to lift his hand when he pressed the door switch on the key fob, locking the vehicle behind them.

"We need to discuss this away from everyone," Palma said. "This is even more sensitive than usual."

"Understood." Andrew brought his satchel with him. The PC was an NSA-issued unit so its contents would be fully encrypted and useless to anyone who might find it. "I assume you mean Ms. Sams."

"Yes, I do."

They continued further and further along an unmarked path through the forest. Andrew stepped carefully over piles of leaves, fallen branches, and animal carcasses. Palma stepped deliberately through everything with just enough thought to keep him moving forward. He had been in these woods before. They were well into the Virginia countryside.

During the Revolutionary War, there was little to no combat this far inland. Palma wondered how a war fought today would work without the reliance on technology. Even deep into these woods they could be found if they needed to be. One day every person on every square inch of the globe would be tracked so no one could ever use information asymmetry as a defense.

But not today.

After a few minutes, Palma looked around. The SUV was far enough in the distance as to be invisible. "Andrew, you do understand that everything we're doing is to satisfy agreements made years ago."

"I don't understand. Is this to discuss the timetable?" Andrew leaned his bag against a tree. "I thought we were going to discuss Magnolia Sams."

"We are," Palma said, "but one agenda item at a time." Palma walked at a deliberate pace before Andrew. He counted his steps as the ground crackled with every footfall. The clouds drifted overhead and covered the sun like a blindfold over the eyes of nature. "The timetable, please."

"Everything is on schedule. Once you told me you had decided to begin clearing out the contractors I notified the proper parties that we are on our way to a successful transfer," Andrew said. "And we are. There will be some contractors working on externalities for the next few weeks, but those are not going to cause any problems whatsoever."

Andrew's brow furrowed. "If you're worried about budget and funding, I can assure you we will take care of everything after that. The U.S. government will not have any expenditures in this project. That was agreed upon many years ago."

"Excellent." Palma stopped and leaned on a tree. "So perhaps now we can talk about the leak."

The air stopped moving. "Please." Andrew's face remained stoic.

"Once the Oversight committee made its recommendation to begin the investigation based on the paperwork they were given, they handed over whatever they had to us, if you recall," Palma said.

"Yes, I have copies of everything," Andrew said.

"Yes, you mostly do." Palma wanted to make sure he had all his facts straight. "You handed them over to the internal team and they began looking into everything Ms. Sams had been doing. It can take weeks, sometimes months, to do the proper auditing, reporting, and analysis." He motioned to Andrew. "But you know how that is."

Silent, Andrew stood at attention. Palma was sure Andrew's passivity belied his confusion and curiosity.

"Anyway, I just received the results of the internal investigation." Palma smiled. "Let me tell you, they were both surprising and expected. Magnolia had a lot more on hand than she gave to the committee. We're very lucky that she was discriminating. She was really only concerned about a select number of programs." Palma grinned. "Bless her heart, she knew which programs were legal and which were questionable." He looked at Andrew. "What should we do?"

"Is that a rhetorical question?"

In other circumstances, Palma would have been amused. He squeezed his right hand opened and closed. "No, Andrew. I would like to know what you would do. I have some ideas on what to do about

Ms. Sams, but the bigger question is: what do we do about the person who leaked the leaks to her?"

"Sir, there is a protocol for everything at the agency. What I think doesn't matter as much as the dictates of protocol," Andrew said.

"Well put. You always default to doing what has been decided by the higher up regardless of whether it makes any sense or solves the problem." Andrew really was a good soldier. He would always do what he was told. Was he instructed to keep the pressure up?

"Finding the source behind the leaks would solve the problem, would it not?"

"Yes, it would. But sometime you just need a level of emotional satisfaction." Palma tilted his head. "You don't ever seem to show a level of emotional satisfaction."

"My job is to ensure a smooth transition. Your job is to give me something to transition."

Palma looked at Andrew's eyes. No tell-tale signs. He would be a great poker player.

"You tell me what to do, and I do it," Andrew said.

"Yet you've been doing a great job at pushing on the project in different ways to give me the impression that I'm not the one in charge."

"You are not. We have waited almost ten years for delivery. We would never do anything to jeopardize it. Where did the leak come from?"

Palma reached behind his jacket. He saw Andrew's face go pale. "The actual source of the leak?" Palma pulled out a gun and held it at his side. "It came from my office. In fact, it came from your computer."

"That is not possible, sir. I assume that your team set up overhead cameras to confirm my treason."

"No reason. The files came from your PC."

"That would hardly be conclusive evidence. Someone else may have been at my keyboard and sent the files." Andrew remained unmoved.

"Maybe. Then perhaps you can explain to me why you met with

Agent Garrison a few days ago out in the middle of nowhere and you chose not to tell me about it?"

Andrew inhaled. "There was a suspicion that he knew about the project. I was instructed to look into what he knew and to report back."

Palma motioned towards Andrew with the gun. "And?"

"His biggest concern was about the funding vehicles," Andrew said. "But you don't really care about that." He started to take a step back and then seemed to think better of it. He walked up to Palma and stopped a few paces away. "I have no reason to sabotage the transfer. I'm here to help, not hinder."

"Perhaps you are, Andrew. And you have been a great help to me these last few months." Palma cocked the chamber. "But you've stepped into the wrong things one too many times."

Palma aimed and fired.

55

SORE EYES

Anna lay covered in scratchy, smelly canvas on the restraining chair in Intake. With a built-in straitjacket, the chair kept its occupant from moving around and hurting themselves. She was certain that if she squirmed enough, she would either tangle herself in a knot or get a rash. She wasn't sure which she was more worried about.

Her bruises throbbed and her face simply hurt. She was going to take a long time to heal.

Lucky for her she had a lot of time to make that happen.

Behind her mask, the tiny fibers of suede lay against her face. Her cheeks were so sensitive she swore she could count the leather strands. She closed her eyes to the smell of old cloth, and the feel of light metal against her throat.

There was a knock on the scratched Plexiglas in front of her. Since the recliner was set back, Anna had to lift her head to see who was there.

Did Dr. Hawking decide to visit? No, it was the Warden. Did he ever wear another suit?

Three rather large, uniformed men stood to his right. They weren't wearing their marshmallow suits. That must mean something.

He pressed the intercom button. "Hello there."

"I'd wave, but I think you understand why I won't," her cyborg voice said.

"We're taking you to interrogation," Coleman said.

"I'd rather you leave me here. It seems that being in my cell or being outside my cell doesn't seem to matter."

Interrogation? What could they ask that they hadn't already?

"You can refuse, but if you do, we'll have to go in and pull you out," Coleman said.

That explained the movers in uniform.

"Your prison, your rules." *If Benson is here, I swear I'll start screaming and never stop. What was his real name again?*

"I like the way you think," Coleman said.

"Persuasion with a gun." *Oh, please, I don't want to go.* Her stomach twisted. Would Hyde be there? Did it matter?

"However you need to see it."

"Can the doc see me first? I think my bruises have bruises," she said.

"I'll have someone put in a kite," Coleman said. "Again, I have to ask, do you understand what I'm telling you?"

She sighed. "Yes." What were they going to do now? "I understand."

They opened the door and three correctional officers came in.

———

Her steps were heavy. No playing this time. Anna felt like every bone in her body hurt, but at least she wasn't strapped in the torture chair.

They had entered an unfamiliar area. The same drab light, dark cream-colored tiles, and beige walls. The back of her head ached. Every so often, she walked with her eyes closed.

The warden stopped in front of a door that looked like so many of the others. "I have to say, this was not my idea. I tried to keep you from having to go through this." He turned toward the door. "I hope you remember that." He grabbed the knob and opened the door outward.

There, in the interrogation room, was FBI Special Agent Terrell Garrison.

———

"I want this mask taken off her," Terrell said.

Oh, no, you don't, Anna thought. *You are not seeing me like this.*

Coleman was insistent. "Special Agent, we discussed this. We have observers in the other room and no one's been cleared."

"Then make them go away. You can sit in the other room instead," Terrell said.

He was wearing civilian clothes. She didn't remember him in anything but his FBI attire.

"Not to make a joke about my weight, but could we consider the elephant in the room?" Anna asked in her electrolarynx voice. She sat on the bare metal chair attached to the floor using a chain that came through the hole in the table.

"Warden, do whatever you need to do. For the next few minutes I'm legally allowed to question her in any way I see fit as long as I don't violate her right to due process."

Coleman narrowed his eyes at Anna, then at Terrell, and left the room.

Terrell made a beeline to Anna.

"No, no, NO!" Anna said. He pulled the mask off and dropped it on her hands. She put her head down and tried to put the mask back on. "Please, oh, please, put it back on." She looked at him and couldn't stop the tears from coming down her face. She wasn't ready for the world to see her even if the world showed up anyway. Hiding her face was all she could do.

"Special Agent, please!" She put her head down on the table and did her best to cover her face with her hands. "Terrell! Please!"

He took the mask, squeezed it in his right hand, lifted her head, and slipped it back on. Anna felt the coarseness of the materials as it slid across her head. He looked into her eyes for a few seconds as she shook the mask into place.

Terrell crouched down next to her. "Are you okay?"

She looked at him and smiled. "Yes." She gave a deep-throated chuckle. "Yes. Please get me out of here."

"What happened to your hair?" They both chuckled, Anna through barely disguised emotion.

Anna felt some of her tears sliding down her cheeks. How could she begin to describe what it felt like to see him? She whispered, "I got your notes. It was," she looked into his eyes for a sliver of truth, "the only thing I looked forward to."

He scanned her eyes, but with the wrong look on his face. Was he looking for understanding? "What notes?"

Anna's shoulders sagged. She sighed and then sighed again. *It wasn't him. I'm still alone.*

Terrell touched her arm the way someone held the arm of a terminally ill patient. "I don't have a lot of time. There were all sorts of things about your case that you don't know about."

"Like the sniper?" Anna asked.

"Like the sniper." He glanced at the two-way mirror and then back at Anna.

Anna peered at the mirror as well. "How does anyone keep secrets anymore?" she asked.

"How do you know about the sniper?" Terrell asked.

"Some guy who said he was a journalist came to talk to me." She took in a deep breath and leaned back. "He was not a journalist."

"What did he ask you about?"

"The same thing everybody asks me about. I'm getting tired of the question."

They both spoke at the same time. "What happened on the roof that day?"

"Yeah, that one," Anna said.

"And?"

"And, nothing. I remembered a few extra sentences and that was all."

Terrell picked up the chair from across the table and brought it next to her. He reached over and held her cold hands. The warmth of his touch melted her. She pulled her hands back.

She told him what she had told the journalist. He didn't seem impressed.

"The guy, Donnell, said that people were dying and that it was my dad's fault." She shook her hands on the table. "It isn't his fault. Whatever it is that man thought Dad did he would never do." She brought her face as close to Terrell as she could. "Never."

"Like you would never kill anyone."

"Oh," she threw her head back, "I didn't kill anyone. Well, I killed him because I held the gun, but I didn't fire it. Find the gun." She fought to find the right words and gave up. "Find the gun."

She looked over her shoulder at the mirror and whispered again. "You're in danger. As long as I tell everyone what I know, whoever put me here can't kill me. You have to tell everyone you can too. He would have to get everyone."

"What are you talking about?"

Anna wasn't sure if she should tell him. "The guy who helped me get to London and then back to the U.S." She leaned in again. "Benson?"

Terrell shook his head.

"I have a photo of him," Anna said. "I had someone look into it."

"What? How?"

"Doesn't matter. Distraction."

"Who is he?"

"Some intelligence guy. Higher-up. Malik something."

56

UNWANTED CAVALRY

A convoy of olive drab trucks pulled up on either side of the entrance to the prison. The officer at the guard's station counted the number of vehicles and stopped at fifty. He picked up the phone and called into the main switchboard to have messages passed to the various administrators of the three prisons.

He wasn't sure, but he was confident that the National Guard had just shown up.

————

Governor Hollingsworth listened to the man on the other end of the line and remembered the day he had won his first election. While he was proficient at shaking hands, he was just as proficient at giving away favors for future use. And rattling cages.

"I'm not sure what's going on, but sending the National Guard to ADX is not the way to get us to cooperate," Bureau of Prisons Director Allan Berry said. "In fact, we're already cooperating."

"I know you feel that way, sir." Hollingsworth looked out the window of the Governor's mansion across the street to the twelve-story high rise, and smiled. "But from where I stand, we have extended every courtesy to you, and BoP has done nothing to allay the fears of the people of Florence. How many more deaths do you need to have before you accept our help?"

"Governor, while your help is appreciated, it is not needed at this time," Director Berry said.

"I understand." Hollingsworth walked back and sat on the deep leather chair behind his desk. "However, Warden Coleman has not been forthcoming with information needed by my officers to do their jobs."

"The warden has explained it all to me."

"And to me as well, but I'm not satisfied," Hollingsworth said. "This is why I'm reaching out to you, personally." He sat and put his feet up on his antique desk. Why did he persist in thinking the most painful shoes he had ever worn were ever going to get better? He popped off the shoes and let them drop onto the area rug that took up most of the room. He stretched his toes.

"Governor, I respectfully ask that you pull the guardsmen away from ADX, and just let the warden do his job," Berry said.

"And I, just as respectfully, must decline. You must see that the state police just want to do their job. We have already confirmed that at least one of the deaths occurred on state land. We have asked for assistance but haven't heard from the FBI at all." *Except for the one call I made sure didn't get returned.* "Don't let the guard get the BOP in a twist. They'll be gone in no time, and everyone can go back to being friends again. In fact, we're still friends," Hollingsworth said.

A few empty closings later, Hollingsworth hung up. It took a number of phone calls, but the National Guard were going to stay there for the moment, maybe a few days. When Berry and the others in BOP stopped acting like a bunch of babies, and give his people the information they needed, he would pull the guard immediately. Maybe now they could find out what was going on.

Hollingsworth almost hoped they wouldn't produce any answers for a long time. He hadn't had this much fun in a while.

57

CALLING IN FAVORS

Unless he was losing his mind, Terrell was sure that the warden, and BOP, didn't know a con if it bit them in the ass.

"Let's see: NHC was lifted, more hours out of her cell, books, I'm assuming all the paper and pens she could handle. She even has a supply of inhalers so she can keep one in her jump suit at all times." He furrowed his brow. "And nobody thought this was strange?" Terrell asked.

Coleman's jaw clenched as his shoulders made a feeble attempt at escape, but regained his composure. He put his hands behind his head.

"Was she ever allowed near a networked PC?" Terrell asked.

Coleman looked insulted. He swiveled forward. "Not on my watch. The inmate computer is in a room with no connectivity." Terrell felt pity for the chair as Coleman crushed its armrests. "Personally, I didn't care if they sent steaks to her every day. She's DOD's problem, not mine. Everything was fine until she attempted suicide."

Terrell felt his heart tighten. *She tried to kill herself.* The woman who saved his life tried to kill herself while hidden in a prison for reasons no one wanted to admit.

"When was this?"

"A few days ago. I would take you to medical, but we sent the doc home," Coleman said.

This only got better. "I was led to believe you were in lockdown due to a homicide. Why would you let anyone out until the shift when it happened was questioned?" Terrell asked.

"Long story, but it involves your friend, Prisoner X."

Coleman stood up and went to a mini-refrigerator in the corner. "Water, Special Agent?"

"Yes, please. What happened?"

Coleman grabbed two bottles, closed the door, and walked over to Terrell.

Coleman made himself comfortable on the edge of his desk. "What happened is that the doc had several private examinations with her. I'm sure they were innocent, but we have no way of knowing what they said or did. Her escort officers would peek in every so often, but he was always just talking and examining."

Terrell's paranoia was coming out to play. An inmate was alone with the facility doctor. This explanation was getting worse and worse. "Warden, what are your standing orders for her?"

"We've had a few run-ins over the last few days so I reinstituted NHC. She attacked a guard. Twice. She was found with contraband." He exhaled through his mouth. "And one of the guards who allegedly tried to rape her turned up dead yesterday."

"She was almost raped? In a maximum-security facility?" Terrell was ready to throw her in his car and take off. He had heard of prisoner rape in low and medium facilities, but in maximum? It was rare, but it did happen.

He would just make sure it didn't happen to her.

"Tell me about the contraband," Terrell said.

There was a knock on the door. Officer Orville Moss walked in. "Excuse me, Warden. I didn't mean to interrupt."

"I guess you did since Angie would have told you I was meeting with someone." Coleman stood and motioned toward Terrell, who stood as well. "Agent Garrison from the FBI.

Correctional Officer Orville Moss."

Terrell reached out and gave Moss a warm handshake. Seemed like a nice enough young guy. What could be so important?

Moss took his hat off and held it against his chest as if for protection. "I'm sorry, Warden, but I just had to come by. It's about Prisoner X."

Terrell saw Coleman close his eyes for a moment. Who was this officer? Terrell said, "Please join us. We were just discussing them." *Let's keep gender out of this for now.*

Coleman walked back to his chair, but Moss remained glued to his spot. "Sir, she needs to be kept in Intake. I know that she isn't a danger to anyone, yet, but it seems that she might be in danger," Moss said.

"I'm sorry, Agent Garrison, I don't mean to avoid your question, but, Warden, please." Moss took a step forward, his hat still covering his chest. "She can't be left in her cell. She needs to be in Intake where there's someone looking over her the whole time she's there. She doesn't need to be restrained."

"She was restrained in Intake?" Terrell asked. "I saw her face for a few seconds. She had massive bruising. Has she been checked for internal bleeding?"

"This is getting out of hand," Coleman said. He turned to Terrell and held out his palm. "Special Agent, I understand your concern and, yes, the doctor on site did a thorough examination."

"The doctor knows who she is?" Terrell asked.

"Please, Warden. Keep her in Intake," Officer Moss said.

"I'm going to send you both packing in a minute," Coleman said.

"Warden, I'm going to need to question this man," Terrell said.

"If you don't keep her in Intake," Moss stopped for a second, "I think she might try to escape."

The room became silent.

Terrell said, "She what?"

"I said: she might try to escape."

58

PINK SLIP

Palma had had enough. The entire operation was spinning out of control, and he was going to bring it back to sanity. He'd already taken the first steps.

First, he had called his contact over at NCS, the National Clandestine Service. An interesting project that NCS had been implementing was a way to plant false clues as to the whereabouts of a given asset. This gave the agency a way to hide someone, while whoever was looking for them was off on a wild goose chase. One way NCS did that was by inserting into airport security cameras images of the asset arriving at the airport, getting on the security line, doing various things like having breakfast or lunch, then going into the bathroom and never coming out. The asset would appear to miss their flight and no one would know where they were.

In fact, the asset had never gone to the airport. Sometimes the assets were escorted out of the U.S. by private plane. Sometimes, they were taken to an unknown location for questioning. Sometimes, they were buried.

Anna Wodehouse had to disappear from Carswell. Everyone would assume an escape, but she would simply disappear. The woman standing in for her at Carswell would also disappear.

Next, he notified the small cadre of men he had worked with over the years on HALON. They would take care of making Andrew Yen disappear. His NSA-issued hardware would be destroyed so even the agency wouldn't be able to trace it back. His cell phone was already shredded, the accounts shutdown remotely. No customer service calls for Andrew. Anyone looking for him would find that Andrew had not come into work one day and the agency had been unable to track him down. Perhaps Andrew had heard about the internal report that accused him of passing secrets to unauthorized persons. Perhaps Andrew was in an unfortunate accident during an unscheduled vacation.

It didn't matter. As long-term goals became short-term goals, it was necessary to re-prioritize and reset expectations. He'd simply reset HALON's goals to the new reality, to the new schedule.

It was time to get everything back on track with a vengeance. It was time to show the buffoons Palma had been shepherding around for years that they would get what they wanted, and they would get it early. Andrew was the price for on-time performance.

With all that, Palma had one other thing he had to take care of. Not because he wanted to, but because allowing others to handle it meant opening up the possibility of unpredictability and failure.

Unpredictability and failure were not in his vocabulary.

He had driven his own vehicle to a clandestine airstrip in the middle of Virginia where two men were waiting for him. There were a number of airstrips around the country run by the various Intelligence agencies and this was one of his. Requisitioned years ago, he had been using it more and more in recent years. Some of the HALON equipment flew out of hidden airstrips like this one; some out of regional airports and some out of larger ones like Reagan International.

The entire team was only ten men altogether (he had purposely discounted having a woman on the team. The hell with diversity) and he needed the others to handle other HALON-related assignments. Things were going to be tight over the next few days and everyone was going to have to pull their own weight.

He parked the black Yukon in the aircraft hangar. There was a white agency plane with a bogus registration number decal on the side of the body, and two men with crew cuts taking boxes out of it. The space echoed every time they put something down. The spotless hanger appeared new but had been in operation for years. If abandoned at a moment's notice, there would be no clues as to who used it, when, or why.

Palma jumped out of the car and walked over to the men who were in their t-shirts. They both put down what was in their hands and saluted.

"At ease," Palma said.

They came over and shook hands with him. They had known each other for years. Family. Strong handshakes. Smiles and pleasantries all around. Strong capable men. Loyal and smart. They had performed much more difficult missions. This one was just going to be a bit messy.

"Don't let me get in your way, gentlemen. When you're done, meet me in the office. You've got a long night ahead of you."

———

Palma put his feet up on the old institutional gray-and- green desk. The top was dusty, but Palma was too distracted to wipe it down. The small room had dirty green walls with no windows so no one could listen in on their conversation using a laser microphone against the glass. He put his hands behind his head, held and released his breath, as the tension left him. He closed his eyes for a moment. The smell of diesel fuel wafted up his nostrils as he relaxed his eyebrows and felt the stress drip from his body. This was always the answer to his anxiety.

Action.

Not talking, not planning.

Action.

He looked down at his shirt. There were a few freckles of blood where his light jacket was open. He flicked at it, but the drops stayed in place. He would burn the shirt and his jacket later. He had another shirt in the car in case of emergencies, and he would buy another jacket. His wife was used to him doing things that deserved attention but would never get any. She was the wife of the King of the Information Vacuum Cleaner. The Ears of the U.S., as she would tease him.

The two men, both tall and muscular, came in and stood at attention in front of the desk. Great pilots. Great sharpshooters. He was glad he would never meet either of them in a bar fight. He knew who would win, and it wouldn't be him.

"I'm going to assume neither of you have been briefed yet since I haven't told anyone why I needed you."

Palma walked over to a map of the U.S. that hung on the wall. It was marked up in different ways, but this time the markings didn't matter. It was about the symbolism. They were doing something in the United States for the United States.

"I need you to go to Florence, Colorado. You're going to pay a visit to the Warden of USP Florence who will be waiting for you. He's going to hand someone over known as Prisoner X. Prisoner X is a dangerous asset.

"You are going to take possession of Prisoner X.

"You are going to chloroform Prisoner X once Prisoner X is on board a Black Hawk you are going to procure from Cheyenne Mountain Air Force Station.

"You are going to fly over the Atlantic with Prisoner X.

"You are going to shoot Prisoner X while Prisoner X is asleep.

"You are then going to throw Prisoner X overboard into the Atlantic and come home.

"Any questions?"

PART IV
---
20 MINUTES

INVESTIGATION INTO THE EVENTS THAT TRANSPIRED AT USP FLORENCE ADMAX, OCTOBER 2012

Official Transcript

Transcript Date: December --, 2013

Speaking
Senator Jeanna Mathias, Chairperson
Admiral Williams Parnell, Director of the National Security Agency

Excerpt (p. 87)

Senator Mathias: Admiral, we only want to clarify a few points if we may.

Admiral Parnell: If I am able to, Senator.

Senator Mathias: I am still struck by the fact that the entire incident took place in less than twenty minutes yet had casualties and property destroyed that would have seemed more like a terrorist attack.

Admiral Parnell: That is certainly one perspective, yes.

Senator Mathias: But it was not a terrorist attack.

Admiral Parnell: No, ma'am.

Senator Mathias: The two men on board the helicopter...

Admiral Parnell: Sergeants Mossberg and Brandt.

Senator Mathias: Excuse me?

Admiral Parnell: The two men who died. They were Sergeant Howard Mossberg and Sergeant Nathan Brandt.

Senator Mathias: Yes. Their names are already on record and our condolences to their families. I expect NSA will cover the $7.4 million cost of replacing the Black Hawk that was borrowed from Cheyenne Mountain. While you explained to me that they were there to collect an asset, you did not explain why they were there.

Admiral Parnell: Ma'am?

Senator Mathias: Why was the asset at USP Florence? And why was it necessary to extract this asset, as you said, at two a.m. that morning?

Admiral Parnell: I am not at liberty to discuss those details at this time.

Senator Mathias: Who was the asset?

Admiral Parnell: I'm sorry, Senator, I am not at liberty to discuss those details at this time.

Senator Mathias: We've received paperwork that states General Palma was involved in the operation and that he sanctioned the use of force. Force on Federal Correctional Officers, on the National Guard...

Admiral Parnell: Ma'am, we have yet to find any proof that they had anything to do with the injuries and unfortunate deaths of anyone at the penitentiary.

Senator Mathias: Then who is, Admiral?

Admiral Parnell: I am not at liberty to discuss those details at this time.

59

LATE NIGHT PICK-UP

The night was a bit chilly so the man had taken a blanket with him and fell asleep inside his car. He left the driver's side window open enough to allow him to hear any ambient noise, and let the cold night air in. His bottled water tasted colder than he liked. It would affect his core body temperature, affecting his sleep pattern. He shivered and waited, taking catnaps at frequent intervals.

He had been prepared to stay awake all night for the last two nights but received word that it wouldn't be necessary. That was good. He wasn't as young as he used to be and sleep was something that he tried to leverage every chance he could. It has been a long time since the military, when sleeping was just as important as training.

He heard the sound of a propeller in the distance. A helicopter.

He tapped his right earpiece. "You were right. Here they come."

He received a reply, but didn't pay attention. If everything went according to plan, it was going to be a long night.

He looked at his watch. Almost 2 a.m.

––––––––

At the helipad outside the administration building of USP Florence, a single correctional officer sat in his duty vehicle waiting for the warden's late night guests. It was a little strange to be receiving a copter so late, but then he'd had stranger encounters with the military when it came to their interactions with the prison system. He was a lifer so he did whatever the duty roster said, and that included doing what he was doing.

The Black Hawk's headlight was off, but its position lights were all in working condition. Without the sound of the rotors, it would be easy to mistake the flying truck for a UFO, given the sharp movement even a large hunk of machinery like a Black Hawk could do. He had never been in a helicopter before. He wondered if he might be able to convince one of the pilots to give him a quick ride sometime.

He had his windows rolled up to avoid the rotor backwash, and to keep the cab warm, and waited until the Black Hawk had completely landed and its rotors slowed down. He exited the dirty, white duty truck, walked over to the copter, and wished he hadn't worn his waist-length unlined light jacket. While he couldn't see frost from his breath yet, he knew that would come soon enough. The weather hinted he should bring his lined leather coat for tomorrow's late night shift.

The Black Hawk was a low riser meant for military transport. The VIP version would never be used to transport a prisoner. Tonight was no exception. Only VIPs in the VIP.

The side door slid open. A man jumped out and scanned the area. He looked the part of a career military man wearing a full operational camouflage uniform. The bulge under his jacket at his right hip concealed his holster.

The soldier took long strides toward the waiting officer and held out his hand. "Good evening! Or should I say good morning?" He smiled and they shook hands. "Sergeant Mossberg."

"Correctional Officer Adams." The rotors of the helicopter were slow enough that the din had gone down a few decibels. "Ken Adams."

"Please, call me Howard," Mossberg said and squeezed Adams' arm.

No glasses. Straight teeth. Square jaw and crew cut. Earpiece in his right ear. Adams didn't expect him to ever feel cold.

"Please, follow me," Adams said. He had left the truck running so the heat would keep the passenger compartment warm. He walked over to the passenger side and opened the door for Mossberg. Mossberg thanked him and closed the door behind him.

Adams entered the vehicle and found that his passenger already had his seatbelt on, with his hands resting on his thighs. "You don't know how many people I have to ask to do that first. Their seat belts," Adams said.

"Safety first, Ken. Safety first." Mossberg looked out the window. "Were those National Guardsmen outside the gate?" Mossberg's brow furrowed.

"Yes, they are," Adams said. "You can ask the warden about that when you meet him in a few minutes." That was going to be an interesting conversation.

"I was told the warden would be here."

"Damn straight. Let's just say there have been a few issues with this inmate." Adams shifted gears and began the slow drive to the maximum-security facility. "There are a few COs who will be happy to see her go," Adams said.

"Her?"

"That's the rumor. Did I mention there have been a few issues with this inmate?"

They drove down the curved road past the rear of FCI Florence, the medium-security facility, and past USP Florence–High, the maximum-security facility. The drive was long.

"Any chance we could get to my prisoner sometime tonight?" Mossberg asked.

"Sorry, Sergeant. House rules. Fifteen miles per hour is the speed limit; otherwise, it attracts the attention of the snipers in the guard towers."

"You have snipers? This is a secure place."

"Just kidding. The guard towers are unmanned." Adams smiled a little. "We're usually understaffed, but the warden runs a right ship. You'll see."

Mossberg nodded.

"Besides, things are very quiet around here," Adams said.

"That's not what I heard. I think the National Guard would agree with me." Mossberg pointed at his window with his thumb. "They seem to think you need help with something."

"Oh. Just for the last few days. This place is usually a tomb."

"I'll remember that the next time a chopper is dispatched to you from Cheyenne Mountain," Mossberg said.

———

Adams pulled into a parking space at the entrance of the prison proper, not the administrative building that would have meant even more driving.

He turned off the truck and both men stepped out into the brisk late evening air. The entrance was on the northeast side of the triangle that constituted ADX proper; the business side of the prison. Mossberg stood at attention and gave the surrounding area a look. Adams walked toward the fence.

The fence door slid open with a low rumble to let them in. If the lamppost within the perimeter fencing had not been working, it would have been too dark to see where they were walking.

"You sure you want Prisoner X?" Adams asked.

"Is that what you call him? Like Racer X?"

"That's the name on the paperwork." Adams just wanted to get inside and have something hot to drink.

"Let's just get a move on," Mossberg said.

60

TUNNEL VISION

The front door of the building just past the fence opened and Mossberg saw a cadre of people standing inside. Good. Everything looked like it should.

They stepped inside and a man wearing a dark suit, white shirt, and tie greeted Mossberg. It was good to see that they held the respect for their positions so seriously.

"Good evening. Sergeant Mossberg?"

"Yes, sir." Mossberg extended his hand.

"I'm Warden Coleman. Glad you could make it." They shook hands.

"Just doing my job, Warden. Just doing my job," Mossberg said. "I'm the taxi." Mossberg regarded the two other correctional officers to Coleman's left in the somewhat cramped room. They weren't as tall as the warden but stood so straight it would be easy to mistake them for being taller than they were. There was a cordoned off area to his right and a guard behind a Plexiglas shielded room to his left.

The warden walked him over to the guard behind the Plexiglas. "Please sign in and hand the guard an acceptable form of identification."

Mossberg understood the requirements. It always made him

uncomfortable. The job entailed both looking normal yet remaining stealthy.

He reached into the pocket of his jacket and pulled out his military ID. "Will this do?" Mossberg asked.

Warden Coleman examined it then placed it into the slot for the guard to process it.

"Is the prisoner ready for transport?"

"In due time. We don't want to move anyone until the last minute." Coleman nodded his head toward an elevator. "Have you had the pleasure of being here before?"

"Can't say I have."

"I didn't expect so." Coleman put his hands in his pockets. The room was a little cold. "We'll take the elevator down a flight and walk a bit to Range 13. The inmate returned to the cell before we received the paperwork. I have a team that will meet at the cell door and will be standing by in case there are any problems. The inmate will be manacled, hands and feet, and both will be attached at the jumpsuit waist to minimize freedom of movement, but still allow for walking."

Mossberg picked up his ID and put it away. "Sounds reasonable to me." As the others took the few steps toward the elevator, Mossberg stepped over to Coleman's right. "You don't expect anything, do you?"

"Not tonight."

———

The elevator door slid open and the five men stepped inside. Coleman glanced at the collection of people within the enclosed room. Three COs to escort Wodehouse to the helicopter, and a DOD rep to ensure that everything went according to plan. Coleman had chosen to attend the hand-off. He would be remiss to come in the next morning to find that his claim to clandestine fame was gone, and he didn't get to see her off.

He had never looked at her file, but what he'd heard in briefings told him enough: her stay had nothing to do with her sentence.

Regardless, ADX was a safe place relatively speaking. She would be safer here than at a facility where she would have to mix with the normal population. That was never fun for someone who wasn't a hardened criminal, even in the federal system.

The doors opened. The men walked out into the corridor.

They were down in the hallway, really a tunnel, that led to the cells above. It was a myth that the cells were below ground. Only these tunnels were. The hallways themselves were as generic as the rest of the facility. The sound of their shoes echoed in the otherwise empty tunnel. If the DOD rep, what was his name? Mossberg, or something? If the DOD rep had worn civilian clothes, Coleman would have been able to pick him out in a crowd. Straight walk, shoulders back. A fighter. Not someone you wanted to cross. Coleman knew men like him. He had a selection of them here at ADX.

CO Adams walked a little faster than they did and arrived at the elevator first to press the call button. Within a few seconds, the familiar ding echoed around them and the doors slid open again.

"You know," Mossberg said, "this reminds me of another place where I used to work."

"You worked at a prison before?"

"No. Not important."

———

Fort Meade, Mossberg thought. *This reminds me of the underground hallways at Fort Meade.*

The elevator doors closed with the men packed snug in its confines. The room had a slight audible vibration that Mossberg felt in the back of his jaw.

The doors opened again and everyone piled out. The warden took the lead so Mossberg decided to keep up with him. He didn't want to share any pleasantries with the boys in the back. There was a reason they were holding up the rear.

They went past row after row of locked cells, spying an officer at a console every so often. *Tough job.* Mossberg tried to peer through the translucent rectangle windows but was unable to catch a glimpse of movement. He guessed that even murderers and traitors had to sleep sometime.

Another turn. More cells. They approached a pair of barred doors. The warden waved at a camera and everyone entered the cordoned area. The door slid shut behind them with a solid thunk. A few seconds later, the next door slid open and they continued their walk.

There appeared to be no better place to hold someone while you decided what to do with their future.

Up ahead, Mossberg saw five people dressed in padded outfits. This must have been the team the warden mentioned. They wouldn't be needed. One of the COs knocked on the door. No one answered. He knocked again. Coleman looked at Mossberg. "Security's confirmed she's in there and asleep. This might take a minute."

The concrete walls and the steel door made for great soundproofing. They waited and nothing happened. The CO knocked again.

"What do you want?" A squeaky voice answered.

How old was this girl?

"You're being moved. Present hands and feet," Coleman said.

A few seconds later, a pair of gloved hands presented themselves in the slot. One officer handcuffed, while another manacled the prisoner.

"Step away from the door." The officer waited a few seconds and unlocked the solid steel door.

Mossberg saw a pair of eyes looking back at him; the only unfamiliar face and the only one in military dress.

"Are you here to kill me?" the robotic voice asked.

61

THE LONG WALK

It had been a while since Anna had walked through this much of the prison. In the last few months she had memorized the number of steps to the pool, how far to Medical, how many steps constituted the size of her cell, and how many approximate seconds to each so she would know both the distance and time to each destination. She thought about how fast a quantum of light would take if it took a straight line or had to go the same route as her.

Little by little, as she cared less and less, she started to forget things. At the age of twenty-five she was simply tired.

It was only in the last few days that she had felt awake again. The black-and-white world, or more accurately, the dark cream and light cream world of ADX was in color again. She noticed things. The hues of people's eyes. The way they walked. Even the bouts of helplessness she felt were tempered by the fact that she could feel people caring.

CrapIsKing. Doctor Hawking. Orville Moss. Who was she that she had somehow earned their friendship and even their trust. Hawking had even let her use his computer! *What a crazy man!*

Anna was conscious of the things around her. She coughed to hear the sound of the electrolarynx bounce off the walls. She counted her steps, and tried to count the number of tiles to the end of a hall (very hard when she was in motion). The endless doors to all the cells were unreal to her. Prison. She was in prison. No amount of repetition took that shame away from her.

But the one thing she knew was that tonight at whatever ungodly hour

it was: she was in the present. There were two guards behind her, one in front of her, the warden and the soldier leading the way. She didn't know what his rank was, but Anna was certain he was here to take her away.

They entered the first elevator. *Breathe in everybody!*

The elevator shook and stopped at the lower floor. She felt someone behind her. The two Cos flanked her on either side. One of them stared at her with empty eyes.

"Excuse me. What time is it?" her cyborg voice asked.

"Just after two." She heard Coleman to her right.

She turned her head just enough so she could acknowledge him, and nod.

As they exited, she looked into the hallway. She didn't remember this path. Had it been that long since she was last in this part of the facility? Must have been. No cells and only the occasional door. The clanking of her chains and the sounds of their footsteps echoed all around her.

She was reminded of *A Christmas Carol*. Was she Christmas Past, Present, or Christmas Yet-to-Come? Not Past, that was for sure.

Present. Definitely Present.

She stared at the back of the soldier's head. Her hair was shorter than his. Did his scalp itch as much as hers? And unbidden: Was she being rescued? This didn't feel like a rescue. Rescues usually consisted of either happy or frantic people, but not calm, composed participants.

There was too much calm in this hallway. The starkness was a touch macabre. She was in for life. Was her stay changed to the death penalty? Donnell's daughter had asked for it, but for some reason the judge chose life. Even if the judge had decided to end her life, it would have taken a year or more for the sentence to be carried out.

She came up with nothing except a bad feeling, and a man with a bulge under his jacket that looked like a gun lived there.

The end of the hall. Another elevator. *OMG. Kill me now!*

"How many more of these do we have?" she asked.

The soldier smiled. It wasn't a friendly, don't-worry-everything-is-going-to-be-okay smile. It was an I've-got-work-to-do-let's-get-this-over-with smile. "I like her. I like the way she thinks."

Anna held back a sigh and shook her hands a little. The chains were noisy and shiny. Stainless steel. *Not getting out of these.*

Into the elevator. Again. The last to come in pressed the floor button. *There are only two buttons. Why isn't the elevator smart enough to go to the opposite floor every time it closes?*

It needs a hint?

More vibrations. Slow progression to the surface. The door opened. The temperature changed. It matched everyone's mood.

They all stepped into the anteroom. Anna didn't remember this area at all. She really had been here a long time.

Coleman turned to her. "Are you alright?"

She nodded.

"It'll be okay," he said.

It will? "Where are we going?" she asked.

"You're coming with me," Coleman said. A few of the others in the elevator gave him a sideways glance. "I think that's enough interaction." He stared straight ahead. "No more talking, please."

"Yes, sir," she said in monotone. She could do a good robot.

It was dark out. It was cold out here. Maybe not as cold as a New York winter, but her orange jumpsuit wasn't lined. She shivered and the muffled sound of the chains reminded her of Marley talking to Scrooge. One CO got into an SUV and everyone else got into a van. Anna was seated in the back, chained to her seat with a guard seated in front of her, the soldier next to the guard, and the warden and other guard in front. The warden didn't drive.

The van swung back and forth on its slow ride along the road.

Anna looked at the soldier. "Seriously. Where are we going?" Walking around at this hour of the night left her feeling disoriented, but concerned. Why couldn't they do this in the morning? She calmed her shallow breathing.

"Feeling scared?" the soldier asked.

Anna preferred to wait for his response.

"Don't be. You're leaving. You're coming with me." He turned toward the front of the compartment.

Not comforting. She stretched her back and clenched her hands open and closed. She hated when her hands got cold. At one point, she tried to stretch her arms and came face to face with the length of her reach. She winced as the handcuff scraped her wrist. Her stomach gurgled. Something was wrong. She didn't know what it was, but she supposed it was just the next step in her humiliation. Might as well just cooperate and get it over with.

The long slow drive came to a halt. The CO who was driving came around and opened the rear door. Anna closed her eyes as a blast of cold air entered the compartment. The CO released the lock holding her to the van.

Anna stepped out and saw a helicopter. *Maybe it is a rescue!*

"You're taking me in that thing?" She pointed at the Black Hawk as the other guards congregated around her. Coleman was walking ahead while the soldier stood by her left side.

"Let's go," Coleman said. He held on to her left elbow and guided her toward the chopper.

"I hope I don't get air sick," Anna said.

"I said no talking." The soldier approached the side door and slid it open. He turned around to look at the warden.

Anna did the same. Now he was on her right side. He'd wish he'd listened if she got sick.

She stood with the helicopter behind her and a view of another facility in front of her. There was no wind. There were so many lights she wondered how much electricity was being wasted when the inmates were locked in cells with no windows.

Should I wave good-bye?

The rotors were starting up. Anna had never been on a helicopter before. Her gut told her not to get on this one.

Behind her she heard a sound not too far off in the distance. *Thump! Thump! Thump!*

Fireworks started to go off. Anna smiled as the first set went off high in the sky in a shower of whites, reds, and greens.

"What the hell is going on?" the soldier asked.

Thump! Thump! Thump!

More fireworks flew into the air, only these now arched and crashed into the facility. First into the dumping area and then into the surrounding buildings. Explosions began to go off, sending sound, color, and shrapnel all around them.

62

CELEBRATION

Two Minutes Earlier

The man was awake. From his position to the north of the golf course, which was north of the prison, he did what he did best: he watched and waited. From his position on Rincon Road he watched the Black Hawk land, but the waiting was over. It was going to take him a few minutes to drive onto State Highway 67, but he had the advantage. He knew why they were there and how long it would take to bring her out. After considering all the different ways the extraction could go he knew how long he had and what he had to do.

He drove as fast as he could until Rincon became Bear Paw Road and Bear Paw intersected with 67. At that point, he reverted to the speed limit. No point getting stopped before the fun began.

As he approached the guard station leading into ADX Florence he saw the line of National Guardsmen. That was going to cost the good folks of Colorado a pretty penny. He wasn't sure who was going to win this pissing contest, the federal government or Colorado, but he didn't care much. It was just passing entertainment, like a two-headed cat, or a train wreck. He drove south on 67 until just before the turn off and then pulled onto the shoulder across from the line of soldiers.

It didn't matter if they saw him or not, or wonder why he would be looking through binoculars into the facility. He would only do that for a few seconds out of sight of the guard at the entrance.

Two cars were approaching the helipad.

He put the binoculars down, pulled out, and made the left turn that would take him in.

The man slowed down, unmolested by the National Guard, and pulled up to the guard's station.

"Good evening, Doc. What are you doing here?" the officer asked.

"Good evening, Willie. How's it going?"

"Has your leave been rescinded? I saw your name on a list somewhere." The officer turned into the hut to look for something. Probably the list.

Hawking turned to his right and flipped the ignition switch on the remote for the fireworks that had been set up just outside the golf course.

Three rockets shot up into the area exploding into gorgeous colors that could be seen for miles.

Here we go.

The next volley came directly onto the grounds of the facility. Willie turned around on his chair and looked at the carnage over at the helipad.

"Doc, you'd better get out here! Get out of here!" Willie picked up the phone and started dialing for help.

"Are you crazy? I can help!" Hawking slammed on the gas and took off toward the helipad.

After all, that was what he was here for.

63

ANALYSIS PARALYSIS

Anna stood frozen solid outside the helicopter. She wanted to run but didn't. She wanted to get in the helicopter but didn't.

Movement instructions short-circuited in her brain.

"Get on!" the soldier yelled.

The smell of gunpowder and burned paper surrounded her. Anna's awareness flared and everything came into sharp focus.

Out of the corner of her eye, Anna saw that the soldier was moving. He yanked the right side of his jacket up and pulled out his gun.

As the gun came up toward her head she stepped in so the gun was past her head and the distance between her and the target of her knee were closer. The gun went off and the officer to her left went down as she kicked the soldier in the groin with as much force as she could. The manacles on her feet gave her just enough length that she felt her knee make serious contact.

When the soldier doubled over, she grabbed his head with both of her hands and slammed it against her knee. Then she twisted his wrist as she forced the gun out of his hand. He fell like a lead balloon.

The two remaining officers were already running up to her and latched onto each of her arms as they arrived. She tried to pull her arms free, but they had her.

Coleman strode up to her. "Stop!" he said.

Anna jumped, using the officers as leverage, and kicked Coleman in the chest with both feet. He went back a few feet and fell to the floor, unconscious from the blow to his head where he landed. The guards stared at Coleman and then at her.

She slammed her right foot into the instep of the guard to her right and pulled her arm back to hit the guard to her left. He took a step back. Anna felt the handcuff scrape against her arm where she'd cut herself. The punch fell short when she ran out of the chain securely attached to her waist. She reached for her arm and squeezed.

The guard to her left stepped in and tried to punch her, but she side-stepped him instead, bringing her closer to him, and she walloped him in the stomach. He doubled over and she kneed him in the face.

She spun to face the other guard who was also reaching for his gun. Anna walked over to him as quickly as she could and whispered, "Sorry!" wrapping her right leg around his left leg and tripping him in the direction of the Black Hawk, where he hit his head and dropped to the floor.

The side door moved. She saw a helmeted head starting to come out. She slammed the door shut as fast as she could and saw the person twitch as it struck the helmet he wore. She slid open the door, and the man, and his gun, fell out onto the helipad.

What was she supposed to do now?

Fireworks crashed and exploded to the east closer than they had been just a few short seconds before. She didn't realize how loud they were up close. She felt the shockwave of the explosions go through her and her anxiety level went up each time. She should run for cover.

No. She couldn't leave the people she had knocked out cold alone. Since she was still cuffed she couldn't do much for them, but she could at least wait until the SORT team, or someone, would come out to rescue everyone, including her. She looked around and cringed with every blast. How much longer would the fireworks go for? She closed her eyes and heard the booming get further and further away like thunder receding on a stormy day.

A fresh volley started to her left with a stream of white sparkles falling all around her as a pair of rockets flew overhead and smashed into the ground well ahead of her.

She pulled her shoulders up and grimaced as the rockets continued to rain down around her, but not coming down on the helipad. This wasn't going to work. She had to get out of the area and into a secure building. She took a few steps forward, and another rocket crashed and burned in the grassy area. She turned around and went back to where Warden

Coleman lay unconscious on the ground.

She couldn't find a comfortable way to sit on the ground, but she did what she could and waited. The ground was hard and what little grass sprouted up went flat without a fight. Maybe she should pull the keys from one of the COs? She could be there for a while unless a rocket hit her first. She should at least be comfortable. What if a rescue team came and found her unrestrained? Would they shoot her? Maybe she should wait in the helicopter.

No, if a rocket hit it, she would be a goner.

So this was how people became paralyzed in an emergency. Overthink everything and do nothing. She had to do something.

"Hey!" A voice called out to her from the direction of the truck loading area.

64

NIGHT SHIFT

In the center master control of ADX Florence, the two night shift officers were pulling out books to determine protocol. All the lights were on in the normally dark room.

Cells were sealed? *Check.*

All officers deployed to the armory to protect and distribute additional weapons? *Ongoing.*

Were state and local authorities notified? *Ongoing.*

They had practiced drills in the past and everything proceeded in a smooth and professional manner. Calls to the warden's phone went unanswered, but they knew that the warden was busy with a prison transfer.

A transfer?

Officer Willsbach turned to his partner. "Did you reach out to state police yet?"

"Hell, yeah."

"Call them back. Cheyenne Mountain, too. Tell them that the warden was in the middle of a prisoner transfer, and this might be an escape."

"Ya think?"

———

Terrell awoke after the first volley of fireworks struck, causing a slight rubble in the ground and a loud explosion in the distance. He tumbled to his left and groaned.

The Super 8 hotel on State Highway 67 positioned him in the center of things: he was just north of the prison and just south of Florence proper. An ideal location for movement at a moment's notice.

His muscles were sore. He had walked up and down the road in an attempt to keep up with his exercise, but it was also obvious to him that the pain he was feeling was from neglect. And a bullet to the shoulder. He knew that was a bit much, but he could feel the anxiety as well.

The incessant travel from the last few days and the stress of the job had started to take its toll. The one thing he had in his favor was that a Federal judge had given him the authority he needed to see Anna since even the CIA had no record of her detention. Only they had the dubious legal authority to render enemy combatants.

Now he just had to make sure that he wrapped her up in enough paperwork to keep her in one spot until he could work out what she had to do with Donnell, and Piercing Ventures. And General Palma.

That was the strangest connection.

Boom!

His eyes popped open. What the hell was that? It sounded like an explosion. More shock waves followed by sound. Through the curtain of his window he could see blazing colors and sparkles even as the glass rumbled its complaint. He pulled the blanket off, ran to the window, and pulled back the curtain.

In the distance, explosion after explosion hit the prison.

You have got to be kidding.

He grabbed his cell phone from the nightstand. Who should he call who hadn't already been called? He dialed the local FBI office and left a message. Then he dialed the Colorado State Police who assured him they had cars on the way. They took down his FBI information. *This is a waste.*

Terrell hung up. He grabbed some clothes, got dressed, and ran to his car.

As he sped down 67 he realized that the line of National Guard was broken. That was fine. He'd need all the help he could get. What the hell was going on over there?

65

KEYS

Anna tried to stand as she recognized the outline of Hyde coming at her from the dark by the truck loading area. *Keys! Keys! Keys!*

As she stood he came barreling at her. She thought to run, but slammed her right elbow up into his face shooting pain up her arm and into her shoulder. She turned to the guard on the ground by the Black Hawk. She ran and hopped onto the helipad as best she could, and tried to move the officer's inert form to look for the keys to her cuffs. Everything was in sharp relief. The explosions were overwhelming, as was the smell and the alternating heat and cold, but they were just part of the sensory overload she felt. Where was Hyde?

She turned around from a crouch to see him pulling himself up.

"Get away from him!" Hyde yelled.

There was the keyring!

Hyde stumbled over the second guard on the ground, the one the soldier had shot instead of her. Anna twirled from her crouch, leaving the keyring behind. She took as many steps forward as she could, grabbed a handle on the inside of the copter, and swung her feet up toward him. Her feet connected with his chest, and he stumbled back far enough for her to land on the guard. She pulled the guard's gun out of its holster and threw it.

Idiot! Why did I just do that?

She got back into a crouch and pulled at the keyring of the dead officer. She felt a knot in her throat. *He would have shot me. I was just standing there and he would have shot me.* She undid the cuff on her left hand and looked up in time to see Hyde stumbling back. *He doesn't know when to quit.*

She stood up, still holding onto the keys when the ring ran out of slack and was pulled out of her hand. Now she had one hand free while the other was still stuck to her belt by the chain. Hyde looked about to jump on her when she retreated to avoid him. She fell when the manacles stopped short of where her center of gravity was. She tucked her head forward as her shoulders landed on the helipad asphalt.

Hyde's head was at her waist. She pulled her hands back and slammed both his ears as hard as she could. Both his hands went up to protect his ears from another attack and he rolled off her. She rolled under the Black Hawk and crawled back to the dead officer. She needed to free her legs, but what she needed the most now was distance.

She pulled herself toward the unmoving body and reached for the keyring again. *Which key? Which key?* Hyde was on the ground holding his head. *I bet that hurt.*

Yes! Her left hand was free. She pulled the keyring off the deceased officer's belt as Hyde ran to the unconscious officer behind her. She jumped into the helicopter and used the bulletproof door as a shield as Hyde popped off a few rounds. She slid the door shut and ran to the door on the opposite side. She looked at the various keys and tried to see which would release her legs. *No. Another one. No. Another one...*

The door slid open wide enough for her to see Hyde sticking his hand in the gap. She grabbed the handle on her side of the door and smashed it on his hand as the gun went off in the compartment. The gunshot echoed, deafening her for a moment as she heard Hyde yell in pain.

The gun was now on the inside of the copter. She snatched it, put it on the floor by her feet, and undid her manacles.

66

POWERLESS

Anna slid the Black Hawk door holding the gun in her right hand, and felt the freedom of movement from both hands and legs. The helicopter was dark and smelled of diesel fuel. She was going to survive this if she had to take down Hyde, and anyone else, to do it. She was not adding to her murder conviction. Assault and battery, perhaps, but that seemed to be the only way she could convince her guardians that she wanted to stay. She didn't start this fight, and she wanted no part of it.

Thoughts of rescue crossed her mind, but all she wanted was to stay. Let her lawyer do her job. *Oh, please, let it not be a rescue. Please, please, please.* She looked around the large, dark olive door to see if anyone was hiding as another triplet of explosions went off behind her.

A car was coming. She hid behind the door again. *Do I surrender? Who do I surrender to? That car doesn't look very official.* The car came around the Black Hawk so she scooted over to the other door and peeked over the window frame.

The car stopped and Hawking came out. *Yes! Doctor Hawking. I can surrender to him. He'll make sure no one shoots me out of nervousness.* She was about to slide open the door when she stopped.

He was holding a gun.

Were doctors allowed to carry a gun on-duty? Was he off-duty? Was it a model that she liked?

He ran over to the warden's unmoving body and touched him with his foot. No movement. She felt a pang of guilt. How was she going to explain that she got caught up in the moment? Her arms hurt and when the men grabbed her muscle memory kicked in, and she kicked out. The warden just happened to be in the way.

That was so lame. Intake was in her future if she survived this.

Hawking came over to the helicopter and examined the unconscious body of the officer to her right. Again, he gave the man a cursory look and left him.

Now Anna couldn't get a good view of him, but she assumed he examined the dead officer as well. Why wasn't he calling anyone? Maybe he didn't have a radio? A cell phone?

He turned the two soldiers over and looked in their pockets. He found ID which he threw on the ground.

He looked up at the door. Anna pulled back. Had he seen her?

She did her best to turn and look without showing too much of her face, but she knew that some part of her would be evident.

He grabbed onto the door handle.

Anna heard the locking mechanism turn.

Then the lights went out.

67

DOUBLE LOCK

Hawking stood there ready to prep the copter when a new level of darkness fell around him. The fireworks flying overhead, and into the buildings on the ground, lit up the area, but the buildings across the facility went dark. The change in lighting was noticeable and he didn't like it. His nose filled with the pungent smell of gunpowder, the air thick with it.

Damn it. If he didn't prep the copter, he wouldn't be able to use it if he needed it. The pilot was unconscious so he couldn't trade the pilot's life for a few minutes of flying time, but maybe he would be conscious when Hawking returned.

Did he care about the power shutting down? Not really, but it was unexpected. He didn't like unexpected. He knew where the power plant for the facility was, but was it worth the distraction?

He ran back to the car. The new destination was nearby. He was certain that none of the rockets had struck it, but he wasn't sure. Hawking didn't like not being sure. The darkness could have been an accident, or by design. He suspected he knew who was giving him a run for his money, but he had to find out. If he was right, Hawking would have to neutralize him in the next few minutes.

He wasn't sure where Anna was, but he was sure he would find her somewhere in the area. Anna might even be with him. Maybe she was on her way to the power station.

Hawking took off in a cloud of dirt and loose pebbles, which struck the undercarriage of his car. The power station was to the north and surrounded by a standard fence, but it wasn't electrified or protected in any real sense. There were cameras and a patrol that checked on it all the time, but tonight he suspected that the nightly patrol might be busy with other things.

He drove up the road with the solar panels to his left and the truck station to his right. If he was careful, no one would be there by the time he arrived. If he was lucky, he would find Anna.

Hawking hoped for lucky.

The car was doing about 80 by the time he got to the end of the truck loading area. He took the turn harder than he should have. The car slid a touch to his left, but he had maneuvered safer going faster under worse conditions.

The two main electrical towers were coming up to his left. The fireworks, as expected, were going over the power station. The lines from the Florence Electricity Department led directly to the main towers, which did the job of stepping down the current for the use of the facility. The hut opposite the other tower receiving an incoming line was where the brains of the beast were. Or at least where the power could be cut to bring the facility into darkness.

Hawking wanted the power going. The cells would all go into automatic lock if they lost power, but the facilities would go dark inside. Not knowing where Anna was meant that he had to make sure there was a modicum of order here, but not too much.

The station was ahead. He pulled to the right and made a jug handle turn so the car was facing the power station fence. The car slowed enough for him to make the turn and he floored the gas. The fence enveloped the front of his car and then flew off since it was still attached to a section of fence that still attached to the ground.

The car came to a sliding stop just before the entrance to the metal building. In the dark, the building had the appearance of a bunker. He had to do this fast. Reinforcement would arrive soon and then it would all be over. Time was a wasting. He had to find Anna.

———

The bare metal door was ajar. There was a strange glow of lights through the gap, daring him to enter. Hawking took a deep breath, gripped his gun, and stepped inside. He closed the door behind him best he could. As large as the power station appeared on the outside, it was quite small on the inside. There was very little room to move and a fight would be a bad one. He took shelter behind one of the racks within a few steps.

"I know you're in here, Dr. Hawking."

So much for the element of surprise.

"Why did I know you would be in here?" Hawking asked.

"You didn't. You came running when you saw the lights go out."

"Not true," Hawking said. "I knew you would be in here." He took a step toward another rack and got closer to the voice. "The General sent me here just like he did you."

"He did?" the voice asked. "That's very interesting. He might have sent me, but he didn't send you. There were two of us being sent and we were given photographs of each other." Hawking heard a slight flutter in the eerie calm of the room. When the room was operational, there would have been too much noise to hear anything, much less have a conversation. "You know, just to make sure we wouldn't work at cross-purposes."

Hawking was silent.

"It wasn't your face. I may be bad with faces," the voice said, "but it wasn't you."

Hawking took another few steps. The room was deep, but the sound came from nearby. He looked at the ground. He cast a strong shadow to his right. That meant that the intruder would cast one away from him. Hawking would see him when it was too late.

"If you come out, I promise to not to kill you," the voice said.

"Thanks. I wish I could say the same." He turned to take cover in between a rack and slammed into a running figure.

Both men dropped their guns, brought their hands up to their respective foreheads, and then ran at each other. The figure wore a mask, but Hawking recognized the voice even muffled.

Hawking's head snapped back as his assailant's fist connected with his exposed jaw. He saw sparks but reached out and clutched the masked man by the throat and threw him against the wall. He pulled his fist back but didn't throw the punch. If he missed, he would slam his fist into the concrete wall.

The delay cost him. The man punched Hawking in the stomach. Hawking came off the ground for a second. He punched Hawking again. And again.

Both men stepped back. The emergency lights flashed. The masked man looked up, and Hawking threw himself at him. Both men fell to the concrete ground with a loud smack. Hawking connected with the man's face once and felt the soft compression of skin against the man's cheekbone.

The man threw Hawking off him, and Hawking slammed into the base of one of the racks. He felt the knobs dig into his back, and the rack swung back and forth, but it didn't fall. Hawking saw the man's shoe about to connect with his face when he grabbed it, twisted it as hard as he could, and brought the man down onto a pipe where the man's chest collided before he bounced off, and crashed on the floor.

Where the hell was his gun?

Hawking stood. He knew he only had a few seconds to act.

There, off to the side. A gun.

He tried to reach but couldn't move one of his feet. He was thrown onto the floor where the side of his face hit the concrete. He snatched the gun and spun around.

He fired as the man ran out the door. Hawking heard the turning of the lock. There was no point firing at the door. It was solid metal.

He pulled himself off the floor and walked to the door. It had a lock that needed a key on the inside.

68

BODIES IN MOTION

Anna watched Hawking pull away and wasn't sure if she was upset or relieved that he had left. He was a doctor, and there were people on the ground who needed doctoring. Didn't he notice the continuing barrage of explosives raining around them?

She slid the Black Hawk door open and jumped down. The unconscious bodies needed to be moved and no one seemed intent on coming over to help. Had these people never seen fireworks before? The helipad seemed to be in a bubble as the fireworks showered the area around her, but not on her. She gave thanks for small favors and wondered who to move first.

The dead officer. She looked down and didn't recognize him. She wasn't sure how she was involved in his death, but she was certain that if she had not been in this facility, he wouldn't be dead now. *Another casualty to my father's disappearance.*

She left him where he fell. It was a crime scene after all.

She went over to the unconscious officer. There was no way she was going to be able to pick him up. She put her hands under his armpits and dragged him onto the grass away from the helipad and toward the solar panels. It was slow work. Her back was sore and her arms were scraped from the loose handcuffs. She looked at his feet as she pulled him along. He didn't leave a groove in the ground the way she would have expected. The ground was too hard even for October. When this was over, there would be nothing to mark that she had been here. Everyone would forget Prisoner X soon enough.

Everyone.

She lowered the officer so that his head wouldn't strike the ground hard and cause him more problems. She hoped that hitting his head against the Black Hawk would be enough to keep him out until this was all over. For some reason she couldn't help but think, *This is somebody's father.*

She ran back to the helipad. Who should she move next? The warden, or the other officer?

She heard running to her left just before another explosion went off behind her. By the light of the fireworks, she saw Hyde running toward her, holding onto a large pipe with his two hands. *What is wrong with that guy? He's throwing himself offbalance before he even gets here.*

Anna ran toward him as he pulled the pipe back, and swung it around toward her with all his might. She waited for the swing to start and tumbled on the ground as the pipe flew by, above where her head would have been. She grabbed his legs with hers, and knocked him over. On his way to the ground, the pipe bounced and struck Anna in the shoulder. A sharp pain ran through her right arm. She clutched where her arm and shoulder met. Inching back from Hyde, she felt something hit her hard enough in the back that she almost fell forward.

Hyde had found a rock, and thrown it at her. She turned and picked it up. *Two can play that game.* She threw the rock back at him, and it went off into the distance.

"You even throw like a girl," Hyde said.

Anna put her hands up. "Look, I know you think that I'm resisting arrest, but I'm not. I am willing to surrender to you.

You just have to stop trying to kill me."

Hyde pulled himself up into a crouch, and then bounded toward her. She took a couple of steps to the side, and he just about passed her, when his hand caught the jumpsuit waistband that accommodated the chains the inmates wore. She fell in toward him but spun herself off his back to his right and landed on the ground. He swung his arm out and hit her in the face.

"The only way I'll be bringing you in is in chains, unconscious, or dead," he said.

"That doesn't make any sense! I'm telling you that I'll surrender to you." Anna looked at the Black Hawk. Could she make it back into the security of the passenger compartment? "I just don't trust you to handcuff me."

"Oh, would you prefer the doc to do it? I'm sure you'd like that."

Anna could feel anger building in her chest. This was why she preferred to be alone. She wanted a minimum-drama life and idiots like Hyde made that impossible. She had a flash of high school and embarrassment she thought she had shaken off. She was done with that.

"Okay, I just offered myself up and you said no. That means nothing I do is going to convince you to do the right thing." She walked toward him as he started to stand. "That means I have to make you do the right thing."

"What do you mean?" He stepped back.

"I'm going to hog tie you and sit on your head until help comes."

Hyde took a swing at her. Anna grasped his arm, twirled herself under him, and yanked down only half as hard as she knew she needed to. Hyde yelled at the top of his lungs as another explosion went off near them. Anna relished the vibrations of the explosions coursing through her every few seconds, sometimes one after another. Subduing Hyde wasn't something she wanted to do, but she was nothing if not thorough.

She spun around again and slammed her right elbow into his jaw. The jaw went back and forth and Anna was sure she'd broken a few teeth. Hyde went down onto the grass, and remained there.

Great. Now I have to move this sack of potatoes over to where the others are just so they can see that I didn't kill anyone.

Anna grabbed him by the armpits. His shirt was soaked in sweat.

Oh, this is so gross. As they approached the area where the other officer lay Anna let go and started to shake her hands in disgust.

She turned away for a moment and started wiping her hands on her jumpsuit. *This is never going to wash off.*

She turned back and she found Hyde standing a few inches in front of her. Her eyes opened wide and she wanted to throw herself back, but she wasn't sure what to do.

He squeezed her throat with both hands and lifted her off the ground. Anna groped for his hands to get leverage to kick him, but the sounds became muffled and her vision blurry. Her hands slipped over his wrists when she saw his head tilt to her right as something exited his head. His grip went slack. She fell to the ground on her knees and reached for her throat. She gulped air through her sore throat.

Sparkles. Explosions. Air.

What the hell? Someone had just shot Hyde.

That someone ran over to her. She felt a hand on her back and the someone to whom the arm belonged to her left. "Are you alright?"

It was Orville.

69

SWEET SURRENDER

Anna threw her arms around his neck. She had never before been so happy to see anyone. The smell of his hair and his neck overpowered the acrid odor of gunpowder and the ground burning all around them. She held him for a few more seconds and then pulled back. She didn't notice when they stood.

"Hello," Orville said. He smiled at her, his blue eyes glittered with the reflection of the flames and sparks surrounding them.

She hugged him again. *Oh, please, let him come with me.* She felt him tugging at her arms. She so wanted to kiss him. Her neck hurt. She looked at his face again. So perfect. What would it be like to be with him all the time? In a few seconds Anna had taken in the texture of his skin, the distance between his eyes, cheekbones, eyebrows, anything she could absorb of his face.

She needed more smell samples. She hugged him again.

"Anna."

Oh yeah, she was not going to be forgetting him any time soon.

"Anna!"

In the midst of all the carnage and chaos, here he was. And he saved her. She was in danger; she was about to die and he saved her. What more could she ask for?

He came back for me.

"What?" She blinked. The sounds around them started to come back. She felt shock wave after shock wave as another volley of rockets blew up far behind her. What were they doing standing there?

"You have to go," he said. A cloud of burnt paper flew overhead.

"Where are we going?"

"You have to go."

"No, I'm surrendering." She put her wrists together behind his head, bringing her closer to his face. She smiled. "Put me in cuffs, Officer."

"I would except for one little thing."

"And that is?"

"You can't stay," he said.

"But I want to."

"You can't. You have to leave."

"No."

"Yes," Orville said.

"No, I'm staying here. I don't want to leave. I want to stay here," Anna said.

"You can't." Orville reached for her arm behind his neck and pulled it in front of him.

She brought her other arm back and put her hand on his chest. His hand covered hers. The sensation of his thumb pressed against her palm sent a bolt of electricity up her arm.

Anna squeezed his thumb. *This might be the only chance I get.*

"I told you that you would be the first to escape. I knew it." He held her hand in his. "Let's go."

70

SHOOT OUT

Hawking checked as much of the power station hut as he could, and decided that Anna wasn't there. That meant that she was still in danger. He had to get out of there. He had banged on the door over and over again in the hope someone would hear him, but that was not going to happen. His fist was sore.

There were no windows, but he could hear the explosions going on as they would for another few minutes. No matter. He would take care of this. He picked the gun up from the floor and aimed at the double-sided lock. Blowing off the doorknob wouldn't help at all.

Someone banged on the door. "Who's in there?"

"This is Dr. Hawking! Can you open the door? Someone locked it from the outside, and there's another lock on this side."

"Sorry, Doc!" the voice on the other side of the door responded. "I'll have to call facilities management and have them send someone over."

Right. "Step away from the door!" Hawking said. He put the gun about two to three inches away from the lock and pulled the trigger multiple times.

Now there was a hole on both sides of the lock.

"You okay out there?" Hawking asked.

"Yes, sir!"

Hawking pushed open the door. His car was where he had left it and the tires were still intact. *What an idiot. Did he really think I would stay trapped in there until this was over?*

Hawking shook hands with the officer. "Thanks for stopping when you saw the car."

"No problem. Since when did they issue you a gun?"

"I'm a hobbyist. I always leave it in my car, but it seems to have come in handy tonight."

"I hear ya, Doc. What should we do?"

"I don't know about you, but I have to get back to help anyone who's been injured. I want you to get on the horn with whoever you can find in facilities, and get the power turned back on. Whoever is doing this is hoping that the added problem of zero visibility in the buildings will work to their advantage. Let's not let that happen."

The officer pulled out his radio while Hawking ran to his car. He started it up and drove back toward USP Florence through the new hole in the fence.

Where the hell is Anna?

71

COORDINATING CHAOS

"I'm sorry, sir, but you have to turn around."

Nine National Guard personnel surrounded Terrell Garrison on State Highway 67 where they had set up a roadblock on the north end of the road. None of them pointed their rifles at him, but several had their fingers near the trigger. Terrell had his right hand on the steering wheel, and his left in a sling.

"My name is Terrell Garrison. While I appreciate your enthusiasm, I need to get in there." Explosions continued at regular intervals to his left. "That's federal land over there, and I'm with the FBI. This just became my crime scene." He cocked his chin at the person standing next to him. He didn't look older than twenty-five. "Can you even shave?"

Looking past the young man, Terrell saw that the entire facility was in darkness while multicolored projectiles struck various buildings and exploded in showers of light and sound. What little wind there was brought the smell of gunpowder and burning grass. *The prison lost power. That was targeted to increase the chaos, I'm sure.*

———

After showing them his ID, Terrell took off for the abandoned guard station at the entrance of USP Florence, and exited his rental car. There were National Guardsmen blocking the road.

"Good morning, gentlemen," he said as he exited his vehicle and held up his ID. "I'm going to need about ten of you to come with me while the rest of you wait for emergency services to arrive." He pointed at various helmeted personnel. "You, you, you,..."

He continued pointing, calling out until he had about ten people. "Alright. When emergency services show up, keep them away from the facility until the shelling stops. Understand?" Everyone around him nodded. "Let's go."

"Sir!" A voice came from behind, running up to him holding a bulletproof vest. "I think you might want one of these."

Terrell took the dark blue vest. The weight was enough that he knew his shoulder was going to complain, but he didn't care. One of the men he had pointed to came over and helped him put it on before they jogged up the road.

"How long have the lights been out? Did power get hit?" Terrell asked.

"Don't know, sir. It went down a couple of minutes ago," the National Guardsman next to him said.

Everything was happening so fast. It was going to take another few minutes before the fire trucks arrived and brought their own collection of lights and piercing noises. They wouldn't make an appearance on the grounds until the explosions stopped. These were the kinds of scenarios that planning and practice made possible. While this had never happened before, everyone involved was at least conversant with what to do in an emergency. Everything was on schedule and, barring any unforeseen events, things would be under control within the next ten minutes or so.

In this case, what had to be done was to keep everyone indoors while they waited for the cavalry to arrive.

Over to his right was FCI Florence, the medium-security facility that had a minimum-security camp next to it. The ground around it smoked with heat from smaller surrounding flames. In fact, the temperature around the prison had gone up about twenty degrees since the attack had started minutes earlier. Terrell was sure that the state police would be arriving any second now, and they would have squad cars as close to the perimeter of the various buildings as they could get. They would also stop just short of entering the blast zone. Whoever was doing this was either dead or using the attack as cover to do whatever it was they were hoping to do.

Thank God, Anna is safe and sound in her cell. This was no place for anyone to be. The rockets came down in waves for a few minutes, and then in hard pairs and triplets that left large craters in the ground. A few of the buildings had fires burning in areas where the rockets had penetrated.

A rocket at ADX wouldn't do very much given the amount of concrete involved in its construction. FCI, on the other hand, was built like a normal prison.

Very flammable.

He jogged across the parking lot to the main entrance of the administration building for FCI with the National Guard close behind. The parking lot hadn't been touched but was almost in the dark. They started banging on the glass doors to get the attention of the officers inside, and one of the COs ran to the door, unlocked it, and let them in.

Terrell looked for anyone dressed in civilian clothes. Not finding such a person, he turned to the CO after showing him his ID. "Who's in charge?"

"The warden and she's home. We've been giving her updates every few minutes. The sergeant-at-arms is running around the facility making sure everything is locked up tight, and that no one is in the areas where we were hit."

"Good. How many non-essential personnel are here?"

"Very few. It's two in the morning so other than a nurse in medical it's all officers and inmates for the most part."

"Good. So everyone is either in a cell or secure area."

"Yes, sir. We've been lucky. Given the hour, the areas that were hit were empty so we've had no casualties so far."

Terrell gave thanks for that, but if there were no casualties at FCI then something was already wrong. The only way there could be no casualties at such an easy target was if FCI wasn't a target to begin with.

This was the work of a pro. The question was, how much time did Terrell have to find him?

"Are there any connecting tunnels to the other facilities?"

"Not to my knowledge."

Terrell looked down the corridors where he stood. The emergency lighting would do until the sun came up. The few lights that would fail wouldn't make a difference. He turned to his escorts. "When emergency services show up, bring them in and take them to the areas that have been hit. Do a search for anyone the officers might have missed, and make sure no one, and I mean no one, does anything stupid." He pointed to the group of men standing before him. "No one dies tonight."

Terrell headed for the door.

"Where are you going, sir?" one of the escorts asked.

"To do something stupid."

Terrell exited the building, and ran down the tree-lined street leading away from the administration building of the medium-security facility. It was hard to see through the smoke and debris except for the flashes of light from the explosions that lit up the grounds like a battlefield. He stopped, took a breath, and coughed. To his right was the maximum-security prison and further south was ADX. He thought for a quick second if he should head down to ADX, and make sure Anna was all right, but he knew she was fine. She wasn't going anywhere.

He, on the other hand, knew he had to see if there was anything he could help with to minimize the loss of life by coordinating whatever resources he could. And maybe find out what the hell was going on.

He would check on Anna after it was over. She was probably

feeling the rumbles of the explosions and wondering what was happening. *Don't you worry, Anna. Everything is going to be fine.*

He jogged in the direction of the maximum-security prison. ADX was too far to the south, and USP Florence High was calling his name. Fires came from the center of its triangle.

72

TAKING SIDES

Anna and Orville turned back toward the helipad. She had led him away a distance, but he was firm in his insistence they head back. Not only was it safer around the helipad, but she would find her way out better from there. After the last few minutes, it was obvious to Anna that whoever had arranged the attack had targeted some areas, but not others. She just didn't want to be around Hyde, and now that he was ex-Hyde even less.

She looked around the area. The invisible perimeter Anna had envisioned around the helipad held, which meant that the survivors of her attack would live. That was good. It might help her in any disciplinary hearings once she got back inside.

Who was she trying to kid? She was already a lifer. They would just lock her away even tighter. No one would ever find her. No one would ever talk to her. No one would ever touch her.

She squeezed Orville's hand. It was warm and rough.

She didn't remember the last time someone held her hand even if it was to lead her back to her cell. She was good with that. She would learn to come to terms with it.

"How's your arm?" she asked. Another set of explosions rocked the medium-security facility to her right. They would be all right. Anna didn't see any more than minor fires around it.

"Stop worrying about me. We have to get you out of here," Orville said. "C'mon." He started running toward the heliport.

"But I don't know how to fly a helicopter much less a Black Hawk."

"Do you always complain so much when people are trying to help you?" Over his shoulder he smiled at her then turned back toward the helipad.

"Yes. Especially when I don't know what they have in mind, and I'm the one who has to live with the consequences," Anna said.

"Oh, c'mon. Have I led you wrong yet?" They approached the helipad from the north. There were two bodies: one was the still unconscious officer and the other was Hyde. Hyde was face-down on the ground.

Orville led her around the bodies, and around the Black Hawk where the others were still out cold.

He let go of her hand and scanned the various people. "How did you do this?"

"It was an accident."

"More like a hurricane." He gave her a crooked smile. "You're dangerous."

Anna felt embarrassed. How would she explain hitting the warden in the chest? That might have killed him! She was sure her luck would hold up, but she also knew that she was probably in denial. And running out of luck. "Look, Orville, can't we just sit right here and wait for some of the officers to come get us?"

"Are you kidding? There are bombs going off all around us. You have to get out of here, and I have to find shelter."

"How am I getting out of here?" she asked.

Orville went over to the soldiers and shook them. He pulled a bottle out of his pocket and held it under the nose of the one wearing a helmet. He was probably the Black Hawk pilot. He had a cool job. She would never get to work in anything that cool. Ever. A sense of helplessness washed over her, but she remembered what had just happened. Maybe with Orville things might be different. Maybe he could be what turned her fate around. Her lawyer could win the appeal, and send her to a prison for females. She could learn something there (law?), and at least feel productive in her own way. She could help wayward girls. She could help someone.

Maybe, one day, she might be released.

"What are you doing?" she asked.

The pilot shook his head and sat up after pushing himself up with his gloved hands. He was in full gear.

Orville patted the man's arm.

"This is a really bad idea, Orville." Anna took a step back and found herself standing very straight. "Those guys wanted to take me away to kill me."

Orville put the bottle under the nose of the other soldier.

"Kill you? They would never do that." Orville walked over to the other man and shook him. "These men are sworn to protect and defend. They came here to help you escape."

The soldier awoke with a start. He was the one who had escorted her out.

Orville trotted over to Anna. "It's alright," Orville said.

She peered over his shoulder at the soldier who had stood up and was rubbing his wrist. The one Anna almost broke disarming him. He gave her a cold look.

"The world has other plans for you, Anna Wodehouse." Orville turned and looked at the soldier. "These men are here to make sure you fulfill your destiny."

Anna felt her chest deflate. "Orville? Why are you doing this?" Her face felt hot.

"What do you mean?" He stood in front of her. "The only way for you to find your destiny is to get in that helicopter and let them show you."

With measured steps that looked painful, the soldier walked over to where they stood.

"I'm sorry," she said to the soldier.

"Don't worry about it." His face strained to smile. "This is what they pay me for."

"And what do they pay you for?" she asked.

"Rescuing damsels in distress," he said.

Anna felt her hackles raise. His words didn't line up. This man was a professional come to do a professional job. She was his job. Anna was a linear thinker most of the time. This time holistic thinking took over. Events. Information. Nonlinear answers. Nothing added up. She wanted to run.

"Orville," Anna retreated an inch, "I'm not going with them."

"What's wrong?"

Orville came closer, and now Anna felt her personal space invaded. Her subconscious was screaming. She remembered standing on the roof of the police car yelling out to her father eight years ago when they'd first ripped her out of her house. *Run!*

She turned and Orville grabbed her left wrist with his free hand. "Where are you going? These guys aren't going to hurt you."

"Let me go."

The soldier drew close.

RUN!

The soldier behind Orville watched her face. His eyes were blank. It was obvious he was waiting to see who would win, and then take over regardless of the outcome.

He looked like he was used to winning.

"Anna, go with these men," Orville said.

Anna wanted to cry. "No. Orville, I told you. I want to stay here, and surrender to the warden. Why are you doing this?" she asked.

She looked past the soldier and saw that the pilot had boarded the Black Hawk. *One less person to worry about.* She gulped lungfuls of air.

"You don't have to do that. Go with them, and everything will work out the way it's supposed to." Orville still held onto her arm. His face wasn't playful. His eyes were empty.

Anna looked at Orville and then at the soldier.

That man wants to kill me.

And so does Orville.

73

LIFE CHOICES

For a split second everything froze.

Orville clutched Anna's arm.

The soldier was a few feet from Orville's back.

The Black Hawk was in front of her a distance away.

Decide: what are you going to do?

Anna slammed her right foot into Orville's left kneecap. She felt the bones break and Orville screamed. Then she took his left hand and dislocated it from his wrist as she spun his hand around, and folded it in a direction it was never meant to go.

She pushed Orville toward the soldier who then pushed him to the ground. Orville hollered, and tried to grab his shattered knee. Anna got a running start, but the soldier caught up with her within a few seconds. He spun her around and tried to punch her in the face. She blocked him once, twice, and tried to slam the palm of her hand into his face, but he pushed her hand out of the way.

How could she do this? He was bigger and stronger. She was smaller and exhausted.

Only one thing to do.

She pushed his arms away and shoved him to the ground. As he reached for her leg she jumped over him and ran back to the helipad. The Black Hawk's rotors had started up.

Orville cried in pain.

She thrust him over onto his injured arm.

The Black Hawk was a large helicopter. It took her a few seconds to run around it to where the bodies lay.

Where she left the gun.

She turned around and saw the soldier catching up. He'd had a nice rest while Anna was busy fighting Hyde. The only difference was she had crushed his genitals while she was still in one piece.

There! She jumped at the gun, spun around, and fired just as he was coming around the copter. The bullet cut through the rear fuselage of the Black Hawk. She aimed at his legs, but he had already leaped out of the way.

This wasn't going to end well. She had to get away from here. She stood up and ran to the south. She had to find somewhere to hide.

Explosions rocked to the west, and then to the south. When was it going to stop? At some point she was going to get killed and then what?

And then what? She wasn't sure. Adrenaline shot through her chest, arms, and legs, lighting up her brain so she didn't have a lot of time to think about existential angst, or betrayal by someone she hardly knew. She just had to get away.

Should she shoot at the Black Hawk? *No, don't waste bullets.*

74

RESCUE ATTEMPT

Every time Anna thought she had found a spot to hide another explosion rang out, followed by a shower of debris. She wanted to get to ADX, but she would never make it. She was at another one of the facilities that looked just like ADX, but wasn't. Didn't matter. She needed to figure out a way to avoid the soldier and his minion. Oh, she was going to make Orville pay if she survived this.

She heard the rotors picking up speed.

Over to her left was a parking lot. Maybe she could hide in between the cars.

Another burst. And another.

Boom! Boom! Colors, lights. Constant bombardment of shock waves. She wondered if the waves pushing through the air were additive or not. It didn't feel like it, but she knew it was.

She thought she heard a car horn, but with all the chaos around her, she knew hearing things was next. The parking lot was so far away. How would she start a car? She had never hotwired a vehicle before.

She slowed down and then just stopped. Anna's mouth felt like someone had shoved a cotton sock in it. Every breath got more and more shallow and drier. She could hardly breathe. She reached into her jumpsuit and pulled out her inhaler. She gave herself two good blasts and put it back in her pocket. Her throat opened a bit, but she couldn't keep doing what she was doing and expect to live if her lungs decided to close up on her.

The cars. She had to get to the cars. What brainchild put the parking lot so far away?

HONK!

WTF? Someone is honking at me! She saw the headlights of a car bouncing up and down on the lawn heading straight for her. She stumbled out of the way just as it came to a halt.

Hawking jumped out of the car and ran toward her. She deflected his reach and did a roundhouse kick toward his face. He blocked it. She threw another kick and he blocked it.

"What are you doing?" he asked. "I'm trying to save you from Orville."

She swung at him, and swung at him. Each time he either deflected her or stepped away.

"A little late for that. He already got what he deserved," Anna said.

"You killed him?"

She stopped. "Of course not!" She crossed her arms. "I broke his leg." What kind of a person did he take her for?

Hawking looked at her. "Oh, his leg." He shook his head. "You broke his leg." He crossed his arms and closed his eyes for an extra second. "Why didn't I think of that?"

"Besides," Anna asked, "what are you doing here?"

"What do you care?"

Anna lunged at him. He continued to deflect her punches until she tangled his legs and he fell. "Get up."

"Why?"

"So I can finish kicking your ass."

"Yes, I can see how well you're doing so far," he said.

"I can shoot you."

"I can deflect bullets," he said.

Anna's brain clicked shut for a second. "Really?"

He looked at her for a second and then stood. "No. There's not a lot of training offered on that particular skill."

"Take your car and get out of here." Anna wondered why she trusted him, but her anger subsided. She hated to admit that the problem was she *did* trust him.

"I can't leave without you," Hawking said.

"Oh, don't tell me you're here to rescue me too."

"No, I'm not, but I'm pretty certain that you're going to have a hard time explaining how you got free in the middle of a fireworks display when you were being transported off prison grounds by a couple of military guys."

"How do you know that?" *WTF? How does he know all that?*

"That you're running free without handcuffs, or other restraints?" He looked her up and down.

"No, all the other stuff." She walked right up to him. "How did you know I was being transferred? And the military guys?" She pushed against his chest.

Hawking grabbed her arms, reached around, and pulled the gun out from her waistband. He pushed her away.

He pointed the gun at her.

"So you are going to kill me."

"No, this is my way of showing you that I'm not." He twirled the gun in his hand so the grip was pointing up. He extended his hand to Anna. "I'm not here to kill you. But Orville is."

"News I could have used yesterday," Anna said.

"Look, you have to get out of here." An explosion of brilliant greens and yellows expanded up into the sky.

"Why does everyone want me to get into worse trouble than I already am? I'm surrendering to the Bureau of Prisons! I will surrender to the master chef at the prison if that's what it'll take. I'll even surrender to you." She put her wrists together again. "Please, put the cuffs on me and take me back inside."

What was wrong with people? Why would they want her to get into more trouble? Orville lied to her and she fell for it. That would never happen again. She would never flirt or even talk to a cute guy. Ever again.

Anna looked in the direction of the helipad. The Black Hawk was taking off. *Yes! They're leaving! I hope they get singed from the fire raining from the sky.* She turned to Hawking. "Okay, maybe I'll trust you enough to take me in."

"I'm not taking you in. I'm getting you out." He started walking back to his car.

"Where are you going?"

"Let's go, Anna." He motioned with his hand toward the car. "Your chariot awaits." Hawking held up the keys, but the jingle was lost in the surrounding detonations.

Anna couldn't help but check out the Black Hawk.

Should she have boarded the helicopter and accepted her fate? Giving up was easier when someone else made the choice for her.

The Black Hawk lifted off the helipad. *Good. So much for that.*

"What are you looking at?" Hawking asked.

What good was being caring and smart if you don't know enough to look around, Anna thought.

It lifted off a few feet from the ground, paused, spun until it was facing in their general direction and started to come at them.

She ran to Hawking and yanked the keys from his hand. "Hide! Don't let them see you!" She pulled open the door and started the car.

"Wait a minute!" Hawking ran to the car as Anna was just giving it gas. He managed to open the passenger door enough to get his foot in, but not his body. He held onto the car door as she picked up speed and the car started to bounce on the bumpy dry grass. "Let me in!"

"Get out!" Anna yelled.

"Let me in!" The car bounced. He almost lost his grip on the door.

"Let go of the door!"

"How fast are you going?"

They hit another bump. Maybe he'd fall off. "Not linearly! My rate of acceleration is accelerating."

"How fast?" Hawking yelled.

"About fifty."

"I'm not letting go!"

75

BLACK HAWK DOWN

Mossberg wore a headset designed to keep out the deafening sound of the Black Hawk, but it was worse with the parade of explosions. He put his arm through one of the straps hanging from the ceiling for balance. From his vantage point, the rockets still came in above them, but landed closer than he wanted. He could tell that Brandt was doing everything he could to keep the Black Hawk steady given the shock waves coming at them from the unending blasts.

He held a rifle in position as he looked for Prisoner X out in the wide-open area of the prison. This was going to be easy. He would take her out, throw her body into the helicopter, and they would still go out over the Atlantic to dispose of it. This op was never meant to be complicated, and he would put it back on its rails if it killed him.

Brandt was still giving him complaints about the incoming rockets, but Mossberg had learned to ignore him years ago. Brandt was an excellent pilot. He would hold up his end of the op.

In the headset, he could hear Cheyenne Mountain asking Brandt for an update. Brandt didn't answer.

———

Anna's palms were sweating. This was going nowhere good, and she still felt foggy from the lack of oxygen due to her asthma. She had the car going as fast as she was comfortable with, and that meant about 70 miles per hour.

Hawking still hung on. Every time he tried to get in she sped up, throwing his balance off. She didn't need him in the car second guessing her.

Could he die? Maybe. He seemed knowledgeable about more than just medicine. Maybe he was knowledgeable enough to hold on tight. Whoever he was.

She looked in the rearview mirror. The helicopter's running lights were getting larger with each passing second. At least the copter didn't have its headlights on. That would have blinded her. What could she do as a first pass at shaking them? The rockets were coming down parallel to her.

"Where the hell are we going?" Hawking asked from his perch.

"Don't worry about it!"

The helicopter should have been overhead. She took her eyes off the rearview mirror for a second and it looked like they'd disappeared. The overpowering sound of detonations covered the whirr of the rotors as she frantically searched for her pursuers.

To her left, on the driver's side, she saw them. The helicopter was just above eye level and parallel to her. The soldier was pointing a rifle at her. She slammed on the brakes without thinking and the bullet meant for her blew out her windshield. She went from 70 to 50 in a few seconds.

"What are you doing?" Hawking yelled. His speed was now relative to hers so he could leverage his balance. He climbed in as she sped up again. "Do you understand how this works? He's going to...what are you doing?"

Anna reached the end of USP Florence High, slowed down into a left turn, and then sped up.

"You're going into the kill zone." Hawking braced his hand against the dashboard. "Do you realize that? You're going to get us both killed," Hawking said.

The Black Hawk slowed down and stopped as she went behind them, entering the corridor between the prisons where the rockets continued to land. She avoided crater after crater and let the car slow down until she turned it around and drove the car up to the fence of the northern most facility.

"What do we do?" Anna asked Hawking.

"Damned if I know." He turned to her. "We are in the kill zone! Do you know why they call it a kill zone? Because we can be killed in it."

Anna wanted to respond but wasn't sure what to do next, much less what to say.

"We need to get out of here," he said, craning his neck far afield. "There are craters as far as the eye can see." A rocket landed to their left and sent clumps of dirt flying onto the car. "Get us out of here!"

Anna stepped on the gas and went back the way they came.

"Ohmigod! Where are you going? Not back there!"

"Where do you want me to go?"

"Anywhere, but back to the guys with the guns," Hawking said.

The Black Hawk hovered in the space between the two facilities. Anna swerved the car left and right in varying amplitudes so the soldier couldn't predict where she would be next. She hoped.

"Anna?" Hawking asked. Her wave pattern was converging.

"Anna, where are you going?"

Later, she tried to remember what kinds of things he said to her while they were in the car. All she knew was that the gap between the ground and the helicopter was narrow, and even though the gap between the two prisons was sizable, she had her target. The Black Hawk was getting closer as she continued to speed up.

Time to play chicken.

"Anna!" Hawking yelled.

She sped under the Black Hawk just as the car hit a bump in the grass. The car slammed into the left wheel of the helicopter, denting the roof behind Anna and Hawking. She knew something bad had happened to the helicopter but couldn't stop long enough to find out.

———

The helicopter listed to one side and Brandt righted it before it became uncontrollable. "We have got to get out of here! We've been here too long and she's leading us by the nose."

"Not yet. If we don't get her in this next pass then we'll retreat," Mossberg said. *Over my dead body.*

———

Anna thought she saw the helicopter move to one side, but she couldn't be sure. What she did see scared her: the Black Hawk righted itself, spun on its axis, and faced her again.

"I could use some ideas right about now," she said.

"Go back the way we came and blow through the fence." Hawking paused for a second. "No, that won't work."

"They'll just follow us. I know." Anna slammed on the brakes. "Do we run?"

"Are you crazy? Keep moving."

A bullet cut through the roof and penetrated the floor between them. Anna floored the gas and the car took off again.

"Where are they?" she asked.

Hawking loosened his seat belt and stuck his head out.

"Coming after us."

Great.

Anna took off for ADX.

Something was wrong. She could hear the rotors.

Boom! Something hit the roof. *Boom!*

The dent become more pronounced now that the Black Hawk was purposely hitting the car roof so it would lose forward momentum.

Anna refused to let physics help them out. She turned the car toward ADX. The fence would gain her some time. They couldn't come that close while she was skimming the wire wall.

Boom! The dent was getting worse. What the hell did she do to deserve this?

Boom! Wait.

The fence.

She was already past the northwest guard tower. She pulled away enough to give them room to strike.

Boom! She let the car drift to the left.

Boom!

"Keep them busy!" she yelled.

"What?"

"Distract the pilot!"

Hawking undid his seat belt and stuck his torso out the passenger window. The helicopter fell behind and then caught up.

She hoped Hawking shot at the pilot as they approached, but he had to come back in once it was over them.

Boom!

The helicopter fell behind again. Hawking shot at the pilot. The Black Hawk swerved, sped up, and came down on them again.

Hawking took a glimpse at where they were heading. "What are you doing? Are you going to crash us into the guard tower?"

"Distract the pilot!"

They were getting closer and closer to the fence.

And running out of distance to the tower.

"Where are they?" she asked.

"Catching up!" Hawking shot toward the pilot again.

BOOM!

Anna swerved the car just another few feet toward the fence as the Black Hawk lifted off again.

She slammed on the brakes enough to slow down to allow for a hard turn to her right and then she floored the gas again.

The Black Hawk's left front tire hit the fence and got caught in the barbed wire. The helicopter stopped all forward motion almost immediately, and flipped in the direction of the prison, pivoting over the fence and crashing down into the ground on the other side.

The destruction of the Black Hawk was audible only because they were close enough to it that even the rockets raining devastation couldn't compete with the sound of the fireball.

76

TMI

"Stop the car," Hawking said.

Anna's hands gripped the steering wheel so tightly that she might have cracked it had she been strong enough. The car bounced over and over again as every rock and bump became an obstacle the car couldn't roll over fast enough. Her foot was in place on the gas pedal, and it wasn't moving.

Hawking put his seatbelt back on.

Before them was the medium-security facility. They were heading straight for it. He looked at the speedometer.

70 miles per hour. Those buildings were going to be a problem.

"Anna."

She wasn't reacting. Damn it! He shook the steering wheel. "Anna!"

She startled out of her focus and gave a short cry. "You have to stop the car. Anna, stop the..." she slammed on the brakes, "car."

She unbuckled her seat belt, and almost fell out of the car when she swung open the door. Hawking undid his seat belt as well and ran around to the driver's side.

Anna kneeled on the ground vomiting.

He knelt next to her and put his arm around her shoulders. She let out a low moan and started to cry. He moved her head to his shoulder, and just held her.

———

What have I done? Oh, what have I done? I just killed two men. They're not going home tonight.

Anna felt the same hole in her chest she felt the day she shot Donnell. She had never killed anyone before and even Donnell's death wasn't deliberate. The gun had simply gone off.

She chose. This time she chose and she took the lives of the men in the helicopter. She and Hawking were alive because she decided that their lives were worth more than the lives of those other men.

She chose. No one else.

Did she choose well?

In the dark warmth of Hawking's chest, she lost all sense of time. Through the corner of her eye, she could see the dry grass on which they were crouched but still only smelled gunpowder and burnt paper. In the rocket's red glare, Hawking smiled at her. She laughed, and cried, and wiped a tear with her dirty hand.

"You alright?" he asked. He almost yelled over the sound of the shelling.

"Why are you here? Why didn't you let them take me away?" Anna asked.

"Because they would have killed you. And that's not allowed."

"Why did you save me? Maybe it would have been for the best," she said.

"Stop feeling sorry for yourself. I didn't save you. Someone else decided you were worth saving."

"And who the hell was that?" She pushed away and pulled herself up by leaning on the car to stand while she steadied her legs.

"It was you, Anna." He smiled at her again. "It was you.

"Welcome back."

———

Safe in the car, Anna was driving again. There was no way she was going to let Hawking drive. She trusted him, but she had no way to verify his intentions. She wiped away a tear every so often, but she was speeding to her new destination: the helipad.

Time to ask Orville a few questions.

She saw him still on the ground writhing in pain. She went at him at full speed and slammed on the brakes just before she would have run him over. She jumped out of the car.

"Oh, Orville, poor thing," she took long steps to him, "it looks like you're in pain."

Orville lay on the ground shivering. How long had it been since she broke his leg at the knee cap? Five minutes? Couldn't be more than that. The pain was still fresh. Hawking remained silent. Orville looked over at him and croaked tiny sounds of pain.

By his shirt collar, Anna dragged Orville to the middle of the helipad on top of the line connecting the two bars to complete the H. She let go and he fell a short distance on his injured arm.

"You see that man over there?" Anna pointed at Hawking. "He doesn't like you." She gave Orville her complete attention. "I don't like you either." She slapped his cheeks with both hands.

Hawking walked over and stood on the edge of the helipad circle. He put his hands in his pockets. He looked relaxed.

Anna held her hand out to Hawking. He gave her his gun. She took it, giving the appearance of weighing it, and then stuck the gun on Orville's other knee. Orville pulled the knee out of the way.

"Good. You're scared. You should be. Who are you, and who sent you? We don't have a lot of time, so don't think too long," Anna said. Orville shook. Anna was sure he wasn't faking it. He reached for the gun, but she moved it away without a thought.

"I was trying to help you," he said. His words came out in staccato. His pain had a rhythm.

"Those guys, your friends, sure showed me how much they cared." She pointed the gun at his kneecap again. "Who sent you?"

"No one. I wanted to help you and they came to me." Orville stared down doing his best not to focus on Hawking.

"Really?" Hawking asked. "So you don't remember shutting down the power? And trying to kill me?"

Orville shook his head. "I was shot. Someone tried to kill you, and I got shot instead."

Anna gave him a sympathetic look. "That's true. I think I'm going to cry." She fired off a shot that missed Orville's leg. He screamed from the inadvertent movement of his left leg. "Damn. I missed." She was getting tired of this. She clutched him by the collar. "I am so fed up with people lying to me, and telling me that they feel for me, and that I have a destiny." She put the gun against his head. "Since you don't want to tell me anything..."

She felt Hawking's hand on her hand. She wanted to scream. How dare he stop her? Who the hell was Orville that he could decide to ruin what little she had of her life? Who was Hawking?

"Stop," Hawking said.

"Let go."

"Stop. Anna, stop."

"Let go!"

"You're not him."

She let go of the gun, and Hawking took it out of her hand. "You'd regret this. It doesn't feel like you would, but I can tell you within a few minutes you'll change your mind and there's no going back."

She shoved Orville onto his back.

"Besides," Hawking said, "you have to go."

Anna stood up. Not that again. "I'm not going anywhere." She took the gun out of Hawking's grip and pointed it at him.

"So you're going to kill me instead?" Hawking asked.

Anna felt the weight of the gun in her hand, and her anger through her arm. "Who are you? Your answer is as good as his."

"I'm just a country doctor doing his duty."

She pushed the gun against his chest.

"You're not going to like it." He gazed into her eyes. "I was sent here to kill you."

77

BIRD IN FLIGHT

Anna took a step back. "All this is a sham?" She pointed the gun at Orville and then at Hawking. "Is that why you don't want me to kill him? So the two of you can find a new way to kill me?"

"No, Anna." Hawking stepped forward and she poked him in the chest with the gun. He put his hands up. "This is not a sham. The man who sent him sent me."

"No, he didn't," Orville said.

Hawking glared at him. "If you want to die, keep talking."

"Are you telling me the truth?" Anna asked.

"Only you can answer that question. I can only tell you what I know." She raised the gun a little higher. "Orville and I have the same master, only not really. Our boss doesn't know I work for someone else. Someone who wants you, who needs you, alive."

"Why?"

"How the hell should I know? I get paid to do something and I do it. I was paid to make sure you got out. If you play your cards right, you get to go on an all-expense paid trip...to Vancouver."

"What?" Anna asked.

"What?" Orville said. "Vancouver?"

Hawking gritted his teeth. "Keep talking." He turned back to Anna. "The only problem is you can't take that car."

"Why not?"

"What do you think?" Hawking asked.

"Everyone knows it?"

"Ah. You really are smart."

"Then how do I...?"

"There's a hotel up the road. There's a car, clothing, and money waiting for you." There was an explosion in the truck area to the north. "It's all yours. Kill me; don't kill me. It doesn't matter. You have to go."

She put the gun down. "So you're still helping me?"

Hawking put down his hands. "Do you really want to stay here and go through this again? Do you think that the people who want you dead are going to stop just because you broke lover boy's leg?"

Anna's cheeks got hot. She pointed the gun back at him. "I take it back," he said.

"So I'm going to walk?" Anna asked.

"Something like that."

"Something like what?"

Hawking grimaced. "You're going to take that jumpsuit off and walk, jog, run, whatever, north as fast as you can through the golf course, past the development, and to the Super 8 hotel. There's a car with license plate AWH-CPP. There are clothes in the trunk, money in the glove compartment, and some snacks in the back. The snacks are a little old, but I think you get the picture."

"What was that license plate?"

"Anna Wodehouse dash Carpenter Poole." He made a license plate just for her? That didn't make any sense.

"Who wants me to go to Vancouver?"

"They'll find you. Don't worry. They always do."

"What if I don't want them to find me?" she asked.

"You can deal with that when they find you."

"I'm not going to Vancouver."

"Your decision once you leave here. Go to Hawaii. I hear the prisons are really nice there."

If she shot both of these men, she might get a medal.

And another cell in isolation. *No Human Contact.* It wasn't appealing.

How would she survive? What was going on? Who wanted her out bad enough they would destroy the prison? Who thought of her enough to send someone to keep her alive?

"Think about this all you want, but you have to go. Take off the jumpsuit," Hawking said.

"But, what are you going to do?"

"Oh, I'll just sit here and keep Orville company. You know how that is. We'll have some man talk. A heart-to-heart."

Anna looked at the two men who meant something to her for the last few days, and knew that Hawking was right. If she stayed, they would come for her again. Maybe this time they would succeed. They would kill her, and she still wouldn't know why.

"Why am I taking off the jumpsuit at two o'clock in the morning?"

Hawking looked at his watch. She would have checked her cell phone. "It's almost two twenty. Take off the jumpsuit."

"Why do I have to run naked through the fields like Tinker Bell banned from Neverland?"

"Why? Because you look like a highway cone, and the authorities will find you from your glow. What do you think? What you have in your favor is that none of the people who meet you will think you came from an all-male prison.

"Now take it off," Hawking said.

This was the moment of truth. Did she believe him and run? Or would she disbelieve him and stay? She gave Orville a glance. She couldn't stay. She shouldn't go.

But she was going to go.

She handed the gun back to Hawking and unzipped her jumpsuit. She slipped out of it, felt the cold wash over her, embarrassed that both Hawking and Orville saw her in her underwear. She slipped the shoes back on and rubbed her arms.

"Thank you," she said, "I think." She started to run to the north.

"Wait!" Hawking called out to her and she came back. He reached into his pocket and pulled something out that looked like thread.

A necklace? He unclasped it and held it out to her.

"Am I running or doing a runway set?"

"Shut up and turn around."

She felt the warmth of his hands on the nape of her neck and heard the explosions erupt around her. She was going to have a killer headache after all this.

The charm on the end of the necklace was a silver bird in flight. She wasn't much for jewelry. Her aunt and uncle had given her rings, necklaces, and watches over the years, but she always managed to lose them. Anna always told them that even the jewelry didn't want to be around her.

The bird was beautiful. And someone who was not related to her gave it to her. She gave Hawking a hug and took off in the direction of the fireworks.

78

PARTY'S OVER

Hawking stood there looking at the scantily clad Anna Wodehouse run toward freedom, as long as no one else saw her undress. He had done his job. She was on her way.

He heard a sound at his feet.

Orville was trying to drag himself away, but every move had to be sending unbelievable pain through his body.

Hawking smiled. *Good.*

Hawking walked over as the fireworks continued to light up the sky and blow up in the two main triangles that constituted USP Florence. As distractions went this was a doozy. He would remember this one until the day he died. Which might be today.

He sat down on the helipad, but far enough away from Orville that the injured man couldn't grab the gun from him. It wouldn't do to screw up this close to the finish line.

"So, Orville," Hawking said, "how's it going?"

Orville's shirt was stained with sweat and his arms shook.

"That leg has got to hurt like hell." Hawking gave Orville's leg a loose kick. Every so often one of the fireworks would go up instead of out and lit the sky with brilliant whites, greens, and reds. He hadn't seen fireworks since he was a young boy. He didn't know how much he'd missed them until now.

"You know, Orville, the first chance I got I ran a DNA test on you like any good father would on his daughter's boyfriend. Now, while I'm not her father, I am nothing if not an attentive friend." He gave Orville's leg another kick. "You're not really that good at this, and today kind of proves it." He motioned behind them with his gun. "I mean, even she saw through you when you needed her to believe you the most."

He thought about some of the assignments he had been on that didn't go well. Luck was with him then. Luck was with him now.

"The General is going to know you did this," Orville said through clenched teeth.

"Oh, the General is just going to know that you failed him. Imagine that," Hawking said. "What you don't realize is that the last few days of your life were spent with a woman the likes of whom you will never see again, even if the General let you live."

Orville looked pale. Was it the pain or thoughts of explaining how he got taken? He had known that Hawking was not the second man, yet he didn't report it. Why not? Hawking learned not to worry about the things he couldn't control.

"Anna Wodehouse is going to either head straight to Vancouver, or somewhere else, but the people who need her will find her." Hawking turned to face Orville. "They always do, and I just made sure of it."

Hawking stood. His muscles were sore. He had to get back to his car so he could get out of here and to his new ride. The one with the unregistered plates and the new identity.

He couldn't afford to be caught on the prison grounds now. The controller to the fireworks was in the car and that would be a bit of a giveaway.

"You, on the other hand, did one thing right. You killed Jekyll. I guess Hyde was next on your list, but you ran out of time once the Black Hawk showed up. Otherwise," Hawking waved the gun back and forth for emphasis, "you screwed up. What you did was unconscionable. You led her along. You broke her heart. Did you see the look of hurt and disappointment in her eyes when she looked at you?"

"Screw you," Orville said.

"If she had wanted to kill you, she would have done it even when I tried to stop her." Hawking pointed the gun toward the ground. It was getting late, but he sometimes enjoyed letting his victims stew in their own juices for a while. "You knew she was never going to kill you. She might have blown a hole in your other leg, or missed a few times, but she would never, ever, have killed you.

"Now, me, on the other hand," Hawking said as he pointed the gun at Orville's head and pulled the trigger.

The fireworks stopped.

Party's over.

79

SOLAR SHARDS

Terrell Garrison wasn't sure what to do next. Should he confront the man who just shot the correctional officer or continue hiding among the solar panels to the west of the helipad? Or should he just shoot him?

———

When Terrell had left FCI Florence, he'd had every intention of getting to the maximum-security building to the north of ADX. His trek up the tree-lined asphalt road from FCI started out well, even with the falling incendiaries, smoke, and fire, but long before he got to the corner he was out of breath. Every detonation sent a shock wave that hurt his shoulder and threatened to knock him over. He finally started to walk in the hope that the rockets would not come down on him. Given the dearth of craters in certain areas, he felt confident enough that he just had to stay on point.

That was until he heard the shots coming from the helipad. He ran in that direction until he saw an orange jumpsuit head in his direction. He pulled out his gun and threw himself on the ground. The patchy grass did nothing to hide him — the prison grounds were very flat — but in the midst of all the confusion he had to stay still enough to become invisible.

An inmate got out? How the hell did that happen? He would sort it out later. The reputation of the residents here did nothing to allay his fears. Terrell prepared to shoot the inmate when he got close enough not to miss.

The white puffy smoke made it impossible for him to get a good view. The man had to come closer. He hoped it wasn't somebody who was in for something like espionage because they were the least dangerous of the inmates, but Terrell was going to shoot him anyway. This was, at least, an escape. Terrell couldn't allow that to happen and the carnage around him was proof that whoever these guys were didn't care about the loss of human life.

The inmate stopped and bent over taking a breath.

Terrell squeezed the trigger.

He pulled the gun back when a car came between him and the inmate. *Damn!* He couldn't see who came out, but after a while the prisoner must have jumped in the driver's seat because the other person ran and leaped onto the car holding onto the passenger door like he was riding a super-powered skateboard.

He still couldn't get a clean shot. If he went back for reinforcements, those bozos might be gone by the time he got back. He decided to wait.

———

The Black Hawk flew past Terrell toward the car. He almost got up and ran after it, but his shoulder was in complete control of his legs. He watched from the sidelines as the helicopter caught up to the car, and hovered at the gap between the two facilities like a hawk waiting for its prey. Whoever was driving that car had ice running in their veins. Even Terrell wouldn't have driven into the gap.

Was there anything he could do? It didn't seem like it.

The car flew back out and struck the helicopter's left front wheel.

Now they were fighting back. If the Black Hawk had been armed, this would have been a short battle.

He then saw the chase along ADX, and in the dark, he didn't have any sense of depth. He didn't see the fence catching up on the Black Hawk. He did see the passenger in the car firing at the helicopter, but that was an exercise in futility.

The car made a sudden turn and put distance between it and the prison as the helicopter pitched to one side, got caught in the fence, and then slammed into the ground before exploding in a fireball.

Terrell pushed himself into a kneeling position and stared at the fire burning within the confines of the maximum-security prison.

Something had to be done. Now good people were dying. Whoever those guys were, Terrell was going to put an end to it.

———

He saw the car speed away and then stop. Something happened, but it seemed to be resolved in a short time. The two people conversed, got back in the car, and raced back to the helipad. They drove right past him.

His shoulder throbbed; his head was a knot of anxiety. Terrell was going to need physical therapy when this was all over.

———

Ohmigod. It's Anna.

From behind the solar panels Terrell saw the prisoner take off his jumpsuit and the sight of panties and a bra stopped him cold. How many female prisoners could they have in this place?

The destruction of the most secure prison in the United States was all about helping Anna Wodehouse escape? Terrell couldn't work out how any of the evening's events made any sense, but he was in it up to his neck now. He took his eyes off her for a second, and when he looked back, he saw her running into the darkness.

He decided to do what he did best: he was taking down her

accomplice. He didn't agree with her being here, but there was no way he was going to shoulder her escape as something acceptable.

The man was talking to an officer who was on the ground in obvious pain.

Then the man shot him.

The bombardment stopped. The silence muffled his hearing. Even his thoughts felt suppressed. The air felt thinner as it didn't push against him anymore.

The man walked to the car Anna had just finished driving.

"FBI! Put your hands up!" Terrell stepped out from behind the panels. He was a good distance away, but he could take the man down no problem. Even with just the one hand holding his Glock.

It was amazing what adrenaline could do.

"Don't shoot!" the man yelled and started shooting around Terrell.

The panels around him exploded into a million shards. Terrell jumped back into the shadows to avoid being shredded.

The man entered the car and continued to shoot through the passenger window until his was out of range.

As the pieces of solar panels fell to the ground Terrell thought, *This is not going to look good in my report.*

There was no point wasting bullets by firing at the receding vehicle. With any luck, the National Guard out front would stop him.

Terrell leaned against the wall behind him as everything around him began to spin. *Oh, please. No more hospital visits.*

PART V

AFTERMATH

80

LOSS OF LIFE

His men were dead. Palma had known them for years. The home-coming he'd planned for them after they returned would now be an unexpected wake. He'd already called their families and promised to call back with details about what happened.

The details would have to change. No one knew Anna Wode-house was there except the people who had to know, and they were going to keep this to themselves. The few guards who had dealt with her would get an early retirement or a transfer to another facility and would be briefed on the importance of silence. They would be reminded of the prison sentence they would receive if they forgot how important it was to forget.

Brandt was a great pilot and a loyal patriot. Mossberg was all that and more. He had run ops around the world that others would have run from and many did.

"Sir?" The young man stood by the door of Palma's office in Fort Meade.

"Yes?" Palma asked.

"The Weather Service. The alerts?"

"Leave them here," Palma said.

"Sir, they're in your email inbox. I just get copies as a reminder."

"Right." Palma nodded at the man. He had already forgotten his name. He would have to ask him later. Palma took pride in remembering the names of the people under him.

"You do have a call waiting."

"Thank you." Palma gave a small wave. "And close the door."

"Yes, sir."

Click.

Palma picked up the phone. "How can I help you, Senator?"

"What the hell happened last night?"

Palma had not heard the Senator incensed before. He bit his tongue as he thought of tearing the Senator a new one. "A Black Hawk crashed at USP Florence last night. Here we're all thinking that it's an attack to free one of the terrorists we have there and it turns out to be a transfer gone wrong. The Bureau of Prisons doesn't know anything about a transfer, and the warden says he was just responding to orders from DOD. What the hell is going on?"

"Well, sir..."

"Don't 'well, sir' me. Was this an attack, an escape...Whatever the hell it is you had better have some Intel for me because this is a big black eye for us."

Palma stood up and gripped the phone. "Senator, in the first place, there are things you don't want to know about. Secondly, the prisoner transfer was being carried out by us." He took a quick breath. "This was a transfer for rendition to ensure that we would stay within the confines of U.S. law. If you insist, I can give you the details, but I can assure you that the details are something you don't want to know about."

Bigelow was silent. "What happened?"

"Sir, I am still getting in reports."

"There were millions of dollars in damage to the prison."

"The loss of life," Palma decided to wait for Bigelow to finish. "The loss of life was minimal. My men took the biggest hit."

"I'm sorry. I know how loyal your people are. And how loyal you are in return," Bigelow said.

"Yes, sir."

"So, you are confirming that this was an op gone wrong."

"Yes, sir, confirming it to you. We are already working with the Bureau of Prisons' press office to release only as much as necessary."

"Have you made your calls?"

"Yes. I called the two families as soon as I had heard that the op had completed unsuccessfully," Palma said.

"Unsuccessfully?" Bigelow exhaled. "Now that's the understatement of the year. You just got your ass handed to you. Now you have a dangerous criminal on the loose and you had better handle this as above board as possible with the FBI."

Palma gritted his teeth. He would look for Wodehouse himself. He had teams. "Yes, sir. I'm already in touch with the proper departments and we are handling this as carefully as possible."

"You understand that you will not be looking for this man alone?"

"Senator Bigelow, the best thing you could allow me to do is have my own men look for this terrorist. We will find him before he does anything."

"You get on the phone with the Bureau. You tell them everything they need to know. Do you understand?" Bigelow asked.

Palma stopped before saying the wrong thing. *Let the man finish. It doesn't matter anyway.*

"Everything," Bigelow said.

"Understood, Senator. We have a good relationship with the Bureau. I know who to call in counter-terrorism." *Yes, I know who to call at the Bureau. No one.* "Please, don't be concerned about the media. There is no way to stop them reporting the event, but they will get palatable details."

"Damn straight. We don't need to start a panic. The damn conspiracy theorists are going to have a field day with this one," Bigelow said.

Palma was counting on it. Let the masses distract themselves while he got his job done. The days of real information were almost gone. The United States was in the age of reality TV and distraction ruled. Even if he told the media the truth no one would notice or care past the first news cycle.

"Not to worry. We have experience with this."

"I'm not worried! You had better worry. Why were you transferring a terrorist legally in a U.S. prison to another country for questioning?"

"When we capture him, I'll be able to let you know everything, Senator. For now, you are better off just letting me handle it."

Bigelow started to object.

"Senator, I promise, you will get a full briefing. We will have this over within a few days at most."

Palma hung up. A few days. HALON would be out of his hair.

If he never heard about it again, it would be too soon.

He picked up his phone and called his assistant.

"Rogers."

"I need to talk to one of the available security teams. I have someone they need to start looking for. Small team," Palma said.

"I'll have someone come down right away."

Palma hung up. The FBI would get in the way. Anna Wodehouse had to be found, and disposed of. He would never be able to keep her alive now. As long as she had been kept apart from population he could let her live. Possibly used later in ways he preferred not to think of. Now, she was a liability for the simple reason that she was still breathing.

His contact had not contacted him. Andrew must have been on a regular check-in schedule and at this point he was late. Very late. Is that why they hadn't called Palma?

He sat down at his terminal and found the email sitting in his inbox. The one he cared about was the report from the investigation on Andrew. He hit Page Down until he found the parts that cut to the reason Andrew was now dead.

Andrew was not the leak. He had been set up. The audit logs showed, without a shadow of a doubt, that the files given to Magnolia Sams had been routed to Andrew's machine without his knowledge. The transfer had happened when Andrew was off-base, done by someone who had knowledge of critical systems, where the bodies were buried, and an understanding of how to hide better than anyone else in the minefield that was the critical systems of the U.S. Intelligence community.

Palma cursed at himself. Only one man came to mind, but he had to be dead.

81

MERITORIOUS INSUBORDINATION

Terrell lay in bed in his neat, but dusty, apartment and wondered. His thin, mustard bedsheets covered his legs and waist. The wide-open curtains let in what little sunlight could squeeze through his less-than-adequate view. He'd tried reading, but his mind wouldn't let him focus. There was probably some sports on TV, but he wasn't up to it. He was a man of few hobbies, but preferred to be as absorbed as possible whenever possible with a few exceptions.

Today was an exception.

The phone rang. It was on the left side of his bed so he had to sit up to answer it, and almost dropped it when he did. The sheet tangled him a little, making the slide a touch treacherous as he did his best not to lean on his left shoulder. His left arm was still in a sling, and still in pain. A bottle of unopened prescription painkillers sat next to an untouched glass of water.

"You know, I think you're one of the only agents I know who is both in trouble and being recognized."

Tolsen was his usual pain-in-the-ass self, but Terrell hoped that he hadn't let him down too hard.

"I'm sure I don't know what you mean," Terrell said.

"Right. Your report is making the round in all sorts of unusual places. It reads like Tom Clancy."

Terrell almost sighed. "What do you want? I'm on administrative leave and I'm not getting paid." Terrell completed his slide off the bed and stood. "And my shoulder hurts."

Days like this he wished he had a girlfriend to take care of him. The problem was he didn't want one the other days.

"The bad news: you're still on leave. The good news: your pay has been reinstated. How's that sound?"

"I like it very much. It makes me feel like I'm being laid off, just not right away."

Terrell wondered why Tolsen bothered calling. He would be getting the letter with his latest status soon enough. He was grateful to have gotten away from the authorities as soon as he did. The more questions asked the easier it would be for the people asking the questions to poke into the dark corners of his story. There were too many dark corners.

"I thought you might like to know that the man you didn't get to shoot was an employee at the prison. Only he wasn't an employee at the prison."

"What are you talking about? You mean they thought he was an employee, and let him in? So they don't know who he is?"

"You got it. Bed rest certainly does clear your mind," Tolsen said. "It turns out that a body had been found a few days ago, but ID couldn't be made. Well, they made it. The dead man's name is David Hawking. Doctor David Hawking. He was supposed to have started at the prison a few weeks ago, but no one noticed he was dead. Or that the guy who showed up wasn't him."

"Hawking had no family who noticed he was missing?"

"Nope. No kids, wife died a few years ago. A loner."

An innocent bystander had been killed to make it possible for Anna Wodehouse to escape. Terrell had been taken after all. He trusted her. He thought she was innocent. He guessed it was true: no one was innocent. Least of all a woman with a troubled past and a definitely troubled future.

"I know I shouldn't ask," Terrell just couldn't get aspects of his case off his mind, "but what's the status on Magnolia Sams?"

"Magnolia Sams? I thought you had heard," Tolsen said.

Terrell gritted his teeth. Another notch on his soul. "She's dead. She never made it to her arraignment. The DC Jail was not a good place for her to be."

"Has the senator been told?"

"Yes. As you would expect, he wasn't happy."

Terrell was sure neither was Magnolia's family. How many more people would he let down?

"He knows your status. He's one of the only things standing between you and the street."

"Oh, please fire me. I'll lose my pension, but I'll make ten times more in the private sector."

"Yeah, I know you won't mind selling your soul for that."

"My soul has been on the chopping block for years. Make me an offer."

"Okay, how's this? You're getting a commendation. The work you did at the prison saved lives."

Terrell started to object. *Magnolia Sams.*

"Yeah, yeah, I know, 'just doing my job, blah, blah, blah'. I know you did your job. And you did a great job. It would have been better if you had stopped the damn rockets from going on for so long, but I'll bust your chops about that when you're feeling better," Tolsen said.

"When the commendation letter arrives, I'll use it as a sleeping aid. There's nothing that puts me down faster than people telling me how great a job I did."

Yeah, great job. Magnolia Sams. This was why he hated cases like this. The guilty parties were surrounded by innocent people who tried to do the right thing, and failed.

Failure. A stabbing sensation pierced his midsection. If only it was hunger.

Magnolia Sams. That name would permeate his consciousness now. He might need some sleeping pills after all.

"I knew you wouldn't be happy about that. It won't save your job when push comes to shove. What would you like me to do?" Tolsen asked.

"How about a raise? Push me up a grade or two." *Damn it. And Anna ran.* Visions of that night at the Supermax flashed like a bulb about to burn out. *She ran. She got away.*

"Talk to you later, Terrell. Feel better."

Is she still a victim caught in the crossfire, or has she become a willing participant? Maybe she always was.

"Yeah."

Magnolia Sams. She would have died a day or so ago. Her family was probably already notified. *We regret to inform you...*

"Oh, and what did you think of your package?" Tolsen asked.

"What package?"

———

FedEx showed up at his apartment later that day and dropped off a large box. He opened the dust-covered corrugated cardboard and found a torn-up box addressed to Prisoner Someone-or-other at ADX Florence. Every inmate had a number and Anna was no exception. The shipping label had her number removed.

Why had the prison shipped this to him? He grabbed a fresh pair of examination gloves from a box in his bathroom. This wasn't the first time evidence that should have gone to forensics ended up on his doorstep.

How did this get to her? There was no return address. The FedEx label had a number. He would have forensics look into who officially sent the package, but he was also sure it would be a dead end.

Someone had torn the box open after it had gone through the prison x-ray machine, and Terrell was going to make sure they were held accountable. The condition of the evidence was abysmal and there was no reason for it.

He would make sure that the lab would get everything he was sent.

Anna Wodehouse.

Would he have to hold her at gunpoint to get her to come in?

He opened the box and pulled out a single item. The massive amount of stuffing surrounding it made it hard to figure out what it was, but it did have some of its original look.

A stuffed squirrel?

82

MORPHINE DRIP

2 *Days Earlier*
3:15 *a.m.*

Anna pulled up to St. Thomas More Hospital about twenty minutes northwest of USP Florence in Canon City. She thought that Hawking, in his wisdom on driving cross-country, would have procured either a very fast car or a long-distance-capable car. What she found was a 2008 used Toyota Corolla of unknown color with a big attitude. And that attitude had a definite smell.

The area just outside the ER was lit up almost as much as the prison was about an hour earlier. She had arrived after the state police and the emergency vehicles had already piled into the parking lot, and sat in the car screwing up her courage. She was sure that the blinking lights and occasional siren bursts were waking the locals.

Was she going to go into the ER where all the police were? There was a definite possibility that they knew what she looked like, and that there would be an APB out on her.

She had been listening to the news on her scratchy reception AM-only radio and wondered how anyone could own or use such a primitive car. The reports of an event at the prison were front and center (pushing out the news on the latest quilting contest, or bear attack, she was sure), but there was no discussion of an escape or a manhunt. Or womanhunt.

To some extent, that made sense. They would know that she might be listening so keeping her in the dark was a great strategy. If she had half a brain, she would already be on her way west. It was a long drive, and she was going to have to stop often enough to fill up, and get snacks. Maybe even pizza.

No. For that she would wait until she could return to New York. No point wasting her time eating less than acceptable pizza.

Canon City was a sleepy place. The odds were good that every last person on payroll was out tonight. Volunteer firefighters, local, and state police. There were more National Guard around than anyone else.

She also knew that he had to be in there and she had to see him.

———

If anyone bothered checking the hospital security cameras later, they would have seen dozens of people coming in and going out. Some to smoke, others to wait for orders on what they should do next. St. Thomas, being one of the only hospitals within reasonable distance from ADX, was the default ER in cases like this. Emergency services would not use the prison's facilities. The grounds looked like the surface of the moon, meaning like Swiss cheese, and since an attack on the prison meant a concerted effort to get in they had to keep everyone out. The National Guard would take care of that part.

All the potential victims of the attack, and when all was said and done there were only a few, were taken to St. Thomas More.

Anna, wearing a blond wig, ran to the registration desk.

"I am so sorry," she said as she pushed a state trooper out of the way, "but I heard all about it on the radio." She gave herself a slight southern accent. "I'm from out of town, but I have a friend who was here to visit with me and the nice people at the prison told me he was sent here."

The duty nurse looked up the name and directed her to one of the rooms off to the side.

The officer she had pushed escorted her. While she felt her palms sweat she touched his right arm once, then twice as he led her to the room.

There he was. "Oh, thank you so much, Officer." Anna didn't look at him. She wanted to remain a blur.

There asleep on the bed was Special Agent-in-Charge Terrell Garrison. Was he unconscious? She pulled his chart. *More illegible writing! Have these people not heard of tablets?*

Terrell started to groan. He was waking up. She moved over to the side of the bed. As he awoke his eyes went wide and he started to call out.

She kissed him. He lay back.

"What are you doing here?" he asked.

"I'm, I'm," she said taking in the details of his face, "not sure." She held his hand. "When I got to the hotel, I asked if you were staying there. Since you came to visit I thought for sure you would stay local and the Super 8 was as close as you could get without sleeping in your car."

"What are you doing here?"

"I had to see how you were doing."

"Anna, you destroyed the prison."

"I had nothing," she lowered her voice, "to do with what happened tonight. I was being handed over to a couple of guys in fatigues who were going to kill me."

"So you killed them?"

"That wasn't my intention."

How could she explain this to him? Everything she said was just going to sound worse and worse.

"They were trying to kill me."

"Anna, they're going to look for you." He glanced toward the door. "You know that, right?"

She looked at the IV lines in his arm. There was a button leading to a box. The morphine drip.

"I didn't kill anyone."

"You mean Garth Donnell? I know that."

"I don't care that you know that. I know that I didn't kill him."

"Anna, why are you here?"

She felt her eyes tear. "Because." She looked away for a second. "Because I'm glad that you know. Even though I don't care."

Terrell squeezed her hand. "Please, stay. Give yourself up."

"Special Agent, they're trying to kill me."

"I can protect you."

She sighed, and looked at the door. "No, you can't."

"Yes, I can."

She grabbed the button and pressed it. Her hand was below his line of sight. It took a few seconds, but his eyes were getting sleepy.

He tried saying something, but jumbled sounds came out.

"I have to go and get answers. I don't know why. I just know that I have to," Anna said.

"You saved me once before. Let me return the favor," he said. His voice was low.

"No, I didn't. Emergency services did."

"No, you saved--" he said as he fell asleep.

Thank you for looking for me when nobody else did. Anna thought about being found, and realized that she had indeed found herself first.

She kissed Terrell again, but this time not to silence him.

EPILOGUE

EXPLAINING ESCAPED APPLES

The man, after leaving USP Florence for the last time and driving ten hours non-stop, arrived at one of the efficiency apartment complexes reserved for the students from Northern Arizona University, in Flagstaff. His money was at least as good as the students. He'd reserved the efficiency a few weeks before, as soon as he had agreed to the job. He paid six months up front. That always made people happy.

After dropping his things off at the studio apartment, he drove to a secluded spot near the Lowell Observatory to the north and pulled out his burner phone. The number was on speed dial.

The voice on the other end was abrupt. "What the hell is wrong with you? You destroyed the prison. This was supposed to be a simple in and out and now the whole world knows that something happened there."

"You're welcome. Sometimes I have fun. Sometimes I don't," the man said. "I don't know, or care, why you're upset."

He took in a deep breath of the afternoon air. It was early and he knew a couple of local spots where he could get some tasty dinner. Maybe even some tasty coed.

"She's on her way."

"How is she?"

"She's fine. She had a few issues with people, but I took care of it," the man said.

"What kind of issues?"

The man weighed truth against consequences. He heard a raptor in the distance. "Boyfriend issues."

"While she was in prison? Are you telling me that she was raped?"

Jesus Christ, he gets wound up. "No, nothing like that. She fell for some guy, one of the guards, and it turns out he wasn't good for her."

"So what did you do?"

"What would you do?" the man asked.

"I'd make sure he stayed away from her."

"Exactly what I did."

"Good for you. The problem, though, is that you killed someone and took his place. That was not part of the agreement. They know about you now. You were just supposed to go in and then disappear."

"Hold on there. How I do my job has always been my business. Palma needed to know who was in charge, and I sent him a really clear sign," the man said. He dug his right shoe into the ground, forming a small cloud of dust.

"And how did that work out?"

"Very well, as far as I can tell," the man said.

"As far as you can tell. Great."

"Could you please show a little gratitude? I got her out. You predicted they were going to get her, and they did. I will assume you were listening to their communications."

"Whatever."

"Look, don't act all high and mighty. I made sure your notes all got there. They were stupid, and left her open to retribution by the warden, but I did it, and you got your way," the man said.

"Will you stop? You liked the challenge. I don't even want to know how you did it."

"Let's just say, I have friends in the laundry room," the man said.

Silence.

"How was she?"

"My updates weren't good enough?" the man asked.

"I know you haven't told me everything."

"I've told you everything there is to know."

"There was a medical emergency a few days ago. What was that about?"

"Nothing. She needed feminine napkins," the man said.

"You're not lying to me about this, are you? Because if you are, I swear..."

"Give it a rest. I did my job. I. Did. My. Job. She's out and she's going as far away from New York as I could send her without it being Guam." The man felt brave. "Why the hell did you leave her in there for so long? What's wrong with you? You left her in there to die, and I saved her." The man let that sink in. "You do realize that, right? I saved her. Not you."

Silence.

"Did she ever..."

"Try killing herself?" the man asked. "Of course not. Who do you take her for?" The man wondered how he would have handled Anna if he could have stayed with her longer. She was head strong, but he liked that. She was different. Someone worth knowing. "She'll be fine in Vancouver. She can take care of herself. I bet she takes the money, and stretches it out for years."

"Of course she would. She's amazing."

"The apple doesn't fall far from the tree," the man said.

"She's nothing like her father."

FREE DOWNLOAD!

Download an excerpt of *Kidnapping Anna: The Montague Tubes*, the third part of the *Kidnapping Anna Trilogy*, by going directly to https://brushedsteelbooks.com/the-montague-tubes-15ch. The first 15 chapters!

OTHER BOOKS BY A.B. ALVAREZ

Please visit your favorite ebook retailer to discover other books by A.B.
Alvarez:

The Kidnapping Anna Trilogy

Book One: Kidnapping Anna

Book Two: Kidnapping Anna: ADX Florence

Book Three: Kidnapping Anna: The Montague Tubes

ACKNOWLEDGMENTS

Many thanks again to Cee Banton, and Nadja Hicks who patiently read this novel without the faintest idea of what they were getting into. Another big shout out to the folks of the Saturday writers group who were nice enough to read excerpts of the manuscript and helped make the story better (that includes Nicole Beverly, Joe Kennedy, David Nierenberg, and Sally Woo among others).

Thanks to my cover focus group: Jessica Lassiter, Lisa Serrano, Melissa Serrano, Cristina Valcarcel, Lindley Valcarcel, Luis Valcarcel, Silvia Velez, Bill Velez, Cathy Velez, Victoria Velez, Elizabeth Velez, Alicia Velez, Casey, and Marina.

Many thanks to my two incredible siblings: Silvia Velez, and Luis Valcarcel.

The incredible cover is due to the hard work of Cathi Stevenson from Book Cover Express, and the wonderful edits to Samantha Stroh Bailey. Thanks, as well, to Glen M. Edelstein from Hudson Valley Book Design for additional visual design on the excerpts.

A big hug and thanks to my daughter Lindley. You are an inspiration to me every day.

The wonderful parts of the book are so because the folks around me stopped me from screwing it up. The mistakes are when, once again, I didn't listen.

A.B. Alvarez
New York City, 2017

ABOUT THE AUTHOR

A.B. Alvarez lives in New York. He doesn't have any cats, dogs, ferrets, or other pets. He does, however, have a daughter whom he did not kidnap.

Discover more great authors, offers you won't find anywhere else, cool merchandise, and more at BrushedSteelBooks.com/tell-me-more

CONNECT WITH A.B. ALVAREZ

Follow me on Bookbub:
https://www.bookbub.com/authors/a-b-alvarez

Follow me on GoodReads: https://www.goodreads.com/author/show/17072140.A_B_Alvarez

Read my blog: https://www.brushedsteelbooks.com/category/authors-blogs/abalvarez/

Visit the Brushed Steel Books web site:
https://www.brushedsteelbooks.com

FIRST PRINT EDITION, February 2018

ISBN-10: 1-947291-04-1

ISBN-13: 978-1-947291-04-1

90425056R00241

Made in the USA
Middletown, DE
23 September 2018